The Seasons of the Wither

Book One of the

Though leaves are many, the root is one;
Through all the lying days of my youth
I swayed my leaves and flowers in the sun;
Now I may wither into the truth.
W.B. Yeats (1865–1939). "The Coming of Wisdom
with Time." *Responsibilities and Other Poems.* 1916.

Jared Kitchens

For Mom and Dad
My time with you wasn't long enough

Schedule

PART 1: FALL

1:00 Prelude to the Fall 11
1:01 Autumn in Auldenton 15
1:02 Seer's Day Festival 27
1:03 The Beginning of the End
of the Beginning 33
1:04 The Once-and-Future Man 39
1:05 Nutberries and Berrynuts 47
1:06 Lithe 51
1:07 Fortune Cookies 59
1:08 The Timister Towers 63
1:09 Oneirotopsis 69
1:10 The Journey du Jour 75
1:11 A Stitch in Time 83
1:12 Manufacturing a Man-Factory 99
1:13 Giants 113
1:14 Threnody and Volare 125
1:15 Prochrons and Metachrons 133
1:16 Death Stalks at Dusk 141

PART 2: WINTER

2:00 Winterlude 149
2:01 The King of the Wolves 153
2:02 Nutberries Do Not Fall Far
From the Family Tree 165
2:03 The Timister Library and
Scientific Research Center 171
2:04 Aori vs. the Ori of Aomori 179
2:05 The Army of the Anachronist
Attacks Again 183
2:06 Tweentime 189
2:07 Educating the Masses 197
2:08 Civility Among Savages 205

2:09 Slipping Through Tweentime 211
2:10 The Singing Glass 217
2:11 The Creators 225
2:12 Connery, Caitlyn, Crowfoot and
the Chronoclysm 231
2:13 The Timister Towers 2.0 239
2:14 Birth of the Bertram-Bot 247
2:15 Time Rolls On and Rolls Over Us All 251

PART 3: SPRING

3:00 Spring Foreword 259
3:01 The Lake of Lament 263
3:02 Take These Broken Wings and
Learn to Fly 273
3:03 Finding Solace 281
3:04 An Evening in the Aeolian House 291
3:05 The Symphony 299
3:06 Insurrection and Resurrection 307
3:07 Unrest Comes to Solace 313
3:08 'Til Death Do Us Part 319
3:09 There is No Harm in Harmony 325
3:10 Ode to the Dorian Elder 331
3:11 *Fellfalla* and Their Larvae 339
3:12 The *Fellfallan* Empire 347
3:13 Emperor Saturn Pavonia 359
3:14 Riddle of the Sphinx 371

PART 4: SUMMER

4:00 Summertime and the Dying is Easy 381
4:01 Life Lessons From a Goddess of Life 385
4:02 The Living Embodiment of Death
Lightens the Mood 393
4:03 Sunrise, Sunset 403
4:04 Time to Die, Time to Kill 413
4:05 The Dead Sea 419
4:06 Hospitality in Hell 425

4:07 Acheron's Call 429
4:08 The Tiny Plastic Sword in the
Sandwich of Time 435
4:09 Stolen Time 439
4:10 War in the Wild Black Yonder 445
4:11 The Future's Not Ours to See 457
4:12 Oroboros 467
4:13 Up the Downward Spiral 473
4:14 Nothing Frees Up Your Schedule
Like the End of the World 483
4:15 The Final Countdown 489

Epilogue 491

PART 1

FALL

Chapter 1:00

Prelude to the Fall

Once upon a time....

Storytellers often open stories with, "Once upon a time," when they mean, "I have no idea how long ago it happened," or, "It doesn't particularly matter when this story happened." It could have been a long time ago, but personally, I remember it like it was yesterday.

Once upon a time, Time collapsed. It now takes just a few minutes to travel across the galaxy, but a three-minute egg takes four lifetimes to cook. It's all very confusing. Don't waste time trying to understand it; I'm a Historian, and the whole thing still gives me a headache.

This is the History of the Anachronist. As a Historian, it is my job to put together the recollections of the past. Of course, how does one differentiate between the past and the every-other-time? Furthermore, how do we separate fact from fiction or clearly represent all the perspectives of one issue? At some point in time, the line between history and storytelling blurred. I am as much a Historian as I am a Storyteller, a Keeper of Lore, and a Seer, of sorts.

We call the confluence of the past, present, and future the *Ever*. Since time is no longer organized, it has become a bit easier for us to perceive events outside our present time.

This has been, or will be, referred to as temporal omniscience, or more plainly, *Eversight.* Someone once said, or will say, "Hindsight is 20/20, but *Eversight* is infinite." Temporal omniscience permits some of the more literary-minded members of our society to tell stories that span many, many lifetimes. However, it does tend to make verb-tenses a bit confusing.

In fact, as you'll find within the course of this story, *Everseers* are infinitely more likely to completely and utterly lose their minds. This is because Time is a very convoluted construct. It helps if we think of it in terms of minutes, hours, days, and so forth, but even that presents problems.

For instance, most people, even though they know that midnight signals the start of a brand new day, will often ask, even at 4:00 A.M., "What are you doing tomorrow?" Overall, people are ignorant when it comes to time. Because of that, and because ignorant people are easily manipulated, Time is and was the greatest manipulator.

Due to the fragile nature of the mind when gazing into the Ever, the higher-ups assigned specifications to each *Everseer.* There are those, like myself, whose job it is to remember, recollect, and reflect on past events. Of course, with the collapse of Time, my job mainly deals with picking out the pieces of past from the Ever and putting them together in an interesting and entertaining manner.

This particular story begins with the last year in the recorded history of the planet Aia. As a Storyteller, I understand that it is my obligation to attempt to avoid spoiling the ending of the book, but there it is, historically. Some believe that Aia began as a fruit on an enormous tree, and that the other planets and stars were fruits, too. Others believe Aia grew from a seed, or it *is* the seed for some other growth. Those who hold no stock in this agricultural perspective on Creation say that it was created by one Supreme Being or Another, which isn't quite as metaphorically literary as the other explanations, but whatever floats your metaphysical boat.

The birth of the planet Aia occurred at roughly the same time as Earth's creation. From that time on, the planets aged quite differently. As children often grow at different rates, so do planets; a mother often wonders why her child cannot speak, when the neighbor's child of the same age speaks in full sentences. It's best not to compare two growing planets, either.

Imagine, if you will, that two humans born at the same second of the same day were then separated and raised on planets with different solar systems. Their orbits around their center stars differ exponentially. That is, one year on Planet A takes 10 times as long as Planet B's solar cycle. Now, I pose this question: If Human A and Human B met on any given day, would they look the same? Person A would be 10 times older in years than Person B, but they were born on the same day!

Fortunately for all of us, the SAT test was destroyed along with the Earth before the collapse of Time, so we don't actually have to find an answer to that question.

For the purpose of telling this story, certain artificial arbitrations must be applied, particularly in the area of telling time on Aia. While the exact orbit of the planet escapes me at the moment, I remember that it was fairly similar to that of Earth's. I find that it's best to avoid the kinds of math problems evidenced above.

Chapter 1:01

Autumn in Auldenton

Seer's Circle in downtown Auldenton bustled with activity for one 24-hour period each year. For the rest of the 8,736 hours in the year, nothing much occurred. In this particular set of twenty-four hours, however, quite a bit happened. The exact ratio of things happening over relative time has never been worked out, partly because it is the importance of the events, rather than the quantity, which matters most, and partly because no one has ever taken the time.

Preparations had to begin months before the Seer's Day Festival, and many able-bodied young men were employed to do the hard work such an event required. Some of the inns and other buildings had to be renovated or remodeled to suit the visiting wizards, seers, soothsayers, witch doctors, or what-have-you. The various booths for the local traders and businesses had to be built or moved in from somewhere else, and all of the banners and decorations had to be displayed. To be sure, it was a year's worth of work that, like a college term paper, had been put off until the last minute.

The lead procrastinator of the crew was a fairly stout man, who was rather ironically named William the Hustler. Of course, the irony lies in the meaning of the term "hustle," rather than that of our contemporary conception of a "hustler." William was not a fast man. Strangely enough, however, he did pretend to be a poor magician while at the same time "hustling" money out of many of the townspeople. He also published a magazine full of inappropriate paintings of women. Go figure.

The bulk of the pressure to meet the deadline weighed upon a hard-working man named Aori Timister. Because of all the work that this festival required, Aori had had no time to work on his farm. Winter was fast approaching, and everything had to be harvested in a painfully short amount of time. Unfortunately, there were not enough hours of daylight left, for this was hundreds of years before the implementation of Daylight Saving Time (DST). The contrivance of DST might have saved the world a lot of turmoil (but seriously annoyed those who lost an hour of sleep) had it been invented or discovered much earlier. However, that is a story for a different time.

Hard work had given Aori a relatively muscular physique, but, like most farmers, prolonged exposure to the sun had prematurely aged his skin. His hair had been grey since the day he was born, much to the dismay of everyone but his parents. Perhaps the Timister family had a genetic deficiency in the production of pigment.

Aori had lived much of his twenty years feeling pressured for time. He studied magic and divination whenever he wasn't working on the farm, tending the sheep, or taking care of his aging parents.

The sun was setting just west of Seer's Circle, where Aori worked as fast as he possibly could. In the dim light of dusk, he slipped off a ladder while hanging up a sign. When he hit the ground, he felt the bone in his arm snap. An injury would cost him valuable time, and his various jobs would not wait for his arm to heal.

William the Hustling Procrastinator eventually walked over to where Aori had fallen. "Young man," he said, "time is money. I cannot afford for you to sit there and moan while there is work to be done."

It is quite possible that William coined that phrase, "time is money," as there are no records of anyone having said it before this time.

"I am aware of the work that must be done, sir. But the time of harvest is coming soon, and there just aren't enough hours in the day to finish in time. I believe I have now injured my arm, as well." He barely had time to finish his sentence before Master William had thrown him off the construction site.

Never mind, Aori thought. *This just leaves more time for other work.*

Aori had taken the job at the request of Bertram Finch, a librarian, teacher, and dear friend of the family. Librarians were regarded as highly as wizards and seers in those times, as few had the ability to read, let alone suggest books for others. As the librarian, Bertram was the Keeper of Knowledge and Lore, which was a powerful position in that day and age. The kids just liked the way he used funny voices when he read.

"Bertram will be quite upset, I'm afraid." Aori headed toward the library, but stopped himself. "I've no time for the library," he muttered. "I still have to tend to the livestock and fix dinner." He cursed the ladder, the sign, and William the Hustler.

It was a good four-hour walk to his home, but he somehow made it in less.

We often refer to the elderly as being "young at heart," but just as often we find the child who wishes nothing more than to be a "grown-up." Quondam Anon, while only eight years old, was such a child.

I suppose one could say that Quondam was the antithesis of Peter Pan, if you understand the anachronistic allusion. The literary character never existed on Aia, of course; nevertheless, Pan chose to remain a boy forever, whereas Quondam... well, you'll see how his story unfolds.

In appearance, Quondam looked different from most of the other boys. His features gave him a distinctly Asian look, but since that continent would not be discovered for many years (and on another planet, mind you), he knew very little of his origins.

In my time of collecting and recollecting, I have discovered several stories involving orphans. More often than not, the unfortunate children never truly experience an ideal childhood but rather a forced-adulthood crammed into a child-sized package. These orphans are often left to fend for or care for themselves, and the absence of a caring nurturer frequently leads to poor socialization.

That is, of course, until the archetypal orphan finds a long-lost family member or benefactor, who removes said orphan from the horrible orphanage, gang of pickpockets, or moisture-farm.

"Leave him alone!"

Quondam faintly heard the words shouted, as if miles away, and, less figuratively, outside the pile of boys now pummeling him repeatedly. Between the thunder of the punches and kicks, Quondam heard more shouts.

"Get offa him!"

"What do you care, you big, dumb ogre?"

Another child joined in with the first. "Yeah, Munder! What's it to you? Is this kid your lunch?" The beating paused as the children focused their attention on the boy they called Munder.

The large boy shouted, "Yeah, maybe he is my lunch. You jerks wanna be my mid-afternoon snack?"

The wee aggressors stared up at Munder as his shadow spread over several of them at once. Collectively, they decided their playground battle had ended. As they left, one of the boys tossed something at Quondam's feet. "Here's your stupid sword, Quon. We didn't want it anyway!"

Munder helped Quondam to his feet and handed him the sword. "What'd you go and do that for, anyway, Quon? They're not worth it."

Quondam spat out some blood that had once been part of his circulatory system. "Did you hear what they were saying about you? ...About your mother?"

"Quon, for all we know, my mother *was* an ogre. I mean, look at me." Upon looking at him, one could easily see that one or the other of his parents might have shared an intimate (though undoubtedly uncomfortable) encounter with an ogre, a giant, or a behemoth of some sort. Munder, as they say, was big for his age. In fact, he was big for any age. At roughly the age of eight (no one was sure exactly when he was born), Munder's height compared rather closely to that of a fully-grown, but freakishly tall, man.

Because of his size, Munder rarely lost a fight, but he tried his best to avoid any brawls whatsoever for the simple reason that he couldn't pick on someone his own size.

"I don't really need you to fight my battles for me, Quon."

Quondam felt angry. He had valiantly stood up to a mob of bloodthirsty ruffians (children, though they were) to defend Munder's honor, and this was the thanks he got? He could feel the skin around his eye swelling shut, and blood still attempted to free itself from several places on his body.

"You could have beaten them all," Quondam grumbled.

Munder frowned and looked up at the orphanage's uppermost tower. "I can't spend another night up there, Quon."

On several occasions, dire situations had necessitated in Munder the need to defend himself. Fighting off the playground taunts and witless barbs of children is altogether different from fighting the adults who were the so-called caretakers of the facility. After every altercation with an adult, Munder was given "Time-Out," or isolation in the tower.

Those who ran the orphanage fit the type found in every orphan story. They cared for the orphans in that they provided meager necessities such as food, water, and shelter, but the Austere Boys' Home of Auldenton left much to be desired.

Origin of the Orphanage

The Austere Boys' Home of Auldenton got its name from the founder, a Sir Frederick Austere of Deficity. As a knight, Sir Frederick was barely able to defend his city against a roving band of were-squirrels. The town of Deficity, which had never been very adequate anyway, was left barren and desolate, and many of the young children were orphaned in the raid. After a rather long time of deliberation, Sir Frederick decided to take the orphans with him to nearby Auldenton, where he forced the children to build and run the orphanage. They also made shoes.

As Quondam and Munder approached the building, it became evident that the other boys had already presented a somewhat one-sided account of the playground fight. A guard, who the boys called Mr. Fist (for reasons which will be, if they are not already, obvious), poked at Munder's chest in that way that archetypal bullies do.

"What have you two been up to?" asked Mr. Fist, clearly and pretentiously indicating that he already knew the answer to the question.

Quondam attempted to explain that the other boys had called Munder names, and beaten him for standing up to them, but Mr. Fist just stared at Munder the whole time, eye-to-eye.

Mr. Fist interrupted his testimony. "I don't want to hear from the slant-eyed runt. I'd like to hear what the ogre has to say—or grunt, that is."

Munder clenched his teeth, and performed a similar motor skill with his fists. "Leave him out of this, Fist. Quon had nothing to do with this."

"Well, I did get beaten up a lot," mumbled Quondam.

Mr. Fist broke his stare away from Munder momentarily to look down his nose at Quondam. Snickering, he sneered,

"Hmm. Where'd you learn to fight? Did your dad teach you how to just stand there and let people hit you?"

Quondam could feel his blood pumping a bit harder in his veins, as if it had taken the insult to its bloodline personally. "Your insults are even less mature than those of these children, Mr. Fist. My father was a great warrior. He died in the War."

"You think you know so much. He was fighting for the wrong side."

Children tend to have a limited perspective when it comes to wars, which stems from their egocentricity. They have yet to learn about other parts of the world, so their perspectives focus on what is around them. Wars are often interpreted with an "us against them" interaction (by some adults as well), without even realizing who makes up the "us" and "them." In this case, Quondam had always believed the Auldentons and their allies to be on the "good" side, ridding the world of the evildoers on the other side. It is often difficult to adjust one's preconceived notions to accommodate for new information.

"Herbovine-dung!" shouted Quondam, as loud as he could.

"What's that?," Mr. Fist retorted. "Munder, I think your friend here is talking about your mother. Wasn't she a herbovine?" I believe it is important to note that,

> **A Brief Word on Herbovines**
> - A herbovine is a fairly ancient, distant cousin of the cow. Although its name sounds very similar to the word "herbivore," it was, in fact, carnivorous. While the modern word "bovine" originated here, the word "herbivore" was invented many years later, and has only a small relation to the animal. Uncannily, it tasted quite a bit like herbs. The area commonly referred to as the rump actually tasted like cabbage.
> - A more important description of the animal lies in its size. The largest herbovine could not fit in a house, while the smallest could still do quite a bit of damage to a front door. Therefore, quite a few fat kids (Munder, for example) were teased by other little boys and compared to herbovines. By the way, pronounce it with the h or without. Temporal omniscience allows us to see all time periods, but we've never seen a pronunciation guide.

while Mr. Fist was, in fact, much older than both of these boys, he was raised and socialized on this very playground, and his only means of communication had always been the childish taunt.

Amazingly, Munder refrained from acting out violently, which was the other most common form of communication at the orphanage. Instead, he and Quondam walked into the building and up to their room.

Munder helped Quondam up to the top bunk, so they could look at each other face-to-face. "Thanks," Munder said.

Quondam shrugged. He was still mad about what Mr. Fist had said, and his swollen, bloody face just added to his bad mood. "One of these days, Munder...." He trailed off, as people often do when using that phrase.

"I know, Quon. You're going to be a brave warrior like your father." He had heard it countless times before, but he tried to drain some of the sarcasm from his voice out of respect. "Maybe I'll be a warrior too. We could be in the same battalion."

Quondam lay back in his bed and stared far past the ceiling and deep into thought. His mind wandered across coastlines, over mountains, to faraway places he didn't even know. A child's fantasy of far-off places and epic battles blasted in his brain, and he was dreaming before he even realized it.

The Great Aian War of Whatever-Time

As a Historian, I feel it is important to provide a few details on the Great Aian War, which was the longest and bloodiest war in Aian history. They might have called it The Hundred Years' War, or perhaps something even more accurate, but no one remembered when it actually began, or, for that matter, *why* it began. The general populace was never entirely sure why they fought, but the soldiers were willing to give their lives for that cause... whatever it may have been.

Geographically, it is difficult to pick sides in the War, because it was more a war between people with differing perspectives than between civilized nations. The people of Auldenton fought alongside the meager army of

Deficity, but they also allied themselves with other small cities and towns. They often fought other nearby cities, but some did get as far as the island village of Aomori, where Quondam's father had lived and died.

Since it is so difficult to understand the antecedents of the War, let's just assume it was like any other war. Many people died for something they believed in, and whether their deaths were justified or necessary is anyone's guess.

In these cases, we often say, "We'll leave it up to History to decide."

As a Historian, I've decided to gloss over the War and get back to the story.

In his dream, Quondam saw a man, who he could only guess was his father, with his back against an enormous tree. As he gazed at the man, imploring him for some clues about his lineage, Quondam took his father's place up against the tree. Arrows flew at him from all sides, and seemingly-familiar faces fought against him.

Meanwhile, miles away, the man named Aori Timister also slept, and dreams brought him similar discomfort. He always dreamt of his parents, and in his mind he watched them grow older and older. He had never known them to be young and vibrant, and many of his memories involved taking care of them. Like Quondam, Aori's childhood had rotted on the vine. Life forced Aori to grow up quickly to take care of his parents after the deaths of his older brothers and sisters.

In his dream, a strong gust of wind shook and rattled the frame of the house like the bones of a skeleton. In a blink, the wood of the house *became* bones, and they continued to rattle. Slowly, Aori watched as the bones began to disintegrate and the wind carried them away as dust. With his house completely obliterated, Aori rushed to protect his parents from the gale-force winds. In seconds, all that he held in his arms was more dust, which he held as long as he could.

He woke in the middle of the night, and his knuckles were white from clutching his bedsheets. He cursed the dream and shuttered to clear the images from his head. His arm looked bruised and swollen, and he felt certain that it was broken. Like some sort of mindless robot, Aori set aside his troubles, lit a lantern, and went straight to his chores despite the darkness outside.

****

Quondam opened his eyes and instinctively reached for his wooden sword. The sword had been a gift from his father, and even though he had no memory of the event, Quondam cherished the toy sword as if it were the greatest weapon of all time.

Suddenly, Quondam realized what had startled him awake; a commotion in the bottom bunk rattled the metal frame of the bed. He gripped his sword tighter and listened. He heard a muffled grunt and sounds of a struggle. "Not this time," Quondam whispered, in that cracked and weak voice one has upon first awakening. The sound stopped and there was a jolt on the underside of the top bunk.

Mr. Fist stood up, rubbing his head. "Quiet, boy. This doesn't concern you."

Quondam felt a strength within him that gave him bravery beyond his years. "Not this time, Fist." He jumped down off the bunk and poked his sword at Fist's chest.

"Stop, Quon," Munder mumbled.

Quondam looked at his large friend, who appeared rather beaten and bruised. In the dim light of their room, it was difficult to tell the full extent of the damage, but something was tied around Munder's throat. How had such a fight gone on without waking him sooner?

He gripped his sword tighter, and tried not to imagine what had happened. Rather, Quondam turned to his enemy. "Is this an alpha male thing? Try to take out the biggest threat to your dominance?"

Mr. Fist didn't really understand. He clenched his fists and puffed up his chest to appear more intimidating.

However, Quondam wasn't thinking like an eight-year-old in a fight with a grown man. To Quondam, this was a balanced fight.

Mr. Fist lunged toward him, and Quondam thrust the wooden sword at his enemy's chest. Much to everyone's surprise, the sword pierced the man's skin. The man fell to his knees in pain, and Quondam reared back for another blow. As he swung downward, Munder caught the blade with his hand and stopped its swing.

As if suddenly pulled back into reality, Quondam looked at his friend and realized what had happened. "I didn't mean to...."

Munder assessed the situation. "He'll live. We have to go." He let go of the sword and noticed blood dripping from his hand.

"What happened?" asked Quondam, worried.

"Just a splinter," said Munder. "It's just a wooden sword, right?"

"Right," said Quondam.

They ran out of the room and out of the building as stealthily as they could. Once outside, they ran into a dark alley.

"Where are we going to go?" Quondam stopped to rest. Tears were streaming down his face, and he caught up with himself enough to realize he was crying.

"It'll be okay," Munder reassured him. "We're just kids. We won't get in trouble. We just have to stay far away from Mr. Fist."

"I'm not a kid," whimpered Quondam unconvincingly.

Despite the fact that it was very late at night, Quondam and Munder were not alone in the streets of Auldenton. As they maneuvered through the dark alley, they came to a street lined with campers eagerly awaiting the opening of the Seer's Day Festival.

"Seer's Day," said Quondam. "I forgot."

"We need to get in there, Quon. Fist would never find us in the Seer's Day crowds."

"And maybe we can get help from a wizard or something," added Quondam.

They walked up to the festival gates, which Aori helped build only days before to prepare for Seer's Day. There was a large sign attached to the front gates that read, "Soothsayer Sue says, 'You must be this tall to enter Seer's Day.'"

Attached to the sign was a life-size picture of a cute, wide-eyed kid who must have been Soothsayer Sue. She wore a precious, little wizard costume complete with a pointy hat covered in stars. Unfortunately, she was about a hat's height taller than Quondam.

Quondam hissed out a string of foul language—mostly having to do with Soothsayer Sue—under his breath. "How are we going to get in?"

Munder stepped up beside Sue and said, "Well... I guess I'm going to the Seer's Day Festival." He laughed as he towered over Sue, Sue's pointy hat, and the gate as well.

Quondam laughed as he joked, "You could pretend I'm your son and buy me a Soothsayer Sue hat!"

"Not a bad idea," said Munder, seriously. "But, I'm not buying you a hat."

If the people of this community had owned watches or clocks at this time, it might have been called six o'clock. However, most of them just referred to it as "early." If alarm clocks had been invented, they would undoubtedly be ringing, for the Seer's Day Festival was about to begin....

Chapter 1:02

Seer's Day Festival

The day began like any other, except for all of the activity in Seer's Circle. The Seer's Day Festival was a sight to behold. Peddlers brought furs, weapons, pottery, and various food items from all around the world for sale or trade. The traders who had not rented a booth from William the Hustler had to set up their goods on the ground beside the booth area. This walkway became known as a "sidewalk," hence the phrase, "Sidewalk Sale."

Besides the traders and sidewalk vendors, one could also find inns, brothels, bars, dining establishments, and amusement park rides. Anyone who wished it could get any number of various meats on a stick. Patrons could smell the unmistakable odor of the steamed herbovine rump

Seer's

Historians have traced the lineage from Seer's Day Festival and Seer's Circle to a similarly named department store. Apparently, they dropped the "circle" part and changed the spelling a bit over the years. That offers a bit of an explanation as to why the Seer's Day peddlers often attempted to sell the citizens of Auldenton on the idea of steel siding and something called a "refrigerator." It might also be important to note, here, that the refrigerator was not named after Refrigerator Perry. He was around much, much later.

from miles away. Most people avoided it and wondered how long ago, and who decided, that eating something that smelled so foul was a good idea.

The main attractions of the Seer's Day Festival were the seers themselves. Among them were various astrologers, apothecaries, alchemists, augurs, diviners, druids, enchanters, evangelists, gurus, mystics, magicians, priests, prognosticators, psychics, psychologists, shaman, soothsayers, sorcerers, warlocks, witches, wizards, and voodoo witch doctors. One person was walking around with a sandwich board sign that read, "THE END IS NEAR," while another had a sign that read, "THERE'S PLENTY OF TIME."

Auldentonite Sandwich
It's a little-known fact that the sandwich was actually named after the sandwich board rather than the Earl of Sandwich. Many considered an Auldentonite sandwich, which consisted of herbovine meat ground into a gooey paste, to be a great delicacy around the world. Of course, they used pieces of sandwich board instead of bread, so it might not appeal to modern senses of taste.

That morning, Aori fed the sheep and herbovine before sunrise. He had only slept a few hours because of all the work he had to do the night before, and the sleep he had had been fraught with dreams. After Aori had fed the livestock, he had to go back inside to feed his parents.

In this time of shorter life spans and disease, passing on the family name was the closest one could get to immortality. Aori had been the last in a long line of brothers and sisters, and his parents were very old. The other siblings were not available to help care for their parents because of various illnesses and accidents that took their lives throughout the years. Therefore, it was Aori's responsibility to carry on the bloodline.

He spooned a mouthful of some sort of mush into his father's mouth and waited as patiently as possible for some sign of swallowing. He looked around for something to do to keep busy while his father chewed and swallowed the food.

The sun was rising quickly, and the Seer's Day Festival was beginning. He loathed being late for the festivities because he hoped some magic might help him find more time. If nothing else, he could learn better time management skills or get therapy for Type-A personality disorder from a psychologist.

He shoved a spoonful of food into his mother's mouth and another into his father's. Anticipation gnawed at him like a herbovine. He could already hear sounds of revelry and excitement coming from the town circle. He tried another spoonful, but mush began oozing out of his father's mouth. He muttered a curse for old age.

"Why must time wage such bitter war on us all, Father?" he asked his silent parent. "Will it just eat away at us forever? When will the torment end?"

As if in answer to Aori's question, his father's Adam's apple moved up and down slowly. He had finally swallowed.

Quondam woke to the sound of someone breathing heavily in his face. "You awake?" asked Munder in a deep whisper.

"I suppose." As he began fumbling with his shoelaces, Quondam remarked, "You know, I don't see how it could be possible, but I think you've grown even bigger overnight."

"Could be. Ready?" Munder asked as he began to run. Quondam just followed.

Aori ran through forests and fields with the speed of a somewhat agile (but injured) person, but with the patience of a person stuck in rush hour traffic for three hours. He longed for a more expedient means of travel and, as he was cursing his mundane feet, a strange object shot through the sky above his head. He slowed his pace for only a second to look at the object. It looked a bit like a bird, but no bird was that large or that fast. He spared a half-second more to watch it land in what he knew to be the center of Seer's Circle before he dashed off towards it.

Quondam and Munder had camped just outside the Seer's Circle, so their journey took far less time. Before long, they stood face to face with one of the guards watching the main gate. "No youths allowed," said the guard when he saw Quondam. He looked at Munder, who was almost his height. "Am I to believe that you're this young man's guardian?"

"Well...." Munder froze. He hadn't really believed that anyone would believe he was over eighteen. *Gotta be the beard*, he thought.

Quondam had considered the beard, which they had drawn on with charcoal, to be a bit much. He just patiently waited for the guard to wise up and make them leave.

"You don't look anything alike," said the guard. Quondam began backing up to leave. He didn't wish to be thrown physically out of the gate area. The guard continued, "You can't just get any adult off the street to pretend to be your dad, kid. You aren't pulling one over on this guard."

"Oh!" spurted Munder, as all of his 8 year-old brain began to work. "You're right. He isn't my son. He's my partner."

"Partner?" questioned the guard.

"Sure," said Quondam, catching on to the revised plan. "We're part of the sideshow. He's the strong-man...."

"And he's the midget," finished Munder. "Haven't you ever seen a wee midget before?"

Whether the guard believed this story or not didn't matter much, because all of a sudden a sleek, silvery bird-like object shot down out of the sky and landed in the center of the circle. In all the confusion and bewilderment, Quondam and Munder slipped inside the gate undetected.

In the center of Seer's Circle, the silver object let out a strange mechanical sigh. A door opened and an old man sprang out with the energy of a five year-old. He looked around at the staring faces of the crowd and then proceeded to walk to a nondescript booth as if nothing out of the ordinary had happened. He stretched a purple tablecloth across the table and started placing several small trinkets upon it. In the center of the table, he set a large hourglass. The sand began to sink slowly from the top of the glass to the bottom.

"Who is that?" whispered someone. The words spread through the crowd like dandelions in one's yard. "Who is that?"

"It's just the clock-maker," answered Aori, who had finally arrived.

"What's a clock?" whispered someone, which started another chain reaction through the crowd. No one was very sure what a clock was, but they figured it had something to do with time, since Aori obviously knew what it was. The Timisters had a reputation for being obsessed with time.

Aori didn't really know what a clock was either, though. He had heard of one somewhere, perhaps in a dream. He assumed it was the answer to all his problems. However, more patience would be required of him today. The crowd had already sprung around the booth like rabbits on a piece of rotting herbovine flesh.

While he waited, Aori searched the other booths. He asked the apothecary for help and was given a strange white powder. If memory served him correctly, this had been what killed his brother Roy. In the prime of his life, Roy had worn a multi-colored coat made of a variety of furs. He was also known as Roy the Free-baser. Few people knew what "free-baser" meant, but a lot of them incorrectly assumed it was similar to freemasonry.

The other so-called "seers" proved just as fruitless. One of them said she was sensing that somebody close to him, maybe a woman, was cheating on him.

"I'm sensing something to do with the letter A. Aurora... no. *Asa?*" she offered.

"My name is Aori," he offered back.

"Oh, that must have been it."

"Anything else?" Aori asked. "I'm a little short on ---"

"TIME!" came a shout from the crowded booth. The sounds of the crowd had stopped completely. Even the mystic at the table in front of Aori seemed strangely silent. He looked around, and noticed that no one was moving. The world seemed perfectly still, except—what was that small thing scampering in the shadows over there?

Quondam hid behind a booth and struggled to get a better view of the strange silver object in the center of the circle. As he was scampering among the shadows, he collided with the knees of a person with large, purple pants. He looked up to see a strange, dark-skinned seer. "I am Zoltar," said the mystic. Zoltar had a dark beard and moustache, and he wore a purple and gold turban. "What is your wish?"

"W-wish?" Quondam stammered, but almost immediately recovered. "I wish I were older... just a couple years, maybe...." He stopped short, startled by the sudden silence of the crowd around him. Was it his imagination, or was the old man with the silver rocket staring straight at him? Zoltar was now completely inanimate. Quondam poked at Zoltar's midsection. No response. He tapped a little harder. Still nothing. Quondam then struck the mystic repeatedly, punching and kicking wildly. When there was still no response, he darted behind a booth to get a better look at what was happening.

Quondam noticed the grey-haired seer from the silver bird-like object was pointing in the direction of some person with a broken arm. He looked around for Munder, but couldn't find him anywhere. Slowly, he made his way towards the old seer's booth. He was careful not to be noticed.

Chapter 1:03

The Beginning of the End
of the Beginning

The old man had long, white hair and a beard to match. Innumerable creases and wrinkles wove through his face, indicative of his age. Strangely, however, the wrinkles seemed to have just mysteriously appeared with no origin or cause.

As all the people seemed to freeze around him, he seemed to be speaking to both Quondam and Aori at the same time. He pointed a long, pale finger at the only person still moving. For a split second, his eyes darted towards and focused on a small being cowering in the shadows.

Aori walked towards the old man and introduced himself. "Hello," he began, "my name is Aori Timister. Who are you?"

The old man waved his hands rapidly, as if brushing away the question. "We don't have time for names, Timister. But, if you must, you may call me Toki."

"Did you finish my sentence for me a moment ago, or was that just a strange—."

"Coincidence? Happenstance? No such thing. Poppycock." The old man seemed to age a bit more in the seconds it took to speak.

"Oh," said Aori, stricken with awe. "Can you read my mind? How do you know what I'm going to say before I say it?"

"That, my good man, is insignificant. Do not tell me that a man as pressed for time as you are has let his thoughts stray to other, less important matters. Focus is the key to getting work done efficiently."

"Yes. That's right. Let me tell you about my problem," Aori began.

"You needn't take the time, master Timister. Your problem is with time. I can help. However, we mustn't beat around the bush. All these good people are waiting on us."

Aori looked around at all the people, who still seemed frozen in time. Out of the corner of his eye, he spotted that same small figure darting behind the old man's booth. He wasn't sure, but he thought Toki had seen it too.

"So…" said Toki, "… would you like to have twice the daylight hours you currently spend so thriftily? Would you like to work as long as you wish, without sacrificing any sleep time? What about your loved ones? Would you like to have more time with them, before they grow any older and… wither away?"

"Seer, your wisdom exceeds all of the wizards and mystics here today," said Aori with a sort of awkward bow. The old man grinned and nodded his head slowly.

"I can help you. I shall cast a spell on you that will give you complete control over your time. If you have ever felt that time was against you, you could change that now. If you need forty-eight hours of straight daylight, it can happen. Then, you can sleep for the next sixty."

"But how?" Aori asked. "Won't the world pass me by while I slumber?"

"Only if you want it to, my good man. You can slow down or speed up the effects of age. You can stop the sands of time while you remain mobile and aware."

Aori looked around at the frozen crowd once more. He noticed that the sand in the hourglass was no longer moving either. He tried to formulate a question about the spell: what side effects or consequences it could have, what would be required of him, et cetera, but all of a sudden, it felt like his vocal chords were stuck. When they began to work again, he heard himself speak in a high-pitched, high-speed voice. The next words out of his mouth were ones he hadn't even planned to say yet. "Yes. Do your magic."

"Now wait a moment," Toki interjected with a grin. "Let's not be hasty. Have you thought it over? You might want to go home and think it over for a day or two."

Aori considered his haste, then immediately thought of all the work he had to do in the next few days. His mind raced from thought to thought—his parents chewing so slowly—his broken arm that would take months to heal—the social life he'd never had time for before… "I don't need time to think about it. How long will the enchantment take? Will I need an artifact? One of these clocks perhaps?" He was proud of the fact that he could identify a clock, even though he still didn't know much about them. Somehow, however, it seemed as if he'd already learned a lot about them, in just the few seconds it took to ask the question.

"Oh no, my good man. You won't need any of these artifacts." Toki began to speak rather loudly, as if he were talking to someone other than Aori. "This artifact here is only useful if you want to grow old very quickly, or change your age. You have no need of that, do you now?"

Aori thought for a fraction of a second about the artifact. "No," he said. "I do not wish to be old just yet. However, it might be useful to my parents…"

Toki smiled. "Believe me; your parents have been taken care of quite nicely. Do not waste time worrying about them. Besides, I cannot give you both the enchantment and the artifact. You must choose."

Aori paused a moment to think of his parents and which choice would serve them best. "Let us continue with the spell, please."

The old man's voice oozed languidly as he spoke some indecipherable words then suddenly zipped around in a high-pitched buzz. As soon as the old man stopped talking, the crowd began to teem with excitement again. The hubbub returned to normal, and the old man was right back in the middle of his sales pitch. It seemed as if nothing had gone amiss during the whole time. Aori wondered if he had imagined it all.

He quickly abandoned that idea, as his mind raced from one thought to another like quicksilver. He thought of the old man, the spell, the crowd, the clocks, the small boy—*yes, that's right, it was a boy—the clocks—one is missing—the boy—where is that boy? And who is that young man crouching behind the Seer? Oh well. I haven't time to worry about that. Must press on. Lots of work to do.*

Normally, the hustle and bustle of the crowd bothered Aori. Everyone was always in his way. Today, however, the rest of the world moved at a leisurely pace and Aori could weave in and out of the chaos as he pleased.

He began walking home, when he noticed a herd of wild horses stampeding across the plains. Oddly, the stampede was moving very slowly. In no time, he came upon the herd and was able to climb upon a wild horse as if it had been standing still.

A thought flashed in Aori's head. *I don't know how to ride a horse. I've never done this before.* Before he had finished the thought, he felt as if he had been riding for years. He had learned a year's worth of information in a split second.

With a horse, it took a lot less time to get home. He completed most of his chores before noon. There were times when he had to wait on the sheep to finish eating or walking across the farm, but he learned to occupy his time with other activities in the meantime.

Aori felt like many days had passed already. He had taken the time to learn a bit of magic, fed and bathed his parents, herded the sheep and herbovine up the hill, read a book or two, learned some sword-fighting techniques, fed and bathed his parents, herded the sheep and herbovine down to the pasture, and – *what? The sun has been up the whole time. I don't think it has set since I got home. But—*

Aori took some time to look around him. The clouds in the sky started moving again. He went inside his house at a normal pace. His parents were both propped up in bed as usual, but their skin was very pale and prunish. It was as if they had been in the bath for a long time, but they hadn't. They had just been given almost a week's worth of baths in one hour. Mushy food was strewn all over their bed, since a week's worth of food couldn't fit in their mouths. Outside, some of the animals had gorged themselves on a week's worth of food consumed in an hour. The grain silos were all empty. Why had it taken him so long to realize what he had done? *I guess time just got away from me*, he thought.

Chapter 1:04

The Once-and-Future Man

From behind the booth of the strange old man, Quondam could clearly see and hear the conversation between the man with the broken arm and the Seer. However, at times their movements seemed to speed up or slow down. There was one instance where it looked like the man with the broken arm was going to say something, but he just froze like the rest of the crowd.

The only words Quondam could easily distinguish in the conversation had something to do with the weird objects on the table in front of him. *The man with the broken arm called them clocks*, he thought. *However, what are clocks?*

The old man started talking very distinctly in Quondam's direction, so the words were clear: "This artifact here is only useful if you want to grow old very quickly, or change your age. You have no need of that, do you now?"

"Yes, I do," said Quondam, forgetting that he was not a part of the conversation.

Apparently the old man forgot he was part of the conversation too, because he began talking to Quondam as if the man with the broken arm wasn't even there. Strangely, the injured man just stood still and waited while the Seer spoke with Quondam. "Yes, you do. You wish you were bigger, older. You had a difficult time getting into the festival today because of your young age, yes? And you would not have been able to get in at all if it weren't for my having arrived at just the right time."

Quondam nodded. He was quite a bit frightened. The old man seemed to know all kinds of things—private things—about him. Having completely forgotten about trying to be sneaky, Quondam rose to his feet.

"Who are you?"

The old man sighed. "I should just wear a nametag next time. Isn't anyone in a hurry anymore? Your people call me Toki."

"My people?"

"Listen, kid. You could wait ten years until you're old enough to come to these festivals alone—and old enough to own land, I might add—but ten years is a long time to wait."

The old man reached for and grabbed one of the more ornate timepieces that he had placed on the purple tablecloth. It was a pocketwatch with beautiful engravings all over it. It had a long chain attached to it, which was just about the perfect size for hanging around one's neck. "This watch, or clock as Aori here put it, can give you the ability to shift up and down your personal timeline. If you want to be twenty years old, you will be. You'll have all the experience, strength, and abilities of your future self. Then, if you want to go back to being an eight year-old, you can. But—and listen to this closely—when you go back to being eight years old, you'll remember being twenty also. You'll retain all that experience and knowledge. Isn't that wonderful, Quondam?"

Quondam felt that he might explode with excitement. He always wished he could see a real wizard or soothsayer, but he never imagined that one would give him a magical artifact. He told Toki how much he would like to have the pocketwatch. The old man smiled, set the watch back down on the table, and went back to his conversation with the man he had called Aori. While no one was looking, he grabbed the pocketwatch. He got a little frightened again as the old man started speaking in a strange and mysterious voice. Then, he put the chain around his neck and looked at the engraving on the watch.

Immediately, chaos collided and crashed over Quondam. He had trouble thinking clearly, but he saw flashes in his mind of the future. However, the images flashed by so quickly that he was unable to ascertain what exactly was happening. He saw himself fighting someone in a swordfight. He saw Munder, but it didn't really look like Munder. Then, an image of his mother's face flashed in front of him. Quondam the Once-and-Future Man was living and reliving his entire life in a cycle.

He tried to clear his head and concentrate. *I don't want to be a baby again,* he thought. *I just want to be older. Maybe eighteen.* The cycling chaos eased up and things felt normal again. Even the crowd returned to their chattering and droning. Quondam looked down at his hands, arms, torso, and legs. They looked a lot bigger than they had a few minutes ago. His clothes were different but vaguely similar to what he had been wearing—the colors matched, but the sizes were definitely larger. He also felt stronger, more agile, and smarter.

He looked up at the man named Aori, who was staring at him with a confused look. Aori then took off as if there were a fire or something. However, there was no fire—if there had been, Quondam could have saved all the townspeople from certain doom with his strength and cunning, for he was now a famous warrior!

Quondam looked down at the engraved letters on the pocketwatch. It read: "YESTERDAY AND TOMORROW – THE ONCE AND FUTURE MAN."

Munder had only looked away for a second, but, much to his surprise, Quondam had disappeared from where he had been only seconds ago. The dark-skinned man with the turban was just standing there, looking confused. Munder scanned the crowd. He noticed a man with a broken arm who must have been in a really big hurry. However, Quondam was nowhere to be found.

He ran from booth to booth, asking the seers if they had seen a little boy. They all immediately went into their sales pitches about all the things they had seen.

"I just need to know where he is now. His name—"

"Begins with a Q. I am sensing something to do with the letter Q," one of the mystics offered.

"No, his name begins with a K, I think. It's some weird spelling. Like this kid Juan, who hates it when I call him Joo-ann. His name is Quondam."

Suddenly, all of the seers, mystics, wizards, sorcerers, gurus, voodoo witch doctors, evangelists, priests, psychics, and psychologists looked over at the eighteen year-old who was standing behind the old wizard from the silver bird-like object. "There," they all said in unison.

"You see him? Where?" Munder asked, as he looked in the direction of the old man's booth. Someone wearing clothes that looked similar, but not identical, to Quondam's clothes was standing and looking at some sort of necklace or something.

Quondam's attention diverted to the twenty or thirty mystics who were staring right at him. He heard a familiar voice and followed it to Munder. When he saw his friend, a strange feeling immediately swept over him. "Munder?" he shouted. "Is that you? I thought you were dead!"

"What? What are you talking about? I've been here the whole time. Who are you?"

Quondam looked a bit puzzled then slowly became aware. He felt as if some younger version of himself was explaining things to him about Munder and how alive he was. As the wave of understanding swept through the eight and eighteen year-old Quondams, they came to a decision.

"Perhaps it will ease your mind if I'm a more familiar age, Munder. I can't change here, however. Follow me." He led Munder out the gate and through the streets of Auldenton.

Munder had yet to assemble all the clues and just assumed that some strange adult was throwing him out of the Seer's Circle. He tried to argue that he had just as much right to be there as anyone else, but he found it hard to speak when he saw the young man suddenly turn into an eight year-old boy.

Quondam's boyish smile showed his once-again missing teeth. "My wish came true. I'm not sure if it was Zoltar, or the old man with the rocket, or just the pocketwatch, but my wish came true. I can make myself older whenever I want."

The explanation didn't seem to be working, so Quondam decided to give another demonstration. He shifted to a twenty-four year-old. "See? Now I'm... twenty-four. It takes a moment for the realization to kick in. But, wait. Munder? Is that you?"

"Of course it's me, you silly, old man. Did your eyesight go bad when you got a little older?" Munder retorted.

"No, it's just that..." Quondam tried unsuccessfully to think of what it was about Munder that was so fundamentally wrong.

"Well, let me see it. I wanna turn older too!"

"NO!" Quondam shouted. Things were becoming clearer now. He had to keep Munder from getting the watch.

Even if I have to kill him.

Kill him?

Whatever it takes.

No, killing him won't help. Just keep him away from it.

It was too late. Munder had overpowered Quondam during the confusion. He ran off with the watch in his hands. He kept running until there was sufficient space between them. He couldn't run any farther anyway; he had come to a cliff in the countryside. It wasn't a long way down, but he didn't want to risk the jump.

Quondam's powerful legs allowed him to catch up with Munder in no time. He was still in the body of a twenty-four year old. He tried to make himself younger, because he thought Munder might respond better to someone his age, but it didn't work. Without the watch, he was stuck as a twenty-four year-old. He had to get it back. Two older versions of him were very certain that it was imperative that Munder give the watch back.

Quondam began to cry. "Please, Munder. Give it back to me. If you don't, something horrible will happen."

"What? You gonna try and fight me? I bet I could take you on; especially if I make myself twenty-six!" Munder countered.

"No, Munder. Something horrible is going to happen to you. Please. You're my best friend in the world. Don't do it."

Munder looked at the watch longingly. "Let me just try it."

"NO!" With all the strength of a man in the prime of his life, Quondam lunged at his friend.

"STOP! Don't move another muscle." Munder held the watch out over the precipice. "Another move and I'll drop it. Then neither of us will have it."

"Munder, don't be stupid. Just give it to me."

"I'm not stupid," he insisted, as he put the chain around his neck.

Immediately, the cycle of chaos crashed down upon him. Quondam watched in horror as his friend turned from ten to eleven all the way up to an old man. Munder's legs began to sway a bit. He lost his balance. He fell.

Quondam scrambled to the edge of the cliff and reached out with his long, muscular arms. He grabbed something. It was the watch. Luckily, Munder was still attached.

Quondam reached for his friend's hand and grabbed it. He held on and began pulling his friend to safety. However, the hand was still uncontrollably cycling older and older. The skin started flaking off, and the bones started cracking. Munder's hand wasted away, but Quondam kept his grip on the pocketwatch.

The cycle started over, and Munder shifted to a small infant. The chain slipped loosely from his neck. Quondam tried, but he could not catch his friend in time and the infant Munder fell to the bottom of the cliff.

An adult Munder, or even the eight year-old version, would have survived that fall, but a tiny baby....

Quondam stepped back a bit, put the watch on, and tried to control the cycle. Gradually, he stopped it at a familiar age. He had been three years old when his mother died, and at the time, he thought he would never stop crying. Now he was reliving that age, and he cried as only a three year-old could.

Chapter 1:05

Nutberries and Berrynuts

My *Eversight* gives me the ability to know how this story ends. I could tell you right now, if it would help. Or, you could turn to the last page of the book. Believe me, though-- it's not all it's cracked up to be. I know what's on the last page when I'm reading the first one. In fact, it's like reading every single page all at once. It just seems like a good time for your humble narrator to step in and offer some insight, seeing as how the last few chapters were so climatic and suspenseful. Don't worry—the silvery aircraft will return.

Clearly, jet planes or rockets did not exist during the time discussed in this book, and space ships will not be a reality until many millennia later. Nonetheless, the old man did, indeed, pilot a spaceship into the Seer's Circle. Obviously, there was more to the old man than just fortune telling. However, that is a story for a different time. The time, as mentioned earlier, was just a few weeks before winter. Animals all over this particular biome were working busily to prepare for the cold months ahead.

Winters were very harsh in the region of hills and forests surrounding Auldenton, partly because things such as earmuffs, toboggans, and central heating had not yet been invented.

Very few of the small woodland animals required earmuffs or central heating, however. They probably would not have turned it down had an extra article of clothing or a cozy fireplace been offered to them, but the minds of these creatures were fairly simple. Very few of them even knew how to start a fire, let alone crochet a woolen cap.

Asalie, the most protective of those forest-dwellers, had inspired the majority of the fearsome and fantastic tales about the area. Although in reality, she was rather small and harmless, she had a fanatic obsession with collecting the berries. She was partial to the nutberries but also collected fruits from other trees.

Asalie systematically gathered the fruits/nuts/berries, catalogued them in a large, red book, and then displayed them, one by one, upon her shelves. She had found over 147 different species of fruits/nuts/berries, all of which looked and tasted uncannily similar. The few visitors she had would peruse her display of fruits/nuts/berries for a

Sali Lumpa

The Sali Lumpa, one of the more clever woodland animals, performed numerous ingenious tasks and probably could have crocheted a complete sweater, had it been so inclined. Instead, the little creatures spent most of their time constructing *avant-garde* sculptures out of twigs, berries, and tree sap. Most passersby or onlookers stopped to inspect the intricate sculptures, made several perplexed looks, and finally proceeded to look on or pass by to another part of the forest. Sali Lumpas were just ahead of their time. Few would fully appreciate their style of art until many thousands of years after their complete decimation and extinction. Their utter annihilation, however, is a sad tale best left for another time.

By far the most popular berry among the Sali Lumpa sculptors was the nutberry. Nutberry trees grew in all parts of the world, but their greatest concentration was in a circular, ring-shaped grove that stretched out in a one-mile radius. The citizens of Auldenton called the area the Nutberry O. Strangely enough, Nutberry O's, the breakfast cereal, did not contain any nutberries. None of the local cereal-makers in Auldenton dared to go to the Nutberry O to gather any. They claimed it was not because of the artsy collection habits of the Sali Lumpa, but rather because of the other denizens of the forest, who were also very protective of the nutberries.

moment or two, stare at her for several minutes with puzzled looks, and then, as with Sali Lumpa sculptures, continue on to another part of the forest. Only a few brave souls had ventured that deep into the woods, but they believed Asalie to be utterly insane.

Most of the time, she stood about four feet high, but folk tales about her reported that she towered over the

> **A Quick Lesson in Aian Botany**
> Closely related to the nutberry trees were the nutfruit, seedberry, nutseed, and fruitberry trees. Shockingly, all of the fruits/nuts/berries tasted exactly alike. They also looked quite similar. Only a connoisseur of fine fruits/nuts/berries, such as Asalie, could distinguish between them all.

tallest trees. In contradiction to her intimidating reputation, to many people she conjured up the image of a grandmother. Asalie looked as if she'd always have cookies baking when you visited, which perhaps explains why some cultures knew her as Granny.

Her skin shared many of the same properties as the trees she loved the most; it had the deep, reddish brown color of mahogany, complete with the wrinkled texture of tree bark. Her hair spread across her shoulders and back like roots seeking moisture, and the gnarled locks were an ashy black color. Overall, she had the appearance of a tree that had burned down long ago but still had life left within it.

This particular morning, as with every morning, Asalie woke and rose with the sun. As the daybreak took its sweet and luxurious time, she smiled and felt as if every living thing around her was new and fresh. As she gathered some berries that had fallen to the ground, Asalie felt a slight chill. She had been preparing, both mentally and physically, for the coming winter, but she was not prepared for what she saw that day. She heard a faint humming sound, and her eyes followed the height of the tallest tree, then up some more. High above the towering Nutberry trees, she saw what appeared to be a large, silvery bird.

She bounded up the tree in order to get a better view. From the top of the tree, she could see very far in all directions. A good distance to the northeast, she saw the object land in the town of Auldenton. Since many of her acquaintances were druids, she was aware of the Seer's Day Festival happening there. She had not wished to leave the Nutberry O even for such a momentous occasion as that festival. Still, she wondered what the arrival of the flying device heralded. She spoke, and her words blended in with the rustle of the falling leaves.

"It seems the Time has come."

Chapter 1:06

Lithe

Tears continued to stream down Quondam's cheeks, which were now pudgy with baby-fat. As three year-olds often do, he worked himself up into such a frenzy that he could barely breathe, which only made him cry harder. Above his dolorous wailing and moaning, one could barely detect the sound of music.

The music reached Quondam's eardrum and immediately calmed him. He blinked his watery eyes as if waking up for the first time. It sounded airy, like a sweet whisper of wind, but changed in pitch to make a tune. Quondam wiped the tears away and began to walk in the direction of the music.

The source of the music took a deep breath and stopped playing. She looked down at Quondam and spoke in a soft melodious voice. It sounded something like a gentle breeze passing through wind chimes. "Hello, little boy. What is your name?"

"Quondam," he answered. His older selves had yet to catch up with his toddling brain, so his awareness was presently a bit limited. When his senses returned, he spoke more like an eighteen year-old. "How did you—What was that—Who— um." Correction: he spoke more like an eighteen year-old talking to a pretty girl.

"I am called Lithe," she sang. "Did you enjoy the song? I learned that one from a man in a faraway town called Hamlin."

"It was very enchanting. Are you a sorceress?"

Lithe smiled. She pinched his chubby, little cheeks. "No. I know a few songs that seem to affect people in a magical way, but I know nothing of spells or sorcery. I just play my instruments and let the songs do what they will. That particular song seems to be a favorite of small children, but most adults find it quite irritating."

Unbeknownst to Lithe or Quondam, the tune has had a lifespan of thousands of years. It is the song that never ends. It just goes on and on, my friend.

Lithe hailed from a large family of musicians. In fact, every member of the Coda species had a natural affinity for music. As a Coda, she had long, nimble fingers that bent in multiple places. This trait, along with their long, prehensile tails, gave them a definite advantage at playing instruments. Most Coda could even play more than one instrument at one time.

She also had the pointed ears and tall stature of an elf, along with the agility and grace of that species. It was widely believed that the Coda had evolved over a long period of time from the Elves. Time had definitely played a part in making their species especially suited for making music.

Upon her belt, she wore numerous picks, reeds, and several other accessories for musical instruments. She also carried pipes and horns of various lengths, which she had strapped to her back as a warrior might wear a sword.

Her face matched her music—soft, fair, and very soothing. In the center of her forehead, she had a distinctive marking that further identified her as a Coda. It had the following shape:

"This is Ariel," Lithe said, introducing the flute she had been playing. She sheathed it in its place behind her back and continued to walk towards Seer's Circle. Quondam tried to speak, but every sound he made seemed painfully cacophonous compared to her voice. She waved to him as she continued to walk. Even her footsteps syncopated in a bit of a musical rhythm.

When silence once again crept into Quondam's ears, his mind functioned more clearly. His thoughts shifted to Munder, and his age shifted back to eight. He slumped down on the steps heading up to Seer's Circle and moped. "I wish Munder was still alive," he whispered, childishly hoping this wish would come true as his last one had. "There must be a way." At that point, he decided to return to the Seer's Day Festival to seek the help of Zoltar or the old wizard. His previous wish had come true, so it seemed logical to him that anything could happen.

By the time he reached the guard at the gate, he had grown ten years. The guard did not question him about his age and allowed him to pass through unhindered.

The first detail (or lack of detail) he noticed about the festival was the absence of the silvery rocket. The child in him wondered what *rocket* meant, but he felt as if he had already learned its meaning. Quondam then turned to where the old man's booth had been, but it was quite absent as well.

He sprinted over to Zoltar, who was still wearing his purple and gold turban. The strange foreigner asked Quondam what he wished. Quondam described the death of his friend in as much detail as he could without giving any information about the pocketwatch. Good sense, or experience, told him to keep it to himself.

When Quondam completed his story, Zoltar bowed his head. "I am sorry," he said. "Most people ask me for great fortune or renown. I am afraid that I cannot help you with that particular wish. That will be three silver pieces, please."

"Three silver?" Quondam gasped. "No wonder everyone wishes for great fortune; they need it just to pay for your 'services.'"

"If you cannot pay, sir," the *swami* said snootily, "I will be forced to call upon the guards to have you removed from the festival!"

Just as all the muscles in Quondam's body tensed and his brow began to sweat, a band of traveling musicians struck up a song that drew all attention to the center of Seer's Circle once again. The music sounded as mystical and exotic as those in attendance at the festival, but the band soon took second fiddle, so to speak, to a lone dancer on a platform in the center of the Circle. As she danced, it seemed that the music flowed from and responded to her movement, instead of the other way around. Her long arms swayed like sea plants in the undercurrent.

"Who is she?" several men in the crowd inquired breathlessly.

"Her name is Lithe," Quondam proclaimed. His eyes, too, had taken on the entranced gleam of a dream-state.

Lithe wound her way through the crowd like a thread weaving through embroidered silk. Even though all eyes were on her, no one noticed her nimble fingers as they prospected the pockets of the more affluent members of her audience. With the skill of an expert thief, she lifted several purses and sacks of silver. Then, just as suddenly as the music began, it ended, and Lithe slipped into the crowd seamlessly. Whatever magic had enthralled the audience now worked to make her unnoticeable.

Casually, she sauntered up to one of the more expensive seers and set down several silver pieces. A large sign above the female seer's head read, "3 silvers for the first minute, 1 silver for each additional minute." Despite her second sight or sixth sense, it took the seer several minutes to notice Lithe right in front of her.

Quondam wandered over to the booth as the seer gazed through her. "Nice trick," he whispered. He had never taken his eyes off her, as the others had. He snatched her arm partly to prevent any theft from his person, but the way it felt made him want to keep holding on indefinitely.

As slippery as an eel, she freed her arm from his grasp with ease. "What trick?" she asked innocently.

"Is the band in on it too, or are they unwitting participants in the ploy of a criminal mastermind?"

Quondam's wordiness astonished even him. He had always had a rich vocabulary for his age, but he now used words he had never heard before. The knowledge of his older brain had gradually seeped into his consciousness.

"Do I know you?" she asked. "You are obviously not a guard, so what business do you have making accusations?"

"Of course you know me! We just met a few minutes ago," he explained. Sudden realization sparked, and he remembered that he had looked like a three-year-old when he met her. Everything suddenly felt very awkward and uncomfortable.

Luckily, Lithe's psychic friend (who, mysteriously, had been a complete stranger before today) came out of her trance and broke the tension. "I am sensing a name. It begins with the letter D. Is there someone or something close to you that begins with a D?"

Lithe thought for a few minutes, but could not think of anyone close to her with a name that began with a D, or any other letter for that matter. Her constant travel and focus on her work tended to separate her from others. She reached behind her back and presented a long tube-like instrument. "Could it be this didgeridoo?"

"Yes, that is it," declared the psychic with bravado. Then, she hesitated. "No. I am sensing something else." A chill shuddered across her, and she felt as if someone had just walked across, tripped, and fallen on her grave. "I can speak no more. I am sorry."

"What? Why? Is it death? Do you see death in my future?"

The psychic friend's mystic aura faded briefly, and she took on a more patronizing, obvious tone. "Yes, of course. Death is inevitable."

"But that is not what you saw," Lithe ventured.

"The vision has passed. Please leave now. Take your money back." The psychic friend gestured to where the money had been on the counter, but it was no longer there. Having already reacquired the coins several minutes ago, Lithe turned from the psychic and Quondam also.

He tried to follow her, but she managed to lose him in the droves of passersby. Looking around, he noticed a tent with a sign that read, "The Neurologist-- Free Lobotomies." Intrigued, he looked inside the tent. The Neurologist took a sharp instrument and forced it upward through a client's eye socket. The instant that the instrument pierced the man's brain, an excruciating, blinding pain coincidentally shot through Quondam's skull. The pain drove him backwards, and he fell violently to the ground.

When he woke up, he was in the fetal position and sucking his thumb. He was also eight years old. Luckily, the Neurologist had been busy at his task, and no one else had seen the transformation either.

"Are you alright, boy?" asked the Neurologist.

Quondam closed his eyes and shook his head, trying to make sense of what had happened. "I think I fainted."

"Aye, boy. This operation is not for the weak of heart. Really, you shouldn't even be in Seer's Circle today. How did you get in here?"

"I..." Quondam could not even think of a good lie.

"Never mind," said the Neurologist. "Let me have a look at your head. Does it hurt?"

Quondam rubbed his temples. "Not anymore. It felt like it was about to explode earlier, though."

The man cupped his palm on Quondam's forehead and closed his eyes. While most of the seers, psychics, and mystics of the Seer's Day Festival were in actuality crooks, liars, and false prophets, the Neurologist possessed an amazing ability that no others could claim. Others professed to read minds, but he could actually see into a patient's brain. It was like performing a CAT scan without all the fancy equipment.

The Neurologist explored Quondam's brain, but he could not find anything out of the ordinary anatomically or medically. However, if he had been able to see the connections between neurons, he might have been surprised to discover that Quondam's brain had already developed well beyond that of a normal eight-year-old brain.

Dismissed with a clean bill of health, Quondam left the tent and immediately sought cover from any prying eyes that would spot an underage child out of place at the fair. He entered the tent of some tree-worshipping druids. With the druids' attention elsewhere, he was able to, once again, shift to an age that was more appropriate for the Seer's Day Festival.

Then Quondam noticed that everyone's attention was focused on Lithe, as usual. The head of the druid order was wearing a Sali Lumpa mask. He sat on a thatched rug with his long legs bent and his knees high off the ground. Many ornate sculptures surrounded him, and berries, twigs, and nuts seemed to have been the artist's media.

"I seek the tree that is known to my people as *timbre*." The sound of the tree's name held on in the air and resonated around the room.

"You have come to the right place, for we are familiar with all trees. Welcome. Please, rest your feet. I am Cypress." He motioned for Lithe to sit upon the floor in front of him. She resituated some of her instruments and sat cross-legged on the floor.

"The tree you seek has many names," he continued. "The Elves called it *asa*, while the forest-people call it *bloodbark*. In the language of the commoners of Auldenton, it is known as the Nutberry tree. It is very tall, broad, and very rare. An entire house could fit inside its trunk."

"Very rare, you say? How rare?" questioned Lithe. She had prepared herself for a difficult journey, but she had already traveled far.

"Worry not, fair minstrel. There is a section of forest not far from here where the trees are rather plentiful.

However, they are very well protected. They are revered, worshipped, and cherished by the druids and other forest-people. Even the tree-eating trolls of Sugarwood avoid the Nutberry O. I hope, for your sake, that you did not wish to carve lumber from the trees."

A melodious, yet painful sigh escaped Lithe's lips. The most important part of her initiation ritual into the Symphony required that she build her own instruments. Only a select few Codas qualified for membership. The Symphony was an esoteric sub-culture in the Codan society, which consisted of the very best musicians. Their music transcended what most people accepted as entertainment. Most Codas worked as street musicians, minstrels, or royal bards, and while some were famous or popular among the public at large, very few understood the deeper, more profound power of the musician.

A Coda could construct mandolins and other instruments from the wood of any number of trees. However, some woods possessed special properties that conducted sound better than others did. The wood of the *timbre* tree not only provided the acoustics necessary for playing music, but many believed the wood to have mystical properties. Lithe could have built her mandolin from maple and rosewood, as most instrument-makers commonly do, but the Coda's vizier and seer had advised her that a mandolin of *timbre* wood would be well worth the time.

Chapter 1:07

Fortune Cookies

Quondam stood outside the druids' hut and absorbed the details of Lithe's situation. He knew nothing of the *timbre* tree, or even the nutberry, for that matter. As he poked and prodded the vague memories of his older selves, he had the strong feeling of being watched.

An elderly woman stood at the door of a nearby tent and stared at the timepiece hanging from Quondam's neck. When he noticed her, she retreated into the tent. Quondam followed. The smell of stewed herbovine immediately burned in his senses.

"Excuse me, kind sir, but do you have the time?" the old woman inquired, as Quondam entered the tent. Her accent sounded foreign, yet somehow familiar to him.

"I beg your pardon? The time to do what?" he responded.

"Your watch. It takes a licking and keeps on ticking."

Quondam's mind could not fathom the woman's strange prattle but noticed, quite suddenly, that the watch did make quite a loud ticking sound indeed. He wondered why he had never noticed it before—perhaps because he had never before heard the word "ticking."

Suddenly, she reached forward and grabbed the pocketwatch with a speed that belied her age. She pulled Quondam closer to her face. Her breath smelled of herbovine meat.

"The time has come," the woman said, "to talk of many things." She released her grip on the watch and he fell backwards. She helped him stand and handed him a cookie.

Quondam studied the cookie very closely but could derive little sense from anything. He took a bite of it, for it seemed the logical thing to do. Then, he noticed a small piece of paper tucked within the cookie. It read, "There was a wise man in the East whose constant prayer was that he might see today with the eyes of tomorrow (Alfred Mercier)."

Quondam still comprehended very little of his current situation, but he gathered that the words referred to him. He realized that he saw things differently with the eyes of an older man—he hoped it would give him the forethought needed to prevent circumstances like the one with Munder. He tried to explain the problem to the old woman, but she often interrupted him with nonsense and gibberish.

"Time to make the donuts!" she exclaimed, as she ran to the back of the tent. She picked up a box full of the little cookies and handed it to Quondam.

From out in the circle came the sound of music. It caught the old woman's attention first, and she scurried around the room in search of something. When she found it, she ran out of the tent like a maniac. Quondam followed her, for he was feeling quite mad himself.

Lithe was standing outside the druid's den and playing one of her many instruments. It was a dulcimer, and it made a sweet, calming sound when Lithe's nimble fingers touched the strings. The old woman ran up to her and gave her a cookie.

Lithe accepted the cookie and opened it just enough to get the slip of paper from it. The paper had been folded many times, but Lithe found that, when unfolded, it was a sheet of musical notes. She put the cookie away and began to play the song on her dulcimer.

As the soft, sweet melody unfurled, the old woman seemed calmer and more lucid. She turned to Quondam and quietly said, "Time goes by so slowly, and time can do so much." She smiled at him, and the weary look of age faded temporarily from her face.

"My name is Ekisha," she began. "I am a time keeper. I gather and recount the exploits of Time in all its many lines. However, my work, and my power, are my curse, for what I collect through Time often seems nonsensical."

"I see." Quondam was still trying to piece things together.

"These are nutberry cookies. Take them, for food will be scarce along your journey."

"Journey?" Quondam had hoped all his problems could be solved in Auldenton.

"Yes. You must seek the stump of the ancient *asa* tree. Its guardian may be able to help you, for she is very familiar with birth, rebirth, and growth." Ekisha then turned to Lithe. "Thank you for the song, my dear. It lulled my addled brain and gave me a brief respite to my toil. You may keep the notes as payment, though I owe you much more. Now, I believe you two have some traveling arrangements to make."

Ekisha returned to her tent. As soon as the song ended, her walk grew more labored. She called out, "This killing Time is killing me."

Quondam re-introduced himself to Lithe and remarked at the strange coincidence of their intertwined quests. As they walked away from the tent, they heard the old woman shout something about the woven tapestries of Time.

The sun began to sink below the horizon.

Chapter 1:08

The Timister Towers

Roughly ten minutes had elapsed since Aori noticed the gorged livestock and wrinkled parents, but he had already completed a month's worth of work. Once he began to comprehend the ratio of real-time versus his time, he could schedule many events around his daily chores (which he learned to do at the appropriate times instead of hundreds of times a day).

His first task was to invent a clock so that he could keep up with the passing of time. He spent a few days taking apart all the simple machines in the household, discovered how they worked, and designed a gear in just a few minutes of real-time. After about an hour of trial and error, he had discovered the system of clockwork. He spent another hour or so of real-time building a workshop and a forge, melted down some metal, and used his homemade molds to fashion his gears and pulleys. The first clock he built was quite large, but it fit nicely in the tower he had built.

The clock would not read the correct time until it could be accurately set, of course. He estimated the time, by the position of the sun in the sky, at around two. By three, he had invented another clock that ran on his personal time, but instead of an hour and minute hand, it had a day and week hand. This soon became obsolete, however, because the time ratio kept growing larger and larger. He had to spend a month or two studying math to keep up with the ratio. By four o'clock, he could complete complex mathematical equations and had written many essays on mathematical theory.

The limited supply of reading material served as the biggest problem Aori encountered. He had already read every book in his parents' small library by late afternoon. He was running out of things to do, and boredom began to surface.

He painted pictures until he ran out of paint, wrote a play about the unheard conversation of an elderly couple, and took up needlepoint. He wrote a book of essays debating the existence of creativity versus time management. In it, he reasoned that creativity and ingenuity derive from having too much time on one's hands. "If ten Sali Lumpas were put in a room with ten quills," he wrote, "in ten years' time they would have recreated the complete literary works of Dolente."

Dolente wrote quite prolifically and steadily for about ten years. Many considered him one of the world's greatest writers at that time. In just ten years, he wrote 47 plays, 14 novels, 3 how-to self-help books, and well over a thousand poems. His last work, *The Complete History of Time*, was never finished; he died of old age while writing the second chapter. Oddly enough, those who knew him swore that he had been only thirty-seven years old at the time.

Aori decided to visit the library of Auldenton. There, he could choose from a wider selection of literature as well as catch up with his old friend and teacher, Bertram. He wrote a letter to his teacher to inform him and set up an appointment for the following day. However, he grew tired of waiting for the letter-carrier to arrive and decided to just surprise Bertram with a visit that day.

When Aori arrived, he greeted his mentor with a firm embrace. "It has been a long time, my old friend."

With a puzzled look, Bertram replied, "Aori, we saw one another just a few days ago during the preparation for the festival. You're not supposed to lose your memory until you get to be my age, young man." He studied his student closely. "It does appear, however, that the time has mistreated you. Are those wrinkles I see?"

Aori looked at himself in the mirror to confirm the wrinkles but quickly changed the subject. "I thought I might borrow some books, Master Bertram. Or, I suppose I could just read them here." He picked a book from the shelf and began to read it. It was a thick book, but he finished before Bertram could even answer the question.

"Something about you seems odd, Aori. Are you getting enough sleep?" Aori thought about Bertram's question very carefully. He felt as if he had been at work for around a month, and he had forgotten all about sleeping. He surmised that external forces, such as the lowering of body temperature in relation to the brightness of the sun, determined his sleep cycle. He postulated a theory about the body's natural cycles, which he termed *circadian rhythms*. Aori completed an essay in his head in the time it took for Bertram to inhale enough breath for his next question:

"You're not using that white powder that killed your brother, are you?"

"No, Bertram. I have merely fine-tuned my time management skills. Proper scheduling is key—Are you hungry, Bertram?" Aori found operating within the normal parameters of time, as was necessary to carry on a conversation with his friend, to be extremely taxing. His mind could not wait for one sentence to finish before beginning the next.

In the seven hours since the old wizard cast the spell on him, Aori had eaten all the food in his house. *Apparently consumption rates and other body functions exist independently of sleep cycles*, he thought.

"Here," Bertram said as he offered Aori a small cookie. "Plenty more where that came from. One of the seers from the festival brought these by earlier today." Looking around the room, Bertram added, "She called my library primitive and out-of-date, the old witch!"

Aori took a bite out of the cookie, and Bertram warned him against choking on the paper message inside. "The messages seem to be mostly short, pretentious sayings by men of whom I have never heard."

Aori read his message aloud, "In time take time while time doth last, for time is no time when time is past. – Anonymous."

"See what I mean? This 'Anonymous' is no Dolente, that's for certain."

"Dolente's work is nothing but bilious, superfluous foofaraw. The expanse of his melancholy is only exceeded by his lack of maturity," Aori opined.

Again, Bertram looked puzzled. Just a few days ago, Aori had borrowed every one of the library's Dolente books, including his surprisingly thick autobiography.

"How about a game of *Epic*?" Aori suggested, in order to divert from the confusion.

Epic was an early form of chess or the even more modern game of *Risk*. The name came from an Elder Elvish word for "unbelievably, painfully long." Each player took his or her turn and then moved their carved figurines one space.

Fortunately, Aori had already carved all the pieces

> **Epic**
>
> Most *Epic* boards consisted of 5,425 spaces, had to be folded several times in order to fit in a house, and required at least six people to lift. The carving of the figurines took the most time, for the materials first had to be gathered from all over the world and then hand-carved using a very dull knife. Most people believed the rules to be a bit absurd, but all agreed that the figurine-carving was an improvement on the previous practice of waiting for the pieces of stone to naturally erode into person-shaped figurines.

for both Bertram and himself. Since he was the youngest of them, he played first. He took a minute or two to plan his move, but it seemed instantaneous to Bertram.

Try as he might, Aori could not adjust his personal time enough to tolerate the time Bertram took for each move. He grew immensely impatient and felt as if he would be an old man before Bertram finished his turn.

A virtual eternity passed (which was only a few minutes real-time), and Bertram moved his piece. Aori immediately moved his piece. "That's it?" asked Bertram. "You didn't even take a second to think about your move! This game is about careful planning and strategy, Aori. You can't just... just..."

The game was over. Aori had won. "Oh, I used strategy, Master Bertram. I studied *Epic* for several weeks while waiting for you to move. I then planned my counter to your move for an hour before making a decision."

"Weeks?" Bertram dubiously questioned. Then, he looked up at his student, who seemed much older than he had just moments earlier.

"Yes. Of course, I didn't just wait here the entire time. I also took a few weeks to read your books. I am afraid that they are a bit out-of-date indeed. I went ahead and translated some of the older texts to a more current manner of speech. Since I had already learned Elder Elvish, Codan, and several other languages, I spent some of the time translating the texts into those languages as well. Codan is a really beautiful language, you know. If done properly, it sounds like singing."

Aori could not wait for Bertram's response. There was much to do. He grabbed a bag full of the fortune cookies and cracked one open. It read, "How poor are they that have no patience! What wound did ever heal but by degrees? – Shakespeare, *Othello*, Act II, Scene 3."

Hmm, Aori thought. *I shall have to read this Shakespeare someday.* Then, his thought shifted to his broken arm. He knew that only a day of real-time had passed, but the injury was fully healed. *What wound did ever heal but by degrees? Why, this one.*

Outside the library, the sun was setting in the east.

Chapter 1:09

Oneirotopsis

Eventually, Bertram rediscovered his ability to speak. "What?" He found that he remained just as dumbfounded. In the few seconds it took to close his eyes and give his head a good shake, Aori had seemingly disappeared. In actuality, he had just walked off at his own leisurely pace.

Bertram picked up a cookie, broke it apart, and nibbled on the crumbs. The message inside read, "Bed-ways is right-ways now. – Burgess." He took the cookie's advice and went to sleep.

Oneiromancy is the practice of divining the future in dreams. In *The Big Book of Dreams*, Dolente wrote the following:

> In dreams, time has no meaning. One minute, everything seems to be going okay; the next minute, a Sali Lumpa is getting to know a sandwich, carnally. And, the next minute, you *are* the sandwich, only you're very old and past your expiration date. Your bread is moldy, your meat is rancid, and your herbovine rump has wilted (Dolente, 412).

So, how does an oneiromancer distinguish the future from the past, present, and downtime if time has no meaning in dreams? Not easily, and not without losing his or her mind completely—that's how.

On his way home, Aori wrote some poems about the moon and stars, knitted a sweater, and cut his hair, beard, and nails for the millionth time that day. He decided to invent something that would slow down the growth of his hair. However, it would have to wait, because he was stuck having to ride his horse home, for he was too tired to walk.

Traveling had always been a time-consuming, wearisome chore, but now that Aori was running out of things to do, it was downright tedious. He focused on his personal timeline and concentrated, trying to shorten the journey. While the spell held no sway over the items and objects around him, he was able to decrease the personal-time to real-time ratio enough that what was left of the four-hour trip seemed to take a fraction of the time. He wished he had thought of that while waiting for Bertram to move his *Epic* piece.

Since most of his body was already asleep, Aori went to bed. Sleep crashed in instantaneously, and he wasted no time cycling into the rapid-eye-movement level of sleep.

As we sleep, some parts of our body shut down, while those on the night shift keep working. Old, dead cells are sloughed off to make room for new ones. Hair and nails 'grow' during sleep in the sense that they are made up of discarded cells. We do most of our aging at night, and, sadly, there is nothing we can do to stop it (Dolente, 918).

Aori had no idea what cells were, but suddenly he was aware that they were growing old and dying inside him. From there, his perspective shifted to a point somewhere outside his body.

As he studied his own face closely, he saw a tiny line appear on his skin between his eyes and his temples. Suddenly, a crow swept down from the sky and scratched his face with its feet. The formerly tiny lines began to extend outward like vines or fissures in stone.

His discursive mind caught on to the analogy, and he watched a tall tree as it experienced the effects of a year's growth in a much shorter amount of time. Buds formed on its branches, grew into leaves, went through various color changes, and eventually plummeted to the ground. The process started over from the beginning, and gradually Aori was aware of a broadening in the girth of the tree. The outward growth would have been all but imperceptible, had it not been for the fact that its bark was enveloping his hand as it held on to the tree.

Instinctively, Aori unsheathed what turned out to be a rather dull butter knife and attacked the tree. After a relatively long period of sawing back and forth with the knife, a nick in the bark spewed forth a thick, crimson substance. The knife turned into a saw, which turned into a herring. When the fish swam away, Aori tenaciously continued his assault on the tree with his bare hands.

A giant cookie fell out of the sky, stopped just inches above the ground, and cracked open like an egg. An egg-yolk dripped out of the cookie and then turned into a large slip of paper. The message read:

> *In time, even an ant may move a mountain, and a tree may be cut down with a butter knife (Anonymous).*

The paper message then sliced through the tree trunk and a sweet, melodic voice shouted "TIMBER!"

Several small men made up of gears and pulleys then carried the tree away and built two tall towers from the wood. Aori recognized his clocks, which were each placed at the top of a tower.

The hands of the real-time clock moved at a normal speed, while the other clock's hands moved so quickly they could not be seen. Aori watched himself age very quickly. His hair turned white, his teeth fell out, and he could no longer walk without a cane. As his heartbeat slowed down, the ticking of the clock did too. Both syncopated sounds stopped at the same time, but the real-time clock kept ticking.

From Aori's point of view, the world seemed to flash in a flurry of images. His parents died and decomposed before his eyes, as did all of his friends and acquaintances. A frozen tear on his face suddenly slid down his cheek and dropped to the ground.

When the dream ended and Aori rose from his bed, he noticed that many of his muscles and joints ached. *Must have worked too hard yesterday*, he thought. He took his time getting up and out of bed, and when he finally walked outside, he noticed that the clock read half-past two. *It must have stopped working yesterday.* Judging by the sun's position in the sky, however, he ascertained that he had slept most of the day away.

Judging by the absence of any living livestock and the thickness of the dust on all the furniture, he surmised that he had actually slept for many days. Quickly, he rushed to his parents' room. His father's beard had grown wild and bushy, and their hair seemed a bit longer as well. *Just how many days have passed? Perhaps a week or more.*

Aori put his ear to his father's chest and listened for a heartbeat. It was very faint, but steady. It sounded a bit like a clock ticking, which reminded him of his dream. His parents' faces were sunken and sallow, and the skin hung loosely from their bones. Again, Aori cursed old age and its debilitating effects. But, his parents were alive and he was thankful for it, despite his sympathy for their suffering.

For the first time since waking, Aori looked at his own skin. It, too, seemed baggier than usual. It was also quite wrinkled and worn. He ran to a mirror as fast as his legs would take him. The reflection looked like his father had around age fifty. *While but a few days passed here*, he thought, *I aged roughly twenty years.*

Therein lay the drawback to the spell. If he lost control of his personal time, he would become old and decrepit like his parents. However, if he slowed down his own aging process, the rest of the world would decay.

Like the gears of a clock, his mind began to work. That day, he set in motion a series of plans and machinations that would change not only his life, but the lives of many others around the world.

Chapter 1:10

The Journey du Jour

The English word *journey* comes from the French word for *day*, regardless of the fact that journeys usually take much longer. The word in the common language of Aia meant something like, "Don't plan to be there by nightfall," which was, of course, far more accurate.

"The sun has set and darkness is coming," sang Lithe. "We shall need to make camp soon, for our journey shall not end tonight."

"Yes," agreed Quondam. "I believe Bed-Time is upon us."

They had only been walking for a few hours, but the ground was rocky, and treacherous slopes had slowed them. The trip had taken them through the base of the cliff from which Munder had fallen, but Quondam had seen no sign of his friend's body.

"You shouldn't worry so much," said Lithe. "Furrowing your brow makes you look old."

The contrast between an adult's ideas of aging to those of a child bewildered Quondam. "I've always wanted to look older."

"What's on your mind?" The sound of her voice beckoned Quondam to empty his every thought. The Coda would (and will, one day) make great psychiatrists.

"My friend, Munder. I watched him fall from one of these cliffs, but we should have found him by now. Do you think we'll be able to help him without the body?"

Lithe furrowed her brow. "Did no one sing for his soul?"

"Um... was I supposed to?"

"When someone dies, my people create music to carry their souls to the next world. Sometimes, our songs give the Coda a bit more time here on Aia. I have even heard of Coda being given a second chance at their own lives, but that is very rare. I've never heard of that working for a human, though." She patted him consolingly on the shoulder.

Some time passed, and the duo experienced what would one day be known as "awkward silence." During these times, those involved have reported that time seemed to slow down and minutes became hours. However, the reasoning escapes even me as to why the god of Time would stoop to manipulating conversations between relative strangers. Those who have experienced the sensation grasp frantically at any conversational scraps in order to fill the silence.

"My father was a great warrior. When I grow up, I'm going to be a great warrior also."

Lithe stared at Quondam with a confused look. "You seem relatively grown up already. How many years have you? In Codan, we would say you are a *ventee*... roughly twenty cycles of the seasons?"

Quondam shrugged. "I don't really remember my birthday. My parents died when I was very young."

"I'm sorry," said Lithe. She understood very little about the life cycles of humans, but she was beginning to understand how grief seemed to surround and drive their preoccupation with death. Whereas the Coda saw the end as just part of Life's Song, the humans she had met in her travels seemed to focus on loss.

In an effort to change the subject, Lithe began, "My mother is an heiress to the Aeolian family, the House of the Air." As she spoke of her mother, Lithe's voice seemed to whistle like a gentle breeze. The breeze even seemed to move through her chestnut colored hair, giving her a very peaceful aura.

"Does that mean she's royalty or something?"

"Well, times have changed since the days of the Ruling Houses. Some still see it as a high status, I suppose." Her voice and demeanor stiffened noticeably. "My father," she said, almost as if speaking through her teeth, "comes from a family with a lengthy heritage. He is what one might call *old-fashioned.*"

Quondam wished he had as much to say about his own parents as Lithe had about hers. Her stories continued for an hour, as they set up camp and settled down for the night. Throughout that time, Quondam remained enraptured by her voice and never tired of hearing her speak.

As night fell on the weary travelers, an even deeper darkness hung over Auldenton. The Seer's Day festivities lasted well past midnight, and the commotion required the full attention of Auldenton's town guards. The bulk of the military was away at war, but for those present, it was like an episode of COPS in New Orleans at Mardi Gras.

If Quondam's eyes could have seen all the way to Auldenton, he might have been interested in the events that took place that evening. At that very time, a small pocket of air in Quondam's former room made a sudden popping sound as time and space twisted like a wet towel. As a wet towel drips water, so too did time and space release a rather large amount of pent-up energy.

When the energy took its normal form, shiny black armor covered its rather large body. On its helm protruded two twisted, black horns, and the image of an hourglass adorned its chest. One of its arms was bare in that it was not armored, but neither was it covered in skin. Rather, the arm seemed carved out of wood.

Quietly and quickly, as if he was following a tight schedule, the armored man left the room and walked down the hall of the orphanage. One of the night-shift workers saw him, shouted, and fell dead with a broad stroke of a battle-axe.

The armored man took only a few steps to traverse the long hall, and he had to duck to get under doorways, but nothing and no one slowed his progress as he marched.

Upon entering the dormitory of Mr. Fist, who had been recuperating from his injury only a few nights ago, the man's wooden hand moved in a manner unexpected of wood. Quite animatedly, the hand clutched Mr. Fist's throat and lifted him several feet from the floor. The armored man squeezed Mr. Fist's throat until bones in his neck began to crumble.

When the armored man was satisfied with the death of Mr. Fist, he looked down at his wrist as one who is pressed for time might do. By pressing a little button on the side of his watch, a dim green glow lit up the darkened room. The light shone off his black armor, and the air around him hummed as time and space twisted again.

In an instant, several other men occupied the room. Some of them wore similar armor, while others seemed to be dressed only in loincloths and excessive amounts of hair. They all looked at their watches nervously.

"You're late," said the armored man. "You'll have to work overtime. Clean up the mess. Erase this place from the History books."

With that, the armored man left just as quickly as he had entered. In just a few seconds time, a large explosion destroyed the entire orphanage. Quite obviously, no one survived. Well, one can assume that those who triggered the blast escaped just in time, but I hardly think that readers or history buffs will be too concerned with the fates of murderers and assassins—that is, except for the fate of the armored man.

"You sleep," Lithe suggested. "I shall take the first watch. I rarely sleep when traveling anyway." Lithe sat down beside a tree and began to play a soft, somnolent tune on her dulcimer. "This should help sleep find you. Sweet dreams."

The lullaby she played weighed down Quondam's eyelids with surprising quickness. He tried to argue that he was big enough to keep watch over himself, but the words faded with his consciousness.

As he slept, the ticking sound of the pocketwatch kept perfect time with the lullaby. He watched his watch as if from a distance, and it swung back and forth from its chain. Tick. Tock. Tick. Tock.

Quondam saw himself in his eight year-old base form. He gradually metamorphosed into the trunk of a large tree. Three large branches extended outwards and upwards from the trunk. Those branches grew into the three, eighteen, and twenty-four year-old versions of him. More branches grew out from the trunk, which represented (and eventually took the form of) Quondam at other ages. Soon, there were roughly a hundred large branches stemming from the main trunk of the tree.

From those branches, many smaller limbs, twigs, and tendrils grew. Somehow, Quondam recognized them as reflections of himself from many alternate timelines. The number of offshoots numbered as countless and infinite as the stars in the sky.

Each version of Quondam wielded a different weapon. His younger forms had the familiar wooden sword that lay sheathed beside his sleeping body. Only hours ago, that sword had pierced the skin of his worst enemy and given Munder a splinter. One thirty year-old version of him was carving a bow and arrows out of its tree branch. An elderly Quondam propped himself up with a long, wooden staff, while one of his offshoots used the staff to cast magical spells. In fact, each and every version of Quondam carried some sort of wooden item; one of the small children even wore wooden clogs on his feet.

The tree grew leaves, which eventually fell off and grew again. The fallen leaves began to pile up, and the younger versions of Quondam jumped and played in them. Gradually, the branches of the tree began to intertwine until all that could be seen of the tree was a very tall, very broad trunk.

Without warning, the man who the old wizard had called Aori attacked the tree and quickly sliced through it. A sweet, melodious voice shouted, "TIMBER!"

The fallen tree metamorphosed back into the Quondam of eight, and he walked up to the stump. As he studied it, he began to cycle through the ages of his lifetime. He thought of Munder as he, too, became so old that pieces of him broke off and turned to dust. His legs gave out and he fell to the ground in the position and form of a fetus. The cycle sped up and then flashed to an image of a sperm cell and an egg cell. The zygote became an embryo, which eventually turned into a seed and, finally, a tree.

As the tree cycled through its various ages, Quondam began to gain consciousness. He opened his eyes to the image of a tree, which convinced him to close them again. He felt a hand with long, slender fingers on his throat.

"Who are you, and what sorcery is this?" shouted Lithe. She had watched Quondam's strange growth cycle for most of the night, and had tried unsuccessfully for hours to wake him.

"Did I turn into dust? Did I turn into a zygote?"

"What? No, you did not turn into a goat. But if you do not explain this strange witchery soon, I shall choke the life out of you, old man."

Quondam looked at his hands, which he noted were, indeed, the hands of an old man. That explained why his eyesight and hearing seemed so impaired. He shifted to a younger age and felt Lithe's grip tighten on his neck. "Okay," he whispered with what little breath he had left. "I'll explain."

He told her about the old man, the rocket, the hourglass, and all the clocks. He explained the mystical properties of his pocketwatch and told her about the unfortunate demise of Munder.

"So you were that young boy who was so drawn to my music?"

"Yes," Quondam replied.

The news surprised Lithe, for the Coda were not an easy species to fool. They had many songs with discordant tones that could break spells and cast away illusions. Despite her initial shock, she felt as if the whole story seemed a bit familiar.

"The old man from your story sounds a bit like the man our people call Tempo," she said, after they had resumed their journey.

"You mean you know him? Where does he live? I really need his help! I think he could help me turn back time and prevent Munder's death!"

"I know *of* him. My relatives often spoke of a wizard or enchanter who visited our people from time to time. The elders of my kin would sing us to sleep with the tales about the wizard."

"Do you remember any of the stories?" asked Quondam.

"I might be able to remember the words if I play a bit of the tune." She reached for her dulcimer and hammered one of the strings. "Alas! The song was not played with a dulcimer, so the tale cannot be recounted."

"What? Why can't you just speak it without music?"

"Unfortunately, the song does not exist without the proper instrument. If the tune does not exist, neither do the words. They are intertwined, like our quests and the branches of this tree. I am sorry."

"What instrument did your elders use?" Quondam asked.

"A stringed instrument called a mandolin."

"And you don't have one of those, among your assort-ment of instruments?" Quondam found that hard to believe, for she carried more instruments than he had seen in his entire life.

"Sadly, no. My quest is to build one out of the very tree we seek. You call it *asa* or nutberry. I call it *timbre*."

Quondam's thoughts immediately drew to his dream. "I think someone else may beat us to it."

Chapter 1:11

A Stitch in Time

Quondam looked worried. "How long is the journey to the Nutberry O?" he asked his companion.

"Depending on our pace, it could be a nine days' journey."

"I fear we may not have nine days," said Quondam.

"We might make it in less time, but I am not familiar with these paths. What do you fear?"

Quondam told her about his dream and the man with the formerly broken arm. "I think my dream was telling me that we have to stop him. Is there no quicker way?"

"Perhaps if we had a map and some other means of travel, we could get there in time," Lithe sang-spoke in a voice that eased Quondam's mind.

"Are there any towns upon this road, where we might find such things?"

"No," she said. The song temporarily left her voice, for she was worried too.

Quondam reached into his bag and brought forth one of the cookies Ekisha had given him. "Are you hungry? Perhaps we should share one, since we may not have enough to last the nine days' journey. Nevertheless, I do feel as though I could travel for many days on one cookie alone. They are very filling, don't you think?"

Lithe agreed and took part of the cookie. Her half contained a folded up piece of paper. "A map!" she exclaimed. "How fortunate!" She unfolded the map completely, and the two of them rested, shared another cookie, and studied the map.

"It looks like we could save some time if we leave the road here," Quondam said as he pointed to the map. "However, we shall have to cut across this wooded area."

"Do you think that is wise?" questioned Lithe. "We don't know what creatures may live in the woods."

Quondam reached down inside him for some sort of sage-like advice. His skin began to wrinkle and his hair grew long and white. A beard and moustache grew from his face. His clouded eyes struggled to read the message from their second shared cookie, which depicted a circular design, so that the beginning and the ending connected:

> **Coinkydink**
> Frequently in stories, an event takes place that seems to happen at just the right time. For instance, one might say, "We'll be fine as long as it doesn't start raining." In that instance, a torrential rainstorm most assuredly follows. Some might call this happpenstance a strange coincidence or even fanciful writing on the part of the storyteller. However, it's important to realize how manipulative the god of Time really is. Timing is everything.

wisdom

with   *with*

wrinkles

Gradually, his boyish innocence left him, and he felt more familiar with the region. "Yes," he said. "I remember now. I have experience with these woods. The woodland beasts should cause us no great harm."

Unbeknownst to Quondam, the woods at this point in time were not as he remembered them. In addition to the tree-eating trolls, there were the pretentiously artsy Sali Lumpa, the wild herbovine, and various tribes of woodland people, none of which took very kindly to strangers.

In fact, the Sali Lumpa were so unfriendly to strangers that they often hid their sculptures and stopped handing out invitations to their art exhibits altogether.

In accordance with the map, the road ahead of them bent just west of the forest. At the intersection of the forest path and the curve, the Auldenton military had set up a checkpoint, or *turnpike*, as the forest-people called it.

As soon as Lithe's keen eyes spotted the soldiers, she hissed a crude epithet in her native tongue. Had Quondam's future self been unfamiliar with the language, he would have thought it a melodious incantation.

"What is it, Lithe?"

"Soldiers," she whispered. "Auldentonian, by the looks of it. How could they...?" She trailed off, unwilling to mention the pockets she had picked. Thievery was not a practice she preferred, but she saw it as a necessary evil for a wandering minstrel. The townspeople of Auldenton in particular held on to their coins like a Sali Lumpa holds on to its nuts. Besides, the Coda were naturally nimble, and the magical qualities of their music went hand-in-hand with a little sleight-of-hand.

"Let's just stay calm," suggested Quondam, which drew to his attention the fact that Lithe seemed to have only two states—calm and stoic. Though she would never admit it, she had inherited that matter-of-fact demeanor from her father. He had been an emotionless rock for most of her upbringing, and her current task had given her the same determined, no-nonsense attitude.

"Halt!" shouted one of the soldiers. "Who goes there?"

Quondam cleared his throat. "I am Quondam, and this is my companion, Lithe."

"Where are you traveling?" asked one of the other soldiers.

"We are headed into the forest," Quondam answered.

The soldiers looked over them suspiciously. "Are there any children traveling with you?"

Quondam had to check himself to see what age he was at that time. "What do you mean, sir? I am obviously an old man, and I have no children."

"What is this about?" asked Lithe, who was relieved to know that they were not looking for pick-pockets.

"Two orphans 'ave gone missin' from the local boys' home," said one of the soldiers, who got a stern look from what must have been his commanding officer.

Something caught in Quondam's throat. He coughed.

"Do you believe that they were kidnapped?" asked Lithe.

"No," said the more forth-coming soldier, who seemed to be ignoring his superior's sideways glances completely. "There's been a tragedy at the orphanage. Seein' as how them kids is the only ones not around…"

"We are speculating that they could have been involved," finished the officer.

Quondam fought the urge to race to his defense, like a child who has just been accused of breaking his mother's favorite vase. "I didn't do it!" he wanted to shout. Instead, he said, "Perhaps the children were escaping some sort of danger themselves."

He tried to remember what had happened when he and Munder left the orphanage, but the recollection was like sifting through sixty or so years of memories. It seemed so long ago, but surely they hadn't murdered anyone during their escape.

Everyone's mind has a tendency to block out the little bits of information that cause more pain, but some minds dissociate from the traumatic experiences altogether. Those with dissociative identity disorder create other identities to deal with memories that the core identity wishes to repress. In Quondam's case, his mind shifted past the trauma much like it shifted through physical pain or fatigue.

Unfortunately, the intense headache he had felt at the festival returned in full force at this inopportune time. The harder he fought to maintain his older image, the more excruciating the pain became.

"If you intend to go through the forest," said the officer, "you need to be extra careful. I care not to venture a guess as to what manner of creature dwells there."

"Dragons, they say, and trolls that eat trees," offered the other soldier.

"Dwight, please," said the officer. "If either of you hears any information about the missing orphans, please report to someone from the Auldentonian Guard."

"We will," said Quondam, as they passed through the checkpoint. The pain threatened to burst through his skull and gave his elderly walk an extra strained appearance.

Regardless of the danger that faced them, Quondam and Lithe left the road and trekked deep into the woods. Once they had passed well beyond the earshot of the soldiers, Lithe whispered, "It is very fortunate that you could change your appearance from that of a young orphan boy."

Quondam swallowed hard. As he reverted to his true age, the pain in his head subsided. "Unfortunately, I guess I can't stay old for too long."

"So you are one of those orphans they seek?"

"Yes," answered Quondam. "Promise you won't tell?"

"We all have our secrets, I suppose," said Lithe. "You have my word."

The wind blew through the treetops above them, but the air that enveloped them hung thickly in place. Even Lithe, whose lungs were naturally suited for sustained singing or piping, found the air here hard to breathe. Talking became all but impossible, and the silence seemed as thick as the air.

"Do you hear that?" asked Lithe breathlessly.

Quondam tried to listen harder, but his ears were not as keen as Lithe's.

"Why are there no birds chirping? The forest should be full of sounds."

He definitely had noticed the absence of sound.

Lithe took from its sheath a thin pipe, which she softly put to her lips. "This is Soffiara," she said, referring to the instrument. "It was given to me by my mother, Aria. Wherever she walked, a gentle, sweet breeze accompanied her. The Codan word for 'air' comes from her name." She then played a light, airy tune on the pipe.

Suddenly, a breeze blew in from the West. It was light and refreshing, and it carried the stagnant air of the forest floor away with it. Quondam and Lithe found it much easier to breathe, and their pace quickened.

Eventually, Lithe's song ended and she took a deep breath. Suddenly, she and Quondam were aware of all the sounds that surrounded them. Birds sang from their perches in the treetops, frogs croaked, Sali Lumpas screeched, and even the trees seemed to rustle with the rhythm of music.

"Do you think the creatures of the forest are responding to your song? Or were they always like this, but inaudible due to the thickness of the air?" asked Quondam.

"I do not know. Perhaps they are singing because they are glad to have fresh air." In addition to the sounds of nature, Lithe could hear the faint sound of drums and chanting. "Do you hear the drums?"

"No," Quondam admitted. It was well known that the Coda people were innately deft at hearing sounds, no matter how soft. Just to get a second opinion, Quondam shifted to a different age. "I believe I hear it now."

"It is getting louder. They are coming this way. They must have heard the pipe."

"Could they be coming to play along with you, perhaps?" Quondam suggested.

"Let us hope so. Be wary, nonetheless. Have you any weapons?"

Quondam thought of his dream and all the weapons his various forms wielded. Unfortunately, his wooden sword was practically useless in a real battle. "None but this." He held the sword aloft. "I'm afraid the worst it can do is give a bad splinter." He could not explain the previous encounter his sword had had with Mr. Fist, and chose, rather, to block it from his memory.

Like when the police put up yellow tape around a murder scene, Quondam's mind had cordoned off that memory. Several older versions of him fought to keep his more fragile selves from reliving past horrors such as the death of his parents, his unfortunate experiences at the orphanage, and even Munder's death. For the good of the whole, memories were sequestered, quarantined, or repressed. The unfortunate side effect, however, was that while Quondam had no trouble remembering skills or knowledge, his memory for events was very poor.

"Let us hope, then, that they are as harmless as you remember, or that there is one among your menagerie who is skilled at fighting with his hands." She listened closely to the tribal music. When she had pinpointed their location, she told Quondam to wait behind a tree while she went to get a better look. As she strode off into the brush, she made no sound whatsoever.

"Her powers over sound are unbelievable," Quondam said to himself. "One minute, she is making beautiful music and then, she wipes out even the sound of her footsteps. And yet, here I am—a brave warrior with no weapon."

Lithe bounded lightly up a tree, using her tail as a Sali Lumpa would. She preferred playing music to acrobatics, but growing up with dancers in the family taught her to be agile and light on her feet. She grabbed a limb with her long fingers and pulled herself to a perfect vantage point.

She watched the group of woodsmen approach. They had not the demeanor of an army going to war. They seemed to be unarmed and only interested in their music.

A rustle in the distance caught Lithe's attention. A teenage boy was scampering through the brush, trying to avoid detection by the rest of his tribe. His feet moved so rapidly that it almost seemed as if he were flying along the ground. *A tagalong*, Lithe presumed.

The teen did not notice Lithe in her perch far above his head, but his sneaking around was getting him closer and closer to Quondam's position. While trying to keep an eye on the advancing party, she leapt to another branch.

Meanwhile, Quondam heard the rustling of feet behind him and wondered why Lithe was no longer suppressing her sound. He turned around, and he and the teenage boy noticed each other at the same time. They exchanged looks for a few seconds. The boy had dark, rough-hewn hair that mingled almost unnoticeably with several dark feathers. His face was dark, and Quondam could not tell if it was his natural coloring or some sort of paint. A necklace of animal bones hung from his neck, and they rattled as the boy circled Quondam. With a sudden, synchronous movement, they lunged at one another.

Eighteen was a fair match for the teenage boy, who had wrestled with the Sali Lumpas for all his life. The two opponents grappled one another and fell to the ground. As they rolled around, Quondam got the advantage and pinned the teenager.

"Crowfoot!" one of the woodmen yelled in the language of the forest.

Suddenly, an arrow hummed through the thickening air and lodged in Quondam's chest barely missing the pocketwatch. He fell backward and noticed the large group of tribesmen encircling him. "Poison arrow," he understood one of the woodmen to say in a strange forest-language as he began to lose consciousness.

The tribesmen moved in closer, and one of them said, "Crowfoot, what are you doing here? How did you get ahead of us?"

"I ran," said the boy, as he kicked Quondam in the ribs. The rest of the tribe attempted to kick him as well, but a sudden shrill noise above incapacitated them.

Lithe leapt from a tree, somersaulted in the air, and landed right next to Quondam's body. She followed up the shrill note with a deep breath. The tribesmen were still clutching their ears when, all of a sudden, they became very frightened and shouted words which Lithe could not understand.

Quondam understood them, though. He rose to his feet as a taller, sturdier man of thirty-six. He pulled the arrow from his chest, winced a bit, and then shifted to a different age. Much to everyone's astonishment, the wound had healed and the effects of the poison had abated. The tribesmen found this, and Quondam's cycling quickly through many different ages, to be quite alarming, which caused them to shout, in their native tongue, "Demon! Sorcerer!"

Quondam's knowledge of the forest-language came from one of his older, more experienced forms. The remarkable healing ability, however, was a first for everyone in his personal timeline. In later years, he would understand that his multiple ages were each taking "shifts," while those not currently working could heal, learn a new skill or language, or just remain in stasis. As long as a wound did not take multiple years to overcome, a recuperated version could take the place of the injured.

"People of the forest," Quondam began in their tongue, "I am no demon or sorcerer. We are... um." He couldn't think of a way to explain his magical power in a way these primitive people could understand.

"Tell them we came to play music and rid their forest of the evil air spirit," suggested Lithe, who could detect stammering in any language. She began to play Soffiara again, since the air had become heavy during the distraction.

"Yes! Good idea!" As the air lightened again, Quondam translated her plan into the forest-language. The woodsmen responded by cheering, chanting, and playing their drums.

As the tribesmen lead the two companions to the tribal campgrounds, Quondam discussed many things with the tribe's bowman. The tribe called the bowman Limbender, because he bent tree-limbs to use as bows. They shared tips and secrets on the subject of archery and made idle chitchat about the weather. Both agreed that the weather had improved considerably since he and Lithe had arrived.

The teenage boy called Crowfoot caught up to them from behind. Limbender said, "Crowfoot, we told you to stay behind in the village. These woods are dangerous."

Crowfoot looked up at Quondam suspiciously. "This man is dangerous."

"You needn't fear me, Crowfoot." Quondam felt that he could identify with the teenage boy. Crowfoot was not yet a man, but he longed to be a part of the tribe's scouting missions. Quondam made a sort of courteous bow, and continued, "It was an honor to spar with you. You fight like a man twice your age."

Crowfoot accepted the compliment gratefully, but he still felt uneasy as he looked at Quondam, who had not been twice his age when they had begun the fight. Furthermore, it seemed to Crowfoot that a dark cloud hovered over the new outsiders.

Primatists

Unbeknownst to Quondam, humans in Auldenton calling themselves the Primatists believed that they were evolutionary descendants of the Sali Lumpas. They formed a religious sect, worshipped their primate ancestors, and created numerous artistic displays using nuts and twigs. Those who disagreed with the Primatists chose to ignore the question, "Where did humans come from?" and focus on disagreeing with the Primatists.

Upon their arrival at the campgrounds, the tribal chieftain approached them suspiciously. "Who are these strangers, Limbender?"

"They are from the city, Chieftain-King," the bowman explained. "They have brought a breeze with them, and it has fought and killed the evil air spirit." He pulled the chieftain to the side. "The older gentleman with the beard and the strange necklace may also be a demon or a sorcerer. He may be a demon-sorcerer."

The chieftain greeted them with a cautious smile, but he shook their hands in the manner of polite citizens in Auldenton. "Welcome," he said.

The chieftain led the two strangers to his tent, which he had stitched together from the hides of wild herbovines. The three of them sat in relative silence (except for the sound of the drums and chanting outside the tent) for around five minutes. Finally, Quondam remarked on the state of the weather.

"Ah, yes," said the chieftain, in the forest-language. "Thank you for bringing your magical breeze. I am sorry for my rudeness. We are not accustomed to having visitors. My name is Albert Leafblower. If it is easier for you, we can speak in the language of Auldenton."

"You speak the common language?" Quondam asked.

"I should hope so," he began, speaking in the common tongue. "I was raised in an orphanage in Auldenton."

"So was I!" Quondam marveled at the coincidence.

Chieftain Leafblower took a minute to reflect, or to inhale the smoke from his pipe. Either way, he exhaled and said, "Were your parents also killed by hunters?"

"No," said Quondam.

Prince Albert in a Can

Readers should thank their lucky stars for temporal omniscience at this point. In recent years, jokes about Prince Albert in a can, which referred to an incident with a young Chieftain Leafblower and a can, have largely been outlawed. Modern, futuristic societies no longer find the joke even slightly humorous or clever. Since it is the objective of this particular Historian to maintain a strict level of cleverness, any such reference to Prince Albert has been omitted.

"Hmm," the old man said, as if disappointed that the orphanage was all they shared in common. He took another long drag of his pipe. "I was born here, among the forest people. My people. My father was the chieftain-king of the forest.

"My people were primitive and uncivilized in the eyes of the outsiders. When the hunters came through the forest looking for pelts, they mistook my parents for Sali Lumpa. I was but a little baby then."

Quondam tried to picture a human who could resemble a Sali Lumpa.

Chieftain Leafblower inhaled from his smoking pipe again. "I was educated in the ways of the city-folk and forgot the ways of the forest. When I returned here, to my home, I experienced a culture shock. Where were the houses, inns, and brothels?"

Apparently, the forest eventually began to grow on him, in the way it does when one stops bathing. "I still miss the brothels," he said.

According to Albert, his tribe found him and told him of his royalty, which he gladly accepted.

The chieftain-king offered the two strangers a wide variety of beverages, for which Lithe was very thankful. Her mouth was very dry and her throat sore from screaming at the tribesmen and playing her pipe for so long.

"I am sorry, but food is rather scarce these days," the chieftain-king explained. "The wild herbovines, as well as many of the other forest animals, have either begun to migrate or hibernate. I'm afraid drinks are all I have to offer."

"That's fine. We each had a cookie not long ago, so we are not hungry." Quite a few hours had passed since Quondam and Lithe shared the two cookies and found the map, but time tends to pass more quickly when poison arrows fly at one's head. "Would you like one? They are quite good."

Chieftain Leafblower accepted a cookie and ate it quite ravenously. The message inside the cookie read, *Prepare ye for the winter to end all winters.* With a slight shiver, he swept up and consumed the last crumbs of the cookie.

"We don't have a lot of the cookies to spare," said Quondam, "but if you would like, we can bring the ingredients back to you after we find the nutberry tree."

"Did you say nutberry?" asked the chieftain-king.

"Yes. We both seek the tree. Our quests are interwoven, you see."

"I hope you don't mean to cut one down for wood, for the *bloodbark* tree is most sacred to our people. Many forest-dwellers have sworn to protect the *bloodbark* with their lives. And don't even consider finding any nutberries this time of year—they have, no doubt, already been picked by the woodland creatures and the green giant of *Bloodbark* Grove."

"Green giant?" Quondam repeated with a ring of incredulity.

"Well, I haven't seen her, but I doubt she's green. That's probably just forest lore. Also, she's not always a giant. If you see her, and you live, then I would be glad to accept your promise of nutberries."

Chieftain Leafblower led them around the village and introduced them to several members of the tribe. In the center of the village stood a tree, and under it lay a large group of villagers. They were on their backs, staring up at the tree's branches.

"What are they doing?" asked Quondam.

"This is the time of the year we call 'Time for the Leaves to Fall.' If I recall, the people of Auldenton have shortened it to just 'fall.'"

Chieftain Leafblower caught a falling leaf, held it in his hand, and gently blew the leaf away. "My people have a custom, or ritual, that we perform this time of year. You may watch if you please."

The old man lay down beside the others and stared up at the falling leaves. When a leaf's descent brought it close enough, he blew with all the breath an elderly smoker could muster. The leaves went on their separate ways, until the breath of others in the tribe changed their paths. Eventually, the descent of the leaves had been rerouted to nice, neat piles on the ground.

Lithe knelt at Chieftain Leafblower's feet. "I believe I have a song that may make the work easier. Do you mind if I play it?"

The chieftain-king paused from his work for a moment, smiled, and waved for her to join them.

Lithe unsheathed her pipe and, as her breath brushed lightly through its holes, another of her mother's tunes filled the air. The song seemed to slow the falling of the leaves, and the breath of the Leafblowers gained more control.

As Quondam listened to the beautiful song and watched the leaves fall, a feeling of peace swept through him. He had always considered the change of the seasons to be an external force that had little to do with him. As he joined the Leafblowers under the tree, he enjoyed a feeling of oneness with nature and its cycles.

The leaves continued to fall, and every once in a while, Lithe would insert a variation on the theme, much to the excitement of the tribe. For, every time she changed the song slightly, a falling leaf would slowly take on the shape of a butterfly or moth and flutter away.

Soon, the leaves stopped falling and the applause of the tribe filled the silence left by the end of Lithe's song. She smiled as she caught one of the butterfly-leaves in her hand. "We call them the *farfalla*."

At this, the young man named Crowfoot stepped forward. "I have heard of the butterfly and moth-people. I have seen one of the moths in a dream. It was an omen of death."

"Crowfoot, please," said one of the older women of the tribe. "Do not speak of such things now. The Singer refers to the fair-folk of times before you were born."

The boy named Crowfoot lowered his head out of respect for the old woman. "We cannot escape Death by changing the subject, Grandmother. Death clings to these two like a shroud. Even now, I can see its dark cloud hovering over their town."

Quondam looked in the direction of Auldenton, and there did seem to be a dark haze in the sky, but it was hard to tell in the dim light of dusk. Moreover, he felt uncomfortable with the idea that some deathly aura had followed them on their journey.

Chapter 1:12

Manufacturing a Man-Factory

Considering that Bed-Time would inevitably draw near once again, Aori knew that he had only a few hours to complete his many tasks. Assuming that sleeping for three days and having such a vivid dream had caused him to age more rapidly, he would have to delay sleep as long as possible. "Sleep wastes precious time," he mumbled as he began to burn a bit of midnight oil.

He searched his parents' inadequate library for books on nocturnal species and natural sleep cycles but found none. The library in Auldenton was much too far away, so he decided that he needed to build one closer. He had already written or translated enough books to fill at least half of a library on his own. Of course, he might require help operating it.

Despite his power over time, he lacked the energy to build everything and do everything by himself. If he hired helpers, such as housekeepers or construction workers, he would have to pay them. Unfortunately, he no longer had a job, and he had very little money of his own.

He stared at his clock for an unreasonably long time. Magically, it always seemed to be in tune with his personal time. After an hour or so had passed on his clock, the gears and simple machines had given him an idea: He would build a servant as he had built the clocks.

His first foray into the creation of man produced a worker that needed to be wound up every two minutes or so. Since it would be counterproductive if he had to stop what he was doing to wind his worker, he built another worker to do the winding. By the third or fourth creation, he had developed a way around the winding problem. The workers were still far from being able to work autonomously, however.

Having used up a lot of the wood supply building his forge, lumber mill, and clock towers, he needed to find some more trees. He sent two of his workers to go find and cut down trees, which reminded him of his dream. In it, cutting down the great tree had been difficult, so he decided to make something that would help expedite the process.

The world's first power tool consisted of several sharp-toothed gears and other simple machines turned by a crank. It was effective at cutting grass that had grown up around Aori's farm, but he doubted that it would cut such a large tree. Through various manipulations and trials, he managed to invent one that ran on magic and steam.

The magic-steam engine helped speed up many mundane tasks and sparked the time-period Historians would eventually call the Aorindustrial Revolution. With the power of magic and steam, Aori built a manufacturing plant where his workers toiled nonstop at creating more workers. Unlike their creator, the mechanical men did not need food, sleep, or even rest. They were more efficient and, since they were part magic, they worked on time relative to Aori's.

The clockworkers, as he named them, looked a bit like humans, but they were all composed of metal and stood about 3 ½ feet tall. Each one left the factory looking identical, but Aori routinely made improvements and considered them all works-in-progress.

Soon, he had manufactured enough employees for an army. He sent his clockwork soldiers out into the world to do the things he could not fit into his schedule. Some did his chores around the farm, while others set out to search the world for literature and books to add to his library.

One clockworker tracked and hunted the wild cats of Smokewood Forest so Aori could study their sleep cycles. One did not have to be a biologist to know that cats did most of their hunting at night and slept in short increments of fifteen or so minutes. Aori referred to these patterns of sleep as "catnaps." He deduced that catnaps might be a good way to prevent the bizarre dreams and prevent his rapid aging.

To ensure that he awoke at the right time, he invented the world's first alarm clock. After fifteen minutes of napping, one of the clockworkers would clang bits of metal together until Aori woke up. He wished that he could wake up to the sound of music, but his workers were naturally not very good musicians.

Using the same basic concept of the clock, Aori invented a music box. Gears turned, and as they did, they moved a large drum as well. On the drum were little pegs that made a tone when they made contact with chimes. Programming the music box to play the right sounds in a proper sequence required many days' worth of trial and error, but eventually, Aori created a song. Unfortunately, he still felt unsatisfied; the music lacked the life of Codan music.

Programming the music box lead Aori to develop a primitive computer that worked on a similar clockwork-and-peg system. He wrote books about programming and even developed the concept that would eventually become binary logic. Despite his brilliant ideas and the months of personal time invested, Aori would never invent the microchip or the personal computer, however. He just had too many other things to do.

In the morning, the clockworkers loaded up several of Aori's inventions into a wagon. Rather than hitching up the horses, however, two clockworkers could pull the heavy load at a much faster pace. Aori held the reins, and a clockworker rode shotgun. Of course, shotguns had not yet been invented, so he armed his mechanical servant with a new contraption Aori called the Aorimatic Alternating Arrow Apparatus. It was something like a cross between a crossbow and a revolver. Arrows could be loaded from a revolving shaft. The weapon held six arrows at a time.

Pride welled up in Aori as he rode into the outskirts of town, drawing the attention of every citizen they passed. The townspeople followed alongside the wagon, trying to catch glimpses of the mysterious objects in the back. "Where are your horses?" shouted one of the citizens.

"I'm afraid they've become quite unnecessary, my good man. My mechanical men have made them obsolete." Aori pretentiously chose words he knew the townspeople would not understand. Since everything in Auldenton had always been obsolete and outdated, they also didn't understand words such as "new-fangled" or "innovative."

Aori drove his wagon straight into Seer's Circle. The festivities of Seer's Day had finally died down, and many of the citizens were still working on cleaning the mess. Aori called down to them, "Stop what you are doing, Auldentonians! Never again will you have to pick up that filthy trash with your bare hands! Let my clockwork servants do that for you!"

The spectacle did not quite match the entrance made by Toki and his silver rocket ship a few days prior, but the people gathered nonetheless. The clockworkers set up the various innovations in a rather attractive display, and Aori continued to speak as if he were a snake-oil- or used-car salesman.

"Do you hate the time it takes to wash all your laundry by hand?"

The crowd indicated that, in fact, they did hate such consumption of time.

"With my invention, the Sensational Cyclical Spic-and-Spanner, you can walk away and let the machine do all the work." The washing machine had a round body, and it looked something like a potbelly stove, which was another handy device someone else had already invented.

It could have been an amazing coincidence that someone else would have the ingenuity to invent devices so closely resembling Franklin's, or it could have been similar necessity driving the creative process. Many believe necessity to be the mother of invention, but really, Time is the father of invention. Yes, Aori needed many of the contraptions he built, but he also had much more time than anyone else did.

"How does it work?" shouted one of the citizens.

"I'm glad you asked. Let me give you a demonstration. First, you load the fuel into this compartment like so, and pull this… lever like so." He struggled a bit with the lever, but as soon as he did, a cloud of purple-tinted steam billowed out of the machine. The Sensational Cyclical Spic-and-Spanner hummed, chugged, and vibrated with mechanical life.

"Does anyone have any soiled clothes?" Aori called out to his audience.

In unison, the crowd turned to the local beggar, who was widely known as being the owner of a certain foul odor that spread throughout the town.

The bum's shirt went into the machine, which continued to issue forth clouds of steam. Aori had to shout above the noise of the machine, "The machine goes through various cycles: it soaks, scrubs, spins, rinses, and repeats the process until your clothes are clean. It may take a few minutes, so I'd like to show you all a few more of my Timister Time-Savers!"

The crowd followed his every word as he explained his other inventions, such as the Timistypist. One of his earlier inventions, the Timistypist was very similar to a typewriter, but it also made copies. He was designing a printing press to aid in the mass-publication of his books, as the Timistypist could not handle the load.

Aori also displayed his version of a lawnmower, which he called the Snappy Grass-Snipper, as well as several tools and gadgets he had developed in order to build other things. He made screws, screwdrivers, nail-guns, and a rather large drill powered by his magic-steam engine. It could fit in the back of his wagon, but, unlike later power drills, one hand could not support its weight.

"Could I get some volunteers from the audience?" Aori pandered.

As Aori photographed some audience members with his Prest-o-Matic Portrait Painter, a very small gnomish girl asked her mother, "What's Prest-o-Matic mean? Is that really a word?"

"Shh, dearie," said the gnomish mother. "Don't ask questions Mommy can't answer." One might describe their voices as distinctly British, if the country had existed at this time. Nonetheless, the accent, along with the high-pitched tone of their voice, set the gnomes apart from the ruckus of the crowd.

"I'll tell you, Daisy," said her older brother. "He made it up. Can't a master inventor tinker around with a few words, too?" Though he spoke with admiration, a slight tinge of envy crept in; he wished that he had invented all the devices himself.

The gnomish girl's given name was Daisychain, but everyone called her Daisy. The term would later take on several different connotations, some of which were quite unbecoming of such an innocent, sweet girl. Her brother's name was Pyrite Pettifogger, and his name fit him quite well. He actually preferred people to call him by his last name, despite the fact that it would eventually mean "a petty scoundrel or lawyer." Her mother's name was Cinquefoil, which was a type of flower. All the women in her family had names that were part flower and part mechanical. The mixture of beautiful flowers with gadgets combined the natural world with the technological in a way only gnomes could truly appreciate. However, there were instances of poor combinations for names, as with the tinker-word *screw* and the nature-word *yew*.

Many believed that gnomish girls sprang out from the ground like vegetables, while the boys were mined out of rock. I'm a bit of a collector of fanciful creation stories, and this one is one of my favorites. Nevertheless, gnomish males had a natural affinity for mining, construction, and inventing.

Pettifogger tried to get a better view of the doodads and gizmos Aori had on display. Daisy followed close behind him, as she often did. She whispered, "I think there are little gnomes inside that drill, making it work. What do you think, Pyrite...?" She hesitated as she noticed her brother's attention was focused on one of the nearby gadgets.

"Pyrite," she whispered. "I know what you are thinking, and you better just forget it. Mother would be cross."

"Hush, Daisychain." Pettifogger tiptoed over to the wagon, which was just out of the spotlight due to the crowd gathered around Aori and his camera.

Daisy followed him, also tiptoeing. "Pyrite, I would rather like to have my portrait painted. Couldn't we get in line, please?"

Pettifogger tried to contain his frustration in a whisper. "Go back to mother, Daisy. You'll get us both caught!"

While their industrial skills made gnomes famous, many, such as Pettifogger, were also very adroit in the practice of picking pockets. Their small stature (the tallest gnome ever was four feet tall), nimble fingers, and wiry frames made them excellent thieves.

Just before Aori moved on to another of his amazing discoveries, Pettifogger pilfered a prototype for a piston. The gnome had no clue what to do with the odd, cylindrical object, but he could sense its technological importance just by feeling it. Tucking the piston into his bag, Pettifogger bolted off into the crowd.

When he finally found his mother among the much taller townspeople, she grabbed him by his rather large ear and pulled. "Pyrite Pettifogger, what have you done now?"

"Nothing," he said through clenched teeth. He shot a look at his sister. "Daisy, you tattle-tale!"

Cinquefoil squeezed her son's ear tighter. "Out with it, mister. What did you take this time?"

Pettifogger produced the cylindrical object. She looked at it, mumbling, "What would your father think, if he could see you now?" Their father was Gneiss Pettifogger, named after a type of metamorphic rock, but the pronunciation "nice" also fit him quite well. Unfortunately, he was the sort of nice that other people loved to manipulate, but that was a long story that eventually ended with his untimely death.

Cinquefoil took the piston from her son and marched up to Aori. "Sir," she said, tugging on Aori's coat tails.

"Madam, you will have to wait in line for your portrait," Aori said to the thin air above Cinquefoil's head. Looking down, he said, "Oh. You must be a gnome."

"I must, and I am, good sir, but I do not wish to have my portrait painted."

Daisy interrupted, "I would, mother!"

Cinquefoil continued, "Mister Timister, I am afraid my son has taken one of your gadgets." She handed over the piston. "I assure you, this will not happen again."

Aori looked down at the young boy, who barely came to his thigh. "Sticky fingers, lad? You look like you have a hand for gadgets, too."

"Two hands, actually, m'lord," said Pettifogger.

Aori laughed.

"My father was a miner and tinkerer," Pettifogger explained.

"You don't say! Why, when you're older, I'm sure I could use your skill in my mines. I have need of all sorts of minerals." Aori gave him one of those patronizing pats on the head—the kind children despise.

"If you'll excuse me," Aori continued, "I have some business to conduct."

"Of course," said Cinquefoil politely. "Good afternoon, Mr. Timister."

Aori gazed over at the clocks he had for sale. "Afternoon already?" He set the clockworkers to operating the Prest-o-matic Portrait Painter, packed up a few of the smaller gadgets in suitcases, and dusted off his jacket. "I think I'll go buy myself some new clothes."

"Pardon, sir," said Cinquefoil, "but my sister, Holly Hocksprocket, is a tailor. She has a shop right over there. She would be more than happy to assist you."

"Why, thank you, Mrs..."

"Pettifogger, sir. Cinquefoil Pettifogger. These are my children, Daisychain and Pyrite."

"Pettifogger," Aori repeated. "I'll have to remember that."

"Here," said Daisy, offering a bunch of bluish, purplish flowers to Aori. "They're forget-me-nots... only these're special." She pushed a button in the center of the bloom and said, "Pettifogger."

"My husband invented them," Cinquefoil explained. "He loved making toys for the children that looked like flowers and whatnot in nature."

"Interesting," said Aori.

The flowers looked natural enough, but upon closer inspection, one could discern tiny rivets and seams in the design. He pressed the button on the flower again, and it repeated, "Pettifogger."

"Amazing!" Aori remarked. "It plays back sound? How truly magnificent! Oh, but I couldn't possibly keep such a memento."

"You can have it," said Daisy. "We have gardens full of them."

Aori smiled at the little girl, bowed politely to her mother, and patted her brother on the head once again. "'Twas a pleasure meeting you all." With a spring in his step, he strode off to Hocksprocket's Haberdashery at the end of the street.

An elderly man approached the gnomes and introduced himself. "Excuse me. My name is Bertram Finch. Did I hear you call that elderly gentleman Timister?"

"Why yes," said Cinquefoil. "Did I mispronounce it?"

"No," said Bertram. "I believe you got it right. It has been years since I have seen Horace. I scarcely recognized him."

"Horace? Was that his name?" pondered the gnome.

"No, mother," said Daisy, whose memory was better than most. "It was Aori."

Bertram's eyes widened. "Silly me," he said, perplexed. "I must have mistaken him for his father. If you'll excuse me...."

Cinquefoil watched as Bertram entered her sister's clothing shop. "Strange sort out today," she said. With a quick look around, she nervously asked, "Where's your brother?"

Bertram entered Hocksprocket's Haberdashery and clasped Aori about the shoulders. "Aori!" Aori turned around, and Bertram got a full view of the beard, wrinkles, and grey hair that could not have possibly belonged to his friend and former student. "What has happened to you, Aori? How could you have aged so much since last I saw you?"

"I'm afraid I have little time to talk, Bertram." Aori continued trying on a fancy, dark grey suit. "There is much to do; it is already afternoon, and I hadn't intended on spending the entire day in Auldenton."

"Aori, I know not what manner of witchcraft has befallen you, but I will help you in whatever way I can."

"Help is what I need," offered Aori, "but I need no cure for the 'witchcraft,' as you call it. I call it power-- power over time!" He paused dramatically. "Bertram, I have served time all my life. I worked diligently to get all my chores and jobs done so that I might have a little free time, but I was still inefficient...unproductive. Here, take a look at this:"

Bertram took the offered cookie and read its message aloud: "Time changes us; we do not change time-- Anonymous."

"Bertram, I now have the power to change time!"

"Yes, well, who is this 'Anonymous' fellow?"

"You're not paying attention!" Aori was growing impatient. "Bertram, look at these clocks." He produced two pocketwatches, both of his own design, which attached by a chain to each pocket of his newly purchased vest. "One is set to your time, while the other runs on my time. Right now, they should be relatively similar. Keep watching, though."

"It still looks normal to--" Bertram paused because all of a sudden, one of the clocks began moving so rapidly that he could not see the hands. He turned to speak to his former student, who seemed to be standing in the same position he had been seconds ago. However, Aori now wore a tall, grey top hat. The entire ensemble made him look very distinguished.

"While only a few seconds passed on your clock just now, I just finished up the rest of my business in town. Did you see the clock move very quickly?"

"Y-yes," Bertram stammered. "Aori, do you..." He stopped speaking, since Aori had already left the shop. "Aori, wait!"

Aori slowed his pace and turned with an exasperated sigh. "Come with me, Bertram. I have need of someone of your intelligence. As we speak, my servants are constructing a library."

"A library?" Bertram found the whole conversation severely bewildering.

"Yes, Bertram. That is where I need your help. Obviously, I cannot run the library, what with all the other plans I have to pursue. It shall be a grand library, Bertram!"

"But, Aori, where will you get the books?"

"That is being taken care of as we speak. My assistants are bringing in books by the trainload!" Aori noticed Bertram's familiar puzzled look. "The train is one of my most recent inventions. It runs on magic and steam! Here," he said, rummaging through one of his suitcases, "I've written a book about it."

Bertram took the book and flipped through the pages. The handwriting was meticulous, as Aori had written and painstakingly rewritten the words very carefully. He understood very little of the technical jargon, despite his high education.

Books of all sorts filled the suitcase. One of the books, entitled *Bed-Time: Sleep Cycles of Beasts and Man* by Aori Timister, detailed the internal timing mechanisms inherent in living organisms. According to the book, birds somehow know when to fly south for the winter, bears know when to hibernate, and the herbovine migrates at the same time each year. Nocturnal animals sleep during the day and prowl at night, despite the natural rhythms of Bed-Time. This behavior has also been found in humans; night watchmen and other people who work at night break the natural cycles of sleep.

"Aori, I am concerned."

"Bertram, old friend, stop talking and get in the wagon." The clockworkers had already loaded up the inventions Aori had not yet sold. Many of the townspeople had put in orders for the fancier equipment, which would have to be delivered later in the week.

With a friendly wave, the wagon rolled out of Auldenton, bound for home. As they traveled alongside the river that ran past their farm, Bertram just watched the clockworkers in wonder. "None of this seems possible. I hope you are being cautious, Aori. Remember what happened to your siblings when they meddled with Time. Furthermore, your parents may never recover. They should be no older than I am, Aori."

Aori could not be bothered by words of caution. Looking back on the merchandise in the wagon, something seemed amiss. Tarps covered much of the larger equipment, but he knew for certain that he had sold one of the drills. Reaching back, he slapped one of the extra lumps with the back of his hand. It moved.

Without the tarp to hide him, Pettifogger smiled nervously. "I... I wasn't stealing anything this time."

Bertram smiled. "It seems you have a stowaway, Aori."

At Aori's command, the clockworkers stopped. "What are you doing here?" He thought of the flower-gadget. "What was your name? Pettifogger?"

"Yes, sir. Pyrite Pettifogger."

"Well, Pettifogger? I don't believe you were invited to take a ride in my wagon."

"Sir, I wanted to help you. I am a tinkerer like my father, and I could help you with your mining."

Aori softened the harsh look on his face. "I could use an apprentice, perhaps. I will need someone to carry on my work, should I become..."

"Too old?" Bertram finished for him. "I believe you are being rash, Mister Timister. Not too long ago, you were *my* student. Listen to your old teacher now, and return the boy to his family."

"No time, Bertram old man. I have too many things to do to go back now. It's decided, Pettifogger. You'll be my pupil, and I'll teach you everything I know."

By evening that same day, the library had been constructed and stocked with books from all over the region. Clockworkers were still searching the rest of Aia for more literature. Eventually, the Timister Railroad encompassed and connected the entire world, thereby providing Aori with a global library.

The clockwork soldiers did encounter resistance in some parts of the world, for most civilizations were not willing to give up their libraries and consequent knowledge to a strange army of mechanical men. However, armies of humans could not take as much damage and required much more in the way of food, water, and sleep, compared to their metal opponents. Global conquest was definitely in Aori's grasp, but all he wanted at that moment was worldly knowledge.

Chapter 1:13

Giants

Quondam and Lithe both slept comfortably that night in separate tents. Quondam's dream was far less complicated this time, but still centered on the tree. This time, however, the seed grew into a green giant. It stomped around, changing colors and chanting the same words over and over: "The beginning is the end is the beginning is the...." And so on. The giant then changed size and shape. The sun set and the world grew dark. Then, as if in another cycle, the light began to grow. Quondam squinted, but the daybreak still hurt his eyes. As the sun rose, it metamorphosed into the green giant, whose skin was actually rather a dark shade of brown.

Quondam woke in the morning feeling more refreshed and less concerned than he had the previous day. From the direction of Lithe's tent, he heard a cheerful, upbeat tune. The song made him feel happier and more energetic. He raced over to her tent like a young boy upon hearing the final school bell of the day.

Lithe sat in a wooden chair with her dulcimer flat in her lap. In each hand, she held a lightweight hammer—the kind used to play a dulcimer, rather than pound a nail. With her tail, she plucked the strings as her hands hammered them. The result was a rich, multi-layered tone, which made a nice accompaniment to her singing. The song was in Codan, but somehow Quondam understood that it was about the coming of dawn. Perhaps she had had a dream similar to Quondam's. He forgot to ask, and she never told him.

The spirit of Lithe's song made the children of the village want to dance and be merry. As the villagers gathered around Lithe's tent, the children of the tribe laughed and played as only those with the energy of young children can do. Several of them tied ropes to the back of their loincloths and pretended to be Codan.

Quondam gazed at them, for he was as enchanted by the children as he was the music. Though he was still only eight years old without the power of the timepiece, he was hardly a child anymore. Besides having seen his only friend die, he had to deal with the memories, thoughts, and jaded bitterness of the people he would one day become. Nothing would ever be as simple as it had been only days prior; when he was eight, and knew nothing of magic, giants, or sacred trees.

With a little hesitation and self-doubt, he shifted to an age around five and joined the tribal children at play. He danced and sang along with Lithe's song, though his voice fell short compared to hers. Quondam played with the inno-cence and energy of a child his age, and the Quondams of the future looked back on that day with the proud smile that goes along with the nostalgic, melancholy feeling of memory.

Lithe sang and played her many instruments for a good part of that morning in order to satisfy her adoring audience. Her songs replaced all the villagers' concerns about the coming winter and famine with a feeling of warmth, happiness, and safety.

Soon, however, her thoughts returned to her quest and the dangers ahead of them. She put away her instruments, said her farewells to the people of the tribe, and then noticed that Quondam was still playing with the tribal children.

"Quondam," she called to him. "It would be wise for us to leave now. We must continue our journey before the winter comes."

"But I'm playing," he whined in a five year-old voice. "I don't want to go."

"Quondam!" Her voice lacked its harmony at this point. The children stopped dancing as if the spell that had enchanted them had suddenly broken.

A solemn look came about Quondam's face. His eyes took on the worn appearance of one who has lived for many difficult years. His brow began to furrow and fold. When he spoke, the voice sounded strained and tragic. "You are right. It would be wise to leave." He paused. "And yet, I do not wish to go any further. My friend is dead, and I see no way that finding some tree will change that. Lithe, I am not a famous warrior. I am an eight year-old boy. A week ago, I was playing with the other children my age, just as I have today. I will only slow you down, and you have no need for a weaponless warrior."

Lithe looked at him questioningly, but she found no argument. Her quest was the most important thing to her, and nothing could detain her. She gathered her things and left the tribal campground.

The overall mood of the tribe shifted dramatically. Many of the children began to weep. Quondam was one of them.

The beat of the drums grew increasingly faint as Lithe walked further away from the village. Quondam had been right; their pace together had been slower than her normal traveling speed. She strode through the forest and leapt over any fallen trees or rocks that blocked her path.

Suddenly a noise caught her attention and slowed her pace. After muting the sound of her breathing and heartbeat, she listened for the noise again. It sounded like metal banging together. *And horses*, she thought. *...At least four. And twice as many men. But the battlefields of war lie far to the north; what army would be traveling so far south? Wooden weapon or no, I* *would feel better if Quondam were here. My dulcimer does not serve me well in battle.*

In an astonishingly short amount of time, the battalion happened upon her. She tried to run, but was unable to move. Archers drew their bows and aimed their arrows at her. A group of spearmen raised their weapons, just as prepared to kill her. The weapons and armor of the battalion were familiar but seemed sturdier and more advanced than any she had seen in all of Aia. From the back of the party came one of the mounted warriors, who Lithe presumed to be their leader. Unlike the other mounted knights, his beast of burden was no horse. The horseman was gigantic—much too big for a normal horse. Instead, he rode a very large bull herbovine.

He wore black armor made of some metal Lithe had never seen before. She noted the hourglass insignia on his chest, which matched the crests on the shields of his soldiers. His wooden arm had taken on a form resembling a battering ram. In his other hand, he carried the same broad battle-axe that had hewn its way through the orphanage the previous night.

"Where is your companion?" the captain asked. His voice was husky and slow.

"I have no companion," Lithe answered.

"Do not lie to me, Coda. Your instruments would not fare well against my army or my steel." As the captain threatened Lithe, one of the other knights put a sword to her throat. "Your voice just wouldn't be the same without your vocal chords."

"I have no companion...now," she confessed. The vocal chords of a Coda were sacred; no secret was worth losing that which gave a Coda power. "We parted ways; I do not know where he is now."

The giant stroked his long, braided beard, as if it helped him think. "You have a song that will draw him here. Play it." Then, he stuffed something into his ears to block out the music.

Lithe took out her dulcimer and sang-spoke, "It may not work, if he is far away." Then, she began to play. The music flowed out of her instrument in soft waves that weaved in and out of the trees. The armored man, who was not a fan of music, eyed her suspiciously.

Before long, many of the soldiers found it difficult to hold their weapons in position. The sword at Lithe's neck drooped a bit. As Lithe continued to play, a few soldiers collapsed into a deep sleep.

The infuriated captain dismounted and swung his great axe at Lithe. As it came down, she barely dodged its giant blade. The axe crashed into the ground with a thud, and the dulcimer fell, in many pieces, from Lithe's hands.

"That wasn't the song. That wasn't even the instrument. Do you think I'm some kind of idiot? Play that painful song that never ends."

Lithe resignedly took Ariel from her sheathe, put the pipe to her lips, and played. The tune annoyingly repeated over and over, much to the chagrin of the awakening soldiers. A few of them attempted to stop the song by force, but their leader prohibited it. "It's working. He's on his way. Keep playing," the captain ordered.

When she had played the song a few days prior, Quondam was not the only child it had affected. Many parents in Auldenton panicked when their children disappeared or simply walked out the door towards town. When the children returned a few minutes later, the parents just assumed that the Seer's Day festivities had drawn them away temporarily.

Quondam sat alone next to Lithe's tent, where he had been since the tribal children got bored and went on to better entertainment. Sobs still shook through his young body.

Quondam noticed the tribe's bowman approaching and tried to dry his eyes. The bowman spoke to him in the forest-language, saying, "Do not cry, Demon-sorcerer. If you go back to being a fierce warrior rather than a slobbering child, I will give you my bow and quiver. Then, you can fight alongside the song maiden again, as it should be."

Suddenly, Quondam's attention was distracted from the bowman or the bow. The sound of a pipe entered his ears. All over the village, children stopped playing and began walking. Quondam grabbed the bow and took off running.

When the rapid pace had drained his energy and sapped his strength, he simply shifted to another, more sprightly age. The race to find Lithe became a one-man relay made up of runners of various ages. Far behind him, the tribal children walked more slowly, followed closely by some confused parents.

The song gradually faded into a similar, but less annoying and repetitive song. It seemed to Quondam to be of a darker, more ominous tone than the previous song. It filled him with a sense of dread. *It must be a warning of danger ahead*, he thought.

One of the soldiers in the battalion had climbed a tree to allow for better scouting. After a few moments of annoyed listening and waiting, he was relieved when Lithe's song seemed to change a bit. Far in the distance, he saw a figure walking towards them. It definitely did not look like a young warrior. As the figure grew nearer, the scout felt certain that it was an old man.

"What do you see, watcher?" the leader called up to the scout in the tree.

"Nothing. Just some old man," the scout answered.

"What would an old man be doing this deep in the forest, so far from the path?" asked one of the horsemen.

The captain took the pipe from Lithe's mouth, removed the earplugs from his ears, and listened for the old man's approach. "It's him! It's the Once-and-Future Man! Seize him!"

Before the captain could finish the first of his words, however, the old man had drawn the bow and fired at the scout. The soldier fell from the tree and landed with a sickening thump. Quondam shifted to a younger, stronger age and drew the bow again. He waited for another soldier to come into his clearing and released the bowstring with a twang. Another soldier fell.

Quondam barely had time to load another arrow before a third soldier came upon him. A fourth followed very closely. The third fell to an arrowshot, but the fourth managed to get in close enough to swing his sword at Quondam. The sword wounded Quondam, but the injury soon shifted away. The fight was something like a tag team match with the odds sorely against Quondam. Luckily, some of the soldiers and all four horses were still very groggy from Lithe's lullaby.

Several soldiers lunged at Quondam all at once, but he evaded them by shifting to a younger, shorter form. The drowsy soldiers found it hard to hit such a small and spirited target. As little Quondam scrambled around their legs, he swung at kneecaps with his wooden sword. Surprisingly, a good number of his targets fell to the ground in agony.

The captain left two of the knights to guard Lithe as he rushed over to join the fray. His giant axe cut a swath through the dense foliage and gave him an advantage over Quondam, who was already fending off the attacks of five or six men at a time. Quondam shifted and dodged the axe just as it whipped by horizontally at neck level. Two of the captain's men fell to his misdirected axe-stroke.

Lithe grabbed one of the thicker strings from her shattered dulcimer, leapt high above a horseman's head, and caught him across the neck with the string. The downward momentum and tension of the string caused a serious gash in the horseman's throat. As he lay bleeding on the ground, Lithe grabbed his saber and plunged it into another rider's torso with musical precision. The other rider's saber sang as Lithe withdrew it from its sheath.

A melodious whistling sound cut through the air as the two swords danced in Lithe's nimble hands. She continued to dazzle and amaze her opponents as she displayed her acrobatic prowess. The music of her weapons blended harmoniously with the battle hymn she began to sing.

Quondam felt his spirit rise when he heard Lithe's song. His fights began to flow into a choreographed dance routine, but the battalion's captain fought as if a different song—one that was offbeat and out of tune—scored his battle.

One of the soldiers swung a sword at Quondam, and he instinctively blocked with his wooden sword. Miraculously, the sword did not shatter into splinters. The wood stopped the metal blade with barely a nick to show for it. Quondam seized the advantage of the miracle in order to parry and to disarm his opponents.

The captain attempted to swing his axe at Quondam several times, but missed repeatedly. The close-quarters provided by his men and the surrounding forest made a proper axe-stroke all but impossible. He discarded the axe and charged Quondam with his battering ram-arm. The ram hit Quondam squarely in the chest as he busily tried to block the attacks of the other soldiers. The force of the captain's charge sent him reeling into the ground first and then a tree. The collision and subsequent hard landing caused him to lose his grip on the wooden sword, which landed somewhere in the underbrush.

Lithe continued to sing as she fought the many soldiers of the battalion. Few of them stood a chance against her Codan reflexes and dexterity. The intensity of her slaying-song seemed to increase as, far in the distance, she heard the sound of drums.

With Quondam removed from the battle, the captain had room to make a sufficient swing of his axe. As the axe blade entered the apex of its swing, an arrow tip plunged into the captain's back. The axe continued to fall, but Quondam managed to evade its blade.

Soon, the sound of drums and flying arrows filled the woods in harmony with Lithe's battle-song. The woodsmen of the Leafblower tribe advanced on the battalion and leapt from the trees at the enemy. Their spears thundered across the shields and their hatchets beat against the armor of the soldiers.

With very few soldiers left to fight for him, the captain made his retreat. In no time at all, the beat of his mount's steps faded completely. Several of the woodsmen tried to follow him, but he had vanished.

Quondam rested on one of the trees that the captain had cut down in his frenzied attack. He secretly wished it were the stump that Ekisha had instructed him to find, for then he could truly rest. "Thank you for your timely arrival, Chieftain-King. And thank you for your swift arrow, Limbender."

"If not for the tribal children and that annoyingly repetitive music, we would not have found you in time," said the chieftain-king. He then instructed the tribe to gather what armor and weapons they could from the bodies of their enemies.

"You might save one of those swords for me," suggested Quondam. "I seem to have lost mine in the battle. Alas! It served me well, for being but a toy."

"If it is but a toy, then it is still lost. But I have found your wooden sword, man of yesterday and tomorrow." The voice came from deep in the woods. Immediately, the Leafblower tribe fell to their knees as one.

"Who goes there?" shouted Quondam. "Who has found my sword?"

"It is the protector of the *bloodbark*, Demon-sorcerer," whispered Limbender. "It is the great green giant of the forest!"

"Not today, people of the wood," said the voice. As she walked out of the woods, they noticed that she was no more than four feet tall. She seemed to be a part of the forest, as if she were any other tree, despite her size. Her hair seemed a tangled mass of moss and vines, and yet flowers added color and beauty to her greenish, brownish locks. Her skin seemed more like the bark of a tree than skin, and a strange organic-looking armor covered most of her body. It had visible veins like human skin, but upon closer inspection, one might decide that the veins were more like vines. Despite the sturdiness of the armor, it bent and flowed as if an extension of her body.

When she spoke, every syllable seemed to resonate throughout the thicket as in some wooden instrument. "You should hold on to this weapon, Quondam. Not every toy sword is composed of such precious material."

"That is not my sword," Quondam remarked. It looked like a simple twig.

"It's not? Hmm. Well, it will be. Give it time." She handed him the sword and continued, "I am Asalie, though some know me by other names. The people of the wood once called me *Daybringer* or *Lightsower* before they came to know me as 'the green giant.'"

"You are the one who plants the seeds of day?" asked one of the tribal children.

"I am."

"And you protect the *asa* tree?" asked Quondam.

"Yes."

"My companion and I…" he stopped, because he noticed that Lithe was not among them. "Where is Lithe?" he cried in panic. Had she fallen in battle?

"She is well," said Asalie. "If you listen, you can hear her song of lament. She mourns the loss of her dulcimer, over there."

Quondam walked towards Lithe, who bent over her shattered dulcimer like a fallen, lithe branch from a tree. She played a solemn tune on a long pipe that Quondam had not seen her play before that time. The pipe consisted of wood from the tree of Willow, and its sound wailed and whimpered as if it grieved the loss itself. The tune was breezy, but it did not give the feeling of lightness that her air-song instilled. Rather, it created an immense weight in Quondam's gut and throat. Tears forced their way from his eyes cathartically.

Asalie joined the two funeral-attendants. "Quondam, the Codan people create their instruments in a way that is not unlike the birth of a child. They name their instruments, and a dulcimer is as much a family member as any other Coda. It is truly a tragedy when an instrument is lost."

"I will help her build another," vowed Quondam.

"If I am right, my friend, it may not be necessary. The materials still exist, shattered as they may be. Eventually, the pieces will grow back together, for nature hates disharmony and destruction as much as we do."

"It will grow back into a dulcimer?" Quondam considered it impossible.

"Yes, as your twig will one day grow back into a sword. It is the natural cycle of life. Things die, decay, and are reborn. Often, one living entity's decomposed remains feed the life of another."

Quondam still looked confused.

"Just as the sun sets, it is reborn each day. Life begins at Dawn. The energy of one formerly living thing may be reborn as another living thing, for few things in nature have the will of the sun. Only those individuals with the will of the sun may be reborn again in the same body. This dulcimer may be one. We shall see. Play on, *Emmeleia*."

Chapter 1:14

Threnody and Volare

Codan folklore told of a female of their species named Threnody who fell in love with a *fairfallan* male named Volare. The term *farfalla*, of which Lithe spoke when among the Leafblower tribe, refers to the larger category of any humanoid resembling a moth or butterfly. Many members of the animal kingdom on Aia had keepers or herders who appeared partly human. The *fairfalla* raised and watched over butterflies, while the *fellfalla* shared more characteristics with the moth. It is important to note the etymology of the names for the beings, as the terms were Codanized versions of Elvish words. Apparently, the Elves thought highly of the beautiful butterflies, while the moths, whose colors were never as bright and cheerful, were vilified and feared. Many years after the last of the fair-folk died, there rose an evolutionary offshoot which many still refer to as the fairy or faerie.

Nevertheless, the *farfalla* were not known for their lifespan. Aian biologists considered them ephemeral beings, in that their lives usually lasted but one season. Their short time on Aia proves particularly important to the following tale, which the Coda recounted as "The Ballad of Threnody and Volare."

Lithe would eventually perform the tale with musical accompaniment during the course of their journey, but as it bears significance to this particular part of the larger story, your Historian will play the role of the storyteller. You will have to imagine the background music, I'm afraid.

Despite the fact that Threnody was a pointy-eared musician with a tail and Volare was a winged butterfly-man, they shared a love that poets and songwriters tried to put into words for centuries after they had both perished. Few loves could enjoy that sort of longevity, to outlive those who spawned it. They actually only knew each other for about ten hours.

Though ten hours may seem like very little time to some, Threnody and Volare managed to fit many years' worth of love and togetherness into that short time, thanks to the intervention of a wizard the Coda knew as Tempo.

Much of their time passed in the air. Volare's wings and Threnody's singing held them aloft for many hours at a time. They flew all over the world in their ten hours and shared the sights of the many oceans and mountains their people had never seen. In fact, much of the world was still unexplored at the time of the events in this book.

Upon Volare's passing, Threnody composed a lamentation that she continued to sing for the rest of her long life. It consisted of two fundamental parts: the *pibroch*, in which a pipe made from the Tree of Willow was played, and the *coronach*, in which the musician sang a mournful elegy made up mostly of sobbing shrieks and tearful moans. The Coda later named the entire lamentation after Threnody, and its practice lasted well past her lifetime.

When she had grown very old and weary of her life, a spirit of death came to her. The spirit introduced himself as Finis, and he signified the End of All Things. Upon hearing her mourning song, he immediately fell in love with her. He asked her to be his bride for eternity.

Much to his dismay, Threnody continued to sing. He realized that the only way she could be happy was to have

Volare back in her life. In a very uncharacteristic move, he appealed to the spirit of the Dawn and asked that Volare be reborn.

Threnody and Volare lived one final day together, and at the end of their lives, they fell from the sky like stars. Many people believe that, every now and then, you can still see them fall. Of course, those are just stars. People will believe anything they hear in folktales. Believe me.

Lithe continued to play the solemn *pibroch* as Asalie tried to explain its finer points to Quondam. When Lithe began the wailing *coronach*, Asalie said, "This is the part I like to call the *ullalulla*. I do so prefer words that have repeating, cyclical sounds, like *ullalulla*. Say it with me, and be sure to curl your tongue."

After the language lesson, Asalie continued, "When someone dies, music is often played at the funeral in order to appeal to the spirit that governs death. It is believed that, if Finis is moved by the music, the deceased will be resurrected."

"Yes! That's exactly what I need! I have come all this way in order to resurrect my friend, Munder. So Lithe can play that song for my friend and he will return?"

Asalie closed her eyes. After a long pause, she spoke again: "You must be patient, Quondam. If the will of the sun is strong in Munder, he may return on his own."

"But I must help him now!"

"Quondam, you are a child no longer. Do not act like one. All things come to those who wait," Asalie concluded. She remained stubbornly silent for the duration of Lithe's song.

As Lithe sang, bits of the broken wood became enchanted. The strings responded to her song like cobras to a snake charmer. As the wood slowly grew back into place, the strings attached to the frame and tightened. Upon her last sorrowful wail, a note rang out of the reconstituted dulcimer. Lithe rested.

After she regained her strength, Lithe and Quondam reformed their traveling group with the addition of Asalie. Two of the battalion's horses had stayed behind with their fallen riders, so Asalie and Quondam shared one, while Lithe rode the other. With the combination of Asalie's small stature, Quondam having shifted to a younger age, and Lithe's innate lightness, the horses could move much more quickly. According to Asalie, the animals were quite relieved at the decrease in weight since their last owners. They still had a good deal of the trip ahead of them, but Asalie was very familiar with the woods, so many shortcuts were available.

"If you are the protector of the *asa* tree," said Quondam at last, "then—and pardon my boldness—why are you so far away from the tree?"

"*Trees*, you mean, for there are many. They do quite well at taking care of themselves. The trees in this part of the forest, however, do not. You undoubtedly noticed the carnage your enemy made of the trees back there; the fallen trees call out to me. It is quite fortunate that, in finding the injured trees, I also found your group."

"Quite a happy accident, indeed," remarked Quondam.

"So it seems." Asalie spoke as if she possessed information unknown to the others. She knew that perfect timing such as they had experienced today usually involved careful manipulation. "So it seems."

The skirmish with the battalion had wasted precious daylight. After saying their goodbyes to the Leafblower tribe a second time, the trio had but five hours of travel time before dusk.

Luckily, by that time they had reached a shady grove by a stream. The entire party found the stream refreshing and the locale quite comfortable. Large deciduous trees of Oak set the perimeter of the grove. Though their leaves were a sickly shade of yellow at this time of year, they gave a feeling of shelter to the travelers.

Asalie fell asleep the moment the sun had set. Lithe and Quondam stayed awake a bit longer to discuss the events of that day and days to come. Lithe had grown more laconic since the battle and subsequent funeral, but the warmth of their fire loosened her tongue a bit.

"Who were those soldiers, Quondam? They had no markings of Auldenton, and yet they seemed to know you and your power."

Quondam had never had mortal enemies before, though as he delved into his past, his thoughts converged on Mr. Fist. Like a photograph gradually developing, the memory surfaced. As they were escaping the orphanage, Quondam had stabbed the man with his wooden sword. Had he truly been responsible for Mr. Fist's death? If so, who was this new enemy with the wooden arm?

"I wish I knew, Lithe." He opened up to her and told the story of the orphanage, and the guilt he felt for his involvement in the murder overwhelmed him.

Lithe tried to comfort him, but it conflicted with her previously unemotional attitude. "Maybe your blow did not kill this Mr. Fist, Quondam. It is, after all, a wooden sword. What if part of your sword broke off in him and turned him into that monster with the wooden arm?"

"I'm confused," said Quondam. "If that was Mr. Fist, then who died in the orphanage?"

"I do not know," admitted Lithe. "Hopefully it will all be clearer in the morning."

"I am quite tired," said Quondam. "Much has happened today."

Lithe sat still for several moments, as if she were letting the day's events percolate in her brain. "My heart is glad to hear that there is more than one *timbre* tree; perhaps my quest will prove easier than I had thought."

"I hope so," said Quondam. "But, I feel fairly certain that Asalie won't allow you to carve any wood from them."

"I agree, and now that we know more, I am loath to do so. How else can I get the wood, though?" The two of them thought for a long time, but neither of them found a solution.

"I'm sure Asalie will know what to do," Quondam resolved. "Of course, I hope this stump I seek provides more help than she has offered. I cannot sit idly by and wait for Munder to grow back, as if he were some fruitberry bush. I don't understand why you can't just do for him what you did for your dulcimer. To think, we had the means to resurrect my friend all along!"

"Quondam, I am sorry I didn't mention the funeral song before. I have had little experience with it myself. I must admit, I was growing doubtful of the tale's power, for the spirit of death had never responded to the song in my lifetime. I am still a bit skeptical as to Finis's involvement in the resurrection of my dulcimer."

"Yes, I believe the dulcimer was more Asalie's style, somehow. Or maybe the song itself enchanted the pieces. If one of your songs can enchant all the children in a tribe, I would think you could have an effect on wood chips as well."

"Perhaps," said Lithe, as the ends of her mouth bent upward. Quondam had seen her smile on only a few occasions since their introduction, and he found himself longing for more. In a child's voice, Quondam asked her for a bedtime story. She played her dulcimer, which sounded better than it ever had, and sang another Codan folk-song-tale. Parts of the song were in her native tongue, but Quondam understood.

> In days gone by, a forest grew
> Within the mountainous terrain
> Of Orchestra and Xanadu
> And in the valley's E-flat Plains.

Lithe's tale continued, mainly in verse form, to recount the story of a damsel with a dulcimer and a pleasure-dome with caves of ice. Thousands of years and miles away, this story (and a lot of opium) served as the inspiration for a poem by Samuel Taylor Coleridge entitled "Kublai Khan." Unfortunately, he never finished the poem. If only he had owned the right instrument, the music would have recalled the words.

Quondam slept and lost himself in a dream. It began, as Lithe's story had, with the Orchestral Mountains and their many cascading waterfalls. His mind followed the water as it flowed through the caverns and became the Vivace River. Far in the distance, he could hear Lithe's voice singing in Codan about a symphony that provided the soundtrack for the construction of a pleasure-dome of ice.

Instead of a dome, however, Quondam saw, in his dream, a pair of twin towers grow out of the ground as if her song itself had called them into being. Eventually, the towers grew into tall trees. One of the trees branched out as in Quondam's previous dream, but the other tree just continued to grow straight upwards.

As his mind reached into the sky, the sight of a small, bird-like object distracted him. As it got closer, Quondam identified it as the silver rocket that had landed in Seer's Circle only a few days ago. Inside the rocket, Quondam was surprised to see his old friend Munder, who busily played with a wooden stick-horse. Suddenly, Munder flinched in pain and held his bleeding hand. A splinter of wood was stuck in his palm, which reminded Quondam of his wooden sword and the splinter it had given Munder a few days ago.

As Quondam examined the splinter, it began to grow. It grew from a small seedling to a mighty tree, and finally returned to a splinter. Munder himself began to grow older, but something interrupted his sleep before the dream finished.

"Get up, Quondam! We must make haste! The battalion is coming!"

Chapter 1:15

Prochrons and Metachrons

The art of war underwent many changes over the span of thousands of years. The evolution of warfare from sticks and rocks to guns occurred similarly on Aia as it did on Earth. Primitive cave-dwellers and woodsmen used sharpened rocks as both tools and weapons. Warfare evolved as humans discovered newer, stronger materials. Some metals mixed with others, which increased their durability.

Eventually, the invention of gunpowder changed the art of war drastically. Sticks evolved into swords, spears, and arrows, which eventually gave way to guns. Catapults evolved into cannons and, in time, grenade or missile launchers.

Warfare on Earth and Aia differed mainly in the area of magic; Aians imbued their swords, arrows, and armor with elemental or spiritual properties to increase their effectiveness. While some mystics existed on Earth, the humans there relied more on technological advances to drive their war-machine.

In the time-period of this story, most armies had abandoned the use of stone, but gunpowder was still years away from invention. However, the battalion that advanced on Quondam and his companions that day consisted of both those technologies and everything in between.

The Army of the Anachronist composed of three groups: the Metachrons, who rode on wooly herbovine and threw rocks; the Prochrons, who fought with rifles and bayonets; and, finally, the armored knights of the present time. The three groups together totaled well over one hundred soldiers.

The sheer number of soldiers approaching was enough to set Quondam aback, but the combination of primitive woodsmen with uniformed musketeers left him mystified. He could barely make them out in the dim light of the moon, but the army looked menacing and full of doom.

Lithe grabbed and pulled him to his feet. "I cannot wake Asalie," she shouted. "Put her on your horse and ride!"

Quondam loaded Asalie and their possessions onto his horse and sped off after Lithe. Looking back, he could see that the captain and his army were dreadfully close behind. He saw smoke rise from a weapon, followed immediately by a loud CRACK. Something whizzed by his head at an incredible speed.

As the riflemen loaded their weapons, archers fired arrows and the Metachrons threw their rocks. Luckily for Quondam, the Army of the Anachronist did not yet have access to scopes or laser targeting on their weapons.

Another advantage in Quondam's favor grew restless in its sheath on his back. The wooden sword spread outward to shield Quondam from enemy projectiles. Despite being made of wood, it turned away even metal arrowheads and bullets.

Behind the three companions and their pursuers, the sun's rays began to peek out over the western horizon. Its gradual rise clashed with the speed of the chase. The sky blazed with various shades of red, orange, and purple and light conquered the darkness yet again.

Meanwhile, the effects of the war below mirrored the radiant sky above. The primitive Metachrons and the soldiers of the present lit arrows or spears on fire and launched them in the air at Quondam. With the increased light and visibility, the Prochrons had an easier target for their muskets. The vision of smoke, sparks, and fire was accompanied by the cacophony of musket-fire, horses galloping, and the hoof beats of grunting, wooly herbovines. Above the raucous din of war, the soldiers could still hear the orders of their captain, who seemed unaffected by the chaos around him.

In the saddle in front of Quondam, Asalie awoke with a similar obliviousness. As her eyes opened to greet the dawn, she seemed unattached from the chase and the battle. Her eyes glanced around and surveyed the land as if taking it all in for the very first time. Flaming arrows whizzed by her head and musket-balls bounced off Quondam's back. The force of the shots caused Quondam to wince, which finally caught Asalie's attention. "Perhaps you should fire back at them, Quondam."

"I have no arrows, Asalie!"

"Be patient; when you need them, they will grow."

"I need them now!" Before his sentence ended, the wooden sword grew from its current form into an arrow. Quondam pulled it out of the quiver where it had grown and studied it as carefully as one can while riding for one's life. The tip was made of wood, but felt sharp to the touch, and dried leaves took the place of feathers.

As he loaded the arrow and tightened the bowstring, he felt as if an older, more experienced version of him guided his hands. His eyes were keen and his vision as acute as a young man's, but these eyes had never seen the horrors of war. They found a target and Quondam's fingers instantly released the string.

The arrow flew for an unnatural range and found its target in the soft neck area of a musketeer. From there, it continued its trajectory into the chest of another soldier who, upon falling from his horse, mistakenly fired his musket at another Prochron.

The other soldiers found aiming at Quondam much more difficult because of a bright glare coming from that area. When they fired, their ammunition, arrows, or rocks seemed to miss both horses every time. The shots that didn't bounce off their enemy's back just seemed to flit away on a tangent.

At that same time, Lithe steadied herself on her speeding horse as she used both hands to play an airy, warbling song on Soffiara. Lithe's past experiences with the song were much less tense than this one, however, and she worried about its effectiveness. The song she had played under the tree in the Leafblower village now raced along with the hooves of the horse.

Quondam knew he had only felt one arrow in his quiver moments ago, but another had already replaced it. In fact, every time he used one, another grew in its place. Quondam saved his questions for later and repeatedly loaded, aimed, and fired arrows at his enemies. As he watched each arrow continuously puncture and slay multiple targets, he tried to ignore the bright light emanating from the front part of his horse.

While soldiers of his battalion fell with increasing frequency, the captain resolutely stayed his course. He looked at his watch as if he were late for some appointment. However, either he was having trouble telling time, or the watch revealed more than just the current time. His gaze appeared to transcend the physical representation of the watch.

All of a sudden, Lithe choked and the song stopped. She grabbed the reins with both hands and pulled with all her strength.

Without the music to divert their paths and the wooden sword acting as a quiver-full of arrows rather than a shield, a few projectiles managed to hit their target. Quondam found shifting between each shot too difficult and eventually tumbled from the horse. The ground rushed up to meet him, and he slammed into it with a less-than-graceful, rolling crash.

The horse immediately responded to Asalie's command to stop, which was fortunate, since the road before them had ended abruptly at the edge of a cliff. Lithe had managed to stop her horse in time as well, but not without some difficulty.

Quondam managed to stand despite the numerous gunshot-wounds and arrows protruding from his body. He looked to his companions for assistance, but they were both transfixed upon the expansive ravine that cut them off from their intended path.

The ravine gashed the landscape as only a thousand years of erosion can do. However, this particular thousand-year-old ravine did not appear on even the most current of maps. Asalie overcame her shocked bewilderment enough to remark, "This cannot be. I walked through here less than two days ago. This kind of chasm requires many lifetimes and ages to…. The river could not have…."

"It doesn't seem to be slowing down the enemy," Quondam pointed out as the battalion rode nearer. He resumed his role as archer and fired off a constant stream of arrows at their pursuers.

"How can we cross it?" asked Lithe. "Not even I could jump that far."

"We must go around; find another path," answered Asalie.

"Impossible. I see no end to the chasm in both directions."

"True enough," Asalie resolved. "Let us not panic. A way will present itself, in time." Unfortunately, this was not a case where something could just grow back eventually. Erosion of Aia's surface was growing increasingly frequent and permanent throughout the planet. This was just one crack, or wrinkle, in a rapidly aging planet.

For a brief instant, Quondam questioned the old woman's sanity. Quickly, however, enemy projectiles lobbed at his person required that he concentrate on shifting accordingly. To make things easier, his wooden sword grew into a large shield that, despite its consistency, even stopped the musket-balls of the Prochrons. The frequent shifting and prolonged abuse began to exhaust Quondam. Soon, the only thing that kept him going was the music he heard in the background.

Lithe had resumed the bouncy, airy song she had been playing during the chase. Immediately, the stones, arrows, and musket-balls began fluttering around like butterflies. The song worked on most inanimate objects, as it had with the falling leaves, and objects already in flight were particularly susceptible.

Lithe grabbed one end of a long dulcimer string and handed the other end to Asalie, who was slowly growing out of her awestricken stupor. Lithe leapt into the air, rested a foot on a fluttering arrow-fly, and leapt again. Using each of the flitting projectiles and her acrobatic grace, she managed to jump her way to the other side of the ravine. She tied the string to a nearby tree trunk.

Asalie tied her end to a tree trunk as well and then grabbed hold of the thin line with both hands. It was obviously too thin and fragile to hold even her small frame, but it had growth potential. This was before instruments were stringed with nylon or metal; this string was made of an organic material that responded well to Asalie's nurturing commands.

She encouraged it to grow, and it did. It grew into a thick cord, then a rope, and as she began to cross it, it got bigger and more complex. By the time she was half-way across the ravine, it had grown into a narrow rope bridge.

Quondam took his attention away from the battalion long enough to notice the bridge and his companions on the other side of the ravine. He hadn't noticed the bridge there before, but he had been preoccupied with not dying from his multiple wounds. Nevertheless, he did not hesitate to run across the bridge as fast as possible.

Quondam had almost crossed the bridge when the battalion arrived. The captain swung his huge axe and chopped down the tree that held that side of the rope bridge. As the rope bridge fell to the opposite wall of the ravine, the captain laughed loudly. "That is the oldest trick in the book...or it will be," he shouted.

Asalie grabbed the rope, planted her feet firmly into the ground, and pulled. When I write, "planted her feet," by the way, the meaning is not figurative. Asalie shared many common characteristics with the trees she protected; for one, she could grow roots and plant herself firmly into the ground, which also gave her the strength of the mighty oak.

When Quondam reached the top of the cliff, the captain of the battalion shouted at him again. "You should have fallen to your doom. It would've served you right. But, we're supposed to take you in alive. Oh well. You guys should go on to the Nutberry O—as it is, you probably won't make it in time. We'll meet up with you later." By the end of his speech, the entire battalion had vanished.

With not so much as a word, the three companions raced towards the Nutberry O. It was still miles away, and they no longer had their horses.

Chapter 1:16

Death Stalks at Dusk

"Honestly, Aori; be reasonable. This is kidnapping."

"Bertram, please," Aori grumbled. "I haven't the time to quibble. I have an appointment today."

Bertram kneaded his peppered brow nervously. "With whom?" he asked.

"Destiny," Aori announced, as if stating something of utmost importance.

Bertram rolled his eyes. "Spare us the drama, Mr. Timister. You and I both know that you have all the time in the world. You have more than enough time to have a rational discussion between a student and his mentor."

Aori deflated a bit. "Why must you belabor the issue? The boy chose to follow us, and he's eager to work for me."

"He is currently slaving away in your mines!"

"...And loving every minute of it!"

Bertram threw his hands in the air. "I shall have none of it. If you cannot slow down enough to let your conscience catch up to you, I will take the boy back myself."

"He won't go. He loves it here; he told me himself."

"Then I shall at least inform his mother of his whereabouts."

Aori paused from his busy tinkering for the first time in their conversation. "You will return, won't you?" Though he could not bear to admit it, Aori had felt a lonely despair during all his time. He felt as though he had spent many years of his life in utter solitude. The acts of fostering the gnome and dragging Bertram here had been his desperate attempt at reaching out to others. *Perhaps*, he considered, *I need him here to play the role of my absent conscience indeed.*

Bertram left without a word.

Meanwhile, in the mines beneath the Timister farm, the pockets of Pyrite Pettifogger bulged with the spoils of a day spent half in work and half in looting. Every stone, ore, or gem was precious to the gnome, and his fingers itched with every discovery.

"Pettifogger?" When Bertram called to him through the darkness of the mineshaft, Pettifogger gave a start and frantically tried to hide the evidence of his crimes.

"Down here!" The gnome's voice echoed in the deep caverns.

Bertram followed the sound and found the gnome suspiciously stuffing his hands in his pockets. Deciding he had no concern for whatever mischief had been committed, he said, "Pettifogger, I have come to relieve you of your duties here."

Pettifogger considered the treasure awaiting him within the mine and managed a polite, "No thank you."

"But, Mr. Pettifogger, this is no place for a child," said Bertram, referring to the mineshaft. Upon deeper reflection, however, he felt that the Timister farm in general had been a corruptive influence on many innocent youths. His memories of Morning Timister, the only daughter of his oldest friends, had faded over the years. While most of the Timister children had traded their souls in one way or another, he remembered Morning as the most innocent and undeserving of her fate.

Lost in his attempt to drudge up memories long since buried, Bertram hardly noticed the gnome sneak away into the darkness. "I take it, then, that you wish to stay?"

"Yes, please," echoed Pettifogger's voice from some hiding place deep within the mine.

"Very well, then; I shall tell your family that you have taken employment here at the farm, and they can reach you here. Will you be needing any personal items from home?"

The echoes of a pickaxe hitting stone served as an answer, and Bertram left.

By four o'clock in the afternoon, Aori had spent four years preparing for what he saw as his destiny. He had studied the maps of the Auldenton area, and workers had built railroad tracks all the way to Nutberry O. It would be a long voyage by foot, but his train, with its magic-steam engine, shortened the travel time considerably.

During the train trip, Aori took many fifteen-minute catnaps, read all he had found on the Nutberry tree and ate a few more cookies. One contained a message, which read, "With time and patience the mulberry leaf becomes a silk gown--Chinese proverb."

"Yes," Aori agreed, "and the Nutberry tree becomes the stately tower."

Meanwhile, many miles away, Quondam, Asalie, and Lithe rested, for they had run for most of the day. Quondam broke apart a cookie, which contained the same message Aori had read: "With time and patience the mulberry leaf becomes a silk gown—Chinese proverb."

Asalie added, "If you are dissatisfied with something, all you need to do is wait around long enough, and it will change."

Since each of them had their own remarkable recuperative abilities, they did not require much rest. Asalie vocalized what had been concerning the others: "We must reach the circle before dusk, or I am afraid I will be of little use to anyone. I can stay awake past sunset, but I will be almost powerless and very weak. We must make haste."

Aori's train arrived at the Nutberry O around six o'clock. He dispatched the clockworkers to cut down the Nutberry trees and load them on the train but instructed them to save the tall, broad tree in the center of the ring for him. The magnificent Nutberry trees were a sight to behold, and the chief among them stretched twice as high as the rest. Two large houses could fit inside the center tree, and one could assume that its roots stretched to the center of the world.

The forest reverberated with the sound of gears turning, steam pumping, and trees falling with a complete absence of harmony. Despite the non-musical nature of the sounds, it enchanted the forest dwellers and forced them to listen. The death throes of the *asa* trees even reached as far as the Leafblower tribe. A war party left that very evening to investigate.

Lithe and Asalie heard the sound as well. By this time, Asalie could no longer run, so Quondam had to carry her. Shifting often allowed him to disperse the weight and conserve energy. They were all very tired, having run for the entire day, but the sound of death and carnage ahead fueled them with determination.

Aori started up his magic-steam gearsaw and commenced his work upon the center tree. As the sharpened gears tore through the thick, reddish bark, a dark, blood-like liquid oozed out. Aori grew impatient and commanded his clockworkers to assist him. Soon, the treeblood poured out of the tree and spilled upon the rich soil.

Though they were still too far away to see the slaughter, Asalie grimaced. She moaned and released a slow, mournful sigh. "Death stalks at dusk," she said.

Lithe, who had sprinted ahead at her top speed, witnessed the fall of the eldest, most majestic tree to ever grow in all of Aia. With all the voice she could muster, she shouted, "*Timbre!*"

By the time Quondam and Lithe reached the Nutberry O with Asalie's unconscious body, not a single tree remained standing. The sun had gone down for the last time that autumn, and everything seemed barren and lifeless.

A cold, harsh wind ravaged the other trees of the forest and stripped them of their last leaves.

Winter had finally arrived.

PART 2

WINTER

Chapter 2:00

Winterlude

Asalie, everyone's favorite tree-hugger and berry/nut/seed collector, brought up an interesting idea in Part 1: If you don't like something, just wait; sooner or later, it will change if given enough time. If you feel like you've had nothing but bad luck all your life, then that will eventually change (if you live long enough). It may not get better, but things always change.

Asalie believed in this philosophy, and had the patience to wait for the cycle of life—it will die, be reborn, and be different the next time. It's evolution, really. Time operates in this manner as well: he didn't like the Elves, and eventually they evolved into Coda. Evolution cannot happen without time. And, what is evolution, if not growth? Therefore, Growth and Time are interdependent.

The same is also true for the folk tale. If one storyteller doesn't like a particular part of a story, he or she can change it. Eventually, it will catch on and everyone will tell it that way. Pretty soon, the story has become completely different. People eventually forget that it was told any other way—and without a historical account of anything different, we have no way of knowing how things really happened.

This happened often throughout the history of writing and telling stories. Children achieve a similar effect with the game known as Telephone or Gossip. A story spreads, by word of mouth, from one storyteller to the next, and only the most interesting bits of a story survive; it's a literary sort of natural selection. The power lies within the storyteller, and anything interesting will eventually be the only truth anyone knows of an event.

Several civilizations have folktales regarding a Great Flood that wiped out all of existence. Some details may seem far-fetched, but how can anyone believe anything else, without proof? Do they have temporal omniscience? No. They don't. Because the fact of the matter is, no one remembers what he or she did five minutes ago, let alone five eons ago.

Let's say the library burns down in an isolated village somewhere—all records of the people there are destroyed in the fire. Without a record of their lives, no one will ever know they existed in the first place. It's like the historical equivalent of salting the earth.

If a tree falls in the forest and no one is there to record it, did it even exist in the first place?

Many libraries burned and many trees fell at this time on the planet Aia. Winter often took out whole populations of Aians who had no historical account of who they had been or how they had died. With such poor record-keeping, many civilizations made the same mistakes and also died.

However, far away on another planet, history continued its survival of the fittest; this history would survive for many millennia. Human life was growing on planet Earth. Its origin and growth varying from human to human, but Time and Growth pretty much weeded out the idea that the first human being sprouted fully-grown from the forehead of a god. Before laughing at another's creation theory, consider this: that far-fetched idea was once believed just as fervently as you believe your own supernatural origin. Your culture and traditions might be very different if the more persuasive storytellers had believed in other creation myths.

On Earth, when the first humans were walking upright after having been cast out of paradise for eating fruit, stealing fire, or learning the secrets of how rain is made, they had many new things to take in and process. The ones in the vicinity of the Fertile Crescent experienced new things like murder, betrayal, fire and/or brimstone, and the strange, silver, rod-shaped object that had flown from the stars and landed in the desert.

Out of the silver spaceship stepped Toki, the Time Lord. Behind him gathered a group of Codan males and females.

"This is Earth," Toki said. "There are humans here, but they are not very advanced. Teach them to make beautiful words and music. However—and this is very important, Codans—you can never speak, write, or sing about Aia or how you got here. Do you understand?" He didn't wait for a response. "I must go. I have to drop off some herbovines in northern Europe and make some other deliveries in Ireland and South America. I would love to stay and watch you grow, but I have to run; I have lots more to accomplish on Aia before the world grows old and dies. See you later!"

The Coda taught music and dance to early cultures on Earth, but they gradually grew out of the tail and pointy ears. Some cultures were more easily influenced than others were; Codan practices and linguistic styles became very popular in Greece and what would one day become Italy. Of course, some thought the Coda to be demons and burned them at the stake. Music critics are almost as old as the music itself. However, that is a story for another time.

On Aia, winters stretched on mercilessly for many lunar cycles. Temperatures normally fell far below freezing, blizzards decimated whole populations, and only the hardiest of species could survive. Many animals migrated to warmer climates leaving little food for the civilizations that relied on hunting. Other animals, such as bears and wolves, hibernated.

Growth, too, took a hiatus. Nothing grew in the wintertime. Trees survived by using up stored food, but most organisms withered and died. This was not a season for change. This was the season of the wither.

Chapter 2:01

The King of the Wolves

Quondam held Asalie in his arms as cold wind whipped through his long, white hair and rattled his old bones. The shock of winter and so much death and sorrow had caused him to involuntarily shift to a very old age. His weary, cataract-ridden eyes attempted to focus on Lithe, who sat in front of him playing her funeral song.

Tears had frozen on her cheeks, and her lungs ached from the cold air, but still she played her willow pipe. She mourned the loss of Asalie, the many regal *timbres*, and for the death that had come with winter. She also cried for the abrupt and tragic end of her lifelong quest, for now there were no *timbres* left for her to use in building her instrument.

Her song lasted throughout that long night until the first light of day. When at last her *coronach* had dwindled to a whimper, Quondam spoke. "I suppose this is the end of our intertwined quests. There are no *asa* trees for your mandolin. And, while there are plenty of the stumps I was told to seek, I somehow feel that they could not help me now; not without Asalie to interpret for them, that is."

Her voice cracked from the strain of her song, but it still carried the life of a comforting song. "Quondam, I know our situation looks as bleak and barren as this landscape, but I feel in my heart that some hope may come with the dawn." She managed a weary smile. "Look at it this way: you came here in search of a stump, not a tree. Perhaps it was meant to turn out this way. Perhaps the answer will come with the new day."

"Maybe you're right," agreed Quondam, "but it may be a moot point anyway."

"What do you mean?"

"The whole point of this quest was to bring Munder back to life, but something tells me I may have no old childhood friend to resurrect." With that, Quondam of ninety-four silently awaited the sunrise.

There was an old Aian saying that went, "A watched sun never rises." Many years later, after people grew impatient waiting for suns to rise or set, the saying grew into, "A watched pot never boils." Both sayings reflect the idea that if one abandons or looks away from something, change will be more readily apparent upon one's return.

Children grow at a remarkable rate if one has not seen them since they were knee-high to a grasshopper. A wound covered by a bandage heals more quickly for many reasons, one of which, it has been out of sight and out of mind.

Recently, this magical occurrence has been demystified as a common way of life, but in truth, it is supernaturally powerful if used correctly.

It is also very difficult to do consciously. Immediately upon trying not to think of something, one will find that it is the only thought that exists. The key lies in an opportune distraction that causes the items to slip out of memory.

As Quondam's eyes began to droop, he questioned whether the sun would ever rise. "Perhaps the sun has died as well, or it cannot rise without Asalie. This could be the Winter to End All Winters."

Lithe unsheathed her twin padded hammers and proceeded to play her daybreak song. As before, it lightened Quondam's heart. He even smiled a bit, and he felt a little warmth and vibrance returning to his body. Soon, he was young again, around eight. He stared at the horizon and waited a little more hopefully.

He waited.

And he waited.

And when he thought he could not wait any longer, it happened.

Not the sunrise, but the opportune distraction.

A large wolf pounced on Quondam ferociously. It was immediately on top of him, and its teeth and claws gnashed and ripped at Quondam's flesh. Before he could shift, two more wolves were upon him.

Lithe's song had also been interrupted by the wolf attack. A pack of ten or twelve wolves fiercely gnawed at both of them, and one wolf was inspecting Asalie's body.

This time of year, wolves had to prey on the very young and weak. The wolves themselves had been weary and exhausted from the night's hunt, but Lithe's song had renewed their vigor.

Try as he might, Quondam could not fend off the attacks or shift to an older age. He could feel sinews being torn and teeth scraping on his bones. As the end drew near, a thin, piercing light caught his eye. It was the sun!

The wolves immediately stopped what they were doing, although it wasn't clear what had startled them more: the break of day, the break of the back of one of their own, or the loud, dominating voice commanding them to "STOP!"

Quondam looked up through the blood and fur to see Asalie, much taller than before, towering over the pack of wolves. Her skin was bright like a blinding light, and her presence was awe-inspiring. In one hand, she carried a large wooden club that appeared almost as if she had just pulled it from the ground. It had roots that were caked with dirt and snow, and blood ran down from the roots. At her feet lay a large wolf in the form of a crumpled mass of fur.

She spoke again in her stern, commanding voice: "Look! The Sun has risen!" The wolves all looked toward the sun, but Quondam fixed his gaze on Asalie. He perceived, for the few seconds that the wolves were preoccupied, that Asalie shrank and the light faded from her skin. She appeared to be the innocent, wide-eyed neophyte Quondam had seen her to be the previous morning.

"Which of you is the leader of this pack? Show yourself, and change!" Asalie commanded.

A grey wolf, which was larger than the rest, lowered its head, as if to bow before Asalie's feet. Gradually, as the light of day stretched across the land, one could tell that the wolf's fur seemed to be thinning everywhere but around its head. Its legs grew longer and thicker near the thigh, while it no longer seemed dependent on its forelegs for balance. The leader rose up on its hind legs and the lupine features of its snout and ravenous jaw regressed to the softer, grey-bearded face of an old man.

"I'm th' leader o' this pack, Granny," said the old man in a voice that sounded something like a growl. He cleared his throat, and his voice changed to suit the calmer expression of his face. "And had I known that y' were livin' and walkin' wit' these two humans, we would'na come here. Please, forgive us." He kept his head low, as if waiting for an axe (or, in Asalie's case, a large walking stick) to fall.

As the old woman looked at him, the roots and tendrils of a wrinkled, yet warm, smile stretched across her face. "Forgive a wild beast for acting on its instincts? We shall see. When a beast has the form of a man, we expect him to show a little better judgment. I realize that food is scarce now that winter has come, but since when do you attack innocent women and children, Master Connery?" questioned Asalie.

Like a dog, the old man's ears pricked up at the sound of his name, but he kept his head low in reverence. Every creature shared a mutual awe and respect for the woman they knew as the grandmother of the woods. "We beg yer pardon, Granny, but we've been out the entire night on a hunt."

"You should learn to gather food before winter hits. Most of your prey sensed its approach and left these woods long ago."

"Actually," the wolf-leader replied, "we've stored enough food t' last 'til the next full moon. Our prey last night was th' metal beast that took yer trees."

"Metal beast? Tell us more."

"The tree-thieves came through our part of th' woods yesterday n' set metal teeth into th' ground. An hour later, a great metal serpent or dragon flew by at an amazin' speed. It flew very close t' th' ground 'n seemed t' follow th' metal teeth.

"I gathered th' fastest wolves in me pack 'n followed the dragon. It spewed forth steam or smoke 'n never slowed its pace. By th' time we caught up with it, it was on its way back. One of me pack tried t' stop th' dragon, but it didn't even slow down as it ripped him apart with its mighty jaws. We noticed th' wood of yer trees strapped t' its back, and what we had thought were scales were actually those metal soldiers riding on th' dragon's back 'n sides.

"I must sound daft, speaking o' metal men 'n dragons, but I had never seen the like in all me many hunts—even in th' lands of Men."

"Some things on Aia have grown past even my under-standing in the last few days, old friend," admitted Asalie.

Connery continued, "We tried t' follow th'...dragon for a few more miles, but we lost it in th' blizzard. The heavy snow obscured th' teeth, and even our keen wolf eyes could not pierce th' dark winter night. Since we could no longer track the scent of our prey, we resolved t' come here t' look for clues."

"I'm afraid these many stumps are the only evidence," offered Quondam, who had shifted away his youth and grievous injuries.

Connery turned his head and bowed to Quondam. For an instant, he marveled at the difference between the weak boy he had attacked and the bold adult that now stood before him. "Apologies, good sir. The night's hunt had left us weary and, regretfully, quite hungry. We must've been so caught up in th' frenzy that we bit first 'n asked questions later."

"The sight of this death and carnage affects us all," added Lithe, who had managed to evade all but one deep gash in her thigh. She rested upon a stump and Asalie rushed over to her.

"Oh, my dear, sweet song! Why didn't you mention this wound earlier? I'm afraid my powers of regrowth and healing are fairly weak this time of year, but I'll see what I can do."

At Asalie's command, Quondam and Connery carried Lithe to a large, hollow *asa* tree that had apparently been overlooked or spared for its lack of wood. As they got closer, Quondam noticed that the tree looked as if it had been damaged in a fire. New growth of grayish-green moss had spread over its blackened bark, so he knew the fire had not been recent.

As Asalie mixed together several nuts, berries, and seeds to form some sort of paste, she told them about her home. "*Asa* trees very rarely die. Despite the carnage out there, you can all rest assured that each of those trees will grow again. This is the only tree of their kind that has ever—well, it's not exactly dead itself. However, I'm afraid that's one long tale that will have to wait."

She rubbed the paste on Lithe's thigh, and at first nothing happened. Lithe had to hum a tune to relieve the pain. Many years ago, there had been a Coda by the name of Anaesthesia, who specialized in making others forget about pain. Fortunately for Lithe, she taught her song to others before dying a long and, quite ironically, painful death.

Asalie rested in a rocking chair that seemed to have grown from the intertwined roots of the tree. As she rocked, Lithe could already feel her skin stretching and growing.

Laboriously, Asalie spoke in a soft, weak voice: "I'm not sure how much more of that I have in me. If anyone else gets hurt, I'm afraid you may have to just let Time heal it. However, he has grown quite unreliable in recent years."

"I agree," said Connery. "I sense he had some hand in all o' this. I could have sworn I caught a glimpse of some white-haired man in th' head o' that dragon."

Thoughts, ideas, and information began to entwine in Quondam's mind like a complex root system. "Time may well have been involved, but the one who cut down the trees was the man from my dreams: the man with the broken arm from the Seer's Day Festival. The wizard who gave me my watch also spoke to him that day. I cannot understand, however, what plans he would have for the lumber." As his mind strained to think about Aori and his plans, Quondam's face wrinkled and his hair grayed.

"Now I'm beginnin' t' understand how it is that y' can change from a small child to an adult. At least one mystery is solved," said Connery.

"Oh, where has my head been? I carry on as if I were born only hours ago and have no sense of manners. You all have not been properly introduced," Asalie realized. "This is Connery, King of the Wolves. He grows into a wolf when one of the moons is full."

"Granny, I grew out o' that phase long ago. I am in complete control o' th' transformations." Connery smiled and stretched out his hand in a rare gesture for one who socializes mainly with animals in the wild.

"Pleased to meet you." Quondam looked him over in the light that poured in through knotholes in the walls. Even in human form, Connery was quite hairy. His long hair and beard had seemed unkempt and wild at first, but had managed to straighten by the time of the introduction. White was the dominant color, but it shown silver when Asalie spoke of his royalty. Quondam stammered, "Um… are you Asalie's grandson?"

"We are all her grandchildren," answered Connery.

"Many of the people and animals in Connery's homeland call me 'Granny.' It comes from *Grania,* their name for the goddess of agriculture. It lacks that repetitive, reverberating tone, but I suppose it fits.

"Back to the introductions," Asalie continued. "The Coda is Emmeleia, though she prefers to be called Lithe. If I had my way, she would Emmeleia. Don't you just love palindromes? I do." As the old woman trailed off, her words were like a windy path through thick woods. "I'm sorry. Sometimes I can get a bit carried away. When you've been around as long as I have, you tend to have quite a large collection of words and languages."

Using the club (which had now grown to a walking stick) for support, she rose to her feet and walked over to Lithe. As one's grandmother might do, Asalie gingerly stroked Lithe's face and gave her a warm, comforting smile. "But, I'll try not to wander in words so. Lithe is here to obtain materials to make her *magnum opus.* My dear, I am sorry you have had to wait so long after traveling so far, but I do admire your patience."

"I have waited my whole lifetime, Asalie. I can wait as long as it takes," Lithe sang-spoke.

Quondam looked out one of the knotholes at the barren field outside. "But can you wait for the trees to grow back, Lithe?"

"Perhaps that will not be necessary," Asalie suggested. "Perhaps we will find another solution, if we wait but a bit longer. First, let us continue with the introductions: Connery, this is Quondam, the Child of the Morning and the Evening. He has come here in search of a stump." A warm smile spread across her face once again. "Come, Quondam. Let us see what the stump has to show us."

They walked back out into the cold weather. Quondam was surprised at how warm and bright the hollow tree had been, despite its lack of a fireplace or such. He shifted to a young age in order to improve his circulation and allow for better absorption of the stump's information.

"This tree has grown here for thousands of years." As Asalie spoke, something caught in her voice. She looked as though she were holding back a deluge of tears. "It has seen many changes in Aia through the ages, and whole species have come and gone in its lifetime. Each ring on the stump represents a year of growth. Do not bother trying to count them; it would take more time than we now possess."

Some rings were thicker than others. Asalie explained, "The wider rings represent years of prosperous growth. Perhaps it rained more that year." As she spoke, she seemed to glow a bit, as one who is remembering the good old days.

"It must have rained a lot in the first half of its life span," Quondam noted. "The rings are the thickest then."

"Yes. Those were happy times. If you bisected me, you might find a similar pattern." Smiling, she turned to Lithe. "I am sure you have heard the story of the *asa* and his bride. You may have heard them called *Timbre* and *Embre*."

"I believe I have heard such a tale as a young girl, but I don't have the proper instrument. It is an ancient, circular harp of some sort, I believe."

"No matter; I remember the story well," Asalie mused. "However, it is a lengthy tale, and I have meandered such in speech already that I fear we do not have time for it now. Let us go back inside, where it is warm."

Before following the others inside the hollow tree, Quondam studied the stump more carefully. He wondered what it had to tell him. In the very center of the tree, the rings seemed to spiral together like a whirlpool. He also detected a pattern in the rings of varying thickness. The pattern seemed to loop continuously up to a point near the bark of the tree. The newer wood of this year's growth broke the pattern. There was also a bit of a notch, which Quondam imagined as his birthday.

"I must go," said Asalie as Quondam entered the hollow tree. "There is still much that you must learn from me, but it will have to wait. You see, for the cycle of growth to perpetuate, I must travel to other parts of Aia. While all is desolate here, new life begins on the other side of the world. Everything revolves, you see."

"But we thought we lost you last night; we cannot bear to lose you again!" Quondam complained, as children often do when their grandmother has to leave.

"You will not lose me, or the information you seek. Already the tiny tendrils in your brain are growing and making connections. I have planted many seeds there, which you can reap after they have grown."

She walked over to some shelves containing her collection of nuts, seeds, berries, and fruits. Meticulously she gathered specific items and tucked them into pouches. She gave a pouch to Quondam and one to Lithe. "These seeds will grow to help you on your way." Ruffling the boy's hair, she continued, "Quondam will come to learn what each of them does as the knowledge grows in his brain."

As Asalie placed a pouch in Lithe's hand, she whispered, "Emmeleia, you will find what you need to build your instrument in that pouch." Gently, she closed Lithe's long fingers around the treasure.

"Oh! I almost forgot!" Asalie tugged at one of her twisted locks of hair, slowly unraveling frayed strands. Each time she found the strand she sought, she pulled it out. Soon, she had a lock of several specific hairs. She placed the lock of hair in Lithe's pouch. "When the time comes, you'll know what to do with that, as well."

Asalie turned to the leader of the wolves. "Sir Connery, I should hope that your path and that of these two travelers should grow together from here. Will you accompany them, old friend?"

"Their path will undoubtedly go through our neck o' th' woods, if they seek th' tree-thieves. I will follow them t' my homeland, at least. I'm certain my brethren will not allow me t' abandon my hunt, though. We all wish t' find th' one responsible fer last night's slaughter."

"Then rest here, all of you. Sleep has missed you as of late, and these may be the last warm beds you will meet for many months. Rest well, my children. I will be gone when you wake."

Chapter 2:02

Nutberries Do Not Fall Far From the Family Tree

As the sun climbed, all those in the hollow tree—human, Coda, and wolf alike—slept the day away. Despite the effects of winter outside, mind-seeds continued to germinate in Quondam's brain. In his dream, he watched as a seed grew into a mighty tree. Many smaller limbs branched out from the trunk, as they had in his previous dreams. This time, there was only one version of him, but other beings were growing out of the limbs.

Two relatively large branches connected to him. Quondam watched as those branches gradually grew into his mother and father. Though he had very few memories of Konban, his father, who had left for the War when Quondam was very young, he recognized his face. The man had noble features and very dark, black hair. Quondam's father had narrow slits for eyes, while his mother's eyes were a bit wider and rounder. Memories of his parents trickled in, as if watering the roots of the family tree.

The memory played out in his dream as if it were a movie flashback. Quondam remembered how Morning, his mother, had been very beautiful when she was young, but she seemed so much older after the day Konban left for the War. As Konban left that day, he gave the wooden sword to Quondam as a gift. Had his father known at the time that it was much more than a toy?

As the memories trickled away and the dream stretched onward, Quondam followed the branches to Konban's side of the tree. Several brave-looking warriors, wearing armor similar to that of a samurai, struck valiant poses as if for a photograph.

As he reflected on the heroic presence of his ancestry, a sudden gust of wind rattled the branches on the other side of the family tree. Quondam studied the wood that represented his mother's family carefully. Every family member seemed older than the next; he estimated the youngest as at least one hundred years old. Upon viewing what must have been Morning's brother, Quondam staggered. A seed of recognition burst open in Quondam's brain and he knew the man to be Aori Timister, the man from his previous dream.

Suddenly, the man cut down the great family tree and it began to fall towards Quondam. Seconds before the tree came crashing down upon him, Quondam was startled out of his dream. The alarming visage of a savage, grey beast loomed inches above his own face. Its mouth gaped open to reveal long, razor-sharp teeth. Words came from the beast's mouth: "Wake up!"

As Quondam's awareness of his surroundings slowly grew, he realized that the beast was the more lupine form of his new ally, Connery. He rushed to his feet and followed the werewolf out of the hollow tree. Night had fallen while they slept. By the full moon's light, Quondam could see the wolves prowling the barren ground of what used to be Nutberry O.

"We must be alert," Connery urged. "Somethin' foul is afoot. We found these tracks all around th' hollow. Someone has been here recently."

"Couldn't they just be Asalie's footprints?" asked Quondam.

"No. There're too many o' them, and it's snowed more since she left."

Lithe scouted around the outside edge of the barren ring. "Those big ones over there—what could have made such large—"

"Herbovines."

"That seems fairly normal," said Quondam.

"All o' th' wild herbovines have migrated already. These're a…different variety," Connery explained. "I 'ave heard of a creature long ago that was very similar t' th' herbovine, but 'twas covered in dense fur, like wool 'r somethin'."

Quondam looked at Lithe. "We are familiar with it. In fact, we have seen them very recently." Briefly, he recounted the events of the previous day, particularly the attack of the Anachronistic Army.

"That explains some o' th' tracks. The sets o' footprints outside th' ring are those o' horses, soldiers with boots, an' the wooly herbovines. However, bare feet made th' tracks inside th' ring and around th' hollow tree."

"Perhaps one of the beast-riders came up on foot?" offered Quondam.

Connery shook his head. "I think not. It seems something kept th' battalion from entering th' circle. Whoever made these particular tracks was not part o' th' battalion."

"Was it friend or foe?" asked Quondam.

One of the wolves returned from a patrol in the woods. After listening to the report, Connery replied to Quondam's question. "I do not know, but it appears that all o' them 'ave gone now. M' wolves 'ave found no trace o' th' battalion or th' barefoot wanderer. Strangely, the tracks just disappear."

Quondam exchanged another knowing look with Lithe. "I'm not surprised," he said. "They tend to escape in the blink of an eye."

Lithe began to gather her things. "No matter what happened here, I feel that we should go. We wasted much of the day, and we must find the *timbre* wood before it is too late."

Everyone agreed, and they left the warmth of the hollow and the relative safety of the Nutberry O. To satisfy his own curiosity, Connery ordered part of his pack to follow the tracks of the barefoot visitor. As they walked past the stump of the great center tree, Quondam took one last look at its rings. "Farewell, *Timbre*. May the spring bring you the growth you so deserve."

The snow was knee-deep in the direction they needed to travel, and none of them could see through the blizzard. The wolves' tracks from that morning had been covered, and the "teeth," or "railroad tracks" as Quondam somehow learned to call them, were completely invisible. However, the clockworkers had cleared a path through the forest in order to lay the tracks, so the travelers just followed the path of tree stumps.

Connery remained deep in thought for much of their journey that night. Meanwhile, Quondam and Lithe discussed his most recent dream. "At least we have a name for our enemy, now," said Lithe.

"Yes. Uncle Aori. I should have known we were connected some way—we share the same roots."

"This father of yours—it sounds like he was a great Orien warrior."

"Aye, man-pup," Connery agreed. "F'r that, y' should be proud. The blood o' many warriors runs through you."

"And the wisdom of the elders flows with it. The two have grown together," Asalie's thought-seeds spoke through Quondam. Her spirit grew up from a nearby tree stump. It looked like Asalie, but her skin was bark and her hair was made of dried leaves. "The Ori live far across the sea. They are a noble, honorable race of beings. Unfortunately, Time has never been on their side. Knowing that the Timisters have forever been servers of Time, the Ori arranged for their finest warrior to marry the eldest Timister daughter. The Ori thought it would improve relations with Toki, their time deity. I believe it helped them in the War, and they have even developed a calendar to keep up with the cycles of the tides and sea storms."

"Did you know my parents, Asalie?" asked Quondam.

"Yes. The Orien elders are revered and respected, and the Ori see aging and personal growth as empowering. Konban also understood the importance of the *asa* and other trees. He raised and grew an *asa* in his hometown. In fact, he died defending it in the War."

"I always wondered how he...died."

"The tree has grown well on the lifeblood and essence of your father. Your father lives forever in those roots. Life continues, even after death, you see."

A sudden gust of cold wind blew the leaves away, and Asalie's image receded into the stump. Quondam and Lithe shivered from the cold. Connery had fur to protect him from the harsh weather, but Quondam and Lithe were not prepared for bitter wind and temperatures below freezing. However, they persevered and kept up a steady pace. Quondam shifted often to stay warm, and Lithe hummed a hymn of warmth that reverberated throughout their bodies.

In the distant woods, six pairs of feral eyes stalked the travelers. The eyes were well adapted for such low visibility, and the creatures wore coats of white fur that blended in with the snow. The largest set of eyes belonged to a feline creature the size of a person. She spoke with a soft, purring voice: "More humans? These days, it seems there are more of those in this forest who walk on two feet than those who walk on four. Perhaps we shall remedy that."

Chapter 2:03

The Timister Library and Scientific Research Center

As the snow began to fall on the tracks of the Timister Railroad, Aori cursed the coming winter. The snow piling up on the tracks would undoubtedly slow their progress. To pass the time, he began whittling a piece of Nutberry wood.

"Can't we speed this thing up any?" he asked of a clockworker. Aori had not yet discovered how to give the mechanical men voices, but he had taught a few of them to communicate with a sort of music-box language, which was not unlike the Morse code that was invented on Earth thousands of years later. The language grew more complex over time, with certain chime-tones representing certain phonemes in the common language. A series of tones could be linked together to form sentences. Often, the combination of tones hurt Aori's ears and gave him a headache.

In the tinny, lifeless music-box language, the clockworker said, "We're at top speed as it is, master."

"We need to get home soon. I'm not getting any younger." Aori was, in fact, aging quite rapidly. His recent ventures had taken him many years, while the rest of the world's population had aged only a few days.

Aori looked down at his wooden carving. His conversation with the clockworker had kept his mind so busy that he had finished the carving without knowing it. It occurred to him that his physical body could use time differently than his mind, but the ramifications of that epiphany were still, as yet, unknown to him.

The carving looked strangely familiar. It was a figure of a young boy with scruffy hair and a wooden sword (of course, the entire carving was wooden, but perhaps the sword looked even more wooden than the rest of the figure). He knew he had seen the boy before, but it seemed like many years ago.

As he studied the figure and tried to recall the memory, the train seemed to pick up speed. He was slowing down his personal time as he had done before, but he could feel his consciousness slowing down as well. Time stopped for him, and his heart stopped beating. For an instant, he glimpsed what seemed like another place or time. A large army poured out of a castle like grains of sand in an hourglass.

Aori's time sprang back to normal. One of his alarm-clockworkers had broken his trance-like coma. As consciousness gradually returned, he noticed that he was at home. His workers had put him to bed. Had he fallen asleep? Was the place between time just part of a dream?

Aori looked down at the carving, which was still in his hand. It had changed. The boy had grown into a young man. The familiarity of the figure tugged at his mind, but his memory was not what it used to be.

Throughout the night, Aori's workers prepared the lumber and finished building the library with the Nutberry wood. Construction of the two clocktowers began at dawn. While Aori waited impatiently for Bertram to wake up, he wrote a philosophy book. The Aori principle of philosophy, according to him, involved knowledge gained through experience. Just as one's level of creativity is directly proportional to his or her amount of free time, knowledge depends on how much has been acquiesced. If time were infinite, one would have limitless knowledge and creative power.

Thousands of years later, philosophers developed the *a priori* principle in a coincidental contradiction to Aori's principle. The *a priori* principle suggests that knowledge is innate—baby birds that have never experienced the act of hatching know to peck their way out of their shells. Of course, those philosophers probably never read Aori's book, and he had no way of knowing about their principle, though I'm sure he would have found it fascinating. He might have also been interested in the fact that Priori was yet another name for Toki, the god of Time.

At three in the morning, Aori grew restless. As any insomniac, graveyard-shift worker, or electroencephalogram will attest, three o'clock is the time when the mind is at its most active. As the brain rages like a turbulent sea-storm, dreams thrash and capsize on its waves and time bends at its apex. As with the watched sun or pot of water, the insomniac finds that clocks refuse to tick. The night stretches on endlessly until, at last, the mind settles.

With no means to pacify his brainstorms, Aori decided to wake Bertram. Twenty alarm clockworkers were set about Bertram's bed, and their music crashed and clashed like a train wreck. Bertram sprang from his bed amidst the chaos and shouted, "Cease that infernal racket at once!"

The music stopped and Aori energetically exclaimed, "Bertram, old man! Your library is complete! Aren't you glad you didn't go back to Auldenton, now? Let us go and tour it!"

"Do you know what time it is, Mister Timister?"

Aori handed him a cookie. Its message, which Aori recited aloud, read, "Does anybody really know what time it is? – Chicago."

As they walked to the library, Aori continued, "Some believe the Witching Hour to be from midnight to the first hour of the morning. However, far more magic happens from three to four o'clock. Furthermore, the most change occurs during the hour before dawn. We shall test that today, old friend."

Bertram eyed the remodeled library with awe and admiration. "Would that your parents could see how you have renovated this building, Aori." He paused, closed his eyes, and corrected himself: "I mean not to suggest that they have passed on, Aori. Only—"

"No need to apologize, Bertram. I, too, think they would be—and are—proud. Most of the original structure is still intact. We just braced some of the older wood and made the whole building bigger."

"Old wood, you say? I remember when the library was first built. I believe it was before your time. Your parents were around the age that you are now.

"Come to think of it," Bertram realized, "they had aged very rapidly, as you have. In fact, all of your family seemed aged beyond their years." The epiphany shocked him, for he should have noticed the connection long ago. Everyone in Auldenton had just assumed that grey hair ran in the family.

"Tell me all you remember of my family, Bertram. How else were they like me?"

Bertram became engrossed in recollection, as if his mind had to retrace its steps back to that time. Finally, he recalled, "The Timisters all possessed your preoccupation with time. One of your forefathers invented the first calendar, so that crops and harvests could be planned around the seasons. Another studied and documented the change of the stars and moons. In fact, the first to propose that the world rotated and revolved around the sun was a Timister."

"Bertram, if their findings were all documented, why is it that I cannot find the books? I've read every book here, and none give any such information. Most of these are about animal or plant life."

Bertram returned to his deep state of recollection. "I know they aren't in my library in Auldenton, so they must be here, somewhere. The Timisters collected and saved many

174

ancient texts." He wandered around the older wing of the library, searching through many years' worth of memories. "When you get to be my age, it is a bit more difficult to remember information from long ago."

"I know, Bertram; all too well," Aori stated very matter-of-factly.

Suddenly, Bertram smiled. "I remember. There should be an old, wooden sundial around here somewhere."

"Yes, the clockworkers discovered it buried under many layers of dirt on the eastern side of the building. But I'm sure it doesn't work now that they've built the building around it."

They found the sundial, which remained in its position in the ground. The clockworkers had just removed the soil that covered it. The hardwood floor surrounding it provided a nice frame for the historical exhibit.

Bertram studied the sundial carefully. "Impossible!"

"What?" asked Aori.

"It seems to have changed over the years. 'Tis not how I remembered it."

"Perhaps it is just the wear of spending many years covered with dirt."

"No. In fact, the wood itself seems in perfect condition. I could have sworn, however, that the text and numerals were in another language, before."

Many languages had come and gone since the dawn of civilization on Aia. The common language spoken by many of the characters in this story grew out of many other languages. Words are very much like living beings; they may stop being used, but they never die. They just grow into something different.

Meanwhile, about twenty feet below them, Pyrite Pettifogger continued to pick away at the dirt in his mine. By this point, he had amassed enough treasure that his pockets could no longer withstand the load. He would need some other place to hoard the gems he had pilfered from the rock.

As he swung his pickaxe into the rock, he heard a dull thud. The ears of gnomes are very sensitive to the varying sounds of rock and metal (not to be confused with the musical genres), and he immediately knew that he had hit something other than stone.

Pulling the rock away, he found a wall made of wood.

Aori's patience wore thin as he waited for Bertram to remember what the sundial had to do with the missing library books. To pass the time, he read a book about the faerie cats of forest lore. In all his time studying the cats of Smokewood Forest, he never witnessed any magical behavior. Other than their sleeping habits, his cats behaved quite normally.

Around noon, Aori's eyes began to droop. The book had been the distraction his mind needed to calm down enough for sleep. In his dream, he watched as a vast forest grew up around his home. The trees sprouted leaves and the landscape was blanketed in verdant growth. Gradually, the trees grew into primitive people of the forest. Eventually, their wooden clubs grew into stone hatchets, which grew into swords. Armor grew around them and they looked like contemporary warriors. Their growth continued until bows and arrows grew into rifles and catapults grew into cannons. Above the din of war, Aori heard Bertram's voice.

"Aori!" The images of war faded and Bertram continued, "I've finally remembered! We need only wait a few minutes."

"Wait for what?"

"Lunch-time."

"I'm not concerned with taking a lunch break right now, Bertram."

"It's the position of the sun that matters, Aori. I cannot remember exactly what will happen. Time will tell."

From outside the library, mechanical music chimed and dinged. Light shot like an arrow into the library through a small crack between the new wooden wall. The beam of light struck the sundial, but nothing happened.

As they watched with anticipation, the crack in the wall began to grow. Over the course of three minutes, it had changed into an opening the size of a fist. As more light poured onto the sundial, a shadow appeared on the word "noon." Directly perpendicular to the shadow, a crack split up the wall of the older part of the library. The hole in the eastern wall gradually grew wider, and the crack in the wall facing it grew proportionately.

By the time the midday sun had risen to its apex, a window had grown in the eastern wall. Inside the library, Aori and Bertram marveled at the door that had grown in the older wall. The sunlight beamed in through the doorway, and a sudden blur of movement caught Aori's eye.

"Is someone there?" Bertram shouted into the shadows of the library's inner sanctum.

A small figure crept out of the darkness and into the sunlight.

"Mr. Pettifogger? Is that you?" Aori squinted, as his eyes no longer functioned well in dim light.

"Yes, Mr. Timister. I am sorry."

"What are you doing here?"

The gnome looked at the floor beneath his feet. "I just stumbled upon this place."

"But how did you get in before we opened the door?" Bertram pulled a lever on the wall, and suddenly the floor beneath them began to rattle and shake. They all felt a sinking sensation as Aia's first elevator took them to the lowest level of the library.

Once the elevator stopped moving, Aori noticed a hole in the wall, just large enough for a gnome. "Your mine led directly into my library?"

"Yes," said Pettifogger.

Aori looked around the room, but in the dim light, he could barely see the books and scrolls that covered the shelves. "Does anyone have a lantern?"

Pettifogger activated the light on his miner's helmet, which illuminated the room. As the light shone on Aori's face, shadows cut deep furrows in his skin. In the few minutes before noon, he had aged at least twenty years. His hair was completely white, and his hands began to tremble. Bertram gasped. "Aori...you have aged...."

"Yes, I've now surpassed you in years, old friend. I can feel it in my bones. I feel my vision blurring and hearing diminishing. I must do something to stop this process, or I shall surely wither away and die."

Chapter 2:04

Aori vs. the Ori of Aomori

While both Aori and most of the vegetation in his hemisphere withered, new leaves sprouted on the magnificent trees in the Orien village of Aomori. As the Ori lived on roughly the opposite side of the planet than Quondam and the others, summer swept in after an uncharacteristically short spring. Flowers were blooming and beautiful cherry-blossoms of pink and white adorned the trees.

One tiny, blossoming flower of a girl stood out from all the rest. She had dark hair like the others, but her eyes were not the usual dark brown of the Ori. Rather, they appeared to change color in certain situations. She wore poorly stitched peasant clothes, and though her hair was pinned up, pieces of it fell haphazardly about her shoulders. Her name was Asia.

Though she did not know it, the roots of her destiny were currently entangling with those of our heroes on the other side of the world. Something inside her had always told her that she was special—that she would one day be the greatest of her people— but it sounded like just one of those things parents tell their children.

Only, the little girl had no parents. She had never known her mother, and her father had died when she was a very young child. Though she had been miles away from the event, it often replayed in her dreams in excruciating detail. Even down to the sizzling scorch of his flesh, she knew almost firsthand how her father had died.

Since that horrible day, when her father died defending the town from a dragon, she felt as if he was watching over her; at times, he seemed to guide her down the right path. She was only eight years old, but people often told her that she had a much older spirit. Somehow, she knew about events that had happened before she was born. The elders called it "history," but she felt as if she had lived it all.

She also had an uncanny ability to beat all of the other children in sparring matches. Very handy with a bamboo stick, she somehow had the skills of an accomplished swordsman. Unfortunately, she had very few skills that the women expected of her, and they often became frustrated with her inability to cook, sew, or dye fabric.

The women of the town often spoke of her in hushed whispers. "No wonder she cannot cook," they would say, "knowing who her mother was." However, the little girl did not know her mother, and she doubted that someone she didn't know could have made her a bad cook. In her mind, her mother was beautiful, noble, and braver than any of the Orien women who spoke ill of her.

Long ago, the Ori had made a pact with Toki, the spirit of Time. Like many civilizations, they had depended on knowing when to plant, when to harvest, and when the rainy season would come. The rainy season often brought with it monsoons, hurricanes, and tsunamis, so it was vital to their survival to learn to predict such weather.

Toki gave them the calendar and taught them to watch the stars for Aia's seasonal cycles. The blessing of the Time god helped them to grow their crops and prepare for even the worst storms.

On one occasion, Toki saved them from a marauding army of barbarians. The barbarians approached by way of several boats, and the Time god brought forth a storm out of season to knock them off course and sink several of the ships. They called the storm *kamikazi*, which means "divine wind" in the Orien language.

The particular influential gust of wind that was currently crashing through the village snapped the oldest remaining *asa* tree like a twig. The tree had stood in the center of Aomori forever, and it was the same tree where Quondam's father had died.

Shouts of "Toki has forsaken us!" were barely audible above the clamor of the wind that violently tore the cherry blossoms from the trees. They had not predicted this storm. However, they would soon learn to blame Aori for all their problems, rather than Toki.

> **What's in a Name?**
> Interestingly, in the Orien language, the word *aori* means "a gust of wind." It can also mean "influence," "change," or "bump," which probably comes from the idea that Aori would soon serve as a kind of bump in the otherwise smooth path of the Orien people's lives. One unfortunate fluke of a storm has a way of changing everything.

In the business of deifying a man, that is, assigning the power of a god to a mere mortal, a handy side effect emerges. The deified man often becomes the scapegoat, because it's much easier to lay the blame on someone you can see than some supernatural entity. One cannot stone a god to death, but mortals crumble under the pain of a blow to the skull.

The great storm hit their village just as the clockwork army arrived. The Ori fought valiantly against the clock-workers, but the mechanical soldiers could better withstand the effects of the weather.

The little girl named Asia ran to the fallen *asa* tree and picked up the largest branch she could lift. As the clockwork soldiers came to harvest the lumber, Asia fought them off as best she could. Her makeshift club knocked them to the side, but could not stop their advance.

As more and more Ori fell against the mechanical onslaught, Asia blacked out.

After the storm abated, the Ori found many of their books and historical documents missing from their library. Hundreds of their people were believed to have perished in the storm or the battle, but many could not be found. The *asa* and all of the other magnificent trees had been taken away to be used for lumber.

Days later, as a seedling began to grow in the center of the broken tree, Asalie visited the barren, lifeless town of Aomori. Brightness and hope seemed to follow her as she walked through the village, and a feeling of warmth permeated even the cold rain of the unseasonable monsoon season.

Asalie called out, in the language of the Ori, "Do not despair! Your village shall thrive once again!" But no one was around to hear her benediction. She placed a hand upon the tree stump to listen to its account of what had transpired. "Aori," she voiced, as she felt a stirring in the very ground around her. "Your influence has spread even here?"

It had been raining for several days, and the ground on the slopes around the village had been very unstable. The subsequent mudslide carried with it the uprooted trees and houses of the Aomori forest village.

When, at last, the ground stopped moving, Asalie found herself buried under several feet of mud. Her planet had turned against her.

Chapter 2:05

The Army of the Anachronist Attacks Again

Throughout history, the relationship between animal and man (or four-legged creature and bipedal humanoid) has been one of domination and submission. Shepherds tend their flocks, but they do not spare the rod, as the saying goes. On Aia (and, later, on parts of Earth), the anthropomorphized beast represented a unification of the conflicting sides. Humans who turn into beasts or vice-versa embody the savagery of the animal and the civilized nature of the bipedal humanoid at the same time. Who better to shepherd the animals than one who is, him- or herself, a sheep?

The guardians of Aia's animal population were known as the Antheri. They were guardians and watchers, but also supreme rulers, not unlike gods to the beasts. The most well-known of the Antheri is perhaps the lycanthrope, or werewolf, who ruled the wolves. Centaurs watched over horses, satyrs guarded goats, and mermaids kept the fish in line. However, if there were a Lord of the Flies or an Ant-man, he or she must not have gotten out much.

Of course, the conflict still exists within the Antheri. Which will dominate—the wolf or the man, for instance? Under ideal circumstances, Connery and most other anthropomorphized creatures could easily maintain balance between the conflicting energies. Transformation from biped to quadruped could occur at will.

Antheri

Some believe the Sali Lumpa to be Antheri guardians of lesser primates, based on the advanced artistic behaviors exhibited by the creatures. Some have even gone so far as to label humans as the Antheri for all primates, but let's not get into that debate right now.

Many of the shape-shifting Antheri of Aia were kings or queens of some animal with a savage side, such as bears, lions, or squirrels (yes, squirrels can be savage). However, some calmer beasts, such as the deer, also had Antheri masters. A human who can change into a deer is commonly called a weredeer, while the female is more specifically called a weredoe. There were also spider-men and bat-men, but they obviously will not be included in this story, for legal reasons.

However, lunar cycles tend to profoundly affect the behavior patterns of humans and animals.

On Aia, there were two moons with separate lunar cycles. For as long as anyone could remember, one moon waxed while the other waned. The combination of the new moon with the full moon balanced the opposing energies very nicely, and all were-creatures could maintain control. Times change.

Connery sniffed the air. His nostrils ached from the bitter cold. The harsh wind had brought a familiar scent to him, but it was gone before he could identify it. He looked up at the sky. The blizzard had stopped, and the light of the full moon poured over the dusky clouds. Oddly, the other moon was also visible that night. A tiny sliver of silvery light shot out from behind another cloud. In all his days, Connery had never seen a full moon and a crescent at the same time. The extra moon-bits gave him an eerie, dreadful feeling.

"What are you growling at?"

Connery snapped back to the here-and-now and noticed that he had, in fact, been growling. His jaws were sore from grinding his teeth. "Perhaps nothing," he said to Quondam, who had already drawn his wooden sword. Connery noticed the sword and asked, "Is that sword made o' wood?"

Thoughtseeds sprouted, and Quondam learned new information about his wooden sword. "It was my father's sword. It came from the *asa* tree he planted in the village of Aomori." He shifted to an older age and the sword changed into a staff. "As I grow, it grows with me."

"For your sake, I hope it does more than cause splinters!" a voice shouted suddenly. In a flash, the battalion once again surrounded them.

The enormous captain had removed his helmet, and the wooden arm now looked more like an arm than a ram. The face looked incredibly familiar to Quondam, and the older parts of his brain soon caught up with him.

"...Munder." The vision of the captain's wooden arm connected with Quondam's memory of the splinter his sword had given Munder. "So the splinter grew, I suppose."

"So did I," Munder shouted. "I grew lots." He was definitely not the boy Quondam remembered. Munder looked to be in his mid-twenties, and his size rivaled that of the Prochrons' wooly herbovines. As they watched, the arm changed back into a battering ram. With a sudden, quick movement, he charged at Quondam.

As Quondam fell to the ground, the attackers approached with weapons drawn. The battalion had decreased in size since their last meeting, and the soldiers seemed primed for stealth. Several Prochrons wore dark war paint and wielded spears. Only a few rode the mighty herbovines. Knights in black armor loomed in the gloomy darkness, but contrasted with the white snow. The musketeers had been replaced by soldiers with dark uniforms and silenced guns. A few of them had night-vision goggles.

The creepy silence shattered with the sound of Lithe's battle music. The Metachrons discovered that their bullets repeatedly missed their targets, so they resigned to hand-to-hand combat. The rest of the battalion found it difficult to see, but Connery and the wolves had experience hunting in darkness.

Lithe moved through the battlefield with speed and grace as she played her battle-pipe. Few of the soldiers could get close to her, and the ones that did met with her dancing saber. As spears and arrows flitted about in the air, she leapt up, caught them, and guided them back at their owners.

Quondam leaned heavily on his staff as he attempted to stand. At that age, the fall had broken his hip. He shifted to another age, but the pain continued. He couldn't shift past the pain. Normally, his various bodies healed from grievous injuries during the shift-change, but the broken bone required setting—perhaps even surgery—and it followed him to all ages.

In this older, wiser form, Quondam felt a kind of magic growing inside him. He called upon the power of Asalie, and thoughtseeds sprouted in his mind. Thorny vines burst from the ground and snatched up a large group of Prochrons.

The wolves were more accustomed to picking off the weaker members of large groups and killing them one by one, but they also had experience with all-out brawls such as this one. They fought the armed soldiers and knights with ferocious tenacity, and nothing could quell their savage frenzy. Connery himself had given in to his savage side when he saw the soldiers attack his pack, and his humanity seemed to fade. He sunk his long teeth into the exposed flesh of a knight and tasted blood. His claws ripped and tore through the knight's armor to get at the canned meat.

Lithe vaulted over a knight and sank her foot into the face of a soldier. She removed the knight's helm with her tail and guided the end of her blade into his uncovered neck. The saber darted from one opponent to another as Lithe continued to play her pipe.

Munder gazed over the heads of the fighters and kicked at the wolves gnawing at his ankles. With a mighty hand, he caught Lithe in mid-leap. The song ended as his iron grip closed off the passage of air through Lithe's windpipe.

A sniper took aim from the top of a distant tree and found Quondam in the sights of his scope. With a loud crack, the bullet found its mark and Quondam fell. Munder released Lithe and looked at his watch. Before Lithe could resume her song, another shot rang out and struck her in the chest.

"Right on time," Munder said, still gazing at his watch. "Come. You two have an appointment."

Chapter 2:06

Tweentime

Quondam regained consciousness and attempted to get his bearings. His hands were bound tight with metal shackles. Soldiers of the future surrounded him, with rifles aimed at his head.

"You can't heal from a gunshot to the head, old man," Munder's voice bellowed. "Just sit still and wait."

Quondam looked around the room. The walls all seemed to be made of glass—some transparent, some translucent. A stained glass mosaic on one of the walls depicted a scene of the battle Quondam had just fought. In the mosaic, Munder towered over the wounded and dying, while the bodies of men and wolves littered the ground.

A ticking sound reverberated through the walls of the room and reminded Quondam of his pocketwatch. He looked down at it and noticed that it had stopped. He tried to shift to clear his head, but nothing happened.

"You're pretty much stuck at that age 'til the master arrives, pops. Get used to it. Just try not to have a stroke or nothin'," Munder mused.

"M-master? Who? You work for Aori?"

"Afraid not, Quondam." The words came from another source in the room. The voice sounded vaguely familiar to

Quondam. "Aori is but my faithful servant, just as all the Timisters were, and as you should be." An old, pompous-looking man walked into Quondam's field of vision.

"You... you're...."

"Yes. I'm the old man from the Seer's Day Festival." Despite the similarity in age, the man looked nothing like he had only a few days ago. That was why the god of Time had so many different names; he manifested himself as a different elderly gentleman each time he made an appearance.

"Toki!" Quondam shouted, as if saying the name aloud might give him some power over the god.

"That's the name your father's people gave me. I've been called by so many names: Tempo, Toki, Time, Chronos, Saturn... I could literally go on for days, but I won't. We have better things to do, and you're not getting any younger! My good man, you have not aged gracefully at all. Be careful, or you might wither away!"

Munder dragged Quondam to his feet. Toki left the room, and Munder followed with Quondam in tow. Quondam noticed more stained-glass mosaics, which combined to form a triptych.

"The three pictures portray the Temporal Trinity," said Toki. "The Past, Present, and Future. The Father, the Son, and the Zeitgeist, or Spirit of the Times."

Quondam recognized one of the figures as Aori. "Aori is your son?" Quondam asked.

"In a way. You see, as powerful as I am, I can't be everywhere at once. *Everywhen*, sure, but not everywhere. I need timekeepers and servants on Aia to do my bidding. That's where you Timisters come in; you're my servants."

"So you are the master of Time?" asked Quondam.

"I prefer *god* of Time, actually. I've worked hard to get to this point, and I deserve a grand title. Would you like to see what your friends are doing, this very second?" He tapped on a stained glass mosaic, and it displayed a snapshot of Lithe in a room full of flashing boxes.

"Where is she?" Quondam demanded with as much bravado as his decrepit form could muster. "What have you done with her? And where is Connery?"

"She is safe. I value the Coda above all else on this planet, save you Timisters. I made them, you know. They were once hoity-toity Elves. They lived forever and caused me all sorts of problems, so I sped up their evolution a bit."

"Evolution is Growth. You would be nothing without Asalie," insisted Quondam in a commanding voice.

The Time-god smiled. "Is that what she told you? Did she plant seeds in your head? She put her thoughts in your brain. Why, she's just as manipulative as I am. One day you will see Asalie as I do: *as a lie.*"

"You are the one who is a liar!" Anger grew in Quondam; he would die defending Asalie as his father had done for the *asa* tree. He reached for his sword, but it was gone.

"Now, Quondam. There is a time and a place for violence. Don't be so hasty. You are weaponless anyway. Let us sit and while away the hours with story and song." He turned to Munder. "Bring her in."

As Munder brought Lithe into the room, Time stood still. Then, he sat down in a large throne. The throne was decorated with various timepieces, and two large hourglasses served as armrests.

"Now, Emmeleia, what was that song your people sang about me?"

The soldiers had taken away Lithe's sabers and stripped her of her many instruments. "I cannot play music for you," she said in a voice devoid of tone but radiating with rage. "You have taken my instruments."

"Fine. I will have one of my own minstrels sing it." Instantly, another Coda appeared. "Dolente, please begin. And do try not to make it so melancholy this time."

The literary community of Auldenton had presumed the poet/author/musician dead for almost a hundred years, yet here he stood in perpetual senescence. Though his long, thin fingers were wrinkled and pale, he showed no signs of debilitation.

The song he played on his mandolin told of the great wizard Tempo's visits to the homeland of the Coda. As he played, the stained glass images moved and changed to depict key events in the tale. In each picture, Tempo was portrayed as some benevolent vizier, sharing key bits of knowledge that would advance their culture. Tempo taught them about time signatures and showed them how to use a metronome to keep time. He gave them rhythm, syncopation, and taught them to hold notes for varied lengths in order to make music.

For two up-and-coming musicians, Tempo provided special, clandestine lessons. One of the Coda, Veloce, was taught to speed up time by playing a fiddle at a rapid tempo. The other, Ritardando, was given the ability to slow down time by singing very slowly.

The duo eventually took advantage of their abilities and became master thieves. Ritardando would slow down their victim just long enough for Veloce to rush in and take the money or valuables. It even worked for burglarizing homes and castles. No one was safe from the Filching Fiddler and the Crooked Crooner.

After they had all the riches they could possibly want, Veloce grew restless. He killed his slow-witted partner and stole his song and power. Of course, as with any good tale, his greediness cost him greatly in the end. The very second that he began to sing Ritardando's song while playing his fiddle, Veloce was frozen in time.

That's why fiddlers never play and sing at the same time—it has nothing to do with the position of their chin on the fiddle making it hard to sing.

The song ended and Dolente wept.

"So the Timisters aren't the only people you've manipulated over the years," Quondam interjected. "Your evil influence has even turned peaceful musicians into heartless murderers!"

Tempo/Toki rose from his seat and stepped toward Quondam. "Oh, come on! You don't know that I turned them into thieves and murderers. They were probably born that way; I just gave them the ability. Besides, I am not evil— manipulative, sure, but not really evil. Am I evil, Munder?"

Munder turned his attention to the time-lord, as if he just got caught daydreaming in class. "Evil? I guess so? I'm no expert."

Toki sighed. "Was it evil for me to save your life, a split second before your helpless body struck the bottom of that cliff back in Auldenton? Or was Quondam the evil one, for letting you fall, and not even checking to see if you had survived?"

The manipulative god paraded out of the room dramatically, waving his arms and gesturing at some primitive pictograms etched into the glass along the hall. Munder pushed Quondam and Lithe after his master and gazed at the child-like etchings. They depicted his story, from the second he touched Quondam's timepiece to the subsequent fall, the timely rescue by Toki, and the years of training that followed.

"Was it evil to take in this unwanted orphan, to bring this giant monstrosity into my... extremely fragile home," Toki gestured to a drawing that showed Munder as a bull in a China shop, "And to give him the education and culture he could never have received in the streets of Auldenton?"

"I actually learned more from just watching TV," Munder mumbled under his breath.

"No," said Toki, completely ignoring Munder. "If I bring out the evil in someone, it was probably there to begin with. It just needed time to grow."

"Grow? You suggest that what Veloce became—or what Munder has become—is growth? Asalie had nothing to do with this!" Quondam gestured violently toward Munder.

"Well," Tempo said, "aren't you the little sycophant, blindly following the great Tumor. She would be nothing without me, for what is Growth without Time?" He sat back down in his throne. "Not all growth is flowers and foliage, you know. There are also weeds."

"Weeds you perverted over time," countered Quondam.

"Hmph. I see now that it was a mistake to bestow such a gift upon one such as you," Tempo said, indicating the pocketwatch. He paused for a moment, as if he were collecting the thoughts of many centuries to come. "But, you shall do much in your lifetime. Perhaps you shall serve me, in time." Tempo rose to his feet again. "Come. I have much to show you."

He led them down another long, glass-walled hall. Through the clear glass, Quondam could see vast spiraling shapes that stretched out forever, like the images of faraway galaxies in Astronomy textbooks. "Don't look out the windows, Pops," Munder told him. "Your brain will explode if you try to understand infinity."

At the end of the hall, they came to a large room decorated with flashing lights and signs. The opposite wall was covered with millions of television screens. Each screen was set to a different channel in a different time. Some showed the past, some the present, and some the future.

"Now, this is how I like to conceptualize the infinite expanse of time. Of course, it's really not like this, but televisions are so… modern. Not as modern as Synaptic Thought Projectors, but so much more practical. I call this part of the palace 'Times Square.'"

Quondam tried to garner some sort of sense out of the images to no avail. One screen showed a couple of people talking about music. "The Timeless Love album has all of my favorite timeless love songs," said one of them.

"Like what?" asked the other.

"Well, like 'Time in a Bottle,' by Jim Croce." As the couple held hands, someone sang:

> If I could save time in a bottle
> The first thing that I'd like to do
> Is save every day

Till Eternity passes away
Just to spend them with you
    (Words and Music by Jim Croce. Copyright 1975,
Atlantic Records)

On another screen, Quondam noticed a young man and
a boy with some strange amulet that reminded him of his
pocketwatch. Tempo walked over to him. "This is a
television program called 'Voyagers!' The little boy and the
man in the ruffled shirt travel through time to fix history."
    "How does history get broken?" asked Quondam.
    "Well, the time stream is fairly chaotic. I have better
things to do than sit around making things all linear and
monotonous. Then, sometimes, I put musketeers and
cavemen in a medieval society and give people the power to
mess with time." Toki pointed at the screen and continued,
"This program, like many others, stars a man with a young
boy for a sidekick. It's also common to have a wise, old
teacher to guide a young novice through a story." He paused
for effect. "You, my good man, are the old man, the younger
man *and* the boy at the same time!"
    Lithe stood enraptured with screens showing music
videos from Earth's 1980's to the 2000's. Some of the music
sounded melodious and captivating, but she found a few of
the musicians to be quite lacking in talent.
    Toki spoke to Lithe of the music of the future. He told
her of concerts, recordings, folk, pop, rap, heavy metal, and
alternative. He told her of millionaire musicians, boy bands,
and divas. "You can have it all, Emmeleia. I will give you the
music of the future—every song, every instrument, and all the
fame and fortune that goes with it."
    Lithe stared at the screens for a long time. Many musical
masterpieces would be created in the millennia to come,
whereas her lifespan might only last a hundred or so more
years. If she agreed, she could have every song at her
disposal, without having to work for them. She could have
instruments of the future, which would allow her access to

never-before-heard music, and the possibilities would be endless. However, she didn't need knowledge of the future to know that the manipulative god she called Tempo would not give the gift freely. Hindsight told her that there would be a catch. She might end up selling her soul to this devil and only get some sappy love song from the 1980's. After careful thought, she answered, "I will create my own music."

Chapter 2:07

Educating the Masses

Feeling that his days were numbered, Aori tried to absorb as much information as he could in the time between his many other projects. When the strain on his eyes became too much, he took time out of his busy schedule to invent a pair of bifocals so that he could continue reading all the ancient texts of his family. He knew the books held some secret to prolonging his life and maintaining what little youth he had left. Somehow, he reasoned, he had to keep from sleeping, because that was when the aging became most severe.

With the knowledge he attained from the ancient texts, he taught himself to meditate, thereby relaxing his mind and body without the danger of losing precious time dreaming. He managed to stop his aging process altogether, but doing so required that he enter a trance-like coma. It cut down on his productivity, which was a painful sacrifice, but kept him from growing old and dying.

The alarm clockworkers roused him from his preservative comas periodically so that he could get his work done. The clock towers were almost completed, and the clockworkers worked fairly autonomously, but Aori's presence was still required. It's basically the same philosophy that work gets done more quickly when the boss is around—except the workers in this case never tired or slowed; they just needed routine maintenance and tune-ups from their master every now and then.

In the mines under the library, similar tuning and tinkering took place. Pettifogger had always had a natural affinity for all things mechanical, and the clockworker guarding him had been following his orders for days. It had aided with the mining and even kept him company in the cold and lonely tunnels, but the latest developments surprised Pettifogger. The machine now seemed more like a man, with a beard made out of rusty wires and even two quartz crystals for its eyes.

Quartz, like other crystals, has a natural resonance that makes it very useful in constructing clocks and watches. Depending on how the crystal is cut, it can store up vibrations of specific frequencies. It is a complex process involving precise electrical charges that are stored up or released at specific intervals of time. The minute details are not as important as the connection between the natural and the mechanical. Such juxtaposition lives and breathes in every gnome, with their innate abilities to work with plants and stone as well as mechanisms and gadgets.

Even though Pettifogger had grown up hearing folktales about living, breathing constructions, the changes in this clockworker were far beyond the blooming mechanical flowers his father had invented. It truly seemed alive and eager to communicate with him. The crystals in its eyes lit up with a beautiful glow, mesmerizing the gnome as he studied it in awe.

Perhaps it was Pettifogger's deep connection with the rocks, but when he lost consciousness, the hard cavern floor embraced him like a lover.

From the library's secret and ancient texts, Aori learned that the Time-god resided in a place between the here, now, then, and there—hence the name Tweentime. He lived in huge, multi-faceted hourglass, and legend told that the palace was conjured by the music of the Coda (the legend is vaguely similar to the story Lithe told of the damsel with the dulcimer and the pleasure-dome with caves of ice). Of course, it was more glass and crystal than ice, but who's counting?

"If that is where Time lives," Aori said to Bertram, "perhaps I should go there." Bertram was preoccupied with cataloging the newer library books, but Aori continued to speak to him. "This Priori, or Tempo, must be the old man from the Seer's Day Festival. But why did he bestow this power upon me, of all people?"

"Well, Aori, you *are* a Timister, and you *do* have an unhealthy obsession with time," Bertram stated in between tasks.

"Efficiency and productivity are not unhealthy, Bertram. Wasting time—squandering it while growing older—*that* is unhealthy. If I age and die before my work is done...."

"What work? What is so important that it must be done right away? Aori, you must learn to stop and smell the roses. Just enjoy life before it is over. No one waits for you at the end to measure your productivity."

"That is where you are wrong, Bertram. Dolente's work may have been predominantly dull, monotonous brooding, but he did accomplish quite a lot. Even though he is no longer around to whine and whimper, his work will live forever. Bertram, I can live forever too, if I just keep creating. You have to stop moving for the gravedigger to put the dirt over you."

Aori ate a cookie with the message, "A rolling stone gathers no moss."

"How timely," Bertram remarked. "Mine says, 'The destruction of a library is the destruction of an entire civilization.'"

Aori thought of all the information stored in his library—the histories of various animals and peoples, the only copies of his theories and inventions—his life's work. If his library burned down, all records of those lost civilizations would be lost. Without his creations to stand the test of time, the world would forget he ever existed. "Indeed," he said pensively. "The death of my library would be the death of me."

As if in response to Aori's thoughts, at that very moment, an ancient Agypsian library burned to the ground in a desert on the other side of the world. Fortunately, the clockwork soldiers who had set the fire had first retrieved the historical records, papyrus documents, and religious texts, which would be preserved for all posterity in Aori's library. Regardless of the clockworkers' apparent disobedience regarding the destruction of the library, the Agypsian culture would not die that day.

Walk Like an Agypsian

For many reasons, the Agypsians would forever be known for their perpetuity. The bodies of their long-dead kings and queens remained unchanged even after death.

The Agypsians used several natural ingredients, most commonly the herb thyme, to embalm bodies after death. The process of mummification kept the rot of bacteria from consuming the organic material in the body. Slowing down decomposition after death was seen as a blessing by their god of death and decay, Osinis (or Finis, as he was known throughout most of the world). It is truly interesting how cultures evolve linguistically. For instance, the people of Egypt on Earth came from Aia's Agypsians, and through an ancient version of a typo in their hieroglyphics, they misinterpreted the spelling for "Osinis" as "Osiris."

The contradiction between Life and Death was important to the Agypsians, as it was to many Aian civilizations. The ankh, which also survived the trip to Earth and Egypt, represents the endless cycle of life and death. While it may seem contradictory to believe in the eternity of life and death at the same time, many cultures hold this to be true. In order to further explain the idea, let us use another symbol sacred to the Agypsians: the moon. The moon (or moons, if you're on Aia) goes through many phases, and many cultures saw this as birth, growth, decay, death, and rebirth. Just as the sun and moon rise and set, so it is with life and death.

The Timister Library also included books on Astronomy. The moons were the first timepieces on Aia. Many cultures studied the lunar cycles, and each culture had its own lore to explain the moons and their changes. Aori's favorite involved two lovers who felt that their lifetimes did not provide enough time together, so they both appealed to the god of Time and were reborn as trees. One tree grew a large, yellow fruit that would grow in the morning and fall off in the evening. The other tree grew two white fruits that sprouted, grew, rotted, fell off, and finally grew back again.

Aori assumed, as his family had, that many legends of the sun and moons were greatly exaggerated. He had already written books about Aia's rotation and revolution around the sun, which debunked the popular theory that the sun moved through the sky. Furthermore, he theorized that the light from the moons came from the sun, and the phases of the moons resulted from the orbits of the moons around Aia. He even predicted that, if the moons continued to change their orbital patterns, both would one day be full at the same time. Aori doubted, however, that he would live to see that.

Underground, the lines between reality and fantasy swirled like paint in a Spin-Art machine. Pettifogger thought he was staring up at the night sky, because he saw two brightly shining moons beaming down on him. As he looked closer, he found that the twinkling lights were the clockworker's quartz eyes. He switched on his headlamp, but illuminating his surroundings only brought more confusion.

The walls glittered like diamonds, but he was no longer inside the mines. Everywhere he looked, he saw the defined cut of crystal, and a faint purple glow emitted from behind the translucent walls. In the dim light, Pettifogger tried to make out the shape of the clockworker. He couldn't be sure, and it seemed impossible, but the machine looked even more like an old man.

"You may not know me, but the elders of your community know my name well. I am Quartz Thymegarden."

Pettifogger shook the fog from his head. "You're a machine. How can you talk?"

"You brought me to life, Pyrite," said the old gnome. "Well, back to life. You acquired the ability from your father, I believe. He was quite adept at making the inanimate animate."

"You're the old tinkerer from the bedtime stories my father used to tell me."

"Like I said, I'm well known among gnomes. I've been around a long time. Come with me, boy. I want to show you something."

As the old gnome led the young down a crystal hallway, Pettifogger caught glimpses of three-dimensional holograms through the walls. The images looked so real that he repeatedly tried to reach out and grab them. In the holograms, he saw clockwork soldiers marching all over the world. He saw them destroying libraries, kidnapping children, and clearing whole forests of trees for lumber.

"What am I seeing?" asked Pettifogger. "Is this really happening?"

"It's difficult to say," answered Quartz. "It might have already happened, or it could be about to happen. I try not to think about it too much. Just keep walking, kid."

"Where am I, anyway? This isn't the mine."

"Brilliant observation, Pyrite; this is not a mine. I realize it's a bit overwhelming, but soon you'll grow quite accustomed to this place. It's a palace between what is, what was, and what will be. Welcome to Tweentime."

From his tower, Aori could easily see the full moon, as well as the small sliver that accompanied it. He logged the size and positions of the moons in his records. One day, if people could look back on his predictions, they would know that he was correct.

Aori often contemplated the limitations of his life and the scope of his influence on Aia. He had already achieved more in the last few days than most people do in an entire lifetime. Of course, he had aged a lifetime in just a few days while working on the achievements.

He feared, however, that his ideas and inventions would be lost to the world someday. Everything he had invented had been created for some personal purpose, but he realized that keeping his work to himself would only doom it to die with him. That night, he proposed an idea to Bertram:

"I want to teach my ideas to the people of Aia."

"What? How? There is a war happening, you know. People don't have time for learning right now." He paused. "Do not. People do not have time.... I have even begun to speak like you, in hasty contractions and such."

"Bertram, I told my clockworkers to find me literature to read, and they went out and got me books from all over the world. Now, I want them to take something back to those civilizations. If I can teach others about clockwork, the magic-steam engine, or mathematics, then at least my ideas will live forever."

Aori rested for a few moments and then concluded, "I have no children, Bertram. I must have some legacy— something to pass on to the next generation. All I have is my work."

Classes began at his library the very next day. He planned for his clockworkers to become missionaries of sorts, traveling around the globe to spread Aori's ideas, inventions, and discoveries. Very soon, he would be well known through-out the world. Of course, lots of the other civilizations wanted him dead.

Aori became obsessed with the future, and the legacy he would leave behind after his death. He worked feverishly to write books, invent new time-saving devices, and make a name for himself globally. One of his latest inventions, which he called the Timister Telescopic Goggles, perfectly symbolized his newfound focus on the faraway future. Of course, he assumed they would work like twin telescopes to make distant objects appear closer. However, some of the greatest inventions of all time have been happy accidents.

Very soon, the goggles would be used to peer into the future. However, even without the goggles, one could easily predict that things were looking pretty bleak for Aia.

Chapter 2:08

Civility Among Savages

Despite the disappearance of their captain and two of their targets, the battalion continued to fight. Bullets started hitting with more accuracy without Lithe's song to divert them, and many wolves were mortally wounded by gunshots.

It took a lot more than bullets, however, to kill an Antheri. The common belief is that only a silver bullet can kill a werewolf, but all Antheri have a supernatural endurance. Any wounds the soldiers, knights, or cavemen could inflict just healed. He would have scars in the morning, but he would win the fight.

At the command of a primitive Prochron, a massive wooly herbovine charged at Connery as he chewed through the black uniform of a Metachron. The herbovine's crescent-shaped horns gored Connery's ribs and pinned him to a tree.

Because the herbovine had cloven hooves and crescent-shaped horns, it was often the object of sacrificial rituals made to the Moons. The hooves, which looked like two crescent moons facing one another, were cut off and given to the hunter who had managed to capture it. The hunter would also affix the horns to a helm or simply use them as swords or boomerangs.

Many cultures believed the herbovine to be a sacred moon animal, but one tribe of forest-people hunted them chiefly for food. The Leafblowers had heard the call of the bloodbark trees as Aori had cut them down, and when they came to investigate, they found herbovine tracks as well. However, at that time, only one member of the tribe had tracked it to this point in the woods.

Crowfoot Darkroot lunged from a tree and stabbed a knife into the back of the giant herbovine. The knife was not his; he had stolen it from a tree-perched sniper. Blood and sweat matted the herbovine's long, wooly hair, which provided a good handle for Crowfoot. The animal bucked and kicked furiously, but Crowfoot held tight to its hair.

Suddenly, darkness washed over him and he darted to one side of the herbovine. A series of bullets perforated the herbovine's thick skin as the Metachrons missed their target. Once again, Crowfoot had mysteriously averted death.

The herbovine provided a rather large shield from the battalion's gunfire, but Crowfoot wondered what would happen when they decided to fight him hand-to-hand. He closed his eyes and waited for the gunfire to cease. When it finally did, he looked for the telltale darkening to signal his death, but it never came.

Instead, he heard the sounds of growling, men screaming, and flesh tearing. Eventually, the sounds of death subsided and were replaced by a hushed rattle, as if a rattlesnake had been wrapped in fabric and placed in a tin can.

As the sound got closer, Crowfoot still saw no darkness. He actually felt relief, and the pleasant sound lightened his mood. Then, he felt the claws penetrate his skin.

"This one with you, Conri?" said a voice that sounded harsh and soft all at once.

"Could be," answered Connery as he attempted to move the dead animal's giant horns from his ribcage. "He attacked this hairy beast, so I am guessing he is not with them."

"I… fight them. They killed my tribe," said Crowfoot in his best common tongue; he had learned bits of the language of Auldenton from the chieftain-king.

"Y' must be th' barefoot walker 'oo made th' tracks 'round th' hollow," deduced Connery. That mystery could finally be put to rest.

"Yes. After they killed my people, I ran to the tallest trees. But the tall bloodbarks were not where I remembered. Just stumps and warm light. The herbovines and warriors did not follow me there. I was safe. Except for the wolves."

Connery surveyed the battleground. It was littered with the lifeless bodies of his pack. Those who survived the battle were severely injured. Connery howled and tore at his hair.

After the woman's claws retracted from his skin, Crowfoot got a better view of the source of all the sounds. She helped him to his feet, but she was not like any woman he had ever seen. A velvety layer of pitch-black fur covered her skin, and she had long ears that pointed up. As she moved, he could see every toned muscle in her body tense and release like a beautiful dance.

"Come. Let us talk, Woodman," she whispered in her harshly soft voice. She sounded like sandpaper rubbing on silk. "The wolf will be howling like that for hours. It is the custom of their kind. My kind too, I suppose, but we rarely die."

"Can you sense the coming of the blackbird too?" asked Crowfoot.

"In a way, I suppose. What is your name, Woodman?"

"Crowfoot. I am named for the spirit of death that comes to the old and weary."

"I see. I am Caitlyn, Queen of Cats. These are my kin." Cats of various sizes and species stepped into the moonlight. Some of them looked almost as big as the herbovine, while the smallest was about the size of one of Connery's wolves. They were all purring quite loudly, and the sound boosted the morale of all those around them, including the human.

Crowfoot looked around at all the death and the moonlight dimmed. He said a prayer so that the blackbird might ferry their souls to the land of death. The prayer involved trilling high notes and drum-like beats, which harmonized well with Connery's howls.

"Conri, are you badly hurt?" asked Caitlyn.

"We shall see in th' morning, Cait."

"You glad to see me, Conri?"

Connery looked at the shredded bodies of the battalion. "Aye, Cait. Quite."

The cats began to lick themselves clean of the blood and death. A few of them gnawed on the flesh of their enemies. Caitlyn looked hungry as well. "Well, Conri, Crowfoot, shall we eat?" Crowfoot looked around at the dead humans hesitantly. Caitlyn noticed his concern: "Not the humans, Crowfoot. We are not all savages." Her words rang with certain ironic tone, for most civilized humans would have considered the three of them to be quite savage indeed. "The herbovine should be fine."

The three bipeds started a fire and cooked the herbovine meat. It was a bit tough and sinewy, since it was born in a time before the herding and domestication of animals, but Caitlyn and Connery found the taste of tendon quite satisfying. Of course, it tasted like tough, sinewy vegetables.

"What sorcery was it that made their weapons spit rocks?" asked Crowfoot.

"Metal, not rocks. An' I 'ave never seen such weapons." Connery kicked at one of the rifles. "Quondam would know, per'aps."

"Quondam? You mean, the demon-sorcerer?" asked Crowfoot.

"I don' think 'e was a demon, though I s'pose he knew a bit o' magic in his old age."

"I fought him when he was young. Then, he grew old and young again. He was very powerful and very wise. He even knew the language of my people."

Connery looked around at the bodies again. "Where could 'e 'ave gone? Quondam, Lithe, an' the giant vanished in th' middle o' th' battle."

"Maybe a spirit carried them away," offered Crowfoot.

"Maybe they died," Caitlyn stopped eating to say. Connery and Crowfoot looked at her with worried looks. "What? Humans do that sort of thing a lot."

Chapter 2:09

Slipping Through Tweentime

Munder escorted Quondam to his cell, which was far away from Lithe's cell. Quondam looked up at his giant, former friend. "Munder?" he called. "Where have you been for the last week or so? I thought you were dead."

"Shut up, Pops. Get in your cell."

"I'm just curious. How did you get so big in such a short time?"

Munder locked the glass door behind him. He pushed Quondam onto a large, flat table. A complex series of gears and machines sat at the head of the table. "How did you get to be such an inquisitive old man in such a short time?"

"Who taught you the word 'inquisitive'? The Munder I knew didn't know any words over a syllable."

"Did too," countered Munder.

"Did not."

"Did too!"

"Did not!" Quondam could not shift his body, but he shifted his voice as much as possible. He sounded like an eight-year-old boy.

"DID TOO!" Munder was angry. He strapped Quondam to the table with shackles that somehow conformed to the size of Quondam's wrist. "Don't even think about making your wrists small enough to get out of these shackles. Even if your precious little watch worked here, the shackle would just tighten around your puny wrist."

"Wouldn't dream of it. I came all this way to bring you back to life, and now here you are! I'm so glad you're alive…and …turning those cranks."

"Yeah, same here. These cranks wind up the clock mechanism. As the second-hand turns, you probably won't feel anything. When the minute-hand moves, you'll feel a slight tug at your arms and legs. As the minutes increase, it'll begin to hurt pretty badly. I have a bet going with the Metachrons that you'll probably only last two hours." Munder walked towards the door.

"Hmm. Good luck on that bet, old pal," said Quondam.

"Thanks." Munder stopped walking and turned around. "Y'know, Quondam, you always wanted to be taller—maybe this machine will stretch you out!" His laugh bellowed down the glass hall and echoed through the entire palace.

In Lithe's cell, the glass walls hummed with the vibration of Munder's laugh. Lithe was bound to the ceiling by her wrists. Tempo entered her room and shut the door.

"Emmeleia, my sweetest song. It's so fortunate that your path has led you here."

"My path leads me to a mandolin and the Symphony. You led me here, Tempo."

"If all you need is a mandolin, I can give you one. Dolente doesn't need his anyway." Tempo produced a digital alarm clock from his many-layered robe and set it upon a shelf. "Just take the mandolin and you can go. Run back home and join the Symphony as it is prophesied." He pressed a series of buttons on the alarm clock.

"No. I must build my own instrument in order to join."

"So take the instrument, go home, and then make your own." Tempo continued to press the buttons. Surprised by her silence, he looked up at her. "I'm giving you permission to leave. You can go at any time."

"I... cannot take Dolente's mandolin. It is linked to his very soul, just as mine will be, and it shall die with him."

"Emmeleia. Lithe. Ethil. Tell me. Why won't you go? Take the mandolin or don't take it. I don't care. I've given you permission to leave. Just say the word and I'll untie you."

Lithe seethed. Tempo obviously wanted her to abandon Quondam and resume her quest. In the beginning, her quest was all that mattered to her. In their time together, however, a bond had grown between them. It wasn't romantic—Lithe was not the love song type. At first, she saw him as a young child in need of parental care. Gradually, however, their relationship had become more complex than that. Maybe she saw him as a father-figure as well.

As if reading her thoughts, Tempo said, "Your family misses you. You may not believe it, but even Ode, your father, prays for your swift return."

She ignored his attempts at finding her emotional soft-spot. Maybe it was her father's cold, emotionless blood that ran through her, but she had no fond feelings in regard to her youth, or her family. For years, she had focused only on the here and now. However, she realized now that she had been self-absorbed in her quest. In addition to her growing bond with Quondam, Lithe felt bonded to the *timbre*. It was important to her to find Aori and the stolen wood, regardless of her mandolin project. Whatever the time-server had planned for the wood, she knew it was more nefarious than the construction of a musical instrument.

"Okay," said Tempo at last. "I'll give you some time to make your decision. I mean, all we have here is time, you know. When this alarm clock beeps, then Quondam will either be dead or in a world of hurt. Then, you can give up on him and leave here. You won't have to make a decision if you just wait around long enough. Of course, I know what you will do, but it's still your choice."

A few minutes had passed, and Quondam could feel a light amount of pressure on his wrists and ankles. There had to be a way to stop the clock and free himself. He had all the wisdom of an aged man, but the incessant ticking made it hard to concentrate.

Toki stepped through the door to Quondam's cell. "Hello, Once-and-Future Man. Are you comfortable? I just came by to see if you're still little Reverend Asalie-Lover, or if you're ready to accept Time into your heart!" He pronounced the last sentence as he had seen television evangelists do, but the joke was completely lost on Quondam.

"That was supposed to be funny, Quondam," Toki iterated. "I'm a funny guy. Let me tell you a joke, to lighten the mood here. Okay, so this guy—let's call him Munder—throws his clock out the window. You see it and ask him, 'What did you do that for?' To which Munder replies, 'I wanted to see Time fly.' You see, my good man, humor is all in the timing."

The minute hand moved to 20 and the slight tug felt more like a jerk. Quondam focused on his emotions, rather than the physical pain. "I can't believe I came all this way with the noble task of bringing back my friend, or at least going back in time to save him, and it had already been done! You could have saved me a lot of time and effort if you had just stayed at the Seer's Festival a bit longer."

"I could have saved you time? Now you're the one who's being funny. I don't do people favors, old man. Time is not on anyone's side. You have the ability of rejuvenation and aging not because I cared about your stupid wish to be bigger. You and your uncle are just pawns; timepieces in my collection. It's time you started realizing that."

"And Munder? What purpose does he serve?"

"Ah... Munder. Now, *he's* a faithful servant. He's not a Timister, and he's hardly worthy of the power I feed through him, but when I saw you push him off that cliff, I just had to do the right thing and save his life."

"I *didn't* push him off that cliff. Your evil little trinket--"

"Did nothing. It was the evil inside Munder that made him try to take it from you, and the evil in you that wanted it back at any cost."

Quondam strained at the shackles, but they just pulled back tighter. "I tried to save him; at that point, I didn't care about the pocketwatch. I knew something bad would happen to him, and I just wanted to stop him from using it."

"You don't have to prove things to me, my good man. Munder's the one to convince."

"What did you do to him?"

"I took the baby out of the canyon and raised him as if he were my own child; my own seriously deranged child, that is. You see, the good thing about having all the time in the world is that you can just sit back and watch things happen of their own accord. I didn't abuse Munder or tell him to be a psychotic killer. Rather, I just told him about you and how you didn't even crawl down into the cavern to see if he had survived the fall.

"I sped up time for him so that he'd age faster and put him on a strict training regimen. His growth amazed even me. I made him captain of my army and brought warriors from other times to fight by his side. His watch really does nothing but communicate with me—I transport him to and from Tweentime, and I'm the one who sped up time for that huge canyon you had to cross. It's hard work paying attention to all the mundane details of what happens on your planet. That's why I have Aori. And you."

Quondam attempted to speak again in defiance, but the pain had increased doubly in the last twenty minutes. Toki smiled and walked out of the cell.

As he walked down a glass hall, Toki's aged and crooked back shortened in length. His body contorted and condensed to a much smaller form, roughly around three and a half feet tall. Two glowing crystals formed where his eyes had been, and his walk became more mechanical.

"Mr. Thymegarden," said Pettifogger as the old man entered the room. "Can I go home now?"

"This is not a prison, Pyrite," said the time-lord he knew as Quartz Thymegarden. "You have escaped, and will escape, much more fortified constructions than this one. Among the many talents you've… attained… over the years, you're an accomplished escape artist, Pyrite. You're good at getting while the getting's good, if you get what I'm saying."

The look on Pettifogger's face made it clear that he was not getting it.

"Whenever you're ready to do as I've asked, you can return to your precious mine-sweet-mine."

"I want to go to my real home, with my mom and sister."

The time-god's quartz eyes flashed. "If you do as I ask, your family will be here waiting for you when you return. They will be safe from Aia's fate."

"I'm not a thief," Pettifogger said in a soft voice.

"You have always been, and always will be, Pyrite. In time, you will steal much more than I've asked, and it will be as natural as breathing in and out. You don't steal the air you breathe, do you, Pyrite?"

"No," the gnome answered.

"Then go back to Aori's tower and steal his goggles. If it makes you feel better, he'll give them to you in the future, so they're practically yours anyway."

Chapter 2:10

The Singing Glass

Half an hour had passed since Tempo left Lithe's cell, and she had been busy. They had taken her instruments and weapons, but they hadn't taken away her voice. The hum of the vibrating glass walls had given her an idea. First, she tried different pitches and frequencies on the ceiling above her. She skillfully modified the volume so as to minimize the damage to the palace as a whole. Destroying all the walls would only result in a long dive through infinity.

She found the right frequency and the glass ceiling shattered. She caught a shard and used it to cut the ropes that bound her wrists. It wouldn't be long before someone upstairs noticed the hole in the floor, so Lithe kicked and broke the locking mechanism on the door. A Metachron in army fatigues stood at attention outside her door, but he didn't make a sound as a shard of glass sliced through his windpipe.

"Focus," she sang in a soft murmur. "Where could he be?" Putting a hand to the wall of the long corridor, she tried to feel the vibrations of sound throughout the complex. If she had Ariel, her flute, she could play her children's song and draw him to her, but she presumed that he was tied up as well, so even that plan would not work.

By drowning out the sounds in her immediate area, Lithe was able to focus on the vibrations in the glass. *People talking,* she thought. —*The drone of the television sets—footsteps—raindrops?* Several typewriters tapped incessantly in a room below, but Lithe could not identify the sound.

As she silently walked down the corridor, she ran her nimble fingers along the glass. She felt distinct vibrations and decoded them into the unmistakable sound of a mandolin. Following the sound brought her to another cell at the end of the corridor. Through the translucent glass, she could easily identify the aged appearance of Dolente.

Placing both hands on the glass door, she began to hum. The frequency for breaking glass transmuted through her hands and into the door. This method would not only pinpoint the shattering effect, but also absorb any crashing sounds.

"Dolente," she sang. He clutched his ears, as if in great pain. Lithe felt her vocal chords to make sure they weren't vibrating at a painful frequency. She murmured, "Come. We will escape. I need your help finding my friend."

Her susurrations echoed through his cell, and Dolente continued to hold his ears. Any and all sounds she made hurt him considerably, and he dared not speak. He held up his hand with his palm facing her with a plaintive look cast about his face.

Lithe placed her palm against his withered, aged skin. Dolente sent vibrations into her hands, which she could translate into words. This was the ancient language of her people, before they learned to sing, and long before the first instrument graced their hands.

In a series of vibrations, Dolente explained, "I have been trapped in this room for many centuries. Tempo lets me out on occasion to sing for him, but most of the time I am songless. Even the softest whisper hurts my ears, and I am sure that if I sang, I would die."

"We can escape, Dolente," answered Lithe by sending the vibrations through her palm. "We must go now."

"There is no escape for me, my child," Dolente replied. "I am old. If I leave Tweentime, I will surely die."

"Then you shall be reborn as the Codan elders are."

"I cannot. I have forsaken my Codan heritage by coming here. I have cheated death and even growth. Nothing grows here; nothing changes, unless he wills it."

Lithe felt the faint vibration of footsteps approaching. "I must go, Dolente. Please join me."

"No, my child. Run. Take this: it will help you, and I cannot use it here." It was a musical instrument constructed out of glass. Eight cylindrical vessels were strung together upon a hollow glass base, and each chamber and antechamber contained various volumes of some sort of liquid.

Lithe handled the instrument carefully and silently paid her respects to the aged Coda. The footsteps got louder as she inched down the corridor. Having discarded her shard of glass, she was weaponless once again. In desperation, she held the instrument in her palms and lightly touched the glass tubes with her fingertips. A beautiful song reverberated through the glass chambers, and suddenly her fingers disappeared!

Upon closer inspection, she noticed that her entire body had become transparent like the glass. She held her hand up to the light and it made a beautiful prismatic pattern. When she waved her fingers the light refracted in a kaleidoscope of colors.

Three soldiers approached and passed by without noticing her glass body. One of them stopped and said, "Do you guys hear something? It sounds a little like singing."

"It's just the glass walls—they hum all the time. Haven't you noticed?" said another.

"This is different, I think."

Not wishing the soldiers to discover her or Dolente's shattered door, Lithe took action. She guided the refracted light to the forehead of one of the soldiers.

"Jim, you have a rainbow on your head."

"What?" Jim was puzzled. "A rainbow?" Lithe bent the light right into Jim's eyes, at which point he gasped at the brilliant spectrum.

While the three soldiers stood mesmerized by the light pattern, Lithe moved in quickly and stabbed her long glass fingers into Jim's eyes. With her tail, she pierced the abdomen of the soldier on her right.

The third soldier managed to grab her glass shoulder, which stopped the reverberation of sound. Lithe immediately reverted to her original form. With a series of fluid movements, she crouched, carefully set the instrument on the floor, and shattered the soldier's kneecap as if it, too, had been made of glass. He fell to the floor in agony.

Lithe grabbed a gun from one of the other soldiers and pointed it at him. Of course, she knew nothing of firearms, but the soldier reacted accordingly. "I need to find my companion… my friend. Do you know where he is being held?"

"P-probably in the lower part of the hourglass," he stammered. "Just f-follow the sand down."

"Directly below here?" Lithe put a hand to the floor.

"Well, yes, but there are other rooms beneath us." The glass floor shattered before he could finish his sentence. Both of them plummeted through the rooms below with a cacophony of crashes and twinkling glass. Lithe managed to grab the glass instrument with one hand while avoiding most of the sharp shards. The soldier, however, was not so fortunate.

Both of them eventually landed in a river of white sand. As they flowed downwards in a spiral, Lithe lost her grip on the soldier and became immersed in the sand.

Because the Coda have so many wind instruments, they are known for their sustained breathing techniques, and that inborn skill kept Lithe alive. Still, her lungs ached as she tried not to breathe in the sand. It emptied into another large chamber, where the sand was keenly distributed throughout the lower portion of the complex. Lithe found a glass tube leading downward at an angle. She assumed the chute filled with sand when the volume rose sufficiently.

As she jumped into the chute, her stomach left her. She rocketed down the smooth surface and lost all orientation. Just when she began to wish she had looked before leaping, the tunnel ended. Lithe landed in an empty room with thick, frosted glass for walls.

With her palms to the floor, she attempted to sense the noises of the palace again. The metallic raindrops were much louder, but the sound of a clock ticking overpowered all other sounds. An agonized scream rang out and reverberated through every room in the lower chamber.

The glass instrument chimed from the vibration of the scream. Lithe noticed that the liquid was vibrating in only one of the glass tubes. As she picked up the instrument and moved around the room, other tubes vibrated. The instrument seemed to be pointing in a specific direction.

The singing glass led Lithe straight to Quondam's cell. It had been almost two hours since Munder had wound the clock, and Quondam felt like his body was ready to snap in two. He tried to smile when he saw Lithe, but the pain was too great.

"How can I get you out of this?" asked Lithe.

Quondam fought back tears to no avail. "I...don't know."

"Maybe I could stop the clock," she began, but the sound of footsteps interrupted her. Quickly, she touched the singing glass as she had before and turned transparent. She hid in a corner and muted the sound of her breathing.

"You alive?" boomed Munder. "That's two hours, Pops. You proved me wrong." He began to walk over and wind the clock some more, but a strange pattern of lights on the wall distracted him. The rainbow of colors enthralled Munder, and he felt compelled to reach out and touch them. The melodic harmonics of the singing glass entranced him even more.

"Disable the device," sang Lithe in a pitch that matched the glass. Munder flipped a lever on the clock mechanism and it stopped ticking. Quondam's body was still under pressure, however. "Loosen the restraints."

"I'm not entirely sure he knows what 'restraints' are, Lithe," mused Quondam.

"Do too," Munder retorted as he wrapped his large hand around Quondam's throat. Despite his hatred for Quondam, he released the shackles.

"Let go of Quondam," sang Lithe. Munder acquiesced. "Now," she sang, "take us back to Aia."

"I can't."

"What?"

"He can't," explained Quondam. "He doesn't have any power of his own."

"Then, just stand there while we devise an escape plan." She continued to play the glass instrument, and as she played, she softly sang a song in Codan about Quondam and Munder. The song told of Munder's "death" and all Quondam had gone through to bring back his friend. Even though Munder couldn't understand the language, it did seem to have a calming effect on the giant, and she hoped that he would get the overall meaning.

Meanwhile, Quondam questioned Munder about other possible escapes.

"Jump out a window."

"Cooperate," Lithe sang.

"No, he's right. If we jump into the time stream, we'll get out of this netherworld."

"But there's no telling where or when you'll come out," Munder smiled.

Lithe touched the floor and wall again, hoping to hear some useful information. Instead, she just heard a man shouting out words over the din of the metallic raindrops. "What is that sound? It sounds like rain on metal."

Munder listened closely. "Typewriters. Mechanical word-makers. They won't be invented for lots of years." He nudged Quondam. "See? I know lots."

Quondam reeled from the powerful nudge and smiled. "Let's investigate. If nothing else, perhaps we'll learn something."

Lithe beckoned Munder to join them, and the trio walked down a glass spiral staircase. The singing glass led them to a dead end.

"Where to now?" asked Quondam. "I can hear the word-makers really well now, but I can't tell where the sound's coming from."

Lithe put her hand to the floor. The emanations were definitely the strongest there. She shattered the glass, and the three of them fell through the floor.

Chapter 2:11

The Creators

The basement of the hourglass palace bustled with activity. Several people were pacing about the room, and two men sat at a table in the center of the room. The seated men relentlessly typed on the mechanical word-makers. A person in the corner of the room spouted off an endless stream of words at the top of his lungs.

Munder was so distracted by the commotion that he was oblivious to the fact that Lithe had stopped playing the glass instrument. He was particularly drawn to the section of the room where a group of Codan musicians were working on a new song.

"It sounds better on the harp," said one of the Coda.

"I think the ending needs some work," said another.

The conductor tapped his baton on a music stand and commenced the performance. Lithe listened incredulously as the band played the song she had written only moments ago.

"Where did you hear that song?" she demanded to know.

"Oh, it's based on a story the writers are working on over there," said the conductor. "Do you like it?"

"Like it? I wrote it!" Lithe insisted.

Quondam inspected the stacks of paper in the center of the typewriter table. The words seemed like gibberish at first, but Quondam managed to piece some words together.

"What language is this?"

"Common," stated one of the writers.

Quondam looked at the paper in the typewriter. It said, in some ancient form of the common language, "Quondam looked at the paper in the typewriter. It said, in some ancient form of the common language...."

"Excuse me," said the typist. "Could you please stop that? You're messing up my train of thought."

"You don't have a train of thought," said the other writer. "You just copy down everything you read off that other typewriter."

Quondam noticed that the other typewriter seemed to be working of its own volition. No one was there to punch the keys, but words still appeared on the paper. It was connected to the other two typewriters by a dense jungle of cords that appeared to have grown out of the ground beneath the basement.

"So?" said the first writer. "You copy everything I type."

The situation began to make sense to Quondam. One writer wrote the present, while the other wrote the past. He could only assume that the empty typewriter was that of the future.

"Who are you, and what are you doing here?" asked the present writer as he continued typing.

A man in the corner of the room shouted, "Quondam!"

"He's the Namer," someone behind Quondam explained. Quondam turned around to find a plump woman wearing a nametag that read, "EXPOSITION." She guided him around the room, explaining everyone's job and background in painful detail. "I was born in a..." Quondam stopped listening.

He gathered that this was the creative hub of Tweentime, and they all worked around the clock on various creative endeavors. As the Namer wrote words on small slips of paper and pronounced them, he was calling those things into existence. Quondam noticed, however, that all the words were ones he had already heard. The Namer wasn't coming up with new words; he was just re-using the old ones.

As Quondam studied the creators, he realized that they were stuck in a loop. None of them were generating new ideas, because nothing ever changed in Tweentime. The absence of growth is the absence of progression.

Exposition continued, "This room was here before the palace. The Time-lord came here trying to influence us—to change history—or the future."

"But nothing changed, because he has no power over growth," Quondam deduced.

"The loop has broken, though. The story is progressing. We get new material here every day," she exposed.

"The missing writer," Quondam realized. "He must have escaped Tweentime, and now he is affecting the future. He's the one who broke the loop."

"How did he escape, though?" asked Lithe.

"Let's find out." Quondam rushed over to the Past-writer's stack. He skipped back quite a bit and shuffled through the history of Aia. Finally, he came to the part about the Future-writer's escape. "Follow me," he said to the crowded room. "Anyone who wants to come with me is welcome."

Lithe walked towards him, but the rest of the room continued their work. Exposition explained, "This is the only existence we know. It's just easier to continue like this than it is to initiate change. It's hard to come up with new ideas."

Quondam peered down the hole in the center of the room. The vine/cords from the typewriters led down into the hole. Quondam grabbed one and lowered himself into the darkness. Using a little musical suggestion, Lithe persuaded Munder to follow him.

The cords had grown out of a large tree, which Quondam proceeded to descend. Massive roots stretched out further than Quondam's eyes could see. Lithe and Munder made it down the tree and joined Quondam at the roots.

"According to the writing, there should be a doorway here somewhere. Here it is." A door had grown into or out of the side of the giant tree.

"It's locked," said Lithe.

"I can knock it down," offered Munder.

"There's a key," read Quondam, "but he took it with him."

Munder got angry again. "So we're stuck here? I'm going back to my room. At least there I had an army of time-tossed soldiers to do my bidding."

"Stand there and be quiet," Lithe sang. Munder complied.

"He planted it near a great tree." Quondam stopped reading and started ruffling through his possessions.

Lithe took the pages from him and read on from that point. "It just says he was reborn, and then goes on to tell about other history." Quondam was looking for something. "Are you worried about your sword? You can get another. We have to get out of here before Tempo finds out we are gone."

"I'm sure he already knows," Quondam said as he rummaged. "He *is* the god of Time, after all."

"Well, if he knew we would escape anyway, he could have made it easier for us," said Lithe. After a moment of thought, she continued, "Now that I think about it, he did make it pretty easy for me; if he wanted me to stay, he would have put me in a sound-proof room like Dolente's."

Finally, Quondam came across a particular seed in his pouch. Luckily, Tempo had not taken them away. "Aha!" He placed the seed in the ground near the roots of the tree.

"What are you doing? Nothing grows here."

Quondam looked worried, but then he remembered that he was standing next to a giant tree. "This tree grew. Maybe all we need is soil."

Sure enough, the seed began to sprout. But the growth was not green and healthy. Rather, it looked like a rotten twig.

"What *is* that?" asked Lithe.

"The key."

"A twig?"

"I guess." Quondam put the twig into the lock on the door. Gradually, the twig conformed to the size of the lock. He turned the key and the door unlocked. Quondam looked at Lithe and walked through the door.

She began to follow him, and then she noticed that Munder was just stubbornly standing there with his arms folded. "Follow me," she sang.

Chapter 2:12

Connery, Caitlyn, Crowfoot and the Chronoclysm

Crowfoot woke up with a strong feeling of dread. His dreams often suggested events of great and gloomy portent, but he could never discern their meaning through the darkness. One image remained clear and haunted him even out of sleep, however: the blackbird. Its dark wings enveloped him like a death shroud. Paradoxically, Crowfoot felt warm and safe in the darkness of the blackbird. He had a strong feeling that it would protect him from the coming doom.

Crowfoot shook the sleep and shadows from his eyes and looked for his fellow savages. He looked up at the sun, which had climbed fairly high while he slept. A dark, charcoal grey cat walked over and began to nuzzle up to his legs. He reached down and petted the animal's soft fur, and the purring lightened his mood.

"I see you've met Felicia."

Crowfoot turned to face the source of the familiar voice, but did not recognize Caitlyn without all the fur. She was a fairly normal-looking humanoid woman. Of course, the average human was not as attractive as Caitlyn, and there was the matter of the pointed ears and cat-eyes.

Connery walked up after her. He also looked relatively normal. His full beard remained, but he had tied up his long hair in a ponytail. Wrinkles played about his eyes but did not weigh him down or make him seem old and weary. Rather, they gave him character.

"Felicia is from the forest of Smokewood," said Caitlyn. "Have you heard of it?"

"I think so." Crowfoot looked in the direction of Smokewood, but was shocked to see a tall structure of some sort far in the distance. He did not recall having seen it before.

"Strange things are happening there," she continued. "Many of my kin have vanished from the woods unexpectedly." She, too, focused on the tall structure. "She escaped and came to tell me directly, because she was too afraid to speak to me with her mind."

"You can do that?" asked Crowfoot.

"Of course. Do you think we communicate with meows?"

"I needn't th' ability t' hear th' distant thoughts o' cats t' know who is responsible," said Connery. "'Tis the same evil man who stole th' trees an' built yon tower." He had noticed the tall structure in the distance sooner than any of them.

"I shall try to communicate with my captured kin, then. Perhaps we can learn something more of this villain." She ignored Felicia's warnings and opened her mind to the kidnapped cats of Smokewood. A low, magical purr emanated from her body.

She saw cats in cages. Men with metal skin beat them violently, and the cats' claws were useless against the metal. The captured cats also told of an old man who watched them sleep.

Caitlyn stopped purring. "We must go."

Caitlyn, Crowfoot, Connery, and all the cats continued down the path of fallen trees. Meanwhile, in a noisy room in the basement of a glass palace, a young woman named Alliteration giggled with satisfaction.

Deep snow still covered the ground, but the temperature had increased a bit. A cold wind blew at them from the northeast, and those that could grew fur. Crowfoot, however, shivered as his bare feet sank into the deep snow.

The sun began to set, and Connery looked concerned. "I'd hoped that we would make it t' m' homeland 'fore nightfall. We've not made enough progress this day."

"Well, if the Woodman hadn't slept all day..." Caitlyn smirked.

"No, that's not it."

"I did sleep late. Sorry." Crowfoot worried about getting on the bad side of those sharp teeth and claws.

Connery assuaged his guilt. "He didn't sleep that long. I think th' sun moved faster than normal."

"What? How?"

"I don' know, but it shouldn'a be time for th' sun t' set. Not yet."

Darkness engulfed the land, and the temperature dropped. Connery began to worry about Crowfoot, who had been softly whimpering for some time.

"We should stop f'r th' night. A good rest an' warm fire would do us all good."

Caitlyn looked him up and down. "You don't look tired, Conri. There is still plenty of moonlight to guide us, and we have a long way to travel."

Connery spoke to her in another language, saying, "He has no fur t' protect him, and his feet are bare. He'll freeze t' death 'fore long."

"So we all have to stop just because he can't grow fur?"

Crowfoot felt bad. He didn't want to slow them down, but his feet had grown numb and black from frostbite. Each step proved more and more difficult, but he felt comfort in the feathered wings of the blackbird. The darkness was pouring down around him, but the blackbird gave him warmth.

As Crowfoot staggered and fell, Connery rushed to his side. "Crowfoot?" he shouted.

"If he dies, can we keep going?"

"Caitlyn!" Connery picked the boy up and carried him into the woods, where the trees might shelter them from the harsh wind. He started a fire and stroked his beard in deep thought. "We shouldn'a've been so hasty this morning. We should've taken th' time t' fashion some clothing out o' th' herbovine hide and hair."

"But we have fur, Conri. Oh—for the boy. Yes. I forget that these humans are so… helpless."

"Y' know, Cait, y' sure have a lot t' say 'bout humans, f'r a creature 'oo grows into one."

"Perhaps you, Conri, are a man who turns into a wolf," she retorted, "but I am a cat first and foremost."

"An' y' care f'r no one but y'rself!"

She snarled. "Look, Conri—I didn't have to save your life last night—I could have left you pinned to that tree." She glared at him. He glared back.

"I have t' find something f'r him t' wear—an' eat. Y' stay here an' keep this fire goin'."

"Where will you go?" she asked.

"If I must, I'll return t' th' dead herbovine."

"You've lost your mind, Conri."

"Not yet, Cait. Not yet."

As he ran through the woods at top speed, he hoped to find some other furry creature. Doubling back all the way to the battlefield would waste precious time. "Why did we leave in such a hurry?" he asked himself. "What was I thinking? I'm a man; I know how th' cold feels on bare skin! At the very least, we should've had th' forethought t' bring some o' th' meat with us."

Connery reached the battlefield in no time. They had traveled until sunset, but it had only been a few hours. Just as he suspected, the days were growing shorter.

He stepped out of the woods into the clearing. The sky had cleared some, and he noticed the full moon once again. "Can it be?" he said aloud. He thought he could see it moving through the sky. Not far away from it, he saw the other moon. It had grown since the previous night, and its movement seemed even faster than the full moon's. As a werewolf, he considered himself knowledgeable in the ways of the moons. This, however, he found highly unusual and alarming.

Connery gathered as much of the herbovine as he could carry, which was quite a bit due to his supernatural strength. Before he left the area, he tried to concentrate and consider whether he was leaving anything important behind.

The sun began to rise, much to his chagrin. He had left Crowfoot out in the cold all night, with only a cruel, selfish cat to care for him. Connery cursed his lack of good sense and focused all his energy on his powerful leg muscles.

"There, there," mewed Caitlyn as she tried to comfort the boy. She patted him on the head as if he were some alien thing. Caring for others—especially humans—was not in her nature. Sure, she had been around young cats that needed attention, but all of her kin had been taught at an early age to be very self-reliant. They cleaned themselves, learned to watch their own backs, and generally looked after themselves as soon as they stopped nursing. Even though Caitlyn usually hunted in groups, it was far more common for her kind to do everything alone.

"Don't freeze to death, Little Woodman. If you do, Conri will probably howl and carry on for hours, and I have places to be." A group of cats sauntered up and she made them gather around Crowfoot to keep him warm.

The sun had been up for an hour or so when Caitlyn suddenly sensed danger. Instinctively, her back arched and her fur stood on end. A hissing sound issued from her mouth. She inched over to where Crowfoot lay sleeping, grabbed the skin on the back of his neck, and dragged him to a more secure location.

When Connery arrived, Caitlyn continued with her defensive behavior. He crept up on all fours with parts of the herbovine carcass hanging out of his mouth and draped over his back. When he saw Caitlyn standing over Crowfoot's bleeding neck, he lunged at her.

Claws and teeth clashed with fur and flesh as the feline and canine fought. Connery sank his teeth into Caitlyn's neck and whipped her around to break the neck bone. Caitlyn's claws tore into his face and he released his grip.

When she was back on her feet, she leapt at him, caught his neck with her teeth, and used her momentum to knock him off his balance. She pinned him to the ground and dug her claws into his wrists.

Connery watched as Caitlyn's irises dilated and contracted in response to the light. It reminded him of the changing moon, and suddenly he became aware of his surroundings. His mental focus was still limited, but he was better able to tell friend from foe.

Caitlyn, however, continued to fight him. He reverted to human form as best he could, but she just saw that as her moment to strike. With her long claws, she tore his gut open and damaged several organs in the process.

Connery recoiled from the pain, and every instinct told him to go berserk again. He managed to keep a level head and said, as calmly as possible, "Look at th' sky." She kept hissing at him, so he grabbed her head and forced her to look up.

The sky was dark, but she knew their fight could not have lasted the entire day. She noticed the moons moving across the sky. One of them was in its waning gibbous phase, while the other was a half-moon. "They... don't add up.

Aren't the two moons supposed to combine to equal one full moon?"

"Good. Y'r able t' use y'r head now." Connery looked down at his gaping gut-wound. "Now get off o' me 'fore I lose control again."

"How long did we fight?" Caitlyn rose to her feet and helped Connery stand.

"No more 'an half an hour, if that. I lose track o' time in m' rages, but I know f'r certain 'twas less 'an a usual day." Connery staggered over to Crowfoot and wrapped him up in the herbovine hide.

Caitlyn searched around in a panic. "Where are the cats? They were here just a while ago—I had them gather around the Woodman to keep him warm."

"How thoughtful o' y'. Couldn't bear t' do it y'rself?"

"Conri, could you please stop fighting with me for one second? I have to find my cats."

"Whatever made us crazy has t' be affecting them, too. T' be sure, they're just mindlessly attacking old men 'n' children."

"They aren't listening to my thoughts, either. What is going on here, Conri?"

"For some reason, th' days 'n' nights are gettin' a wee bit shorter. Times, they are a-changin'." He walked out into the clearing and stared off to the northeast. In the distance, he could see another tower being built next to the one he had seen before. "Aori!" he growled.

Chapter 2:13

The Timister Towers 2.0

Like two twigs in a pond, the clocktowers on Aori's estate created a ripple effect. Although, rather than merely vibrating the surface of water, the effects of Aori's tinkering with time peaked at the center and spread outwards throughout the globe. As will soon become increasingly evident, those closest in proximity to Aori felt the worst of Time's effects.

"Aori!" shouted Bertram. "Snap out of whatever trance you are in and look at this!"

Aori opened his eyes and reverted to normal time. Real-time seemed to crawl. "What is it, Bertram? Make it quick."

"Well, much has happened while you slept."

"I wasn't sleeping, Bertram. I stopped time."

"Yes, I noticed that your clock stopped moving. That is part of what I wanted to show you. Here." He held an old book up to the light so Aori could read it. "It is a picture of the very clocktowers you are building."

"Why, you're right, Bertram! Funny; I don't remember writing that book. Where did it come from?"

"Well, that's just it, Master Timister."

"What? You're wasting my time, Bertram! Get on with it!"

Bertram got on with it. "I found it in the library. The old part of the library."

"So my family knew I would build the towers," Aori assumed.

"Or they had the idea just as you did, but they were less successful."

"Yes. Perhaps, my parents could not build the towers because they got too old." Bertram, I must go back to my meditation. I must not age another day until my towers are complete!"

"But Master Timister, perhaps you should find out the purpose of the towers before you—oh, never mind." Bertram gave up; Aori was too deep in concentration to hear him.

Far below, on ground level, a long train pulled into Aori's station. Several clockworkers filed out and were followed by a large group of foreigners. The clockworkers guided them in a single line to a large school building. The travelers looked ragged and worn out from the trip, and many of them had difficulty walking. When they fell, the clock-workers would drag or beat them.

Bertram watched them from a window of Aori's tower. "What have you done, Aori? Are those students or prisoners?" The entranced time-server did not respond.

Many other trains from around the world were headed for Aori's station with the only survivors of their civilizations on board. When the other nations had not accepted the books and teachings of Aori, or when communication with the mute clockworkers broke down, the conflicts became unnecessarily violent. Those who survived were crammed into boxcars and taken to school by force.

On one train, a neatly dressed Orien girl tried to speak above the sounds of the train. She found the tight space distressing, and she wished to be free. "Listen to me!" she shouted in the Orien language. "We must escape. I do not know what awaits us at the end of this journey, but I fear the worst."

The other passengers refused to respond. They had already grown weak and complacent in the short time they had been away from their homeland. "We cannot fight them, Asia," said one of the passengers. "We have no power so far from home."

"Yes you do! The power is within us all! We are Ori!" She raised her hands up as high as the confined space would allow, and a faint glow emanated from within her. The light spread to all the other passengers in that boxcar and to the other boxcars as well. Soon, the entire train was alive with the power of the Ori.

Suddenly, the train jumped off the tracks and derailed, causing a horrible collision. The boxcars crumpled into one another, and the magic-steam engine burst in a massive magical explosion.

Every one of the clockworkers was destroyed in the blast. In addition, the explosion killed any passengers who had survived the crash. Death and fire reigned over that portion of the Smokewood forest, and the fire was spreading.

The smoke from the forest fire could be seen clearly from the top of Aori's tower. Bertram thought little of it, since Smokewood was known for the dark, mystical smoke that gathered there. He was, however, concerned with the second tower, which was nearing completion.

Over the last few days, he had noticed many strange occurrences. For one, the sum of the moons no longer equaled one whole. He was unable to find anything in any of the books in his library to explain the oddity. In Aori's room, however, he discovered several drawings and diagrams of the moons and their phases. He worried that Aori was somehow responsible for the phenomenon.

Furthermore, Bertram felt different. In the last few days, he had experienced more memory loss, fatigue, arthritis, and other health problems associated with age. The change in his appearance was too gradual for him to fully comprehend, but he felt older. When he tried to recall his life prior to being appointed as Aori's librarian, it was as if he were sifting through years and years of memories.

As he searched his recollection of the past few days' events, Bertram's thoughts settled on the first of Aori's captives—Pettifogger. Though the aches in his body discouraged a trip down into the mines, he hoped to find the industrious gnome in better condition than the rest of the inhabitants of the Timister estate. He also hoped to find him nearby and preferably not underground.

Fortunately for the aged librarian, Pettifogger had the presence of mind to save Bertram the trip. He caught the old man at the top of a staircase and helped Bertram back towards his room. They exchanged pleasantries, and Pettifogger eased him into his bed.

As Bertram attempted to focus his weary eyes, he thought he noticed Aori's goggles sitting atop the gnome's head. "My dear Mr. Pettifogger, what is that you're wearing?" Pettifogger caught himself and quickly removed the goggles, hiding them behind his back. "They're not important, sir—just my mining goggles."

Bertram suddenly had the feeling that everyone he knew thought him to be an utter fool—and treated him as such. "Pyrite, watch yourself. I would hate for you to get caught up in a Timister's troubles."

"I'll be fine, sir. Now, please... rest." The gnome's compassion for Bertram's well-being resounded in the cracking tone of his voice. As he left the room, he whispered, "Good-bye, Bertram."

When Aori drifted back to consciousness, he was pleased to find the second tower fully completed. Both towers were the same height and were constructed chiefly out of the wood from the Nutberry trees. The first tower held the clock showing Aori's time, while the second tower displayed the time for the Auldenton region. At the moment, Aori noted that, for the first time since he built them, the real-time clock was moving faster than his clock.

From his tower, he could witness all the effects of his work. The clockworkers were moving at an amazing speed, the clouds rushed across the sky, and dawn gave way to dusk in a span of about three minutes.

Of course, the passage of time is relative, so it can only be judged from a distance. Once the second tower was completed, the population of Aia thought time went back to normal. However, to an onlooker such as Aori, who was removed from that relative time flow, days and nights passed by in just a few minutes. The whole thing causes quite a massive headache, so people try to avoid thinking about it.

Aori manipulated his personal time so that it mirrored real-time. Everything around him slowed down to a relatively normal speed and the two clocks ticked in synchrony.

"Bertram," he called out as he entered the library. "I did it! I conquered Time!"

"That's...nice. Good for you, Master Timister." Bertram's voice rattled out of his throat like dry sand and gravel. He was seated at the foot of his bed, unable to stand. A thin layer of dust covered the stacks of books, as Bertram had not recently felt up to maintaining his work.

"How about a quick game of *Epic*? I think I can tolerate the time it takes for you to play your hand, now." Aori laughed and began gathering the game pieces.

Bertram made a futile attempt to walk, but his atrophied muscles would not support his weight. "I'm afraid we'll have to play in here, Master Timister."

Aori had experience with the debilitating effects of aging, but he refused to accept them in Bertram. "Fine, Bertram. Be a lazy old bum. The clockworkers can carry the table in there. They never shirk their duties."

"Or get old," finished Bertram.

"Neither do we, old chum. You know, the brain gets more wrinkles as you learn. The same must be true for our skin!"

"Perhaps. Though how do you explain the pain? The weariness? The shortness of breath? Does that come from learning also, Aori?"

Aori swallowed hard. He ignored the decay of his friend and, instead, moved his game piece. "We don't have to worry about it anymore, Bertram. I have conquered Time!" He looked up at Bertram and did his best to smile. "Your move, old friend."

Bertram gathered his strength and breath in order to speak. "Unless you can make it turn backwards, I think Time has conquered me."

Aori lowered his head. He increased the flow of his personal time so that he could gain his composure before Bertram noticed. "You…" he paused for a moment to wipe away some tears. "You won't die, Bertram. I can slow down time so that you'll stop aging. That's the power of the second clock tower, you see!"

"Aori, if you can really control time, then you should stop for a moment to look at all you've done."

"I have, Bertram," Aori interrupted. "Look at all these books I've written!"

"No. Look at the so-called students you've imprisoned in your school. Look at the decimated forests. Look at me!"

Aori tried to look, but he could not see through the tears. He looked up at the second clock tower and tried to make its hands stop moving. "STOP!" he shouted. "I am your master, and I command you to stop!"

All of the clockworkers suddenly stopped. Relief swept over Aori, until he noticed that the clouds, trees, and the clock hands were still moving. "Come here," he ordered one of the workers. "Bring me one of the students from the school."

Bertram took another deep breath and strained. "Your move."

"Is it? Then why do I feel so out of control?"

"Perhaps you are *his* game piece, Aori."

"But, I built the tower. I studied, learned. I have accomplished so much. Have I been just a puppet this entire time?"

The clockworker arrived with a ragged Agypsian slave in tow. He was an old man with dark, weathered skin that was marked by bruises and lacerations. Aori spoke to him in his language: "Good day, sir. I am Aori." The Agypsian prostrated himself at Aori's feet and proceeded to beg for the time god's forgiveness.

"I am not the time god," said Aori. "But I am the one who is guilty here. I wanted to spread my knowledge across the world, and instead I have ripped you from your homes!"

He turned to his clockworker and said, "This cannot continue. You all have sorely misinterpreted my orders. No harm should come to these students, do you understand?"

The clockworker answered with a sequence of music box sounds.

Aori buried his head in his hands. He cursed the effects of time. A thousand thoughts raced in his head. "How can I stop this? What can I do to fix things? What other evil has been done while I stood still?" His eyes opened wide and flooded with tears.

"My parents!"

Despite his aged legs, he managed to get to his parents' room in little time. Much to his surprise, his parents looked the same as they had for years. "I see," he said. "You learned to halt your growth as well. That explains much. But, I need your help! Wake up! I need you to help me fix everything!"

Chapter 2:14

Birth of the Bertram-Bot

Many days passed while Aori waited for his parents to wake. Meanwhile, the clockworkers continued their various tasks, the cold wind continued to blow, and the world continued to turn at its increased pace.

Aori wiped his eyes and stared up at the moons. They had grown very close together, and both were now at their fullest. Since the dawn of creation on Aia, two full moons had never shared the same sky. Aori tried not to think about the consequences and denied any responsibility.

From his parents' bedside, Aori watched the moons for hours. He sped up his personal time so they wouldn't set or change in any way. The two moons filled him with a sense of wholeness despite his feelings of guilt.

Deep in his meditation, Aori felt that his mind was soaring towards the full

---

Mind and Body

Mystics and philosophers believed that the moon of the mind was the key to enlightenment, and transcendence could only be achieved if both moons were full (which had never happened before).

Leaving one's body during the waning of the body-moon resulted in death of the corporeal form, but two full moons meant the energy could be distributed evenly.

moon. All at once, he became aware of new, exciting knowledge and power. He felt as if he had left the physical world behind.

"Welcome," said another spirit. Aori knew at once that he stood before his parents. "We all finally made it."

"But you must go back soon, Aori," said his mother. "Time is passing quickly there, and the moon will soon change."

"Come with me," Aori pleaded.

"We cannot. We will let our bodies wane. It is for the best. Only here will we be at rest."

Aori looked at his surroundings. Swirling energy flowed around him, and he suddenly knew where he was. "This is where *he* lives. I must stop him."

"You cannot, Aori," said his father.

"He is infinite," said his mother.

"Go now. Make the best of your time left on Aia. You will need it."

"But, how can I control time and fix what I have broken?" Before Aori could wait for their answer, Tween-time faded and he was back on Aia, staring up at the sky. The moons had already changed.

Aori sat down at the *Epic* board and moved his piece. "Giant worm to E4. I just engaged in battle with your Orien princess." He waited for Bertram to make his move. This time, he would be patient. "Your turn, Bertram."

He looked at his only friend with tear-soaked eyes. With a final, dramatic gesture, he removed Bertram's game piece from the board. His gaze panned over to the second clock tower, and he focused all his energy on making the hands turn backwards.

"Bertram, what was that story about the faerie and the Coda? You remember: the one where the Coda plays music to bring her fallen love back from the dead? If I can't turn back the hands of time, then maybe I can just resurrect everyone: You, my parents, and all the people my clockworkers have killed in my name. I will fill the world with beautiful music and fix all my wrongs!"

At that moment, a clockworker marched in with clanky footsteps. It spoke in the music-box-language, which gave Aori a bit of a headache. Aori ignored the worker's report, which was something about a wrecked train, and focused on the musical part. If he could program the right series of bell sounds, he might bring his family and friend back to life.

Over the next few days, he developed many automated musical instruments. He invented one that consisted of a variety of levers attached to hammers, and each hammer struck a different string in a sequence. An intricate pattern of punched holes in a roll of parchment determined which lever was pulled. Essentially, it was an early form of the Autoharp or player piano, and Aori could program it to play wondrous, beautiful music.

Other instruments could be played automatically as well: bells, drums, chimes, or even pieces of glass. In time, he had a complex machine that sounded like a fairly large ensemble of musicians. Programming each instrument to play the right notes or beats in synchronicity proved tedious, but Aori took his time.

"It is quite beautiful, but will it work?" asked Bertram. Of course, it wasn't actually Bertram, but a clockworker Aori had programmed to look and behave like him. The robotic librarian wore Bertram's clothes, catalogued the books, and now, it even seemed to fill Bertram's role as Aori's conscience.

Aori had no idea how the mechanical man had managed to speak, and he wondered if it was all a delusion, but his deteriorating mind filled in the gaps in reality. He found himself doing that more and more these days, as yesterday's normal had been replaced with a new and much more confusing version.

"Music is music, Bertram. I'm simply taking the Coda out of the equation," Aori stated.

"But Master Timister, life cannot come from lifeless music. This is more math than music; more machine than musician."

Aori sighed. "How can I give the music life, though? Music is not alive; it is a series of vibrations our brain translates into sounds. It is not a living thing; it does not breathe or walk around. You must look at it reasonably, Bertram—with logic!"

"The Coda are living things. Music comes from the Coda. Therefore, their music is a living thing," reasoned the mechanical Bertram.

Aori snapped and threw one of his instruments across the room. Glass and chimes danced about the walls and floor with a melodic twinkling song. The sound soothed his addled brain, and he said, "Then I shall get a Coda to help me."

Hidden in a dark corner of Aori's room, Pettifogger listened to every word. As a child, he had watched with meticulous interest as his father turned bits of metal or rock into flowers that grew and propagated like any other in their garden. Unbeknownst to him, the young thief had taken a bit of that ability for himself.

Days ago, when he had first come across Aori's pathetic and lifeless reconstruction of Bertram—the only person to have shown him compassion since he came to this home away from home—he just wanted to be able to thank the librarian again. He never expected the mechanical man to spring to life and reply, "It was nothing."

Chapter 2:15

Time Rolls On and Rolls Over Us All

The Chronoclysm seriously affected the Aian way of life. The planet's rotation and revolution had sped up, resulting in a serious strain upon the axis and fault lines. Days and nights lasted only a quarter of the time. Plants had to photosynthesize all their food in only a few hours. People who were paid by the hour found a considerable difference in their take-home pay for those days, and everyone overslept.

As one might expect, the changes in the moons' orbits sent the oceans' tides into chaotic turmoil. Whole civilizations were wiped out by the unexpected tidal waves or typhoons. Air currents shifted, resulting in bizarre weather patterns around the world. Seasons were cut short, leaving many populations on the southern hemisphere with no crops and little food for winter.

Those who knew of him blamed Aori, but many others assumed the shortened growth season meant they had fallen out of favor with their gods or goddesses of agriculture. They prayed for forgiveness and hoped that some miracle would give them enough food to survive the months to come.

Asalie dug her way out of deep mud and struggled to find solid ground. The sun was rising in the east, but it still gave her little comfort. Aia had tried to bury her, but somehow a seed always finds the surface.

With a tired, worried look, she surveyed the effects of the storm and mudslide. There seemed to be no life left of any kind. She closed her eyes and sat down cross-legged. With her palms flat upon the ground, she searched for some sign of life.

Deep under the mud and soil, she sensed a small child. She focused all of her energy on the roots and undergrowth in an attempt to bring the child to the surface. Quite unexpectedly, her power waned and she lost the child's essence. She opened her eyes and what she saw startled and confused her.

Night had fallen. How could she have worked all day trying to free the child? She tried to stand, but her weakened state just left her face down in the mud. After managing to roll over, she was stricken with the image of the unbalanced moons. "How can it be?" she asked herself. "I control the changing moons." Tears streamed down her face, rinsing it clean of the mud and filth. "I say when the two moons grow into one, not him! He cannot... I..." she trailed off. Her world was changing without her. "Aia is decaying. That can only mean...."

Asalie curled up into a fetal position and waited to be born again.

Crowfoot woke up feeling much warmer than he had in days. Looking around, he noticed that much of the snow had melted, and the clear night sky looked beautiful and serene. A loud howl startled him and interrupted his stargazing. Suddenly, he thought of Connery and Caitlyn. They had obviously been there recently, because the embers of the campfire were still burning, but his companions were no-where in sight. There were signs of a struggle and a trail of fresh blood leading off in one direction—the direction of the howling sound.

Crowfoot resolved to follow the tracks, which he knew to be lupine in origin. He wondered why there seemed to be no tracks for Caitlyn or the other cats. After walking for only a few hours, he remarked at the brightness of the sky. It seemed that morning was breaking already.

By the time he found the end of the tracks, the sun had been up for an hour or so. Connery lay crumpled and bleeding beside a tree. His hair was a mess and his eyes pierced Crowfoot with a wild, faraway look. "Connery? What happened?"

Connery's eyes seemed to focus a bit. He looked at Crowfoot, then the sky, and finally back to Crowfoot. He smiled and said, "I'm glad y're alive, boy. Y' had us worried."

"I feel fine. My feet are sore, but... Connery, what happened to you?"

Connery searched his memory for the event that caused his injury, but it seemed like many days ago. "I don't... remember."

"How long have I been asleep, Connery?"

"Days an' days.... I've lost track, but many days have come an' gone since y' fell. I made y' a coat out o' th' herbovine. Do y' like it?"

"Yes," said Crowfoot as he felt the thick hair of the herbovine. He also felt for the first time as if he had horns growing out of his head.

"I made y' a headdress using th' horns, as well. I didn't know if y'r people did that, but I've seen many great warriors decorated with th' bones an' horns o' their kills."

"I am no great warrior, Connery," said the boy. "If Caitlyn had not arrived when she did, I would have been no match for those soldiers."

"Caitlyn," Connery said the name as if he had just remembered something. He called out, "Caitlyn! Here, kitty!"

"Where did she go?" asked Crowfoot.

"I lost track o' her. It all got so confusing." He looked around him in a nervous way, and then noticed the darkening of the sky.

Crowfoot thought he heard the old man whimper like a beaten pup. "Connery? Are you okay? We need to do something about the bleeding. That cannot be…." His words were cut short when two furry hands grasped his shoulders.

"Run," Connery strained to sound as human as possible. "There isn't much time."

"What? Why?"

"RUN!" Connery's voice turned into a growl and his claws dug into the skin of Crowfoot's shoulders.

With the widened eyes of a trapped deer, Crowfoot remained transfixed. Darkness bled through his vision, and he heeded Connery's advice. He ran back in the direction he had walked the night before. As he ran, he could hear the footfalls and heavy breathing of a savage animal behind him. But what would make Connery attack him?

The pain in his feet slowed him down, and eventually Crowfoot stumbled and crashed into a tree stump. As he tried to right himself, he heard the sounds of a whole pack of wolves gathering around him. He searched their faces for some trace of his friend, but all he saw were wild animals.

A large one leapt out of the crowd and pinned Crowfoot to the ground. He stared up at its gaping maw and knew that death awaited him. Through the veil of darkness, he could barely make out the light of day.

The darkness dissipated and Crowfoot watched the wolf turn more human. Connery eased off of Crowfoot and the two struggled to their feet. Smelling Connery's fresh wound, the other wolves attacked. Despite his injuries and disorientation, Connery remained King of the Wolves and displayed his dominance with a combined nobility and brutality.

When the fight was over, Connery wheezed, "These're dark days indeed, when m' own pack doesn't know me."

"Connery, tell me what is going on before night falls and everyone goes berserk again," Crowfoot insisted.

"I've not had m' wits about me long enough t' figure it out, but look at yon tower." Even from this distance, they could see both of Aori's towers standing tall. "I believe Aori's responsible f'r this shortening o' days an' nights. The moons've changed as well, an' th' balance between humanity an' savagery has been thrown into chaos."

Crowfoot struggled with the concept of altered time. "So only a few hours have passed since I passed out, but for you it has been several days?"

Connery struggled with the concept as well. In fact, people all over the world were struggling with the concept. Connery shook away the confusion and said, "Y' must go. Find Asalie, or Quondam. I'll try t' stay th' beast inside me long enough, but y'll have t' run fast."

Crowfoot slowly got to his feet, and Connery added, "Don't look back, boy. Just run." As Crowfoot began to fade, Connery shouted, "A' watch out f'r th' cats as well!"

Only a few minutes had passed when the sun once again began to set. Connery felt himself changing uncontrollably again. The wolf in him picked up Crowfoot's scent easily, and the hunt resumed.

Meanwhile, back in the barren Nutberry O, something stirred. From the center of the great *asa* sprouted a vibrant, green seedling. Trees all over the forest were growing small buds at the tips of their branches. Confused birds were returning from their short trip to the south for the winter, and bears were coming out of hibernation.

Spring had arrived.

PART 3

SPRING

Chapter 3:00

Spring Foreword

In Earth's United States, lawmakers decided to alter time for about six months out of the year. Using the powerful incantation, "Spring forward, fall back," farmers and other outdoor-laborers were given an extra hour of daylight to finish their chores and such. The ramifications of the time change were widespread; for one day out of the year, many laborers would be late for work or church. The loss of an hour of sleep in spring wreaked havoc on the sleeping cycles of Americans, while those who work the graveyard shift in the fall clocked in an extra hour of work. Of course, Arizonans and those from Indiana were spared the dire consequences, for they chose not to tamper with the time-stream.

For the first few days of Daylight Saving Time, one could perceive the changes through the Outsider Effect. "The reason I'm so sleepy right now is because it's really 10:00," one might have said. All of a sudden, the sun blinded drivers going to work instead of from work, and people were often caught completely by surprise at the darkness of nightfall.

Eventually, however, the novelty decayed and people grew into the different time. Unless one were traveling through Arizona, the time shift gradually became imperceptible (that is, until it was time to change again). The same thing happened when one visited or moved to another time zone or country; at first, time was compared to his or her previous time, and the magic effects of "Jet Lag" could cause grievous changes to one's physiology. It took people a few days to get over thinking of time as "our time" versus "their time," but everyone eventually grows into his or her environment.

Living things all over Aia were experiencing the time change in a similar way, except most of them had no computers or TV weathermen to tell them to change their clocks. The last days of Aia were beginning at this point, and the results of the time change would be more drastic and catastrophic than waking up late for church or even feeling the effects of jet lag.

Before our story can continue, we must ask the question, "What would it take to change time?" If every single human in a given culture sets his or her watch ahead one hour in the spring, are those people really creating an extra hour of time? The answer, unfortunately, is, "No; it's merely a trick to use time more efficiently."

You are aware, I am sure, of the effects of seasons on the amount of daylight each day. This is not, as many Aians believed, because Asalie chooses to wake up earlier and go to bed later. Indeed, it has more to do with the angle of the planet's tilt. You may also be aware, or find it surprising, that different parts of the planet experience different amounts of light and darkness depending on their location. Since I have the convenience of having experienced daily life on planet Earth, I am familiar, as you may be as well, with places that know no summer at all. It's simply cold there all year-round.

In order to alter an entire planet's time, one would have to either change the tilt of its axis, the speed of its daily rotation, or the rate of annual revolution around the sun. Very soon, Aori Timister will research this very idea, and perhaps shed some more light on our conundrum. I, of course, know how it will turn out, but isn't the curiosity positively fascinating?

Thus continues the raging whirlpool at the end of time, beginning with a ripple.

Chapter 3:01

The Lake of Lament

Tiny waves rippled across the Lake of Lament as a warm breeze skimmed its tranquil surface. Far overhead, a flock of birds circled the area in preparation to land. The Lake of Lament was the seasonal home of the Tear Ducks of Southern Woe. The call of the ducks sounded a lot like crying. Lore spoke of the ducks as a tortured, depressed lot, and their suicide rate was the highest of the entire animal kingdom.

The dismal, gloomy land of Woe served as the winter home of the ducks, which migrated more for psychological reasons than instinctual. The Lake of Lament, despite its lethargic stillness and depressing background, seemed a bright and cheerful sight for the sore and teary eyes of the Woebegone ducks.

As the ducks circled high above the lake's languid surface, something fell from the sky and landed in the water with a noticeable splash. The ducks just dismissed it as another suicidal member of their flock. It was followed by another falling object, which barely made any splash at all. By the third object, the ducks ruled out a suicide, since no duck could be so large and make such an enormous splash. Some of the more pessimistic members of the flock wondered if there would be anything left of the lake after that great splash. Of course, those are the types who see the lake as half empty.

Quondam felt his surroundings change from the dark, humid center of the tree and the cold, suffocating unreality of the time stream, all the way through to the feeling of falling and painfully hitting the surface of water. The entire range of feeling took place in just a few seconds, and as Quondam struggled to swim to the surface, he hoped for some other change.

The water closed in around him with astounding pressure, and Quondam felt hope wash away to be replaced by utter despair. Guilt crashed in around him as he thought of Lithe and Munder—into what mad dimension of time or space had he dragged them?

Lithe experienced mild disorientation, but quickly got her bearings as she saw the lake's surface suddenly approaching. She worked her fall into a dive and balanced her Eustachian tubes equally in order to protect her precious eardrums from the pressure of the water and to orient herself to the surface.

Munder, who was accustomed to the jaunt between time and space, expected all the range of feelings except the falling and crashing in water. It reminded him of his experience early in life, when he plummeted to certain doom at the hands of Quondam. Once he realized he could stand in the water despite its depth, he sought out his once and future friend.

As Munder searched for Quondam through the gloomy depths, Lithe dove under for a better look. She moved through the water with grace and speed, but feelings of hopelessness soon overwhelmed her. It would be impossible to find Quondam in such a deep, immense body of water. *He's already dead*, she thought as she blamed herself.

Munder reached a massive hand into the abyss and plucked Quondam out like a fish. He carried Quondam to the lakeside, where he dropped the old man with a huff. "Get up, old man."

Quondam coughed a bit, and his eyes immediately filled with tears at the sight of Munder. "You made it. You're alive."

"Yep," said Munder. Then, he punched Quondam's grinning face with his massive, wooden fist.

Quondam rocketed into the air and slammed into a rock. He felt his old bones shatter into a million pieces, and knew they'd never heal properly. He was about to give in to the feelings of despair, when Munder kicked him in the stomach. With a forceful spurt, Quondam's body expunged several liters of lake water.

As Munder continued to beat him repeatedly, Quondam's mind returned from the depths of depression. Of course, the feelings of despair were quickly replaced by intense pain at the beating, but Quondam managed to think fairly clearly.

As his face became buried in the dirt, Quondam got an idea. With a bloody, broken hand, he reached into his seed pouch and blindly felt for a particular seed. When he found it, he plunged it into the soil.

All of a sudden, a staff sprouted out of the ground with enough force to knock Munder back. Quondam grabbed it and laboriously pulled himself to his feet. He focused on an incantation that sent Munder reeling into the lake.

"I should have known you hadn't changed, Munder. I had hoped there was more to your new attitude than just Lithe's song." As he said her name, he began to worry. "Lithe!"

Using the staff for support, he limped and strained to reach the water's edge. He tried again to shift past the broken bones, but they seemed to weigh him down and anchor him to his eighties. All his efforts to find Lithe proved just as fruitless.

Despondently, he cast his staff into the water and crumpled to the ground. Immediately the staff started growing. At first, it looked like a log floating in the water. Eventually, however, it grew into a small boat. With all the effort of an elderly man climbing into a boat, Quondam managed to board the vessel and weakly paddled away from the shore.

Meanwhile, deep in the Lake of Lament, Lithe struggled with the pressure around her. She thought about what would happen if the water ruptured her eardrums—how could she ever play music again? She looked up at the sun shining through the lake's surface and decided that trying to swim to safety was not worth the effort.

As Lithe stared into the murky depths that would become her tomb, she noticed the wailing faces of tortured spirits all around her. Their plaintive, mournful songs echoed through the water in an eerie manner that sent chills throughout Lithe's body.

Despite the depressive nature of the songs, they reminded Lithe that the water pressure had not yet damaged her hearing. Instead of dwelling on the gloom of the song, she focused on her creative power to arrange instrumental accompaniment. Of course, she had only the glass singer, and its music could not be heard underwater, but the sheer act of creating gave her the will to survive. With a determined stroke of her long, lissome limbs, she broke through the surface of the water and gasped for air.

Quondam reached out, grabbed her, and pulled her aboard his boat. With a paternal kindness, he caressed her forehead and wiped her tears away. "I'm glad you're alive, Emmeleia."

"And I you, old man," she replied with a strained smile.

Quondam's thoughts shifted to Munder. "We have to go. Munder is here, and he's not our friend."

She reached for her glass singer and touched the cylinders with her fingers. Of course, the volumes of liquid inside were no longer accurate, and the water of the lake diluted their sound.

"I don't think it's going to work--." A sudden thrashing from beneath them in the water interrupted Quondam's words. A hand shot up from the gloom and grabbed the side of their boat, capsizing it and sending them back into the drink.

Munder grabbed Quondam and held him by his throat. Tears streamed down Munder's giant face. He sobbed, "All I wanted was to play with it for a little while! I wasn't gonna steal it! You didn't have to throw me off that cliff!" He threw Quondam to the shore.

Lithe managed to climb back aboard the boat and paddled it to shore. Once there, she tried again to calm the rampaging, weepy giant with her glass singer. Without the glass walls of Tempo's palace to carry the sound, the instrument had as little magic as it had music.

Munder waded to shore and immediately proceeded to pummel Quondam into the ground. He bawled like a child the entire time while shouting, "It's all your fault! You left me to die, and now you've taken me away from the only father I've ever had!"

In between beatings, Quondam winced, "Toki is not your father. He distorted you... deformed you." He fumbled for the wood of the boat and it changed into a sword, which he stabbed into Munder's side.

Munder rolled off of him and Quondam managed to stand once again. He held the wooden sword up and pointed it at Munder. "I did not kill you that day when we were children, but so help me, I will kill you today, if I must!"

With a strained thrust, Quondam swung the sword at Munder's body. Munder easily defended the attack with his battering ram, and the sword became lodged in his arm. As the two opponents watched in wonder, the sword and the battering ram grew into one another. Munder's wooden arm and the blade became intertwined, and the growth eventually spread to Quondam's hand.

In time, Munder and Quondam were bound at their arms with an overgrowth of wood and vine. They tried to free themselves from the organic shackle, but it just kept pulling them closer.

From there, the bond grew beyond the physical into the psychological. Dendrites from nerves in Quondam's brain cells merged with Munder's, and thoughts flowed from one to the other. All at once, Quondam was aware of all Munder had endured under the custody of the time lord. Years of pain and torment accompanied intense training and conditioning, but the memory of the fall overshadowed all of it.

As Quondam remembered the event that took his only friend from him, Munder shared his thoughts. Suddenly, they both remembered how Quondam had tried to warn him of the danger and had held onto him until his bones withered away. Munder saw himself through his friend's eyes as he slipped out of the timepiece's chain and fell. Together, they shared in the grief that Quondam had once endured alone.

Lithe started a fire, which dried their tear- and lake-soaked clothes and finally rid them of the lake's chill and despair. Lithe informed them that the lachrymose lake was not far from her homeland. "My people have many songs about the Lake of Lament. The rivers that flow from the Orchestral Mountains are said to be tears. The songs of the Coda make the surrounding mountains weep, and those tears gather here, at the Lake of Lament."

"You're not going to sing one of those songs now, are you?" asked Munder.

"No, Munder," she replied. "You may unplug your ears. I think I shall sing nothing but my own music now; I do not wish to perpetuate the cycle of creation."

Her words were lost on Munder, who was playfully throwing sticks into the fire. "Besides," she continued, "I have no instruments."

"Wait," Quondam interrupted. "Let me see the sack of seeds Asalie gave you." She handed it to him and he rummaged through it for a few minutes. As he explained the seeds, he took on the air of one's Grandfather. "These are

Songseeds, here," he said, pointing to a group of small, lightweight seeds. "And this," he held up a rather large nut, "is your mandolinut. Of course, it will grow into other instruments, depending on the song. Try it."

Lithe took the mandolinut and placed it in the ground. She sang a hymn of growth to help it along; she improvised the song, which was made up of several chords in a progression. As she sang, she gradually increased the intensity of the progression. The crescendo resulted in a song that seemed to be growing.

Eventually, the seed sprouted a long vine that spread out along the surface of the ground. The vine slowly produced a fruit or gourd, which was round and fat at the bottom and long and slender near the vine. The gourd kept growing until it was the proper size, at which point Lithe reached out and touched it. In response to her touch, the round end of the fruit became hollow and the neck slowly grew notches or frets. One side of the round part flattened at her touch, and the gourd began to look more like an instrument.

Lithe looked at the instrument proudly, but she couldn't play it. "I have no strings for it," she said solemnly.

"Yes you do," Quondam assured her. "Check your pouch again."

"Oh yes! I almost forgot!" She reached in her bag and retrieved the lock of hairs Asalie had given her. With Quondam's help, she chose eight specific strands of the hair and threaded them through the bridge of the instrument. Gradually, the hairs grew into strings and tightened themselves until they were in tune with one another.

A chord rang through the instrument harmoniously, which gave the trio a sense of wholeness and unity. As Lithe's nimble fingers found their way around the instrument, Quondam said, "I know you intended to carve your totemic instrument out of wood and build it yourself, but this should suit your needs. From the instant you touched it, the instrument began adapting to you; it is as unique to you as your fingerprint and will respond only to you. In a way, the instrument will become an extension of your essence, just as Munder's arm has grown to be a part of him."

"It's become a part of you, too, Pops," Munder retorted.

"Yes, well, in the morning, we shall see if we can do something about that. It appears that spring has come in the time we were gone, so Asalie should be returning to these parts very soon."

"How could we have been gone for so long?" Lithe pondered. "Winter was only a few days old when we were abducted."

"And while our time in Toki's palace seemed long, it could not have been more than a few days. Perhaps the time stream deposited us a few months in the future," suggested Quondam.

"Nope," Munder disagreed. "Going to the future is hard. The time stream dumps you in the present by default."

"So you're suggesting that four months went by in the time we were gone?"

"Yep."

"What makes you think that?"

Munder looked at his watch. Somehow, it was attuned to the actual time rather than the arbitrary system most clocks used. "It's definitely four lunar cycles later, but only a few days have passed since my battalion attacked you guys."

"How is it," Quondam asked Lithe, "that this simpleton is now confusing *me*? Has the world gone totally mad?"

Munder raised his arm, causing Quondam to levitate a few feet from the ground. "If the geezer will kindly shut his mouth, I will explain."

"Go ahead," Lithe encouraged.

"Before we left, days lasted about twenty-four hours. Now, they last about six hours. You just can't tell the difference because you weren't here during the change."

Quondam added, "We had no relative comparison, since Tweentime had no time to speak of."

"Right," Munder confirmed.

"So is this the work of Tempo?" asked Lithe.

"Yes," answered Quondam.
"Indirectly," Munder suggested.
"Aori," the trio said in harmony.

Chapter 3:02

Take These Broken Wings and Learn to Fly

Crowfoot started a fire and rested beside it. He had been running for several days with no sleep, and he was quite hungry. While he rested, he reached out with his mind to sense the animals of the forest, just as his tribe did before the hunt.

Much to his surprise and dismay, the animals surrounded him. The hunters in his tribe might have been pleased with the finding, but Crowfoot would rather avoid the wild beasts. If he could not trust his friends, he assumed the rest of the forest would be out to get him as well.

"It must be spring now," Crowfoot said to himself. "The animals have returned from their winter homes. I hope they are not *all* insane." The distant sound of footsteps made him stop talking. In fact, many of the sounds in the forest were hushed. Were the rest of the animals as frightened as Crowfoot was?

An old woman with grey hair stepped out of the darkness. "Rest easy, child. I am but a toothless old crone. I do not plan to gum you to death."

Crowfoot exhaled and put his knife away. "Would you like to sit down and warm yourself by my fire?"

"Thank you, dear boy. You know, these woods are not a good place for children. Are you all alone?" She pulled back her hood and Crowfoot could do nothing but stare at her eyes. They were completely grey, cold, and lifeless.

"Yes," Crowfoot strained to answer. "Well, I had two companions, but I fear they have gone mad and wish to kill me."

"Many of the animals are acting differently these days. Even the squirrels have a thirst for blood." She pulled a pair of squirrels from her tattered robes and set them beside the fire. "I may be old and toothless, but it takes more than a couple squirrels to take down Griselda Grimalkin!"

Crowfoot offered his knife to the elderly woman, who skinned the animals and cooked them over the fire. She then gave one of the squirrels to Crowfoot. "Eat up, little blackbird. We have much to discuss!"

"How did you…?" Crowfoot marveled. He had never told anyone about his visions of the blackbird.

"There is much that I know about you. You are a savage on the run from savages; too wild for civilized culture, but too civilized to live with the wild beasts. You are also my ferry to freedom."

"What?"

"Look at me and tell me what you see."

Crowfoot studied her closely. Wrinkles covered her skin, and her grey hair looked brittle and worn. "I see… a wise old woman." He had always been taught to preface the word *old* with *wise* in order to soften the blow.

"Look deeper, boy," she instructed.

Upon closer inspection, he noticed that a dull grey glow seemed to emanate from her skin, which seemed to be growing thin hair as he watched. Soon, the old woman was nothing more than a small, grey housecat. "You're a cat," he remarked.

"I suppose that is true, in a sense. However, I was hoping you would see more. Perhaps you are not what I thought you were." She seemed disappointed.

"I am sorry if I have offended you. I find that humans who turn into cats are not as surprising or remarkable as they once were. But, what do you mean, 'in a sense?'"

"Well, I'm not a true cat. Not like your companions, at least. I'm actually a witch."

Crowfoot stood up and took a few steps back. "A witch? Are you evil?"

"Evil?" She seemed to ponder the question for some time, as if the word were foreign to her. "No, not evil."

Crowfoot breathed a bit more easily and returned to his seat.

"But, I am not good, either," Grimalkin continued. "I exist in between such polar opposites as good and evil, black and white, human and beast…." She continued to list extremes for some time.

A sound in the forest put Crowfoot back on his guard. He found no comfort in Grimalkin's company or anywhere else. He longed for the warmth and safety of the blackbird.

As if called by his longing, the shadow of wings covered the ground in front of Crowfoot. A thin veil of darkness seemed to hover in front of Grimalkin just as she said, "life and death."

She stopped. "You see it now, little bird. Do you not?"

"I…do. You're not alive," he surmised.

"And yet, not dead. It's not quite a curse, but not a blessing either. For my entire life, I dabbled in the two extremes of White Magic and Black. I worshipped both the gods of life and death. As a result of my actions, I was made into this nether-being. But, you can help me, Crowfoot."

"How can I help? I'm just a boy." Crowfoot had never considered himself to be "just a boy" before. In the past, he had always wanted to be a part of the hunts or other adult activities. Very recently, however, he wished he were just playing with the other children in his village.

"You see it, boy. The blackbird heeds your call. It will deliver me from this nether-world."

Crowfoot heard rustling in the underbrush around him. He began to panic. "They're coming."

"The animals cannot harm you, Crowfoot. I have seen to that. You and I are in the spirit world; they cannot even see us."

A wildcat circled the area around Crowfoot's camp. It sniffed at the ground, puzzled by Crowfoot's scentless aura. Other large cats joined the inspection but made no more sense of it than the first. Bringing up the rear, Caitlyn sauntered over to the fire. Her fur was now her natural reddish-brown. She looked at the bones of the squirrels, sniffed the air, and hissed.

"Can they smell us?" asked Crowfoot nervously.

"No. We exist a bit in the material realm and a bit in the astral or spectral realm, but not enough to be detected in either. Even Caitlyn's formidable mind and second sight could not sense us here. That is, if she still has a mind. I fear she's all animal now."

Caitlyn looked directly at Grimalkin and said, "I can hear you, *Riabhag*! Come out, and bring the bird with you!"

"Why does she think I'm a bird?" whispered Crowfoot.

"Because you are, lad. Look."

Crowfoot waved his hand in front of his face, but he saw black pinions in place of his fingers. Feathers covered the entirety of his arms and body, which was more bird than human.

Grimalkin continued, "Your people have totems or animal spirits, do they not?"

"Yes, but...."

"Your spirit animal is a blackbird. You carry the souls of the dead away from the material realm. You can take me away from here."

As they spoke, Caitlyn clawed at their "ghosts." The smaller cats jumped and pounced on nothing, as cats often do. Caitlyn's ears pricked up as she heard a howl in the distance. Her back arched and her fur bristled.

Crowfoot watched from his perch in the nether world as Connery and a pack of wolves entered the grove. The wolves and cats immediately began fighting, while Connery and Caitlyn circled one another as if in a duel.

"We must act quickly, Crowfoot," said Grimalkin. "The ritual must be performed while the moons are full."

Crowfoot watched his former companions staring and growling at one another. He was glad to not be directly involved. "What must I do?" he asked her.

"You must leave your corporeal form behind," Grimalkin explained. "Shuffle off the mortal coil and accept your spiritual existence."

Crowfoot stared at her blankly. He had not learned enough of the common language to make sense of the witch's vernacular. She continued, "You must embrace the black-bird…"

The blackbird's wings filled him with a sense of comfort and safety, but he felt conflicted by the sight of his former friends in an all-out brawl. He looked at Connery and Caitlyn, then back at Grimalkin as she finished her sentence. "…and die."

"Die? But I'm just a boy!" he insisted.

"Not just a boy—a vessel. Your spirit is much stronger than your weak human body could ever be, Crowfoot. Leave it behind!" She noticed that his mind was preoccupied with the fight happening all around them. "Leave *them* behind!"

"I…can't. They helped me. They need me!"

"They want you dead, Crowfoot! You are just food to them! But, you're so much more to me!"

"Yes; it seems everyone wants me dead." He knew his fate; one way or another, his material form would die, and he would finally feel the comfort of the blackbird's wings. He resolved, "I will help you. I will take you and all other spirits to the land of the dead, but first, you must allow me to try to save the lives of my friends."

Grimalkin frowned and nodded in a feline, yet also human, sort of way. A black mist fell around Crowfoot's ghost and brought it back to the land of the living. Immediately, he sprang to his feet and drew his blade.

A large wildcat pounced on his back, but he knocked it loose with a stiff elbow. He fought the wolves and cats with the savage, reckless abandon of one whom no longer fears death. Grievous wounds tore through his body, but he persevered.

"STOP!" he shouted, when he finally reached Connery and Caitlyn. Even though both stood taller than the boy, his presence made them cower. He separated them physically with a wide, but human, wingspan. "Listen to me. You must stop this. You are friends. We are all friends here. The moons are driving you mad, but you must control your-selves!"

As Crowfoot spoke to them, Caitlyn and Connery heard only the squawking of a bird. Communication broke down completely, and Caitlyn snapped at Crowfoot's hand. Her large paws batted at the boy; she scratched and played violently as only a cat can. When she had beaten the fight and squawk out of him, she went in for the kill.

As her large, sharp teeth stabbed into Crowfoot's neck, darkness filled his vision. He welcomed the comfort and safety of the blackbird's wings. His blackened, frostbitten feet became crow's feet, and he soared into the air with a crow's wings. Crowfoot perched on a nearby branch to watch the death below.

Just as Caitlyn recoiled at the taste of human flesh, Connery caught her off guard and threw her to the ground. He held her down and barked at her viciously, to which she replied, "I know! I know! He's not a bird! I don't know what was wrong with me, but if you don't let me up soon, I'll… I'll…" her words trailed off, and she broke down crying.

Connery reverted to a more human form and eased off of her. She stood up on two feet, which she had not done for days, and walked towards the corpse. With a gentleness that seemed out of character, she picked Crowfoot up and held his body in her arms. "Why is he dead? Why won't he just come back?"

"Well," said Connery, "f'r starters, y' killed 'im." He placed a comforting hand on her back to console her. "Not everyone 'as more than one life, Cait."

Caitlyn reeled at all the dead wolves and cats around them. "It took all this death for our senses to return...."

"I'm afraid th' worst is yet t' come, Cait. There are still a few more days o' full moons left. Let us now grieve f'r our losses while we can."

As the howling and wailing began, Crowfoot's shadow blanketed the area, and he beckoned the souls of the animals to join him in his flight. He felt he had much work to do; he sensed death all around him.

"So," said the old grey she-cat, "the wings of death have given life. For good or ill, you have saved them. Congratulations."

"Thank you," he squawked.

"Now, will you honor our agreement?"

"Yes."

A fine grey mist rose from the ghost-cat, and Crowfoot inhaled it. As the fog cleared, only a small bit of grey fur remained. The darkness lifted and Crowfoot ascended on the wings of death.

Chapter 3:03

Finding Solace

Crowfoot's campfire continued to burn even after his death. Long after the flapping of the blackbird's wings had faded, the sound was replaced by a different sort of fluttering. On dusty, tattered wings, hundreds of moths filled the air around the macabre scene. They swarmed the grove where Crowfoot died, drawn as much to the death as the blazing campfire.

They hovered over the hallowed ground in search of something in particular. Eventually, the moths gave up and flew straight into the campfire. The flames popped and hissed as the moths were consumed wholly.

Far away, in the distant Smokewood forest, a similar scene of death and fire continued to play out in morbid detail. The only survivors of an entire race of people had been snuffed out in a bizarre train accident, and the magic flames had burned for many days.

The flames began to pop and hiss as, all of a sudden, the moths appeared. They fluttered out of the fire completely unscathed and continued their meticulous inspection of the death scene.

Despite the prominence of fire and death, the moths seemed unsatisfied. Gradually, they began to fly closer and closer together, until no space existed between their flapping wings. The moths merged into one large, imposing creature. It had the wings of a moth, but certain humanistic qualities as well. Its demeanor was like that of a crypt—cold, lifeless, and solemn.

Silently, the creature moved through the burning wreckage with no concern for the danger of the fire itself. It drew a great axe from its pale, tattered cloak and split open one of the train cars. Hidden among the charred and long-dead bodies of the Ori grew a small, bright flower of a girl.

The creature studied the girl as if bewildered by her presence then disregarded it completely. Despite the carnage, there were no souls to consume that day.

As the giant moth listlessly kicked at the chunks of metal that used to be clockworkers, it sensed the approach of a kindred spirit. Immediately, it took flight and, from the higher vantage point, it spied an enormous caterpillar crawling towards the wreckage. It hesitated for a moment, as if puzzled by the caterpillar's presence. Of course, the kindred spirit it had detected was a blackbird, which was drawn to this point for the same reason.

From there, the moth flew to the towers of Aori, where it hovered for some time. The sound of pipes playing a funeral dirge drew its attention, and it lingered around the top of the first tower. As if it suddenly remembered its task at hand, the creature hastily sprang into the air once again, this time flying westward.

"Could somebody explain to me why we're going this way, when we should be going to crush Aori? I mean, you're the crazy kids with the map, but I think I'm right and you're wrong this time."

"Munder, stop shouting," sang Lithe.

Munder continued to shout. "Look, could you stop singing for just a second? Please? It makes my brain hurt."

"Munder, if you don't stop shouting this instant, you'll be hurting a lot more than that."

"Clever threat, old man. I just don't understand why we'd be going out of our way to visit a bunch of stupid musicians!"

"It's mainly because we know how much you hate music, Munder," Quondam jibed.

"I have traveled for too long and endured too much already, Munder. Now that I have my instrument, I must return to my homeland to join the Symphony."

"What will you do then?" Munder asked. The words were his, but the underlying concern belonged to Quondam.

Quondam attempted to hide his desperation. "What we mean is, what does the Symphony do, exactly?"

"Besides play annoying music, of course?" added Munder.

"No one knows for sure. They protect us from harm, keep vigilance over the land of Concord, and perform other tasks, I suppose. Not much is known of them, but it is considered the highest honor to join their ranks."

"So, after you join, do you think the Symphony might help us stop Aori?" Quondam suggested.

"Quite possibly. First, however, I'll have to be accepted."

The trio walked along the River of Tears towards the Orchestral mountain range. Since Quondam's hip and other bones had not yet mended, he put most of his weight on Munder, who grudgingly obliged. As time passed and Quondam became weaker, Munder resolved to carry him.

Lithe smiled as she looked upon the tired old man in the arms of his former friend. "There are healers among my people who may be able to help you. I have never seen a crippled Coda in all my years."

The Codan land of Concord consisted of five major communities surrounded by a landscape of majestic mountains, mellifluous rivers, and cascading waterfalls. The

Orchestral mountain range formed a C-shape around Concord, and eight waterfalls, collectively known as the Octave, poured down from the mountains. The Coda believed, and sophisticated sound detection equipment might have proven, that each fall made a progressively higher-pitched tone.

The waterfalls encircled the area, and the water converged at the bottom to form the *Cascata Concordia,* or Concordance Falls. The individual tones (and water) of the Octave blended harmoniously to form the Concordance Falls.

However, most people just called them the Falls of Catharsis. The reason was two-fold: A) Most people could not hear the harmony of the rushing water and thought it just sounded like a very loud waterfall, and B) the water crashed very loudly, as if releasing pent-up emotion cathartically, but eventually slowed down to form the River of Tears. Apparently, the Namer had extra time on his hands that day.

As they neared the Falls of Catharsis, the sound of rushing water drowned out their voices, but Lithe's excitement communicated well. After they passed behind the waterfall and entered a dark cave, they could hear one another speak.

"That's odd. This chamber is usually illuminated," remarked Lithe.

"Perhaps they forgot to pay the bill," Munder quipped. Of course, no one understood the reference, as the electric bill would not be invented until much later. "Sorry," he added, "before your time. Er…after."

Lithe began to sing an ancient Codan candlelight song, and the room suddenly lit up with the flicker of candles. At the end of the massive cave was a small, round room. As they walked toward it, Lithe explained, "We are currently many hundreds of measures below the feet of the Octave. There are two ways to Solace; we could scale the steep cliff the whole way up…."

"With no rope?" Munder interrupted, "I think not."

"Or, we can use the levitation chamber at the end of this passage."

"Levitation chamber?" questioned Munder.

"Step inside this room and you shall understand." They entered the room, which was large enough to fit even one so massive as Munder. It stretched up in a cylindrical shape as far as the eye could see. The floor was decorated with various runes, which represented the five communities of the Coda. The seal depicted the eight rivers of the Octave, which stylistically flowed in a whirlpool towards the center. Two runes near the center of the design stood out more prominently than the others.

"What do those two symbols represent?" asked Quondam.

Lithe looked down at the floor and studied the runes as if for the first time. "I am not sure. I have seen the symbols before, but not here. These runes must have been carved into the floor since I left...."

They all agreed that that was very strange, and Lithe's concern was particularly noticeable. "We should continue. I am eager to see what else has changed." She picked up a flute from a pedestal in the center of the room and began to play. The song consisted of a progression of higher- and higher-pitched notes, the result of which created a sense of climbing.

The floor beneath their feet began to rise and carry them up the cylinder. As it ascended, they could see sunlight shining in through windows. When they had climbed high enough to reach the top of the Concordance Falls, the windows provided a beautiful view of the Octave. The first fall of the Octave was half the size of the eighth and tallest waterfall, but both shared the same name. Apparently the Namer got fed up by the time he got to *Do.*

The eight waterfalls formed the borders of each *tone*, or community, with Lithe's hometown of Solace being the third largest in the series. Long ago, there was a hierarchical system of government, where the largest *tone* ruled over each smaller community. However, for the past few centuries, all the townships were equal.

Despite the unity of the *tones*, the old walls that helped to divide them remained. Lithe explained, "The Elders said the walls were originally erected to keep the towns from flooding, but they also served to separate the greater from the lesser communities. Of course, Harmony changed all that. She brought the towns together."

"I suppose there will always be the risk of flood, though," said Quondam.

"I suppose," Lithe replied. "Let's go. The gates to the Tone of Solace are right this way."

The tonal gates were magnificently designed; two metal rivers convened in a large V-shape, while a series of musical notes were embedded in the upper framework. Lithe explained that the notes formed a song of sealing, which kept intruders from entering the gates without permission. "But …" she said, "The gates haven't been sealed for centuries."

As they approached the gates, two large men pointed sharp spears in their direction. "Halt! No one is permitted to enter the Tone of Solace today."

Lithe exploded. "What? This town is my home, and I will enter whenever I please!"

"You will address us with respect, young lady," shouted the guard, "or you will enter your home in a funeral procession!"

Munder began to reach for his axe, but Lithe stopped him. She sang, "I am Emmeleia of the House of Air. If I must, I will play my family's crest-tune."

"I am afraid you must, Emmeleia," said the other guard. His tone was much more apologetic. "Times have changed since you left."

"Do I know you--?" A smile spread across her face when she recognized him. "Rallentando? What are you doing guarding the gate?"

"They thought I'd be useful. I finally learned my forefather's Hymn of Hindrance."

"That's wonderful, Rally!" She paused and gave him a serious look. "You're being careful, aren't you?" She turned to Quondam and whispered, "Rallentando is a descendent of Ritardando, the Crooked Crooner."

"Look, young lady," shouted the other guard, "I don't know what you're insinuating about my partner, but…" he trailed off as his words suddenly started slowing down to match his wit.

"Forte is very strong and very loud," said Rallentando, "but sometimes he needs to slow down so his brain can catch up with him."

Lithe laughed, but then remembered her concern. Her brow furrowed as she asked, "What is going on, Rally? Why are the gates sealed?"

"I'm not exactly at liberty to speak of it, but there's a bit of a civil war going on."

"The towns are divided again? But, what of Harmony?"

Rallentando spoke very softly and at a slow pace. "I don't really know that much about it, Em. You should probably ask your family."

Lithe started to press on the gates. "Fine, then. Let me in."

"Whoa, there," Rally sang. "Slow down. You know you can't open these gates without the right song. Besides, I'm not too sure about these humans."

Munder glared at the guard and put a hand on his axe. Quondam tugged at him slightly with their conjoined arm. "Easy," he whispered.

"These are my companions—part of my ensemble. They are my backup singers." She flashed a smile at Munder, who glared back at her. Lithe hastily made the introductions, and proceeded to play the song that would open the gates to Solace. The song was like a musical birth certificate and passport all in one. It was a medley of her family crest-tune and the Song of Solace, including variations on thematic progression of the Sealing-Song.

In response to her music, the gates opened. Lithe walked through unhindered, but the guards stopped Quondam and Munder from entering. "They will have to wait here for permission to enter."

"We shall wait, Lithe," said Quondam. "Please go."

As Lithe passed through the streets of Solace, she immediately noticed several changes. Normally, the Coda would be dancing in the streets and playing music together. This day, however, the streets were empty, save for the armed guards on patrol. In response to her tightened nerves, her mandolin began to play a suspenseful tune of its own accord. It startled her at first, but she worried more about the music she heard coming from the *tone* square. There were no musicians anywhere in the streets, yet some strange music filled the air. Warily, she continued to walk.

One of her younger sisters met her in the street not far from her house. "Emmeleia, is it really you?" she whispered as she ran to embrace Lithe.

"Rhapsody!" The two embraced, and Lithe burst into tears. When she gained her composure, she said, "What's going on here? And how did you know I was here?"

"The whole town is hooked up on loudspeakers, as if the acoustics here weren't good enough already. We heard your entry-song from our house. We're so glad you're here, Em! Come on!"

Lithe paused for a moment to say, "Loudspeakers? Rhapsody, what are loudspeakers?" But, her sister was too far away to hear her.

The sisters ran to their house, where another gate barred their way. Rhapsody sang a password, and the gate unlocked.

An exasperated sigh escaped Lithe's lungs, but the sight of her house lightened her spirit once again. She knocked on her front door excitedly.

The door stood still. Rhapsody explained, "We had to change the knock." She rapped a different rhythm on the door, and it opened. "A lot has changed since you left."

As she walked through her front door, Lithe worried. "Mother and father... are they....?"

"They are well. Come." Rhapsody led her into the main room of the house, where their mother rested upon a sofa.

Actually, the word at that time was "faso," rather than "sofa." The furniture was actually created in the nearby Tone of Fasol. Because of strange import/export laws and such, the name was changed to "sofa" and the bagpipes were removed. At one time, however, the faso was one of the most comfortable musical instruments ever created.

Chapter 3:04

An Evening in the Aeolian House

Quondam leaned heavily on Munder, while the giant sat cross-legged on the ground and occasionally tossed a pebble at the slow-moving guard. "Munder," said Quondam, "stop that."

Munder threw another pebble at Forte. If the guard noticed, he wasn't too quick to respond to it. As he reached to pick up another pebble, his hand barely moved at all.

"Cease your childish behavior," sang Rallentando.

"Yes, Munder," agreed Quondam. "If you get in a fight, I'm not going to even try to stop them from beating you to a bloody pulp." He sat down on the ground as if the sentence had taken all of his energy.

"Fine," Munder huffed. He discarded the pebble and looked over at Quondam. "She's not coming back, you know. She's probably already forgotten about us."

Just as Quondam was about to respond, the guards snapped to attention and the gates opened. He snickered, "I believe you're wrong, Munder."

A tall, haughty figure in an ornate uniform stepped through the gate and approached the visitors. His hair was powdered white and tied back in a ponytail. He spoke in a very proud, pompous tone. "Greetings. Welcome to Solace. I am Baroque. You may enter the city now." The strange man bowed in a grandiose flourish.

Quondam stopped to bow respectfully, but Munder dragged him through the gates. "You guys must not get a lot of visitors, eh?" Munder asked. "Fancy place like this— seems like you'd have tourists year-round."

"Not lately, Mister... Munder, is it?"

"Must be all that singing and dancing you guys do," Munder chuckled. He felt the tendon-roots in his wooden arm tighten. "Look," he cut to the chase; "you can skip the grand tour of your fine c'munity and just show us to Lithe's place."

"I assure you, sir..." Baroque began.

"Let's go then, prim," insisted Munder. Then, turning to Quondam, he grumbled, "Stop dragging your feet, Pops!"

When they arrived at the gates of the House of Air, the atmosphere felt fresh and crisp. A light breeze seemed to be scored with its own musical accompaniment. Though Munder grimaced at the ever-present background music, he began to wonder if the song had caused the breeze or the other way around. Upon closer inspection of the house's gates, Munder found his answer. Within the intricate framework of the gate, several harp-strings vibrated with the breeze. Similar harp-strings could be found throughout the fence and exterior of the house.

"Welcome to the last of the great Aeolian houses," Baroque told them. "In this house, air and music exist as one." Baroque began to sing in a falsetto voice nothing like his speaking voice. The song was meant to alert Lithe's family to their arrival and introduce the visitors. It seemed to be quite a lot more extravagant than necessary.

"You folks ever hear of a doorbell?" asked Munder.

Lithe stepped out of the front door and walked toward the gate. She was dressed in the livery of her family: a long dress made of light fabric that seemed to carry her aloft as she walked. She softly sang the password that opened the gate and, with a light, airy gesture, motioned them to follow. Munder noticed, as they walked up the porch steps, that the house seemed to be floating a few feet off the ground.

As they entered the house, a fresh breeze swept over them, thereby alleviating all the wear and strain of their journey. Munder winced as he looked around him and felt like he had entered one of those flamboyant song and dance numbers from a movie musical of the future. The house attendants danced and sang as they did their work, and everything seemed to be choreographed. Even the inanimate objects, such as dishes and napkins, seemed to dance on air.

Rhapsody danced into the room and sang, "You must be famished. Please, follow me to the dining room."

Lithe looked at Munder and laughed. "I told them all to sing as much as possible, just for you."

Munder narrowed his eyes and tugged at Quondam to follow. Quondam just stood there listening to the music and enjoying the dance. He hadn't heard a word of what was said.

They all sat down with the rest of the family at a long, floating table. At the head of the table sat Ode, Lithe's father. His lack of flourish made him stand out in the crowd. In contrast, he seemed a bit dusty and reserved—much like an old piece of pottery.

Lithe's mother appeared as if full of life, with a perpetual breeze blowing through her hair. However, there seemed to be a distant look in Aria's eyes, as if a breeze blew through her head as well.

Lithe sat across from Munder, and Rhapsody sat beside him. All of Rhapsody's movements were enthusiastic, and she seemed completely weightless in mood and behavior.

"Excuse me," she sang in a breathy tone, "I'll go get Dirge."

"Didn't you tell him dinner was ready?" asked Lithe.

"Well, yes, but he was busy playing that guitar of his. I'm not sure if he heard me." Despite the subtext of mild disdain, Rhapsody spoke with a blissful lack of concern.

"Guitar?" asked Lithe. "What's a guitar?"

Munder smiled. He liked knowing things other people didn't. The guitar had not been invented yet, although it existed on Aia in its earlier forms as a zither or lute. Some people played stringed instruments that very closely resembled the guitar, but none of them sounded like what Lithe's little brother was playing. "That," explained Munder, "is an *electric* guitar."

"What?"

Munder thought about explaining, but he was stricken with the fact that candles and oil lamps provided their light; how did the kid have an electric guitar if the house didn't have electricity?

As Dirge walked in the room, the light seemed to dim around him. In contrast to Rhapsody and the rest of the inhabitants of the house, he seemed barely able to move with the weight of his body and spirit. Despite his demeanor, he couldn't have been more than five years old—not far from Munder and Quondam's real ages. He sat down at the end of the table in a slump.

Rhapsody introduced the visitors to her brother. "Dirge has been really busy lately. He plays that guitar all day long, and when he's not playing that, he's trying one of the other house instruments."

Lithe's mother added, "Yes. He's very productive for his age." Her words carried with them a light, refreshing breeze.

Quondam stared blankly at Dirge for a considerable length of time. Dirge returned his stare, and as he looked upon the old man, his eyes drooped and his forehead crinkled. "What is wrong with him?" the little boy asked.

Everyone looked at Quondam, who didn't seem to respond to the attention at all. Rather, he continued to stare unblinkingly at Dirge. Unbeknownst to the rest of the group, he had aged quite a lot since their return to Aia. Of course, everyone had aged, since the days and nights went by more quickly, but it seemed to affect Quondam more drastically.

"Hurry, Rhapsody," shouted Lithe. "Call a healer. Mother, get him some air."

Aria sang, and air circled around Quondam, making him rise out of his seat and filling his lungs with oxygen. A vacant smile spread about his face. Meanwhile, Munder's wooden arm felt as light as air.

Rhapsody returned moments later with the house healer, who was an olive-skinned Coda with deep-set, soulful eyes and ashen hair. His features were more gaunt and bony than most Coda, and he wore flowing, white robes. As he entered the room, he floated toward Quondam and placed a hand on his head. His song consisted mainly of chanting and humming combined with deep breathing.

Soon, Quondam found himself floating high above the room, and his surroundings seemed to bleed away. The healer held out a hand and spoke to Quondam without moving his lips. "Take my hand." His words reverberated in Quondam's head, and he seemed to be speaking several languages at once.

Quondam looked up and saw two large, full moons. He suddenly felt aware of the other life essences throughout the world. He was drawn specifically to Aori, who was experiencing a similar transcendence at that time.

The healer chanted, "Your body has limited you, Child of the Morning and Evening. Your brain has aged, but your spirit is still very young. If you do not regain your youth soon, your body will waste away."

In the distance, Quondam saw a great blackbird flying his way. The healer continued, "Death is approaching. The end is calling to you, beckoning you. Will you go with him?"

The moon changed and Quondam's spirit returned to his body.

The healer approached Lithe. "Your friend has several broken bones and internal injuries. I will require your aid if I am to heal him properly."

"I can help," offered Dirge, as small children often do.

"I may require your help too, child. Let us hope not, however." The healer turned back to Lithe. "Just play along with my song, and watch me for the changes."

The healer began to sing again, and Lithe accompanied him with her mandolin. The first part to the song was a psalm of circulation, designed to ease the flow of blood to the brain and other parts of the body. Next, the reel of restoration mended his bones and failed organs.

The song ended, and the healer spoke. "He will need rest, now."

Munder walked alongside as Quondam's body floated off to a bedroom. "Will he be okay?" he asked the healer.

"He would be dead now, if not for his youthful spirit. You must not allow him to strain himself so much. And, as soon as he is able, encourage him to return his body to his spirit's age."

Munder felt a bit uneasy with everything the healer seemed to know about them, but agreed to look after his friend. As he sat by Quondam's bed, he focused on the mass of roots and growth that bound their arms together.

"Quondam," he said, "If you need my strength or energy, just take it. You know I don't know how to send it to you, but maybe you do."

Lithe walked into the room. "Do you think he can hear you?"

"I… don't know. I think so."

Lithe sat down beside them. "Munder," she began, "did you notice anything odd about my family?"

"You mean, besides the weird singing and dancing? No."

"Munder, I'm seriously worried. I didn't know Dirge very well, since he was so young when I left, but the rest of my family seems to have changed a lot."

"I didn't know them before, but you shouldn't be surprised if they're different. You were gone for a long time, right?"

"I suppose so. But, it's not just my family—everything seems strange."

"Like that guy that brought us here—Baroque. What's that wacko's story?"

Lithe smiled. "He's a bit ostentatious, but he's harmless. Actually, he seems to be the only thing that hasn't changed."

In the morning, Lithe and Rhapsody went for a walk around the neighborhood. Rhapsody seemed a bit hesitant, but she maintained her blissful outlook. "We probably shouldn't walk near the walls, though," she said. "It's just not safe these days."

"Why, Rhapsody? What is going on?"

"We're not supposed to talk about it." Her voice sounded very naïve and innocent, as if she had spent her life sheltered from the harsh realities of the world.

"Rhapsody, why are you talking like a child? You're almost an adult now; you should know what is happening in your *tone*!"

Rhapsody began to softly whimper. "I don't know, Emmeleia! I just don't know!"

Lithe comforted her sister, but something in the corner of her eye distracted her. A dark figure slipped into the shadows. They were being watched. "Well," Lithe resolved, "if you can't tell me what's happening, I'll have to find someone who will."

She darted off in the direction of the shadowy figure. As she dashed through the darkened streets of her hometown, her mandolin automatically began playing suspenseful music again. The tune became more involved as the mandolin began to change into other instruments. Soon, it seemed like a complete ensemble was accompanying Lithe as she ran.

As the music began its crescendo, Lithe felt a sense of impending danger. She came to a dead end in an alley, and the shadowy figure was nowhere in sight. Suddenly, the mandolin struck a loud, dissonant chord. Lithe ducked just as a burst of energy shot over her and exploded on the wall behind her in a shower of sparks.

Five figures stepped out of the shadows and attacked Lithe with a fury of kicks and punches. She managed to deflect most of the attacks with the heightened sense of awareness the mandolin's song gave her. However, her attackers and even the shadows around her seemed to dance in response to distant music. Soon, she was completely blinded by the dancing shadows, and the attackers got the better of her.

"The music of the night is very beautiful, is it not?" The voice came from the direction of the music, which now seemed much closer. "Do not fight, Emmeleia. We are not your enemies."

"Then give me back my sight!" Lithe demanded. The shadows slowly lifted from her vision, and she saw a dark-clothed man playing a large pipe organ. She was no longer in the dark alley; somehow, they had transported her inside a large, dimly lit room. The man at the organ had long, black hair and skin that seemed to blend in with the shadows.

"You came here seeking answers to your questions. I can help you. My name is Notturno. Welcome to the Symphony."

Chapter 3:05

The Symphony

"First of all," began Notturno, "I would like to congratulate you on your successful instrument-quest. It seems you have made a nice place for yourself within our group. I am pleased. We have had our eye on you for a long time."

"You've been watching me?" Lithe was shocked. She had dreamt of being a part of the secret society of the Symphony all her life, but never considered that they might approach *her*.

"Watching *over* you. And your family; particularly your little brother. Your family is famous here, Emmeleia. Surely you know of the great work your mother did with our organization."

"I... always suspected...."

"It is truly a tragedy, what happened to her."

"What do you mean, *what happened to her?*"

"Perhaps I should start at the beginning, Emmeleia—or at least fill you in on what has transpired in your absence. You see, much has changed since you left."

"So I've noticed."

Notturno folded his hands behind his back in a stately manner and paced around the room. "There are two factions in Concord now, competing for dominance over all the communities. Some might label this a 'class war,' but it's not as simple as that. Harmony brought the communities together and erased every glimmer of stratification that existed, leaving us with a unified nation of Coda people. But, that peace soon ended and two factions rose from the unified nation."

"The peace ended? But Harmony--."

"Died." Notturno continued, "She died of old age, Emmeleia. She had lived for many centuries already."

"But didn't her life's song have a coda? She should have been given an extension on life, as is our heritage!"

"She had been living her coda for the last twenty years, all the while maintaining peace and unity among the *tones*."

"So when she died, the *tones* split apart again?" supposed Lithe.

"No. The two lower communities chose the Bass faction, while the two highest chose the Treble faction. As of yet, the Tone of Solace has remained neutral. Because of this, both factions seek control—we have gathered here to protect the citizens from the war outside."

"And to cloud their minds?" Lithe ventured to ask.

Notturno's dark eyes sank. "It is necessary to keep the citizens in the dark about a few things, Emmeleia. If they knew what went on outside their borders, they might be tempted to join one side or the other. We cannot risk Solace falling into the hands of either group. Especially since Harmony lives in this *tone*."

"Harmony? But you said she was dead!"

"No," said Notturno. "I said she *died*. She has been given an *encore;* she has been reborn!"

"How?"

"Perhaps you should ask your little brother." Notturno smiled the smile of the knowing.

Lithe reeled. "Dirge? But he's just a child!"

"The spirit of Threnody is very strong in him, Emmeleia. Of course, he has had some help, no doubt."

"Help? From whom?" Lithe asked.

"While you were gone, the vizier came and bestowed upon us gifts from the future."

"Tempo gave the Coda gifts?" Concern grew in Lithe's heart; she had refused his offer of the music of the future, but her people blindly accepted the great manipulator's gifts. "What did he give you?"

One of the other members of the Symphony joined in: "He gave us boxes imbued with magic that amplifies the sound of our music, devices that 'record' our songs to be played back later, and other equipment that allows us to synthesize sounds no instrument could ever make."

Lithe's concern continued to grow. She asked Notturno, "Were you not wary of taking gifts from Tempo? Has he not manipulated us before?" She played the introduction to the story of Ritardando and Veloce, since the story had a way of being forgotten. She then embellished on the story with elements of her own experiences with Tempo.

Realization struck Notturno suddenly. "That explains the shortening of days a few months ago. Nights went by in just a few hours, causing the citizens to panic. If the Symphony had not been here to maintain order, I feel certain the land of Concord would have slipped into chaos."

"We believe there is another guilty party involved. His name is Aori Timister."

In a brief song, she conveyed the story of all Aori had done recently. When she finished, Notturno said, "Thank you for this information. We are fortunate to be able to count you among our resources." He held out a slender hand, and shadows seemed to cling to it like skin. "Now," he continued, "you should return to your home. Your little brother needs you."

"But, wait. You never told me what happened to my mother. I just saw her, and though she behaved a bit strangely, she seemed fairly healthy."

"You mean she's--?" Notturno seemed uncomfortable discussing the matter. "I'm not sure I should tell you."

"She deserves to know, sir," said one of the others.

"Emmeleia," Notturno began, but hesitated. "If you have your family, then that is all you need. You do not need to know anything more. Now, I have much work to do; I must go." With that, he faded into the shadows.

The Symphony member who spoke earlier remained. "I shall show you out and accompany you home."

"I don't need a bodyguard, or help finding my house," insisted Lithe.

"Believe me; I understand your desire to be alone. However, you don't even know where you are right now," the man replied. "Besides, I have more information for you."

Lithe stared at him, trying to recognize him in the dim light. "Solo?"

"I hoped you'd recognize me, sooner or later. Shall we go?"

"Lead on."

Solo led her through the dark passageways of the secret lair of the Symphony, and she attempted to record the directions in her memory. Occasionally, she touched a wall or surface to encode the distinct vibrations of the area, which would allow her to find her way back through the maze again later.

As they walked, he told her about the tragedy that struck her family. "Not long after Harmony died, fighting broke out between the factions. Your mother was our only agent in Solace, and worked for years to gain information on the work of the factions in our community. She convinced Notturno to abandon the previous Symphony headquarters to take up residence here, which we did.

"When the Treble faction learned that your mother was trying to keep Solace neutral, they kidnapped your family. Only Dirge escaped capture, because Notturno had cloaked his presence."

"Why just Dirge? Why didn't he cloak my whole family? And, why couldn't they prevent the attack?"

"I don't know, Lithe. Maybe it was less obvious to have a lullaby playing for a baby than for an entire family. I've wondered that myself. Maybe Notturno just saw your brother as an *Obbligato*—one of the chosen who are indispensable to our cause."

"And my mother—my family—they were expendable?"

Solo lowered his head. "Your mother would have wanted it that way also."

"What did they do to her?" Lithe demanded to know.

"We don't know for sure. We believe your family got caught in the crossfire between the warring factions. The Symphony found their bodies strung up on the gate, with a note demanding that the citizens of Solace choose a side in the war."

"But... they aren't dead," Lithe insisted. "I just saw them. They aren't the same, but they aren't dead!"

"That's what I don't understand, Lithe. The Symphony knows everything that goes on in all of Concord. I don't see how we could have missed... I mean, I was there when we found the bodies! I went to their funeral!"

Lithe struggled to keep her composure. "Excuse me, Solo. I need to speak with my brother."

Lithe walked into her house and marched straight up to Dirge's room. "Dirge," she shouted through his locked door, "we need to talk."

His door was decorated with all sorts of macabre images of skulls and a picture of a gravestone that read, "Here lies Dirge; he has finally met his end." Lithe banged on the door even harder. How could a mere five year old be so obsessed with death?

She placed her hands on the door and sang a hymn of opening. The door fell off of its hinges and she stepped inside his room. Codan skulls littered the floor, along with sheets of music and miscellaneous musical instruments. Lithe picked up one of her brother's songs and began to read it.

All of a sudden, Dirge walked in and shouted, "What are you doing in my room? I don't go in your room! How did you get past my lock?"

"Dirge, I've been writing counter-songs for locks longer than you've been alive. But, I'm sorry I came in without permission. I was just worried about you. What's going on here, Dirge?"

"What do you mean? I'm just writing music, like everyone else does."

"Well, for starters, most Coda don't write this sort of music at age five... and, for that matter, most five year olds don't have Codan skulls in their rooms, or their headstone decorating their door."

Dirge sat down on a toy replica of a herbovine and began to rock back and forth. Lithe marveled at the stark contrast in her brother's behavior. In some ways, he was very much a child, but at the same time, seeing all the death of the world had obviously aged him psychologically.

Suddenly, and with little transition, Dirge began sobbing big five-year-old tears. "Where were you? If you're my sister, where were you when Mommy and Daddy died?"

A wave of grief washed through Lithe, and chills ran down her spine. Crumbling into an emotional wreck, she rushed over to him. He scampered away and hid inside a coffin that was way too big for him.

Placing a hand on the coffin lid, she vibrated words through the wood, "Dirge, I didn't know they were dead. If I had known, I would have rushed back here as fast as possible. I don't know how so much could have happened in such a short amount of time!"

She opened the coffin wide. "Dirge, honey, please get out of that coffin. It's morbid and wrong. Death should be respected—hallowed—not used as decoration."

Dirge sniffed. "It's not decoration, Em. I'm bringing them back. I'm bringing them *all* back!"

Lithe looked around the room at the bones and necromantic paraphernalia. The cold reality of her family's reappearance had finally settled, like the bony hand of a cadaver on her shoulder. Dirge had been playing the music of the dead. He had resurrected his family—was he also responsible for the return of Harmony? "Did you bring Mother and Father back from the dead?"

"Yes!" he beamed.

Another Aside from Your Faithful Historyteller

I realize this is a rather dramatic moment I may, perhaps, ruin, and the reader is undoubtedly more concerned with questions such as, "What are the ramifications of bringing the dead back to life?" or "Is this foreshadowing of 'The End of All Things' really as bad as it sounds?" Those are all valid questions, but to answer the most obvious one on everyone's minds, "Yes. Dirge's musical style would one day become known as 'Death Metal.'"

"I just played my music, and it worked!"

"And Harmony?"

Dirge seemed puzzled. "I just played my guitar."

"But, Dirge, they're different. They're not the same people they were."

"Yes they are. They're even better!" Dirge ran out of the room and down the stairs to where his family rested lethargically around the living room. With a clap of his hands, they and all the house servants sprang to life.

Aria floated over to him and picked him up with a gust of wind. She softly blew on his eyelids, as she had when he was a baby. Her breath filled him with a hopeful elation.

He looked up at Lithe, who was slowly creeping down the stairs. "See? Mommy still has her breath—the wind that keeps *him* away."

"Who? Keeps who away, Dirge?"

"The End of All Things. Finis."

Chapter 3:06

Insurrection and Resurrection

"Are you sure you can handle it?" Lithe asked.

"Lithe, I've fought warriors from the past, present, and future. I've overcome senility and a broken hip."

"And I've been thrown off a cliff--."

"Ahem. You fell," Quondam interrupted.

"Okay, I've fallen off a cliff, been raised by a time-crazed maniac to be a super-soldier, and learned how to play *Epic*."

"*Epic* for Kids," corrected Quondam.

Munder shot him a mean look. "Still, I think we can handle watching a little kid for a couple hours. I'm sure the time will just fly past."

"If Munder says it, it has to be true," Quondam added. "He knows Time personally."

"Okay. If you need me... well, you won't be able to reach me, because I'll be in a secret underground base, but..."

Quondam led her to the door. "We won't need you, Lithe. Go. Learn how to be a secret agent."

"Tell James Bond we said, 'Hello,'" Munder added in his best British accent. Everyone in the room just stared at him in confusion. "You guys need to watch more TV!"

Lithe walked out of the front door, stopped, and turned around. In a voice only Quondam and Munder could hear, she said, "Watch over them, too." She looked through the doorway at her undead family. "I guess he doesn't really need caretakers—they are all he has had for the last few years." She placed her hand on the wood between Quondam and Munder and looked them in the eyes. "He's special, though. Protect him."

"With our lives," promised Quondam.

Lithe left and the duo walked back into the house. Quondam looked around the room and said, "Where's Dirge?"

Meanwhile, outside the safety of Solace's walls, battles raged between the Treble soldiers and those of the Bass faction. Songs and swords clashed in a cacophony of sounds the likes of which the land of Concord had never seen. Codan soldiers were slain by the hundreds every day.

Each faction's forces consisted of drummers and marching bands, various ensembles of foot soldiers, and the canon. The drummers and marching bands set up the initial defenses and boosted morale within the ranks, while the foot soldiers performed individual melodies and fought with weapons. Finally, the canon took up the rear of the faction's forces and served as the "big guns." This group was made up of the maestros, conductors, and composers—the highest-ranking officers and elders of the community, and they sang the orders and volleyed bursts of magical energy at the opposing forces. Their songs could level entire buildings and cause massive destruction.

Dirge surveyed the spoils of war from high above his house, courtesy of a motherly updraft. Each time a Coda died in one of the battles, Dirge heard a distinct tone. As he watched the two factions wage war on one another, the din of death-knells became raucous and deafening. Dissonant chords racked his brain as whole ensembles were slain in one blast from a canonical maestro.

"Dirge, get down here!" shouted Quondam, but Dirge could not hear him above the cacophony of death-tones. Munder could reach the roof if he stretched, but Dirge was many feet above the rooftop. Quondam shouted again, "Aria, you have to put him down. It's not safe for him to be up there."

Aria blew a gust of wind at Quondam, but Munder anchored him to the ground. Aria sang, "Do not tell me how to raise my child, stranger!"

Quondam began to shout something back at her, but Munder stopped him. "You're having an argument with a dead person. I don't think you'll change her mind. We'll have to…."

"Incapacitate her," Quondam finished. In a unified movement, Munder stretched his wooden arm towards the roof, using Quondam as a kind of mace. The branches that bound them together grew long enough to reach the highest portion of the roof. Quondam shifted to his tallest age and, with a swift kick to her solar plexus, sent Aria reeling and gasping for breath.

Dirge immediately fell from his perch. Quondam tried to catch the boy, but he only had one arm, so Munder and Aria had to help. Everyone managed to escape with only a few bruises and scrapes.

When they returned to the house, Dirge moped around in a dismal mood. Quondam and Munder tried unsuccessfully to cheer him up, but it was Rhapsody's blissful song that finally managed to pull him out of his slump.

Munder and Dirge enjoyed a long game of *Epic* for Kids, with Quondam occasionally sending strategic tips through their linked limbs. All of a sudden, Munder lashed out and slammed his large fist on the gaming table. Pieces flew everywhere as Munder whined, "He's cheating!"

"Munder, don't be a tattletale," said Quondam.

Munder shouted, "You can't keep putting your dead players back on the board, you little brat!"

Quondam managed to calm Munder down, but Dirge ran out of the room crying. Loud, amplified guitar music streamed out from Dirge's room, and the rest of the re-animated members of the household proceeded to cry like little five-year-olds as well.

"Munder, I think you should stick to the role of protector. You never were a very good playmate." Quondam slumped in his seat.

Meanwhile, in the secret base of the Symphony, Lithe received her first lesson in musical weaponry. Solo worked with her one-on-one. "Up until now, you've used songs for defense and support, but we will teach you to use offensive songs and weapons." As he lectured, he thrust a large sword in her direction.

"I think you'll find that I'm a fairly experienced fighter already, Solo." She dodged his attack and used his momen-tum to trip him with her tail.

"So I see," he said, as he leapt to his feet. "Let's move on to weapons." He handed her his sword, which was very large and heavy. "It gets lighter when you sing to it. If used properly, it can take down multiple opponents at once."

"I see why you chose it; you always have preferred to have the odds against you."

"Let's look at lighter weapons." He walked over to the weapons-rack and grabbed two small blades. The blade was shaped like the letter C with a line cut through it vertically. "These are *alla breve* blades. They are specially designed for doing all the damage of a sword, or other weapon, in half the time."

Lithe took the blades by the handles and immediately felt an increase in the movement rate of her hands. "These blades must have been gifts from Tempo; they seem to cut time in half." She put them back on the weapons-rack. "I would rather rely on my natural ability, rather than some augmentation of time."

Solo took a braided whip from his belt and cracked it in the air. "We call this the chord. This particular chord is braided with notes of poison, silence, and pain." With a flick of his wrist, the whip coiled. "Any notes can be braided in a chord, as long as they are in tune with one another; one cannot braid fire and ice in the same chord."

Notturno stepped into the training room through the shadows. "Have you showed her any staves yet?" he asked Solo.

"Not yet."

Notturno held his staff up and it began to glow. "This is a Staff of the Night. It can either cast forth one strong attack, as such:" he demonstrated by aiming the staff at a training dummy, which was immediately enveloped in a large sphere of darkness. When the sphere dissipated into smaller shadows, the dummy was gone. "Or, it can attack multiple targets for a fraction of the damage. Here are four quarter notes." He fired four shots at the same time from the staff, and four candles dimmed at the same time.

Solo handed Lithe another staff. "This," he told her, "is the Staff of Air."

"It was your mother's," said Notturno. "Now, it is yours, Emmeleia."

Lithe took the staff, which felt almost weightless in her hands. It had several holes in it, which gave it the look and feel of a long flute. "Thank you."

Notturno held out a hand for her to grab. "Come. I have someone to show you." She grabbed his hand and felt the vibrations of his song.

They stepped into the shadows of the training room and emerged in a completely different room. The shadows around them fell away and Lithe could see a young girl playing with a toy xylophone. Upon closer inspection, Lithe noticed that the child was not striking the bars of the xylophone; rather, she was making them vibrate with her mind.

"What is your name, little girl?" asked Lithe.

The girl looked up from her work and smiled. When she spoke, it sounded like an entire choir of singers. "Harmony."

Lithe suddenly felt like all the troubles of the world would soon end. She spoke to Notturno about her as adults often do around children, as if they aren't really there. "So, my brother brought her back to life?"

Notturno smiled, and his teeth shone in contrast to his dark skin. "We believe so, yes. He must have appealed to Finis, the Spirit of Death. Just as he rewarded Volare with extra life, Finis has given Harmony her *encore*. It is rare, but Coda have been given *encores* before."

Dirge slipped out of the house and ran towards the Solace Cemetery. He sank to his knees beside a grave and continued to wail and cry. A fell wind suddenly blew through the tombs and ancient sepulchers of the Coda. The ashes, dust, and remains of the ancient Codan warriors were stirred up by the wind and carried out of the mausoleums.

As Dirge continued his requiem for the casualties of war, the wind blew the dust over the walls of Solace. It whirled and whispered the songs of the dead as it blew. Their cries were plaintive and somber, like the wails of the Banshee.

The whirlwind settled in the center of the main battle-field, where the Treble forces were clashing with the Bass faction. The soldiers struggled to stand their ground amidst the gale-force winds. The whirlwind did not grievously harm the Coda, but it did serve to delay them and distract them from killing one another.

After the winds subsided and the dust settled, the soldiers were left in a confused state. Before the Treble and Bass factions could resume their fighting, Dirge's breath of life resurrected the fallen warriors from the dust. Dirge's army of the dead numbered in the hundreds, which was more than enough to give the factions pause.

Chapter 3:07

Unrest Comes to Solace

"Stop killing each other!" The captain of the dead spoke to the factions in a breathy, sepulchral tone, but the words were those of a five-year-old.

The lesser soldiers slowly sheathed their swords and instruments, but the generals of the canon were not so easily intimidated. The leader of the Bass faction shouted, "Our quarrel is not with you, O Hallowed One. Why have you come here, and why do you wear the ancient livery of the warriors of Solace?"

"That's easy," chanted the dead. "We *are* the warriors of Solace, dummy!"

"Then, Solace has entered the fray after all," the leader of the Treble forces surmised. "Where lies your allegiance, Solacian?"

"I... don't know," the undead captain stammered.

"Treble or Bass?" asked a Bass general.

In the long silence that followed, the tension in the ranks rose. Musicians nervously fiddled with their instruments, and patience wore thin. One of the lesser soldiers picked up his weapon and, with a single piercing blow from his spear, turned the undead captain back to dust.

Soldiers of Treble and Bass alike fought against Dirge's undead army. When their opponents had all reverted to ashes and dust, the canons led their soldiers towards Solace. A baritone from the Bass canon concluded, "The Coda of Solace wish to overpower us both, in order to gain total control over Concord. Their neutrality was but a ruse so they could defeat us all." The canon of the Bass faction immediately began a low song that vibrated the ground around them. The walls surrounding Solace began to crack.

"We are too civilized to break down the walls," said a soprano of the Treble canon. We shall enter through the front gates. Bring forth the Clef."

One of the foot soldiers brought forth a sacred chest and handed it to the soprano. Several of the elite officers tried to open the chest to no avail. "It's locked," said an alto.

"We locked the chest that holds the key?"

"It's an ancient artifact. We didn't want it to get stolen."

The head general, whose name was Maestoso, released a long, labored sigh. "Do we have a spare key?"

Unfortunately for the Treble forces, the coat hanger had not yet been invented. Meanwhile, the Bass faction had successfully destroyed much of the wall that had been designed to protect Solace from invasion. One of the leaders, a Codan male named Vibrato, led the first wave of soldiers into the *tone*. As they marched through the rubble that once was a wall, the ground shook.

"Halt!" shouted Forte as the Treble forces approached the front gate.

Maestoso rode forth on horseback. "You will stand aside and let us enter," he sang.

Forte immediately turned to open the gate, but Rallentando slowed him down. "First," sang Rallentando slowly, "let us think this through. Why must you enter the *tone* of Solace?"

No longer feeling the pressure of time, one of the sopranos calmly pointed out, "You wish to side against us and take control of Concord."

"Solace is and will remain neutral, no matter what you do," vowed Rallentando. Suddenly, a blur of movement caught his eye.

"Your song has no effect on me," said the blur.

As one might recall from Lithe's story way back in Part 1, the time god Tempo manipulated the lives of two Coda, Ritardando and Veloce. Many, many years after their deaths, their descendants faced off against one another in front of the gates of Solace. Before Rallentando could fully grasp the significance of their meeting, the Treble foot-soldier known as Rapida slashed his throat.

Forte, as strong as he was, hardly resisted the commanding notes of Maestoso's song. He placed a hand upon the door and sang the counter-melody to the song of sealing. The gates opened and the Treble forces rushed upon Forte, as he remained in a daze. He fought valiantly, but all his strength and volume proved no match for the advancing forces of the Treble faction.

Notturno had intended to protect the citizens of Solace with his *canta oscura*, but for many, it proved their undoing. Many Coda of Solace perished in the onslaught before they even knew the *tone* was under attack.

The Symphony scrambled to halt the progression of the enemy, but Notturno remained transfixed by his grievous error. "I should not have sheltered them from the conflict outside; they are not prepared for this. None of them are."

Perched atop a tall cathedral, one of the Symphony's best spies watched the Treble and Bass factions enter the city. With eyes like an eagle's, Fermata could easily see well past the walls of Solace. Still, she cursed herself for not having seen them sooner.

Fermata began to sing in a special frequency only the Symphony could hear and interpret. She alerted them to where the different factions were and how many musicians each faction had. She sustained the last note of her song, which served to hold the advancing armies in place long enough for the Symphony to reach them.

Solo raced on ahead of the rest of the group and reached the canon before Fermata ran out of breath. His chord lashed out and caught the throat of an alto of the Treble canon. The alto tried to cry out in pain, but the chord had poisoned her with silence.

Before the rest of the canon even knew of Solo's presence, he had slashed five or six throats with his *alla breve* blades. His intent was to take out the most powerful singers of the canon before they had a chance to inflict serious damage on the *tone* and Coda of Solace.

By the end of Fermata's note, the rest of the Symphony met the Treble infantry in battle. Though the foot-soldiers of the factions were trained in fighting as an army, they lacked the cohesive teamwork of the Symphony. Some agents waited in the wings and played a backup role for those who fought with weapons on the front lines. Their songs instilled courage, strength, and agility in the Symphony while creating adverse effects in their enemies.

The foot-soldiers fought with spears, which bore the Treble clef insignia as the spearhead. Of course, their skill was shadowed by the prowess of the Symphony. All Coda were innately skilled in creating music, but none were as skilled with weapons as the Symphony.

The Treble foot-soldier known as Rapida darted from one house to another in the community, slaying defenseless Coda with the sharpened bow of her fiddle. She ran down a dark alley and quickly turned around when she noticed the dead end. However, as she tried to escape, the shadows on the ground seemed to grasp her feet. She panicked and tried to move to brighter areas of the alley. As she moved, the shadows moved with her, until their movements seemed a sort of dance.

"Run as fast as you can; you will never outrun your shadow." Notturno stepped out of the shadows and held out the palm of his hand. "The Coda of Solace will have nothing to do with your petty wars."

Just before Rapida reached for his hand, Notturno closed his fist. "I do not offer you the comfort of the open hand, fiddler. You will share the fate of your forefather." As he clenched his fist tight, the shadows wrapped around Rapida and crushed the life out of her.

As the Symphony clashed with the Treble forces in battle, Lithe worried more about the enemies that were marching towards her house. When she approached the invading Bass army, the vibrations knocked her off her feet. Windows shattered and buildings collapsed as the bassists thundered through the streets of Solace.

Lithe held her staff in her hands and prepared herself for the fight. She blew across the mouth of the staff and it whistled sweetly. She aimed the staff at the advancing army and imagined the soldiers scattering like leaves in the wind.

The result was less dramatic. When the power of the staff was divided among so many targets, it hit them more like a gentle breeze. Lithe sighed and rushed to meet them in combat. The staff had not been very effective as a weapon of mass destruction, but it worked well as a staff. With her usual precision and dexterity, she managed to knock the wind out of several baritone singers and destroy a bass drum.

The battle seemed to be going her way when, all of a sudden, the ground collapsed beneath her. Lithe struggled to maintain her balance, but an enormous bassist rammed into her and sent her crashing into the cracked ground. Fist after massive fist pummeled her into unconsciousness.

Tremolo of the Bass canon wiped the blood off his fists and rejoined the marching band of baritones and other bassists. They stomped through the streets of Solace and destroyed every house with their thundering songs.

As a massive ensemble of the Bass faction approached a large house at the end of the street, strong gusts of wind held them in place. Even the largest of the soldiers found it difficult to keep his or her footing in the face of the hurricane-force winds. The smaller bassists rolled back down the street like tumbleweeds.

They had reached the House of Air.

Chapter 3:08

'Til Death Do Us Part

Munder looked restless. He shifted his weight back and forth in his seat. "Quondam," he whispered, "Why are we still here? We're on a mission to stop Aori. We shouldn't be here. We're fighters, not babysitters." He started tapping his foot in a hyperactive sort of way.

Quondam listened to Munder speak, but he was preoccupied with the fact that everyone in the house seemed to be moving to the beat of the distant drums. Several people, including Munder and Quondam himself, were each tapping a foot rhythmically.

"Munder," he said finally, "I think we should stay. We are needed here. I have a feeling that, right now, this is more important than Aori. Now—could you please stop tapping your foot?"

As Munder began to realize that he was in syncopated rhythm with the rest of the house, he dashed to the window and peeked outside. The sound of singing could now be heard along with the beat of drums. Disgustedly, Munder grumbled, "Carolers."

Dragging Quondam with him, Munder met the drummers of the Bass faction at the house gates. Since the gates would not open, he reached his long arm between the bars and grabbed the bass drummer. "I hate carolers," he said, as he choked the life out of the bass drummer. The rest of the drummers ran away.

As the sound of the carolers faded out, Munder and Quondam could hear other music approaching. Munder grumbled, "I hate marching bands, too."

The ground began to shake beneath their feet. "I think it's more than that, Munder." Quondam pulled his gigantic friend inside the house.

Plates rattled on the shelves of the kitchen, and the walls and windows began to crack. Pieces of the house fell off in chunks. Quondam struggled to grab falling dishes and flowerpots, as Munder reached up to brace the ceiling.

"What is happening?" shouted Quondam above the thundering music outside.

"The Bass faction," whispered Aria softly. She began to sing a forceful but airy tune, and Rhapsody accompanied her on clarinet. All the denizens of the house picked up a wind instrument of some sort and began to play. Unlike the others, Ode sang in a deep, solemn voice.

Munder grumbled, "Great. And me without my piccolo." The music got louder inside the house and drowned out the Bass faction's marching tune. "Or earplugs," Munder finished.

Great winds began to blow outside, and the advancing ensemble stood helpless in their fury. "We cannot pass," shouted a baritone of the canon.

Vibrato struggled to remain standing, but shouted, "It is the wind-witch!"

"But, she's dead!"

Vibrato lost his balance, but the smaller baritone broke his fall. "Portamento!"

From the back of the group, a smaller, spindlier Coda began to play trills on a flute. As the animated song danced from one trilling melody to another, Portamento would disappear and reappear closer to the general of the Bass.

Vibrato turned to face him. "Stop moving around like that. Stand in one place and listen to me." Portamento obeyed, and Vibrato continued, "I thought you Trebles killed that spy from the House of Air."

Portamento stammered, "We did. I believe Maestoso did it himself."

"Well," shouted Vibrato, "her windsong is keeping us from getting in. I want you to do something about that."

Portamento's Trill of Transportation began again, and in an instant he was inside the house gates. With a slight change of key, he was transported inside the house.

Everyone in the house looked at the Treble in alarm, as Portamento grabbed the headmistress by the neck. He stood behind her and held his flute tight against her windpipe. "Nobody moves," he sang in a lilting voice, "or the wind-witch loses her breath."

Outside, the winds died down, and the Bass ensemble could move once again. The gates crumbled at the intense vibrations of their music. Several Aeolian servants ran out to stop the invaders, but the ground wobbled tremulously beneath them.

A doorman of the house stood resolutely in the face of the ensemble. He shouted, "You shall not enter!"

Vibrato smiled. "All is well, little man. We have a key." He reached to his belt and produced a weapon, which looked like a sharpened bass clef. With a low-pitched, bellowing laugh, he threw the clef at the doorman's throat.

Inside the house, Quondam and Munder tugged at the branching wood that bound them together. "Outside," mumbled Munder under his breath, though he knew Quondam would not leave Aria in distress.

Quondam pulled with all his strength at the wooden arm that linked him to Munder. He shifted to a stronger age and jerked, which caused the wood to grow back into his wooden sword. Quondam tumbled to the floor, and Munder crashed through the front door.

All the activity made Portamento nervous, so he trilled his flute in reflex. Immediately, he and Aria were teleported high into the air above the house. The air was very thin, and neither of them could breathe.

Aria floated downward like a feather, but Portamento fell much faster. As soon as he could breathe, he trilled his flute again and teleported safely to the ground. He breathed a sigh of relief and put the flute to his lips again. Before he could blow across its mouthpiece, however, his breath stopped abruptly. A rusty metal hand clamped down on his throat and cut off the flow of oxygen to his brain.

From his position on the ground where he had landed, Munder noticed the large and dominating forms of the enemy all around him. As he reached for his axe and sprang to his feet, he shouted at Quondam, "I bet you could have done that all along!" With a grand, sweeping arc, he cut a swath through several bassists all at once. "You knew all you had to do was turn the wood back into a sword." With his massive wooden arm, he shattered the rib cage of another soldier.

"I did not," shouted Quondam, who had joined the fight with his sword in hand. The sword had grown to accommodate for the size of his enemy, and he now had to hold it with two hands. "Believe me; if I had known I could be separated from you, I would have done that a lot sooner."

Munder elbowed a baritone in the windpipe and said, "What's that buzzing noise?"

All of a sudden, Munder and Quondam, along with the rest of the community, were swarmed by thousands of flying insects. Locusts, bees, wasps, cicadas, and various other winged pests stung them repeatedly.

Meanwhile, on the other side of Solace, an alto of the Treble canon named Drone played a buzzing, irritating song on a kazoo. The insects were drawn to Drone's music and performed his every command. Several Coda of the Symphony became so swollen with insect bites that they could no longer sing or play instruments, and the air was thick with the concentration of bugs.

Scattered amidst the buzzing, membranous wings of the locusts and bees fluttered the tattered and cloth-like wings of moths. As the moths flapped their wings closer together, a large cloud of dust filled the air and choked out the swarms of insects. The moths gathered into a grey cluster of dust and fabric, and all that could be seen through the dark haze of dust was the ominous visage of Death.

A skull's face and two vacant eyes loomed before Drone and the musician immediately knew that he had crossed a line in trying to control flying insects. He attempted to apologize to Death's consort, but words failed him. At the moment of his asphyxiation, the insects returned to their usual habits and stopped trying to kill Coda.

The moth scattered and took to the air once again. It was drawn to the stench of death floating above the House of Air. The moths gathered all over Aria's lifeless body and began to chew on the decaying flesh. The bitter taste of reanimated corpse made them choke, and they fluttered off in search of other food.

Aria continued her feather-like descent, and as she approached the House of Air, the breath of life returned to her lungs. A gust of wind caught her and carried her safely to the ground.

Not far from where Aria landed, the bow of a double bass scraped and sawed across its strings. The song caused the entire house to burst into flames. On a historical side note, a famous man by the name of Nero would eventually use a similar instrument to burn Rome. However, that story will have to wait.

The instant the house caught fire, Aria acted on a child-like impulse to blow out the candles. Instead of extinguishing the fire, she made it spread and burn hotter. She tried to run inside to save her family, but Munder stopped her. Aria fell limp in his arms, and soon even her heavy sobs faded away. Her decayed flesh quickly crumbled to dust and the wind scattered her remains. As Munder tried in vain to hold her together, a sudden gust swirled the last particle high into the sky.

Quondam noticed the bassist who had started the fire, grew an arrow, and fired it. The arrow made a satisfying hum as it cut through the hot air and pierced the chest of the bassist. The fire continued to blaze long after the song had ended, but justice seemed to have been served after Munder cast the bassist's body into the fire.

As the last of the elder houses of Concord burned to the ground, Quondam thought of Dirge—had he been inside the house? Guilt crashed down around him and all sounds seemed to fade away. In their place, Quondam heard the flapping of wings. A haze settled upon him, and his last sight was the unmistakable face of death.

The moth's tattered wings and cloak cast another cloud of dust that choked all those around him, including Quondam. In the instant before the moth's wiry hand grabbed him, Quondam thought of the time many nights ago, when Dirge had stared at him in much the same way.

Munder caught a quick glimpse of the cloaked, winged figure in the cloud of dust. For the first time in his life, Munder stood paralyzed with fear, and all he could do was watch as the moth took flight and carried Quondam into the fire. As if pulled by the wood that had once linked them together, Munder followed them into the inferno. Again, he watched helplessly as the fire consumed Quondam's body.

The stench of burning flesh and seared moth's wing lingered in the air, but nothing remained of either of their bodies.

Chapter 3:09

There is No Harm
in Harmony

Lithe woke to the sound of her mandolin once again playing of its own accord. The song gave her the energy and strength to stand, and she could feel her broken bones mending. She felt as if the mandolin was speaking to her, urging her to continue on her way to reach her house.

When she saw Tremolo's ensemble in the distance, she raised the staff to her lips once again. After charging it up with her breath, she aimed and released a tornado that overtook the party, swallowed Tremolo whole, and carried him off with it.

The rest of the ensemble escaped the windstorm with minimal damage. They rose to their feet and began marching toward Lithe. Her mandolin tried to warn her of danger, but she ignored it; she was already aware of the advancing ensemble.

However, she, like the ensemble, had not been prepared for the marauding clockwork soldiers, against which songs and weapons had little effect. The ensemble of the Bass faction attempted to fight the mechanical army, but soon became ensnared in some strange sort of wire webbing.

Their instruments and weapons were taken away, and iron muzzles were clamped on their jaws to prevent them from singing.

As they carried the Coda away, Lithe breathed. She had escaped detection at the last minute by playing her glass singer. In her transparent glass form, she blended in just enough to fool the clockworkers' rudimentary sensors. Lithe debated following the bassists and their captors, but a sudden twang of the mandolin convinced her to go home instead.

The invading clockworkers just added to the problems already facing the Coda of Solace. The civil war still raged on between the Symphony and the Treble faction, while most of the Bass faction had already either been killed or kidnapped.

Maestoso, the commander and maestro of the Treble forces, conducted the battle from a safe distance. The would-be king of the Coda had a very stately, gentlemanly look about him. When he sang, his voice commanded respect and obedience. He had complete control over those around him, and even the battle seemed to flow as if arranged by him.

He made sharp, quick gestures with his hands, and the musicians in his faction responded. With a simple flick of his fingers, cymbals crashed, horns blared, and buildings exploded. Maestoso was aware of all that went on in the battle, including Fermata's manipulations of his army. With a raucous musical fanfare, her watchtower burst into flames.

Fermata's dying song screeched through the ears and hearts of every agent of the Symphony. With a dramatic expression of anger, Solo drove his *alla breve* blades into two opponents and let his hands fall loosely at his sides. He scanned the battlefield for the conductor, but many soldiers and a great distance separated them.

Solo's grand sword rang out as he drew it from its sheath. He held the sword close to his mouth and sang to it. As the sound of his voice resonated in the metal, the sword glowed with a magical light. He threw his head back and raised his voice above the clamor of battle.

Solo charged at the bulk of the Treble forces and bellowed his battle hymn. One wide swing of his great sword slew at least ten Coda and injured even more. Sound waves rocked against his opponents and sent them crashing into the ground.

With a sweeping downward movement, Solo dispatched a few more trebles and pinned another to the ground. Using the full length of the sword, he vaulted over the crowd and sprinted towards Maestoso.

The sword glowed and sang as it carved a path to the leader of the Treble faction. As soon as he reached Maestoso, Solo raised the sword above his head with two hands. Maestoso smiled, and Solo felt something tug at his wrists. His arms went numb and a feeling of intense cold spread throughout his body.

All of Solo's bravado and confidence quickly escaped through the chord that bound his hands. Nervously, he followed the chord with his eyes to another agent of the Symphony. "Sonata?" he questioned. "How could you?"

The rest of the Symphony stepped up and readied their weapons or instruments. Maestoso sang, "Kill him," and the Symphony aimed their weapons at Solo.

Meanwhile, as the last house of the Aeolian Coda burned, Munder lingered inside the front atrium. Only a few days had passed since he had walked through here and been inundated by the house's music. As he desperately searched for signs of life, he caught himself wishing he could hear the music again. The silence behind the roar of the fire haunted him in a way he had never felt before. Quite surprisingly, Munder began to sing.

His voice cracked with the heat and inhalation of smoke, but he felt a little better. The grief he felt was as weighty as it was inexplicable; he had not felt compassion for others in many years. And yet, he bore the intense heat for a bunch of annoying singers! "When did I lose all sense of reason?" he sang.

"I was not aware you ever had it," sang the counter-melody. Long, slender fingers wrapped around his wrist and pulled him towards the door. "Come on!"

"I can't," shouted Munder. "I have to find them!" With all his strength, he braced a load-bearing beam in the ceiling. "You go. The house is falling."

"Munder," Lithe sang. "Follow me. Now." She led him out of the house, and the ceiling crashed down behind them. All the while, the mandolin played protective hymns to shield them from the burning debris.

Abruptly, the song of the mandolin changed key. Lithe looked up to find the entire house surrounded by mechanical soldiers. The sound of ticking syncopated with the crackling of the fire to create a most unpleasant cadence.

Lithe sighed. "Perfect timing," she mumbled.

The feeling slowly returned to Solo's hand, and he gripped his sword tighter. He gazed around at the faces of his fellow musicians of the Symphony; their eyes looked back apologetically, but their bodies were primed for battle.

As they charged at him, Solo focused all his energy on reaching Maestoso. His former allies held him and beat him, but he refused to fight back. Instead, he defended and tried to free himself from their grasping hands.

When he finally caught up with Maestoso, the conductor blocked his attack. Every move Solo made was met with a counter-move, yet he refused to surrender to the maestro of the Treble faction. "I will not let you take this *tone*," he belted out in tune.

Maestoso sang back, in a higher-pitched voice, "One man cannot stop an entire orchestra! You have no chance!"

Their swords crashed together with a resounding tone that echoed through the desolate battlefield and hung on the air for several minutes. In that short span of time, all the sounds in the area, from Solo and Maestoso's singing to the grunts of tired soldiers, resonated harmonically.

Time seemed to stand still as everyone watched a small figure in the distance. As it came closer, the sounds grew louder and even more in tune with one another. All Coda in the immediate vicinity stopped fighting and began to sing.

"It is a child," sang one chorus.

"It is a little girl," sang another.

"Could it be?"

"We thought her dead!"

"It must be!" "It is!" "It is she!" "Harmony!" The music welled up inside them all and burst forth beautifully.

She sang, and the voices of every Coda in all of Concord simultaneously sang with her. "Cease this conflict. Unite against the common foe." Her words were simple and to the point, and every Coda immediately understood.

Outside the burning House of Air, the clockworkers readied their weapons and closed in on Munder and Lithe. As they approached, the ticking sound seemed to bleed into the ambient sounds of the environment, and soon it was overpowered by the sound of singing.

Vibrato and the other remaining bassists rose from the oppression of the clockworkers and fought against them. The ground cracked and swallowed two of the mechanical soldiers whole. With great hammers, the Bass canon crashed down upon the clockworkers, giving Lithe and Munder a chance to escape.

Meanwhile, Coda all over Concord rose up against the mechanical menace. Several musicians fell or were kidnapped by the resilient machines, but the important part was that they were united. Even as the Coda were loaded onto trains and carried away, they sang harmoniously together.

Solo's sword easily tore through the metal skin of the clockworkers, leaving behind lifeless springs, gears, and heaps of scrap. In time, the *battaglia*, or song of battle, died away, and Solo found himself all alone with the clockworkers. The incessant ticking set the rhythm of his rage, and Solo destroyed a large portion of the clockwork army.

Of course, the mechanical monsters would not stop until they had captured all of the Coda, so Solo had a long fight ahead of him. For every three he destroyed, five more attacked. Just when he was beginning to fill overwhelmed by the odds, he noticed a familiar shadow on the ground.

The long shadows cast by the setting sun seemed to be infected by the approaching shade, which had no source of its own. Soon, all of the darkness in the area had grown together and took on a life of its own. It rose in the dominating form of a monstrous face, which swallowed up much of the clockwork soldiers.

"Notturno?" Solo searched for his leader, but found only shadows. "Accigliato, where is your *maestro*?" In response to Solo's question, the shadows slipped beneath him, and he fell into the darkness.

Chapter 3:10

Ode to the Dorian Elder

"I hate to leave a battle as much as you do, Munder, but neither of us could stand a chance against them now." Lithe dragged the burned giant along with her, as the mandolin played music to lighten her load. "We must find Dirge and the others."

"All dead," mumbled Munder. His wooden arm still smoldered and hissed. It was charred and black, while his skin had bubbled up like cheese on some sort of casserole. "Quondam... everyone... burned."

Lithe squeezed her eyelids shut and exhaled slowly. "Everyone? No one escaped?" Munder shook his head. "And you found no one inside?"

Tears streamed down his face, soothing his blistering skin. "Ashes. And this." He held in his hand a stone, blackened from soot and fire. Despite having been in the burning house, it was cool to the touch. "Could you tell it to stop singing, please?"

Lithe's somber face brightened at the words. She grabbed the stone and put it to her ear. Munder felt a painful heat return to his body, and all his skin seared. "Oh!" Lithe exclaimed. She placed the stone back in his hand and explained, "This is my father's singing stone. His essence remains in it. No fire could ever burn through his cold resolve. I guess it protected you from the heat... saved your life."

Lithe touched the stone fondly. "It didn't save him, though... Why?" The Odestone vibrated with its song, and she had her answer.

"Without Dirge, our bodies returned to ashes and dust," the stone sang. "But I will remain always, as a tribute to those who died this day."

"Dirge?" Lithe could not complete her question.

"You will meet him, in the end."

"And Quondam?" asked Munder.

"You will meet... the end."

Munder shook the stone, as one would do a broken radio or remote control. "I think it's broken."

"Seek the Elder," sang the Odestone. "You will find answers there."

"The Elder? But, Father... are there any left?"

Under the cloak of night, Solo stealthily approached the train tracks of the Timister Railroad. As he stalked the train, Notturno's pet shadows clung to his body like a shroud. He placed a hand on the metal track and tried to read the vibrations, but the barrage of grinding tones knocked him back.

A dull pain throbbed in his head, but the shadows pulled him onward. The train passed through the walls of Solace, and Solo jumped from the broken wall to the top of the speeding train. It headed westbound, through a dark tunnel that cut through the Orchestral Mountains.

Many miles away, on another set of tracks, or rather beside them, the train of the captured Ori still burned. The fire had burned for many weeks now, and the train was hardly identifiable. Deep within the death and destruction of the train wreck, life stirred.

The bright, beautiful flower of a girl rose from her burning tomb and looked around. She was frightened and a little jumpy, which is normal for those who have just been resurrected. Even the gentle breeze caused her to recoil in fear. "What has happened to me?" she asked in a thousand voices all at once.

One voice spoke above the rest, saying, "You are Asia, the Child of the Resurrection."

Where is my mother? Father? Where are my children? Voices rang out in Asia's head, and she fell to the ground in pain. *Am I dead? Where are we? I want to go home!*

The helpful voice spoke again, "I am Ekisha. I will be your guide."

"Who are the others? There are so many..."

In a calm voice that seemed to silence the madding crowd, Ekisha said, "They are the Ori. You are the Ori. The people and the power of your homeland live on in you, my dear."

"Our power made the train explode. I remember now. I was a princess...and a queen, a merchant, an old man, a little girl." Asia walked around the wreckage. "Where are our bodies? Our clothes? My doll?"

"The bodies of your people have burned," said Ekisha. "Only the spirits remain. They are a part of you, and you will carry them with you."

Asia sensed that something was watching her. She was drawn to a scorched, black tree near the site of the crash. A large blackbird perched on one of the lifeless branches. "You came for our spirits."

A small voice interrupted, "Well, you're not getting mine!"

Crowfoot just silently cocked his head to the side and watched the strange girl. The dark shroud of death seemed to hover about her, but it never touched her. He spread his wings to carry away the weight of death, but the little girl just reached out and petted them.

"Such nice, pretty feathers," said Asia. "Fly away, birdie. There is only life here."

With one last puzzled glance, Crowfoot took flight.

Many thousands of years ago, Time manipulated the lives of seven elves. Those seven elves were allowed to remain on Aia, while many of the others were slain or exiled. The Seven were no longer immortal, but their names lived on in their many children.

Their offspring became the Coda, and because Time favored them, they were given extensions on life. However, the Seven Elders eventually grew old, and all but one wasted away. The last of the Seven had left society long ago, and he lived in a secluded hermitage in the mountains of Orchestra.

The trek to the house of the Elder took Lithe and Munder two days. When they reached the house gates, they were greeted by a hairless, somber Coda with brown robes. "I am Mantra," he chanted. "You seek the Elder Dorian?"

"Yes," chanted Lithe. Munder groaned.

The house was rather small, but many Coda had made pilgrimages there to seek the wisdom of the ancients. The monks of the House of Dorian could sing three notes at once, thereby blending bass and treble and interspersing melody with harmony. Other than that, they mainly just sat around doing nothing.

While Lithe entered the chamber of the Elder, the monks took Munder aside to treat his wounds. The singing Odestone continued to stabilize his feeling of pain, as the monks scraped away his blistered skin. They smeared a strange, oily substance on his skin, which seemed to hum and vibrate. "If it hums, you know it's working," chanted one of the monks. Throughout their work, the monks sang a monotonous chant. Normally, the chant would have sent Munder into a rage of irritation, but he accepted it this time.

"Welcome, Aeolian." Dorian's voice sounded ancient and solemn, which gave him a demeanor very similar to

Lithe's father. However, despite his many thousands of years, he surprisingly looked very young. "Songs of your adventures have traveled far upon the air of your foremother, Aeolia. Lo, I have missed her these many years."

"I gather that you have heard the fate of the House of Air?" Lithe assumed.

"I have. It pains me greatly to watch the great houses of the Elders die. It was said that the spirits of the Seven would live forever in the bodies of their descendants, but their blood has intermingled much over the years. Do you know of your heritage, Emmeleia?"

"I do, Elder. My father was a loremaster of the Dorian mode."

The Elder's seemingly stone face cracked a bit of a smile. "My blood was strong in Ode. And, as much as you might deny it, I see it in you as well. Dirge, however, is an entirely different story. It's an interesting story, and I hope to see it through to the end."

Lithe's grim expression matched that of her forefather. "Is he dead?"

"No." Despite the pleasant news, Dorian's tone of voice did not change. "He was not in the house when it caught fire."

Munder made an apologetic shrug. "He's shifty, that one. Must have crept off somewhere while we were playing *Epi---* er, fighting to the death."

Lithe added, "We also seek news of our companion, Quondam. He was taken by what we think may have been one of the *fairfalla*. It had wings, but its face was like a skull. We thought you would be the one to ask, since..."

"Since I am old enough to remember the days when the *fairfalla* filled the air? Yes, I remember those days as if they happened but hours ago. Time does not flow the same for me as it does for you."

Lithe and Munder squirmed a bit at the mention of time. If the Elder noticed their discomfort, nothing about his rocky exterior showed it. He continued, "Your companion, he is of the line of Timister, is he not?" He didn't even wait for a reply. "Time flows differently for that one, as well. Odd, isn't it, how all things seem connected in one way or another? But, I digress.

"The Kingdom of the Faeries fell long ago, I'm afraid. Some still remain, though their twisted cousins, the *fellfalla*, are more abundant. 'Twas most likely a darker faerie that stole your friend."

Dorian made an almost indistinguishable nod to Mantra, who then left the room. "Mantra will show you the way to the former kingdom. It is not far from here, as the faeries and the Coda were great friends of old."

Mantra returned with his traveling gear. Dorian continued, "Go now, my child. You may still find your friend in time." His face changed ever so slightly, and he concluded, "And do give my regards to Aori."

Lithe stopped short in her exit from the room. She looked at the Elder and longed to stay and hear everything he might know of her family, Aori, and, most of all, Tempo.

The monks chanted words in an ancient form of the Codan language, which sounded more like Elvish. Lithe knew the overall meaning of their chant to be, "time is of the essence."

High above the battlefield in Solace, a dark bird circled in the air. It spiraled downward to the hallowed ground where so many Coda had recently died. The *tone* of Solace was barren and lifeless, and Crowfoot foresaw quite a heavy cargo in his future.

Regardless of their faction, rank, or *tone* of origin, Death had leveled the playing field. The corpses of Maestoso, Fermata, and countless other Coda now decayed equally.

With a sharp intake of stale air, Crowfoot spread his wings wide and invited the tragic spirits of the fallen Coda to join him.

He flew to the blackened heap of charcoal and ash that remained of the House of Air, where he perched on a scorched Aeolian harp. As he flapped his wings, the wind caused the harp to play a very somber tune.

Crowfoot picked around at the ashes in search of the source of the familiar feeling that tugged at his brain. He felt connected to the death here, in one way or another. With a flustered flap of his wings, he cast the nagging feelings and ashes away.

Then, he flew off into the darkness again.

Chapter 3:11

Fellfalla and Their Larvae

"Where do we go from here?" Asia asked herself.

"We could follow these tracks back home," she answered herself.

"No," another voice inside her replied. "We are like the tortoise. We carry our home with us." Ekisha then offered the following aphorism: "Home is where you hang your hat."

"You should write fortune cookies," chuckled a voice from the darkness.

Asia recoiled, for it was the first voice she had heard outside her head in some time. Even though they were far from home, the mystery voice spoke in the language of the Ori. "Who goes there?" Asia shouted in the commanding voice of a dead warrior.

"Do not be afraid." A startling cluster of shining eyes suddenly came into view. The largest set of eyes would have somewhat resembled a hubcap, had hubcaps been invented at this time. Of course, only Ekisha made that comparison.

"Who are you?" inquired a small Asian girl.

"I am your consort, Lady Asia. I have crawled very far, and yet I managed to make it here on time."

"No, you're late, as always," Ekisha snapped.

The creature came closer to Asia, and she could barely make out the shape of two long horns protruding from its head. Long whiskers fell from its face. Its body stretched far into the darkness, but she could see similar hairs all along its sides.

"Are you a… dragon?" asked the little girl.

"No, he is a worm," replied another voice in Asia's head.

"A caterpillar, to be exact. I am Osoi, of the Orien Saddlebacks."

"You are an Ori, like us?"

"We prefer Asian, now."

"We do?"

"Yes."

"Er…" interrupted Osoi, "could you stop that, please?" He rattled his head and his long whiskers flopped from side to side. "When you have conversations with yourself like that, it gives me a rather large headache."

"Sorry," a thousand voices said simultaneously.

Osoi the Orien Saddleback circled Asia and studied her carefully. "You'll need clothes before we go."

"Go? Where are we going?"

The caterpillar answered, "We have an appointment. Everything is scheduled. Why, even this train-wreck was scheduled. Didn't Ekisha explain this?"

The voice of Ekisha said, "I was waiting for the right time."

"Well, Asia, lots of things are happening. The Ori, er… Asians, will play a big part in the days to come. Ekisha has seen it all."

"Time and time again," said Ekisha poignantly.

Never before in the history of confusion had so many different people been so confused all at once. Asia tried to ask for more explanation, but a whole civilization's worth of questions came up at once. Only one word made it through the congestion: "Oh?"

"Yes. Now: A dress? Pants? Capris?"

Asia crinkled her forehead at the caterpillar. "Capris? What are capris?"

Ekisha told Asia all about the fashions of the future, from hip-huggers to bellbottoms to skorts. "The skort was, or will be, the evolution of women's fashion. It should have made skirts and shorts obsolete, but alas!"

The caterpillar wound itself into a coil around Asia and went to work. She panicked, thinking the fuzzy worm meant to squeeze her to death. She struggled, but found that her arms and legs were held tight with some strange threadlike substance.

"Silk," said a voice in Asia's head. "Like the silkworms back home make."

"Yes, but I'm the one who taught them how," boasted Osoi. With a few more whipping, fastidious movements with his hair/appendages, Osoi's work was done. Crawling away to survey his work, he mused, "Very pretty."

Asia looked down and saw the most beautiful, silk dress she had ever seen. It fit perfectly, and as she walked, she felt as if she were walking through clouds. "It's so soft... so smooth."

"Yes, yes. Now, we must be going, if we are to stay on schedule. Hop on."

"On your back?"

"Yes, they don't call me a Saddleback for nothing, you know."

Asia grabbed one of the long hairs, which was stiff and sharp at the point. She used the spiked hairs like steps and climbed onto the giant caterpillar's back. Osoi had a marking on his back that actually looked more like an hourglass than a saddle.

"Why don't they call you an hourglass-back?" asked Asia.

"Good point. Now, stop asking questions and hang on." Though the saddle was part of Osoi's body, it felt padded and very comfortable. The hairs on his back made exceptionally good handles, and Asia held on for dear life.

Of course, when Osoi began to crawl away, she found that the ride was quite smooth and rather slow. She loosened her grip and began to enjoy herself.

"Are we there yet?"

"Munder, stop asking that," Lithe snapped.

Munder breathed a painful sigh. His skin was still blistered, and the cold mountain air bit at it ferociously. "I just don't get why it's taking so long. We could clearly see the kingdom from the top of the mountain. How far could it be?"

"Shortcut," chanted Mantra. "Must be patient." The monk was at least 20 meters in front of them. His feet could not be seen under his long robes, so it looked as if he were gliding along the rocky ground.

"Shortcut?" repeated Munder. He whispered, "If I didn't know better, I'd say this guy is wasting our time."

"I, too, am suspicious, Munder. However, neither of us know the way to the *Fairfallan* Kingdom. We must rely on Mantra."

"Quondam's going to be dead by the time we get there... if he's not dead already. I could have sworn I saw his ashes in that fire."

Lithe lowered her head. Somberly, she said, "With the remains of so many of my house-family, I wonder how you could tell them apart."

In as consoling a voice as possible, Munder said, "Dirge is alive, at least. Maybe that moth took him, too."

Lithe looked out over a snowy summit to the wide expanse of land to the east. There she was, on a journey to find Quondam, when she knew nothing of her little brother's location or fate. She cast away the more dismal thoughts with the rationalization that if he were dead, someone or some feeling would have told her. "He's out there," she said aloud, "and I feel like I'm going the wrong way." After a pause, she continued, "I feel like I should be out looking for Dirge, but..."

Munder mumbled a strained sound of agreement. "You feel pressed to find Quondam. You know that, if you were dead or missing, he'd go out of his way to find you or bring you back from the dead."

Lithe solemnly agreed. Feeling a song coming on, she took out her mandolin. Before she could begin to play, it started without her. The song was another suspenseful warning tune.

"What is it, Mandy?" asked Munder with a laugh.

Lithe glared at him. "Don't start naming my instruments."

"Oh, come on. Mandy the Mandolin. It has such a nice ring!"

"SHHH!" Lithe's tone suddenly turned urgent. She put a long finger to her lips, gesturing Munder to be quiet. She pointed to the cliffs overhead and softly whispered, "Avalanche. No sound."

With but a thought, she used her innate ability to dampen the sound around them. Even their footsteps were muted. Munder tried to remark at the utter silence, but the sound of his words was just absorbed.

Mantra, however, had separated himself far beyond Lithe's sphere of influence. Though he was aware of the danger involved, he continued his constant chanting. Lithe and Munder could hear him over the distance, but could barely make out the words: "*tempo tempori chronos sonos mutanti.*"

The ice on the cliff wall began to vibrate, and though noiseless, Lithe sensed the familiar warning song of her mandolin. From high atop the mountain, ice cracked and snow began to move. With the power of many centuries' worth of glacial movement, ice and snow crashed down on the chanting martyr and the two mutes.

Despite Munder's massive density, he lost his footing and all sight of Lithe. The avalanche carried him far down the mountain and buried him deep under the snow. His blistered skin took the sudden shock of cold quite well. In fact, Munder felt relatively normal in spite of his dire situation. He wasn't panicked or overly concerned. His demeanor was one of stoic acceptance.

"Oh well," he said to himself, "best to have patience. The ice will melt eventually." He resigned to rest his eyes and sleep.

As sleep covered him in a luke-warm feeling of complacency, his cold, iron grip loosened, and the singing stone dropped from his hand. Suddenly, he woke with an intense feeling of panic. His skin seared with the pain of fire and ice all at once. He clawed at the snow around him, as he tried to get his bearings and find the surface.

Munder's hands ached from the cold, so he reached for the stone to use as a digging tool. As soon as he touched it, the stone resumed its song. He no longer felt any urge to escape his surroundings.

High above the mountain, a giant moth just happened to be wandering by when she sensed the moving glacier. In a desperate act of altruistic heroism, the moth dove toward the path. Realizing she'd never make it with the giant, she opted for rescuing the small-framed Coda.

Evolution had always rooted for the fellowship of the Coda and the *Farfalla*. Physiologically, the Coda's thin and lightweight bones made them perfect passengers, and their songs removed all the effort of flying. As the moth carried Lithe away from danger, both of them felt equally thankful for their symbiotic relationship.

The moth settled on a flat surface far from the piled snow. She set Lithe down, lowered her head, and slowly backed away. She seemed to prostrate herself in reverence to Lithe, who looked upon her in wonder.

"Are you a *fairfalla*?" Lithe asked.

The moth shuddered, as if in answer to Lithe's question. A cloud of dust rose in the air, which caused Lithe to choke and cough. Before the moth realized what she had done, Lithe had passed out.

"Sorry," she said in a raspy, throaty voice. "Reflex." A shadow passed along the ground as another moth flew overhead. She covered Lithe with one of her wings, which were like layers of woven tapestries. The whiteness of her wings blended in with the snow, but a wavy pattern of dark brown lines added complexity to her style.

She helped Lithe to her feet and said, "I am Lymantria Dispar, but you can call me Gypsy." The moth stood up and threw her wings back like a cape. "And, to answer your previous question, no. I'm not a *fairfalla*; I'm a *fellfalla*. I understand if you're disappointed. We get that a lot."

"My apologies; I meant no offense. I've never met any of your kind."

"Perhaps you are fortunate, then. I'm afraid our nasty reputation is fairly accurate. My tribe in particular is quite well known for their brutality and vileness. In fact, that's why I left. Actually, I was banished. I've been wandering ever since."

"How is it that you speak the common language?" asked Lithe.

"I speak many languages, actually. I have been all over this great land. It is actually quite fortunate that I happened by when I did; I rarely travel this close to my homeland."

"Very fortunate indeed," agreed Lithe. "But, did you see what happened to my large companion?"

Chapter 3:12

The *Fellfallan* Empire

Before we continue, here's a handy chart for remembering the differences between your basic faerie folk of Aia:

Farfalla	
General term for the Antheri responsible for the flying insects in the order *lepidoptera*	
Fairfalla	**Fellfalla**
Guard and Resemble Butterflies	Guard and Resemble Moths
Governed by Monarchy	Governed by Empire
Cleaner-looking	Furrier and dusty
Diurnal	Nocturnal
Wings fold upward at rest	Wings rest downward
Bright, ostentatious colors	Darker, understated colors

One of the furriest moths is the *cerura vinula*, or puss moth. Its fur and wings are both a pale, snowy color, with darker grey and black patterns layered among the white. For this reason, the giant *fellfallan* version of the puss moth could hardly be seen against the snow of the fallen avalanche. He had great, sweeping, comb-like antennae, which he used to gather sensory information. Some strange vibration and sound was coming from the snow beneath him. More like a ravenous beast than an insect, he bore his fangs and growled.

Another giant puss moth approached with a human carcass in tow. It had already begun consuming the flesh, but these monstrous moths hunted in packs. Since their population had increased beyond the supply of leaves and plants, it had become necessary to the propagation of their species that the *fellfalla* find other food.

With huge, sharp claws on the ends of its appendages, the first moth dug through the snow and ice to get to the noise. He found the Odestone, ripped it from Munder's hand, and took flight.

Pain immediately rushed to fill the loss of the stone, and Munder screamed in agony. He reached up, grabbed a tuft of moth hair, and held on tight. The moth took him high above the ground in spite of his massive weight. Looking down, Munder noticed several other moths gathered around what appeared to be Mantra's body.

As Munder struggled to maintain his grip on the moth's fur, he was inundated with a dusty fog. In between coughs and gags, he launched several attacks on the flying beast. However, his wooden ram-arm did little to stop the hulking moth. He clambered up where he could reach the moth's back, so that he could get closer to the moth's head. With a jerk of the antennae, he got the monster's attention.

The giant moth performed several evasive aerial man-euvers, none of which could shake its passenger. Eventually, Munder fell from the moth's back, but held his grip on the antennae. When Munder felt his feet touch the ground, he took a second to rediscover his center of gravity before pulling down hard on the antennae. The creature crashed into the snow and ice.

Munder stomped the moth's face, but the move was countered when the moth sank his teeth into Munder's foot. Much of his foot was mauled before Munder could get to his axe and put a stop to the problem ultimately. When the moth stopped chewing on him, Munder grabbed the Odestone and immediately felt much more stable. The frenzy of battle subsided along with the pain of his burns and injured foot.

Of course, there was still the problem of the other moths. Munder supported all of his weight on his one good foot. As the moths approached, he felt fairly indifferent about the fight. "Ode, could you stop singing for a bit? I might need to survive this one." The moths gathered around him, baring their monstrous teeth. Their fur was matted and stained with Mantra's blood, which, despite the violent nature of the image, failed to incite any intense feelings in Munder. He whispered to the stone, "Any time now... that is, if it's not too much trouble..."

Just before the ferocious moths pounced on him, something swooped down and picked him up. Gypsy struggled with the great mass of her cargo, but managed to stay aloft. She flew very close to the ground in hopes of conserving energy. Unfortunately, the tribe of puss moths took flight after her. She tried to speed up or out-maneuver her pursuers, but the added weight limited her options.

Gypsy shouted at Munder, "Why don't you make yourself useful and—I don't know—throw that rock at them or something?"

"Oh, that's okay," said Munder passively. "If we just wait long enough, they'll give up and fly away eventually."

One of the enemy moths caught up to them and nicked one of Gypsy's wings with a razor-sharp appendage. She tumbled to the ground in a heap of blood-speckled, white tapestry. The Odestone slipped from Munder's hand in the crash, and pain exploded in him again.

Instinctively, he reached for his axe. A deep, hearty grunt passed his lips, as if in reply to the guttural, bestial dialog of the approaching moths. Several of the frightening creatures landed on him at once in a blur of flapping wings and slashing claws. He found it difficult to see through the dust and fog generated by his enemies, but his fury needed no sense of sight. He lashed out at all around him, and his axe tore through the wings of his enemies.

A great whirlwind came suddenly, blew away all of the dust, and carried the moths high up in the air. Despite the newfound clarity and absence of enemies, Munder found it difficult to relax. Slowly, the rage gave way to agony once again and he fell to his knees. A gentle, nimble hand touched his forehead, and Lithe softly sang, "Sleep, Munder." And, he slept.

While Munder slept, Lithe helped tend Gypsy's injured wing. "The wings of the *farfalla* are made of a material not unlike fabric," Gypsy explained. "We spend many months as larva spinning the fibers needed." She tore some cloth from her long, flowing robes, which were white with a similar pattern to match her wings. She wove the strips of cloth into her wing and continued, "Some moths scavenge materials from others, but I think that's just horrid. That's why I weave extra fabric in my spare time."

"Your design is very pretty," Lithe smiled.

"Thank you. We don't hear that sort of thing very often. The *fairfalla* are the truly beautiful ones. You should have seen them, in the olden times. Of course, I wasn't born yet, myself, but I have heard many stories."

"So there are no *fairfalla* left? What happened to the kingdom?"

Gypsy lowered her head and drooped her long, hair-like antennae. "The Kingdom of the Fair Folk fell many years ago. There is only the Empire, now. The Emperor rules over all the families of *fellfalla*. I vowed never to return there, but I will help you in your journey. I hope for a day when the Coda and the *farfalla* will live together again, though I fear we fallen ones will never be accepted."

Night fell again, and Lithe started a campfire. Gypsy sat and watched the fire in utter silence for several hours. The flames reflected in her dark eyes, which seemed like deep pools of black water. Lithe looked on in wonder, and finally commented on the moth's strange behavior. "You look as if you see something we do not. What is it, Gypsy?"

"Everything." She never took her eyes off of the fire, but continued her conversation with Lithe. "It is all connected, you know. In my wanderings, I have met many people and learned much about our world. I see the world in the fire. Every flicker of flame shows a different part; I will visit them all before I die."

"I would like to visit them as well," admitted Lithe. "Solace is my home, but it will never be the same for me."

"Let us go, then." Gypsy rose to her feet and reached out towards the flames.

"What, now? I cannot go now."

Gypsy looked concerned. "We must go now, if we are to see it all before I die. I haven't much longer to live."

Lithe suddenly remembered the story of Threnody and Volare, and of the ephemeral lives of the *farfalla*. She began to understand why the Coda and the faeries lost touch; their dissonant life spans drove them apart. Though she had known Gypsy for only a few hours, she felt that watching her new friend die would be much too hard to take. She tried to communicate her feelings without dwelling too much on the subject of death.

"The Fair Ones had that effect on others, but moths usually die before they grow on you. You have paid me a great compliment, Lithe. Thank you." Gypsy beamed in the flickering light of the fire. "It has always been my plan to seize every moment of the day, since my time on Aia is so short.

"Speaking of which," she continued, "we should be moving. We cannot dally here, if you are to find your friend."

"Yes; time *is* short." Lithe rushed to gather her things. "Why do I keep forgetting that? Why am I so passive about time, when the consequences are so dire?"

"It's this rock," said Munder, half-asleep. "Your father's song dampens our feelings and senses."

Lithe picked up the rock and held it in her palms. "Why, Father? Why do you deny us our emotions?"

The Odestone suddenly stopped singing, and Lithe felt as if she had lost her father once again. If not for the urgency of their quest, she would have given in to the grief. Rather, she put the stone in her pocket and said, "Let us go. We still have far to travel, and I fear that Gypsy cannot carry us both. Are you able to walk, Munder?"

Without the analgesic qualities of the Odestone, Munder felt the pain of all his injuries, but they no longer seemed to hinder him. "Yes," he said. "I think I'm a bit glad to have the pain; it gives me that edge I need to keep going."

Gypsy said, "You will not need to walk, Lithe. Though you are right, and I cannot carry you both, there are other ways. Walk with me into the fire."

"I think I've been burned enough already," Munder replied.

"Is it safe, Gypsy?" asked Lithe, wanting to trust her new friend implicitly.

"My people do it all the time. It is the way we travel."

Munder looked confused. "You mean, you have wings, and yet you need some other way to travel?"

"Flying long distances takes too much energy," Gypsy explained.

"So does walking! We really could have used wings a few days ago; we'd already be done with this journey." Munder grumbled for a long time after that, but no one listened.

Gypsy took them both under her wings, and the mysterious fabric protected them from the flames. The fire roared up around them, but they felt no pain. The very next second, they were standing inside a fireplace in a small cottage.

"Where are we?" asked Munder as he stepped out of the fireplace.

"A house in the Fell Empire," Gypsy answered. "All houses have fireplaces, so we can travel to and fro. It's much easier than trying to fly by light of day. Moths prefer the night, anyway."

Lithe worried, "Will the owner of this house be angry that we have settled here without permission?"

"I don't know. Ask him." Gypsy gestured toward a decrepit-looking moth in the corner of the room. He was covered in ashes and soot, and his thin fur was a dirty brown color mottled with grey ash. Gypsy ran over and greeted him excitedly.

"You know him?" asked Munder.

"Everyone knows him, or everyone should. He's a Chimney Sweep." Gypsy turned to the old moth and spoke to him in another language. His reply sounded more like coughing than speaking. Gypsy patted him on his back and whispered some strange words to comfort him.

"He is very old, and the smoke of many years has caught up with him. He is dying." Gypsy exhaled a labored sigh of resignation. "Alas! So is the way of our people."

"Ask him if he knows a moth with a skull for a face," Munder insisted.

"Munder!" Lithe snapped. She turned to Gypsy. "Is there anything we can do to help him? Is he in any pain?"

From outside the house, there came a loud commotion. The old moth sat up in his chair and coughed some words at Gypsy. She responded and looked concerned. The Chimney Sweep spread his wings, which were grey and tattered at the edges. With a rapid movement that defied his age, he leapt towards Munder.

Shocked, Munder said, "Sorry! I didn't mean—OOF!" The old moth carried him away and up the chimney, while Gypsy and Lithe followed.

On the roof, Gypsy and the Chimney Sweep spoke in hushed whispers. Gypsy explained, "Footmen of the Empire."

"What do they want with the old guy?" asked Munder.

"Not him. Us. They are aware of our arrival."

"How?" asked Lithe.

"The Emperor has eyes throughout the Empire."

"Can't we just talk to them? If they know where Quondam is…"

"Munder," Lithe interrupted. "I don't think they've come to talk." The footmen had surrounded the house and were shouting angry words. Suddenly, the Odestone began to vibrate in Lithe's pocket. She felt the vibrations and interpreted them into the Codan language. Her father was translating the *Fellfallan* language for her.

> **Footmen Moths**
> There are many different types of moth called footmen. The common name of each moth has a different adjective to describe its appearance; for instance, the four-spotted footman has four spots, the speckled footman is speckled, and so on. In the *Fellfallan* Empire, the footmen patrolled the streets, delivered goods, and did various odd jobs.

"There is no escape," said Gypsy.

"We will fight them!" Munder exclaimed.

"There are too many…" said Lithe, "…even for you."

Munder looked at her incredulously.

She continued, "Okay, even if you could fight them all, I don't think we'll get the information we need by killing everyone."

The Chimney Sweep stood up and began flapping his wings wildly. "What's he doing?" shouted Munder. "He's giving away our position!"

"No," said Lithe. "Look!" As the old moth's wings fluttered, he stirred up a haze of ash and smoke. With their movements hidden by the cloud of smoke, Gypsy took Lithe and Munder and leapt to the next building. She tried to fly, but the weight was too much for her to bear.

"We'll never get away if we can't fly," said Lithe. The mandolin let out a ringing chord, as if it were speaking to her. She understood, and the instrument began to change in response to her touch. It grew into a woodwind instrument that remarkably resembled her long-lost Soffiara.

As Lithe played, Gypsy felt her load lighten dramatically. She soared high into the air, far beyond the reach of the footmen. From this vantage point, they could see the entire *Fellfallan* Empire. Many of the houses looked dilapidated and worn. Even the stately palaces of the Emperor seemed to have decayed over the years.

"The Empire is a far cry from the beautiful architecture of the *Fairfallan* Kingdom," said Gypsy. "The grand forests have all been consumed, mainly by my greedy family. Once, there were wondrous gardens built by the Fair folk. They realized the importance of replenishing what is eaten."

They landed on a rooftop, and Gypsy continued, "There is a fable among my people of a silkworm who worked day and night to sew beautiful clothing for all the people. Then, on the next day, she ate up everything she had worked so long to create."

"Yes," said Lithe. "I have heard songs that told of that story."

"Perhaps you should sing it for my family. I'm afraid they don't understand the concepts of preservation or moderation. I was banished simply because I refused to ravage the forests of Aia for food."

She opened a trap door in the roof and led them down a spiraling set of marble steps. The ornate banister needed a dust and polish, but it hearkened back to a day long since past, when the Kingdom of the Butterflies flourished. Gypsy looked around in awe. "This is the last remnant of the great Kingdom. I have heard that the Monarchs still live, though I have never seen them myself. If we are to find your friend, we will find the Fair Ones the most helpful."

"If the royal family of the *Fairfalla* still live, then why are they no longer in power?" asked Lithe.

"Perhaps we shall soon find out," answered Gypsy. They walked through several lavishly decorated, yet neglected, rooms. Finally, they reached the royal chambers of the Monarchs.

The magnificence of the great butterflies left them speechless. The King and Queen of the ancient *Fairfalla* were seated upon ornamental thrones made up of precious jewels. Their wings, which spread upward at rest (unlike the *Fellfalla*, whose wings rested downward), seemed to be just as precious and valuable as the gems. Black outlined a translucent orange material, giving the wings the look of a stained-glass mosaic. Their bodies were thin, yet regal, and they reminded Lithe of the descriptions of Elves she had heard all her life. Each of them wore a grandiose crown, which bore a design similar to the pattern of their wings.

Gypsy bowed low, and Lithe followed suit. "Your majesties," Gypsy addressed the Monarchs, "I have brought this Coda to pay tribute to the bygone days of the Alliance." She whispered to a surprised Lithe, who fumbled with her mandolin.

Lithe began to improvise a song using elements she remembered from children's stories about the *Fairfalla*. She combined that wondrous imagery with the conflicting despair and decay of the Empire. All in all, it was quite a masterpiece.

Of course, Munder wanted nothing to do with it. He wandered around the room, inspecting the highly ornate decorations and paintings of butterflies and caterpillars. An obvious motif spread consistently throughout the Monarch's décor: every painting contained an eye.

Munder eased up to Lithe as she continued to play her ode to the *Fairfalla*. He tapped her on the shoulder and whispered, "I think we should get out of here."

Eyes Everywhere?
In the wild, many insects (and other animals) exhibit distinctive coloration in the form of spots, called eyespots, in order to fool predators. The eyespots of the owl moth, for example, give it the appearance of an owl, which would be more intimidating to possible predators than the appearance of a small, defenseless moth. In the *Fellfallan* Empire, the eyespots served a different, although similarly sneaky, purpose.

356

"Not now, Munder. Can't you see I'm playing?"

"But, I think we're being watched."

Gypsy sprang up and said, "Did you say 'watched?'" She looked around the room at the various eyespots on butterflies and caterpillars. "The Emperor must have eyes here, as well."

She rushed over to the Monarchs and urged them to rise. "It is not safe here, your majesties. We must—!" Before she could finish her sentence, a pair of strong hands grabbed her by her forewings.

Several moths with sleek wing-designs sped in from out of nowhere. Their flight had been so swift that no one had even sensed their approach. When they landed, their wings folded back to resemble stately capes of a reddish brown color.

One of the Herald moths shouted, "Kindly step away from the Viceroys, Lymantria Dispar."

Gypsy looked at the butterflies in shock. "Viceroys?"

"Of course. You didn't think we would let commoners in to see the real Monarchs, do you? The Viceroys stand in for the long-dead King and Queen, and the common folk come pay their respects every week. You should see how much these gullible moths are willing to give for the cause of the so-called 'Restoration.'"

"That's enough," said another of the Heralds. He seemed to be the captain of the squadron. He walked over to Gypsy and gestured for the release of her wings. "Lymantria," he said, "you should not have returned!"

"The *Libatrix* class of Imperial soldiers," Gypsy explained to Lithe. "They are the Emperor's Herald-Moths."

"The Emperor wishes to speak with the visitors, Lymantria. Resist if you wish, but you cannot possibly match the speed of the *Libatrix*."

"If he just wishes to speak with them, why have they met such violence at the hands of the *Fellfalla*?" Gypsy shouted defiantly.

357

"The Emperor's business is none of your concern, Outsider. Go back to your wanderings, and he may show you mercy this time. Linger here, and you will surely die before your time."

Lithe put a hand on Gypsy's shoulder. She whispered, "We will fight them, if you wish. We may die in the attempt, but we will not let them kill you."

"No," said Gypsy. "They are right. I do not belong here. I will go." She turned to the leader of the Heralds. "Do I have your solemn word that no harm will come to them?"

The Herald raised his arm and held his hand with its palm facing Gypsy. "As I am a moth of my word, no harm will come to them. Despite the current state of the old Kingdom, some honor still exists."

"If that were true," said Gypsy, "you would not be working for that disreputable tyrant."

Several of the Heralds readied their weapons, but their captain ordered them to stop. "I would watch my tongue if I were you, Lymantria. There are few alive today who share your sympathies towards the old Kingdom."

"And too many who blindly follow the emperor," Gypsy mumbled under her breath.

The Herald reached out and shook her hand in a sign of respect. Lowering his voice, he continued, "You've been gone too long, Gypsy. Even Oleander, your old flame, has joined the Empire. It's pointless to fight. Now go, before my soldiers defy my orders and kill you here and now."

Gypsy bade her new friends a fond farewell, exited the building, and took to the skies. She felt as if she had done the wrong thing in leaving Lithe in the hands of the Empire, but she could not let her feelings anchor her to one place for too long. She had much to do before the Death's Head Moth came for her.

Chapter 3:13

Emperor Saturn Pavonia

"I am Harold," said the leader of the *Libatrices* as he escorted Lithe and Munder out of the vice-royal palace.

"Harold the Herald?" Munder had to fight back a chuckle.

"Laugh if you wish," said Harold, "but *his* name is Gerald." He gestured towards one of the other Heralds and smiled.

Munder's roaring laughter was interrupted by Gerald's halberd poised at the thick space where his neck should be. Munder looked to Lithe for permission to fight, but she just shook her head.

Though the Heralds were strong flyers, one alone could not carry the giant's weight. Two of them each took one of Munder's arms and shot into the air. As they rocketed through the sky, Munder was reminded of Toki's silver spaceship. On a few occasions, his master had allowed him to fly it. *Good times*, he thought, recalling the short-lived days of his youth. As the ground rushed past him at breakneck speeds and he was hurtling to some unknown fate, he briefly wondered why he had agreed to join Quondam in the first place.

When they landed, several guards in imperial armor were waiting for them. Like the Heralds, the guards wore helmets of a sleek, futuristic design. Their wings, in their folded-down position, gave them the appearance of some high-tech spaceship. Each of them wore ceremonial necklaces bearing an eye, which was the Emperor's insignia.

Harold stepped up to the leader, whose wing pattern consisted of several smooth, sweeping shades of green. While most moths appeared to have layers upon layers of tattered fabric, the colors of the imperial hawk moths were more like a stylistic paintjob on metal wings.

"Oleander," Harold said to the leader of the guard. He spoke in the language of the *Fellfalla*, but it sounded more proper and less guttural than before. The Odestone vibrated in Lithe's pocket and translated their words for her. "These are the visitors. One of them is a Coda." He spoke very quietly, as if his words carried some great portent only Oleander could understand. "They were looking for the Monarchs."

Oleander looked them up and down. "I have never seen a Coda, in all my days."

"There is something else, Oleander," edged Harold. "They were brought here by a moth."

"It is not yet a crime to bring Coda to our land. I am sure the Empire will treat him justly. Who was it?"

"Lymantria, the Gypsy."

Oleander's antennae pricked up at the sound of the name. He hoped the others had not detected his reaction, but he had trained them to be very perceptive. "Where is she now?" He tried to cover his eagerness with concern for justice. "She was not to return to this place."

"I sent her away. Much to my surprise, she abandoned the visitors. I thought, surely, she would want to accompany them here, to ensure their safety."

Oleander looked out over the horizon, hoping to catch a glimpse of the Gypsy moth. "Lymantria has little concern for others; she has a wanderer's heart."

Harold felt a mild discomfort at the subtle display of feelings in a *Nerium* of the Imperial Guard. "Make haste, Oleander. The Emperor is waiting."

The guards searched Lithe and Munder and confiscated their weapons. "You will get them back," Oleander told them. As he spoke the common language, his voice sounded very sophisticated and noble. "You will not need them inside; I assure you."

The Imperial Hawk Moths led them down several long, vertical passageways with no steps or ladders. Their wings all but vanished in the rapid flutter of their descent. "If you thought the Heralds were fast," boasted Oleander, "you should see the Hawks in flight." He continued, "No moth has ever matched our speed."

"Or strength," added a rather large, but pink, Hawk moth. Its pattern was much different from the rest of the guards but maintained the sleek, aerodynamic style.

"Very true, Elpenor." Oleander sped on ahead of the group in a blur of motion. He arrived at the end of a hallway, where he met a wide set of doors. The doors, which displayed an elaborate pattern of colored lines and eyespots of various shapes, spread open like wings.

Oleander crouched on one knee and bowed his head in reverence. "Emperor Saturn Pavonia," he announced in as much a greeting as an introduction for the visitors. "Empress Miranda." He rose to his feet and beckoned for Lithe and Munder to step forward. "My Emperor, these are the visitors."

Upon looking at Emperor Saturn, it was quite difficult to find his true eyes amidst all of the convincing eyespots. His wings folded down into a cape of various shades of rust and brown. If not for the unmistakable eye design, his wings and attire would have seemed fairly dull. In the middle of his forehead rested another eye, which seemed just as aware as any of the others. Around his neck, he wore a strange amulet of some sort.

Empress Miranda also sported the eyespot design scheme, but her features were much fairer. Her eyespots were purple with a pale yellow background, and her antennae were purple as well. Like most of the nobles, her wings were not tattered or worn, which set her apart from most moths. In fact, her appearance was more reminiscent of the *Fairfalla*.

"It is a pleasure to meet you, Emperor. I am Emmeleia of the Aeolian Coda. My companion is Munder of... undoubtedly large parents." She curtsied and nudged her grumbling companion to bow.

Emperor Saturn spoke in a booming voice. "You have come to seek the *Fairfallan* Monarchs. I am afraid you have wasted your time."

"You're telling me!" Munder blurted. "All we've done lately is waste time. The little songbird here carried on for about an hour with some royal tribute before we found out we had the wrong butterflies!"

An enormous moth stomped out of a corner and shoved Munder across the room. "You will address Emperor Saturn with respect, Dog!" The moth spread its wings in a showy display of bravado, and his wingspan stretched to each wall of the imperial chamber. At the upper tips of each wing, snakes hissed violently and snapped at Munder.

"Attacus, stand down!" shouted Emperor Saturn. The great moth folded down his wings, and the serpents went back to an inanimate state. "You must excuse my Atlas moth, here. He is very protective. Attacus, the human meant no disrespect. Our friend Munder was not raised in our culture...or our time."

Lithe and Munder exchanged glances again, as they had when Dorian used the word "time" in a similar way. Munder felt even more uncomfortable with the information Saturn seemed to have on his upbringing.

Emperor Saturn spoke at length, "I will overlook the acts of violence against the puss moths, as well as the rebellion against my footmen. However, you must understand that the Wingless are not very well accepted in the Empire—especially when they attempt to incite a revolution among the *Fell* society!"

"What?" Munder shouted. "We didn't do that!" He paused, looked at Lithe, and asked, "Did we do that?"

"The Kingdom of the *Fair* is dead, Coda. Any attempts at overthrowing the imperial government will not restore your precious butterflies to power. They have withered away, as has everything else on this godforsaken planet!"

"Look," said Munder. He started to approach the emperor's throne, but the snakes of the Atlas hissed at him. "We came here to find the moth that took our friend. I could personally care less for butterflies *or* moths!"

The snakes began to coil around Munder, and his vision immediately became distorted with surrealistic images of eyes and strange animals. A winged tiger growled at him, accompanied by a pink elephant and a green hawk. A phoenix flew out of a fire and dissolved into ashes when it struck Munder.

"Illusions," the emperor explained. "However, I think you'll find the fate that awaits you very real." He pulled a lever on his throne and the floor fell out from under Lithe and Munder.

They fell for several feet before landing in a large, round pit. The sounds of laughter echoed above them. Munder rubbed at his eyes, but the images of those eyespots would not disappear. "He's got eyes in my head, now," he said with a shudder.

Lithe sang in a soothing voice, "Munder, calm down. We have to figure out where we are." She placed a hand upon the floor and felt it writhe with movement. She sang a song which, when translated from Coda, sounded something like "This Little Light of Mine." Her long, slender finger began to glow in response to the song, and she could tell that the floor was covered in larvae of various sizes.

A shudder ran down her spine as Lithe leapt to her feet. "Caterpillars. They have fed us to their young."

"It'll take days for these little things to eat us," said Munder.

"I'm not so sure. Look!" In a corner of the room, a very large caterpillar looked ready to strike. It had various markings on its face that gave it a rather intimidating presence. A large, black spike protruded from the opposite side.

Several other caterpillars crawled out of holes in the walls. All of them sported some distinctive markings to make them seem more than just a fuzzy worm, as if their sheer size wasn't enough of a deterrent. One had huge eyespots and a pattern resembling the teeth of some fierce toothy creature. Another had a single horn coming out of its head.

"The one with the horn is a Unicorn caterpillar," said one of the creatures. The speaker had yellow, spikey hairs all along its body, which was mainly green. "Welcome to the Nursery."

The voice sounded strangely familiar. "What, do you not recognize me?" With but a thought, the caterpillar underwent a year's worth of metamorphosis without the cocoon.

Several eyes shone in the darkness of the Nursery. "Saturn?" Munder guessed. "Why wouldn't you just kill us up in your throne room?"

"To feed the young. They could munch on a giant like you for years!"

As the writhing, squirming larvae encircled them, Munder made a disgusted retching sound. "And why follow us down? You couldn't just wait for them to do your dirty work?"

"I suppose if we're really honest, it'd be because of pride. Those simpletons up there wouldn't understand my power, but something tells me you will. You see, I was given the gift of metamorphosis at will. It is a wonderful trick, is it not?"

"Seen it," said Munder. "It tends to get less interesting every time."

"Just as I assumed. The prophecies foretold of your coming. Where is it? Let me see your amulet!" Prying eyes darted all around Munder.

"What? I don't…"

With her innate command over sound, Lithe silenced Munder. Then, she said, "Why do you need to see it, if you have one of your own?"

Emperor Saturn spread his wings, and the caterpillars surged with movement. "I need it! Look around you! What do you see?"

"A bunch of worms," Munder stated plainly.

"Not worms. Larvae. They should be fully-grown moths! Butterflies, even!" The emperor cycled through various stages of development in order to demonstrate the growth of the *Fellfalla*. It was a very effective visual aid, indeed.

"I don't understand," said Munder. "If they're supposed to be moths, where are their wings and things?"

Lithe began to piece the information together. "They didn't have enough time. The seasons changed too quickly, and these *fell* creatures are stuck in larval state."

"Exactly," said a chrysalis in Emperor Saturn's voice. "It appears I have fallen out of Time's favor."

"We have found that many servants of time eventually find that fate, Saturn," Lithe said pointedly. "He is the great Manipulator, and he has ruined your people as he did the *Fairfalla* before you."

Anger burst inside the chrysalis. "I am not ruined! I will stand strong and ageless forever! Now, give me the amulet, so that I may give my people the metamorphosis they deserve!"

Defiantly, Munder said, "I'm afraid we can't do that, Saturn."

"Then I will instruct my larvae to tear it from your cold, dead hands." As he commanded, the caterpillars attacked. Several stinging hairs jabbed into Munder's skin, and numbness spread throughout his body. The Unicorn dove at his chest like a dart, but Munder deflected the attack with his wooden arm.

A rather appalling larva issued out of another hole. It had twelve leg-like appendages, which were covered in stinging hairs. "Phoebetron Pithecium," the emperor introduced, "Larva of the Hag." The pithy creature whipped its hairs at Lithe, but she dodged and leapt gracefully out of reach. A whirlwind of a kick sent Phoebetron and her stinging hairs hurtling into the emperor's cocoon.

Lithe landed next to the larva with the spiked end. With a quick, snapping kick, she broke the spike off and stabbed the hissing caterpillar in its head. Then, she dove for the paralyzed emperor's chrysalis. She picked it up and held the sharp spike against the soft outer layers of the cocoon. "Stop!" she shouted, with the commanding power of music behind her voice.

When it seemed that she had everyone's attention, she said, "Emperor Saturn, I assure you, if you attempt any metamorphosis, I *will* stop you. You will find death much worse than the paralyzing sting of your Hag. Furthermore, if any larva or moth tries to fight us, your emperor will not live long."

Lithe placed a hand on the chrysalis, and the unmistakable ticking of the amulet vibrated as if it were calling out to her. "Munder," she called, "come and get this."

"We're taking the emperor with us?"

"Yes," Lithe answered. "Any tool of Tempo left in the wrong hands could be disastrous. Just look at Aori."

Munder picked up the bulky chrysalis with ease. "Couldn't we just carve it out? The shock of those stinging hairs is going to wear off any second now—how are we going to keep him from changing?"

As if in reply to his question, an odd-looking caterpillar nuzzled up to Munder's leg. Several long, spiraling horns or hairs protruded from its head and tail end, but the horns did not appear intimidating whatsoever. Rather, they looked like strange dreadlocks or black branches on a tree.

Munder looked down at the caterpillar in bewilderment. "Why isn't it attacking?"

"Maybe it is not in his nature to attack."

Again, the caterpillar seemed to reply. Its strange hairs branched out and stabbed into the chrysalis. "He won't try to change with a horn stuck in him, I'd wager," said Munder. He picked up the larva and draped it over his shoulder. "Let's go."

They took one of the larger tunnels out of the Nursery and followed it around many twists and turns. "We have to come to open air soon," Lithe assumed. "It's not like a moth to stay cooped up inside a tunnel."

"It looks dark up ahead," Munder noted. "I don't see any end to these catacombs."

"No," said Lithe. "Feel that breeze? The exit must be up ahead." They both fell silent. "What's that sound?"

"Hissing," said Munder. "Snakes. Why'd it have to be snakes?"

They raced for the exit, in hopes that they would outrun the giant snakes. What Lithe's keen ears should have detected, however, was that the sound was coming from outside the tunnels. As they reached the exit, two gigantic hands grabbed them and pulled them out of the tunnel.

The giant Atlas moth threw them against the ground in the withered palace garden. With his wings fully out-stretched, he towered over them ten meters or so. In fact, he seemed to be growing larger by the second. The serpents writhed and struck blindly at the air, while Attacus shouted bitter words in his native tongue.

Lithe rose to her feet and gripped her spike-weapon tighter. "Munder," she said, "do you think you can throw me high enough to reach those snakes?"

"No problem," said Munder. He set the chrysalis and his newfound larva friend on the ground and hurled Lithe high into the air.

She soared high into the sky, and the perplexed Atlas moth groped clumsily at the air around her. Grabbing a layer of material in the moth's wing pattern, she was able to hoist herself high enough to reach one of the serpents. With a quick jab of the spike, the snake's hiss faded to silence.

From there, Lithe rebounded off the wing and dove for the moth's head. She caught one of his antennae and vaulted high into the air. As she descended upon the hissing snake, a buzzing sound filled her ears.

In a blur of motion, Oleander came out of nowhere, snatched her up, and lifted her into the sky. He carried her so high that she found breathing difficult and fighting nearly impossible. "Please," he implored her. "You mustn't kill the Atlas."

The G-forces made her head pound, and every word she attempted to say failed. Oleander decelerated and began a slow descent. "I know you were only defending yourself against what you saw as a threat, but Attacus was doing the same." His wings hummed as they beat an unseen rhythm. "I cannot allow you to kill him, for the world would, most assuredly, collapse. There are very few of his kind left, and they are the ones who hold the world together." As he hovered about Attacus's head, he spoke in a calm whisper, and Lithe could not make out the words.

Slowly, the giant Atlas returned to a more manageable size. Oleander produced an axe, a long staff, and a mandolin from his cape. "I believe these are yours," he said to Lithe and Munder. "I promised to return them. I wrongfully assumed you would not need them. I was unaware of Emperor Saturn's intentions."

He strolled over to the chrysalis and placed a firm hand upon it. "He meant well, I suppose, in his plan to help the larvae. However, he hid his own amulet's power from us all those years, instead of using it for the good of our people."

Oleander patted the head of Munder's larva-friend and said, "This is the larva of the Brahma. When it matures, you will find that it is more magnificent than any other moth. I dare say it will be more marvelous than the *Fairfalla* of old.

Long ago, the Brahmae were the holy-moths of the *Fellfalla*, for only they could fly to the heavens."

"So," said Munder at last, "what do we do with the timepiece?"

"Emperor Saturn must not have it," said Lithe. "It is too dangerous."

"I agree," said Oleander. "Though I wish it could be used to help the larvae, I am sure more ill would come of it."

After a moment's thought, Lithe said, "Perhaps we can find another way to help your larvae. The man responsible for the alteration of time is Aori Timister. We seek to put an end to his madness once and for all."

"Good," Oleander replied. "I would be glad to offer my services, when the time comes. However, at present, there is much to fix in these lands. I would like the Empire to thrive as it did in the days of the Kingdom. We can never bring back the dead *Fairfalla*, but perhaps we can live more in tune with their ways. Above all else, we will rebuild our relations with the Coda!"

Behind them, a group of moths beat their wings together in celebration. "All hail Oleander!" they shouted in the *Fellfallan* tongue. The Odestone vibrated and Lithe understood their words of praise.

One of the Hawk moths of the Imperial Guard stepped forward. She had a similar pattern, but her features were more slender and feminine. "You have won the respect of the Empire, brother. They have been oppressed by Emperor Saturn for far too long!"

Attacus started to grow again out of loyalty to his emperor, but Oleander stopped him. "Daphni is right, Attacus. You needn't defend him any longer. Saturn's day has passed."

S-a-t-u-r-d-a-y Night!

As a result, the day when the emperor was deposed became
known as "Saturn's Day," which eventually led to the name
"Saturday." Of course, some bickering about the day's origin
came about hundreds of years later on Earth, where the name
is traced back to the Roman god Saturn. One might find it
interesting that the Roman Saturn is the same as the Greek
Cronos, and both are depicted as long-bearded gods of time
and harvest. Whether or not their Saturn was named after the
Fellfallan emperor remains to be discovered, but the link
between Emperor Saturn and the time-god of this story is very
clear.

Chapter 3:14

Riddle of the Sphinx

"My liege," Harold honored Oleander with a formal bow and folded-wing salute.

"Please, Harold. Rise. I am not royalty. The parties that deserve the praise here are these two." Oleander gestured towards Lithe and Munder. Without his imperial helm, he seemed a much more personable fellow. His long, elegant hair matched the green of his wings and armor. While most *Fellfalla* had eyes of one solid color with no distinction between pupil, iris or white, various shades of green swirled in Oleander's eyes.

"Perhaps you *should* be king," said the Herald. "You are one of the few noble moths left in this land."

Oleander shook his head. "I think we should let the public decide who Saturn's successor will be. They have been ignored for too long."

The Herald spoke, "I will gather my finest, fastest moths. We will spread the word around the land and gauge their response."

"Gather the Heralds, but I have another task for you. It requires a moth of great speed, and I remember many races of old when you gave me quite a challenge." Oleander smiled and patted Harold on the shoulder. He hesitated, and the smile quickly faded.

"What is the task, my lord?"

He spoke very softly, but he could not escape Lithe's keen hearing. "Find her," he whispered. "Tell Lymantria her exile has been removed and she is free to return whenever she pleases."

Harold nodded. "With all my speed, Emperor Oleander of the Nerii." With a salute to the rest of the party, he launched into the sky like a rocket.

Oleander turned to Lithe. "I am sorry to have taken up so much of your time. I will take you at once to the Great Sphinx. He is very ancient and wise in the ways of the *Fellfalla*, whereas most of us are but a few years old. It is a rather long voyage, but we Nerii can make it in no time."

The former imperial guards, who became known as the Hawk-Knights of the Nerii, prepared the supplies for the trip. Lithe and Munder were outfitted with helmets to stabilize their breathing and armor to cut down on the pressure of gravity. Daphni, the new emperor's sister, gathered a small band of knights to accompany Lithe and Munder on their quest-within-a-journey-within-a-quest.

Munder gripped the former emperor's chrysalis like a football. He made several references to 20th century American quarterbacks, but the anachronisms were lost on all those around him. Along with the chrysalis came the Brahma caterpillar, which eagerly draped itself across Munder's shoulders like a feather boa.

"You seem to have found a friend, Munder," Lithe joked as she helped him with his *Fellfallan* armor. Munder patted the caterpillar on its head.

As the knights soared over a great portion of the Aian landscape, Lithe's stone lore-master and father attempted to act as a travel guide, but he vibrated so slowly that, by the time he explained everything about the decimated forests of Pavonia, they had passed far from the borders of the *Fellfallan*

Empire. Every forest, river, ocean, and mountain zipped past them in a blur of speed.

They crossed a vast ocean, which eventually met up with a sandy beach. The sand continued long after the shoreline had passed out of sight. Situated amidst the dry desert sands, they came across a very black body of water, which the Odestone identified as the Dead Sea. "It is so deep," he vibrated, "the people here believe that it stretches to the Underworld...or further."

As they descended, they could feel the heat radiate upward, giving the illusion of wavy serpents dancing on the sand. "It is very hot here throughout the year," explained the Odestone. "This is one place where the shifts in seasons have had little effect."

The *Fellfallan* knights landed and Daphni said, "We must rest. No energy." The long flight had severely taxed them, and they rested in utter silence for many minutes. When they spoke, they used very few words and always in the *Fellfallan* language.

Munder grew impatient and began playing in the sand like a child. He built a sand castle, which he later remodeled into the *Fellfallan* palace. After that, he worked as if possessed. He created two tall towers with clocks at the top. Lithe and the moths gathered around him in amazement.

Lithe felt like she knew the answer, but she asked, "What are you building, Munder?"

Munder looked down at his creation, as if it should be obvious. "The Grandfather Clocks of the Time Lord. Aori lives there. That is where we must go. Quickly." He rose to his feet and stomped the structure into a pile of sand.

"We will," said Lithe. "First, however, we must find this Sphinx. Hopefully, he can tell us where to find Quondam."

Daphni looked around. "I am uncertain as to where the Sphinx lives. Our records indicate that his temple was once on this seashore. I see nothing now."

"Maybe it blew away," said Munder as he blew a handful of sand from his palm. He went back to work playing in the sand, while the others looked around for some clues.

"There was a great civilization here, at one time," the Odestone vibrated. "The Agypsians were a people of lasting presence. Tempo looked fondly on them for many eons. It appears that the sands of Time have now covered them completely."

Lithe looked puzzled. "Why would Tempo have forsaken his chosen people?" The knights, who had not heard the Odestone's explanation-vibration, thought the question rather odd and unfounded.

"She's talking to her rock," Munder explained. "And it's talking back to her. In case you were wondering, the answer is 'yes, we have all gone insane.'"

Everyone looked at Munder, who added, "What? What did I say this time?"

Munder followed their gazes to his sand sculptures, which depicted an entire Agypsian civilization. In the center stood a grand pyramid with a strange lionesque creature at its foot. "Did I do that?" he asked.

There came a great rumbling under the ground, and the moths defensively took to the air. Munder's sand pyramid got larger and larger, until at last, it stood full-size on the barren sand. It stretched for quite a distance on all four sides, and the enormous lion looked very intimidating with its giant human head.

A large door slid open in the lion's torso, beckoning them to enter. Nervously, they stepped into the belly of the great beast and walked down a dark passage. They came to a chamber lit with several torches. The walls were covered with strange pictures, which seemed to depict a story of some sort. Seated in a broken, eroded throne, a mummified corpse filled the air with the stench of death.

Suddenly, the corpse rose to its feet, disturbing the cobwebs and dust that had settled on it for hundreds of years. It opened its mouth to speak, and hundreds of tiny moths fluttered out of it. Even the brave Hawk Knights were startled, and shivers ran down spines. "What do you seek?" It spoke a dead language in a withered, decaying voice, and only the Odestone fully understood.

"We seek the great Sphinx," answered Lithe after interpreting the stone's translation. Her voice, too, sounded dusty and old, and the others could not understand her words. She was holding the Odestone to her voice box, and her father was speaking for her.

"The Sphingidian Moth is many years deceased," replied the mummy. "You should not have come here. There is only death and disease in the land of Agyp."

"We seek answers only the Sphinx can give," Ode continued.

In the mummy's silence, Munder listlessly surveyed the chamber. He looked at the pictures on the walls, which showed many dark birds gathered around a dead body in a coffin. On one side of the coffin stood a man with a raven's head and feet. A great moth stood on the other side. Munder immediately recognized the man/moth as the one that took Quondam. Its haunting countenance made the blood drain from Munder's face. "Hey!" he shouted. "This is the moth."

The others gathered around to get a better look. The knights discussed the nightmares of their larva stages and agreed that this had been the moth that plagued their most frightening dreams.

The mummy fell back into its rotted throne. "The Sphinx will see you now." A passage opened between the pictures of the moth and raven. Torches lined the walkway, and they saw more pictures of birds and moths on the walls. At the end of a long hall, a cross-like symbol with a loop at the top glistened in the firelight.

"The symbol is an Ankh," Ode explained with Lithe's voice. "It is the symbol of the great cycle of life, death, and rebirth."

A voice echoed through the chamber. "You know much of what is ancient and long-dead." What seemed to be another corpse slowly shuffled out of a tomb. Its worn, tattered clothing draped about its body in many layers and dragged along the floor. Cobwebs and dust covered the fur of its face, and its antennae sagged with age.

"The Sphinx," gasped several voices in unison.

Its voice creaked again, "I will give you the answers you seek." He paused. "But first, you must answer me this riddle: What walks on four legs early in the morning, two legs during the day, and three legs in the evening?"

The Odestone vibrated excitedly. "Man!" Ode shouted with Lithe's voice. Lithe added, "Or Woman. Early in life, she crawls on all fours. As she grows up, she walks on two legs. And, at the evening of her life, she must use a cane or staff to walk; that is the third leg."

The Sphinx spread its rotted wings and a cloud of sand blew around the room. His uncovered body could be seen as that of a lion with matted fur. Several dusty moths fluttered about in a flurry of excitement. The Sphinx creaked, "That is true." Everyone breathed a sigh of relief. "However," its voice echoed, "that is not the answer I was looking for. Does anyone care to elaborate on that?"

"Elaborate?" scoffed Ode. "That's the whole answer!"

"No," said Munder. "Here's the answer: The riddle describes the man we're looking for: Quondam. He is the crawling child, the walking man, and the old cripple all at once. He is the Man of Yesterday and Tomorrow."

The Sphinx's face creaked and cracked as a smile spread across it. "I knew, one day, the answer would come. Now, I may rest." He folded down his wings and rested back in his sarcophagus. Little did he know that his riddling services would be required thousands of years later on Earth, when he met the future King Oedipus of Thebes. Furthermore, his spirit would live on every time that riddle was asked, and his image would be seen everywhere from the pyramids of Egypt to the casinos of Las Vegas.

"You can't rest yet," shouted Munder. "You have to tell us where Quondam is!"

The Sphinx's eyes creaked open again. "My apologies. I thought you knew all of the answers, Riddle-Solver." He wrapped his tattered wings around his body and got comfortable. "Your friend is dead."

Everyone in the room stopped breathing. The Sphinx continued. "The moth that took him was Acheron, the Death's Head."

The knights whispered the name nervously, finally able to identify the horror of their larval nightmares. If they knew its name, it would have less power over them.

"Quondam is in the land of Death, now. All your trouble has been in vain."

A different kind of summer had arrived.

PART 4

SUMMER

Chapter 4:00

Summertime and the Dying is Easy

Aian religions, throughout history, vary similarly to those on Earth. Religion has always been (and will be until the end of recorded history) a point of contention between living things. Wars have been fought over beliefs for as long as anyone can remember, and for those of us who are blessed with Hindsight, that's a long time.

For the purpose of historical discussion, I must remain as religiously unbiased as possible. Of course, I was raised Church of Chronos, which is just an offshoot of Timism, which holds Time up as a supreme being. Notice, here, that I did not write *the* Supreme Being, as Timists rarely name Toki or Tempo as the Creator. Some other being started writing the song and he just set the tempo.

While the discussion of religion throughout the ages is one that fascinates me to the very core of my being, our focus must remain specifically on Aian religion insofar as it relates to this story. I do not wish to generate a great existential debate on evolution vs. creationism in and of themselves; this is the history of Aia and its evolutionary creation.

Aians have many different stories for how the planet was created, and I have seen enough to judge most of the stories as fairly accurate. The closest and most widely-shared story involves a seed, enough energy to germinate the seed, and the continuous, cyclical distribution of that energy throughout multitudes of other life-forms. Some believe the Supreme Being to be a mighty tree, upon which Aia is a fruit or nut. Obviously, those believers are also quite fond of Asalie. In fact, they believe her to be a goddess, which brings us to the next point.

Polytheism is the belief in many gods. Most polytheistic pantheons have a main, patriarchal god that rules over lesser deities. The interesting thing about polytheism is its compartmentalized nature. The hierarchy of gods on Aia, for instance, has the central god delegating several responsibilities to his/her/its workforce. Asalie is the goddess of the dawn, while the god of the sunset is Finis. There is a god of war and a goddess of peace, as well as gods of happiness, depression, and that feeling you get after a good, hearty meal. There is a goddess of the hunt, the midday feast, and I've even heard of some who pray to a different deity for each other meal of the day. Really, they can get quite unbelievable, these beliefs. There came a time in Aian history when regular old humans were just declaring themselves the god of this, that, or the other, and thereby starting their own religions.

It is considered, by most cultures, to be more sophisticated to worship one deity who is, in turn, in charge of every little thing in the universe, from breakfast to dinner and everything in between. For the purpose of telling this story, however, let us just go ahead and label Aia as unsophisticated. Regardless of the true source of their beliefs, Aians worshipped their gods and goddesses and told stories about them, which gave them power. All anyone needs to be a god is one follower.

Asalie had many followers. Many believed her to be the reason why the planet had seasons. In truth, she was a wanderer, and she did possess many powers over the forces of nature. It was said that, without Asalie, the sun would not rise in the morning. Of course, it has become obvious that the sun "rises" because of the planet's rotation, which contradicts many fine stories of deities carrying the sun across the sky.

It is fact, however, that Asalie is at her most powerful in the early morning and Finis is strongest at dusk. Theoretically, if, in her wanderings, Asalie could walk fast enough to keep up with the sunrise, she would always be at the peak of her power.

Now, are these beings the source of the power? It seems that they are not, and Part 4 of this tale will shed more light on that subject. However, let it be known that on Aia, and on several other planets, it becomes necessary for mankind to deify one of their own. The gods work in such mysterious ways that, to truly understand them, we have to humanize them or bring them into the material world in one way or another. Some religions have inanimate objects as idols, while others make humans into idols. On Aia, Aori Timister was waking up to the idea that he, too, was a god in human form.

Of course, there are others who believe that Asalie, Finis, and Aori were all completely insane. Perhaps the gods were not working through them or condescending to a human level so as to be more reachable. However, with the Hindsight of the history of all religions, it is rather nice to have this material connection to the spiritual world.

If you find this sort of religious discussion interesting, you might also be interested to know that, quite ironically, the First Unified Church of Aia, was founded during Aia's final summer. For about a day of real time, every single religion on Aia came together in peace and loving harmony under the unified prospect that the end of the world wouldn't be such a swell idea.

Chapter 4:01

Life Lessons from
a Goddess of Life

Bertram, or the mechanical construction Aori called
Bertram, rang a loud bell to rouse his master. Aori jaunted
back to the normal flow of time with a start. Coming out of a
self-induced, time-halting coma was enough to cause a rather
large headache. "How long was I out that time?"

"A whole season has come and gone," came the reply.

"Really, which one?" Aori said groggily.

"Spring."

Aori flinched at the unfamiliar voice. It didn't sound like
Bertram's, or even the strange, unexplained simulation of a
voice that he had come to recognize from the robot. Someone else was speaking through the replica of his former
friend.

"Spring is my absolute favorite of Time's manipulations.
You have ruined it."

Aori panicked as he noticed that his arms and legs were
bound to his chair. It was as if the wood of the chair had
grown and rooted him in one place. "What is going on here?
Bertram?"

Bertram looked at him helplessly as vines and roots choked off all of his moving parts. Weeds sprouted between his seams and tore through the metal plates as if they were tough soil. Asalie's form grew out of the woodwork. Her skin looked as if it were completely made of wood and living plants. Her eyebrows were moss, and her eyes were flowers.

"Who are you?" Aori screamed.

"I am Growth incarnate," said Asalie. "I am Birth and Rebirth. I am the Dawn."

"You make the sun rise?"

"So they say," Asalie hedged.

"But, do *they* know that the sun does not actually rise? Rather, the planet revolves around it. Therefore, if you make the sun rise, you would spend your entire existence making it rise in different parts of Aia. In fact, shouldn't you be doing that somewhere right now?"

Asalie smiled despite Aori's assault. "So, the trapped fox now growls at its captor. You cannot hope to escape your bonds with insults, villain!"

"You call *me* a villain? Did I come into your home and attack you?"

"Yes," said Asalie. "The very wood that makes your home was stolen from mine! Your mechanical minions have pillaged the entire planet. There is not a single *asa* still standing!"

Aori looked shaken, but said, "They are but trees. They will grow back."

"Do not tell me of growth, Aori Timister!" she shouted in a booming voice. Aori cowered in his chair. "Impertinent beast! I have lived with the trees for thousands of years. I have watched them grow. In a few seconds' time, you wiped out several millennia of hard work!"

Aori looked far away, as if he could see his past actions in retrospect. "I… things seem to have slipped out of control." He paused for many minutes and contemplated his situation for many hours of his personal time. "It seems so long ago. I was so young and brazen then." He looked up at

Asalie imploringly. "Look at all I have done, though! I have done several millennia of hard work in a few seconds' time!"

Asalie's face resumed its wizened, nurturing look. She looked upon Aori as a grandmother would an errant grandchild; his actions were ill advised, but she loved him unconditionally. "You have done much, Aori." She gazed out the window and surveyed his manufacturing plants, libraries, roads, irrigation systems, and mechanical workers. "You have taken the Life out of Creation, Aori. You have soulless automatons working in factories to mass-produce other soulless creations. Nothing here has breath… or Life!"

Aori looked upon the lifeless Bertram-contraption, which was now teeming with living vines and flowers. He thought of the musical instruments he built, and how their music had been useless in returning his deceased friends and family to him. The utter absence of life reflected brightly in his eyes, and he wept.

Suddenly, a large group of clockworkers rushed into the room and cast a clinging, metal net around Asalie. She put up no resistance. "Do they act upon your will, Aori?" His tears continued, and Asalie finished, "I wonder. It seems they have taken on a life of their own, and you aren't even sure what your will is."

Sun Gods a Plenty

Various Aian civilizations believed in a number of different sun gods. As we have seen earlier, there was Asalie (though not all civilizations called her that), who was born every day at dawn, and the god of dusk, who watched as the sun set. However, many also believed in Zenith, a goddess who represented the sun at its peak. Of course, since the sun actually remained in a relatively fixed position while the planet revolved around it, the powers of these gods and goddesses were probably a bit exaggerated over the years. Time has a way of elaborating on a story.

As snow melted on the peaks of the Orchestral Mountains, a lone bird of ebon pinions soared on the wings of deliverance. Its flight spiraled downward, and the bird landed on the torn and mangled frame of Mantra. The bird picked at Mantra's bones and sensed the stench of puss and dust on his remains.

"Moths," said Crowfoot. "Always an ill omen." He noticed several melted bloodstains on the snow and ice. "There were others here." When he had gathered all the available clues and still could not divine any answers, he spread his great wings and covered the area in darkness. The darkness absorbed the spirits of the Codan monk and the decaying puss moth; then, it faded, and only the faint sound of flapping wings could be heard.

Meanwhile, a similar darkness hovered about the lone Coda, Solo. There were no shadows at this time of day, so his dark shroud looked totally out of place. The speed of the train made it difficult to keep his grip, but his long, slender fingers and tail managed to find seams between the "dragon's" metal scales.

An image in the distance seemed to grow larger by the second. Two grand towers shot up into the clouds. Like two great gnomons on a sundial, their shadows (or lack thereof) reflected the position of the sun in the sky. It was at its zenith.

Solo stared up at the goddess Zenith and said, in a hushed whisper, "I will wait until nightfall. Then, I shall tear this train apart and free my fellow Coda!" As the train began to slow down, that plan seemed to shrivel up like a raisin in the sun.

The two clocktowers were now very close, and Solo could see a bustle of activity all around them. People from foreign lands worked beside the metal men at several different projects. Some labored in barren fields, while others mined for ore. No one seemed to stop for rest.

The train's wheels sang as the metal of the brakes, wheels, and tracks scraped together. The train's song hurt Solo's sensitive ears and sounded out like an alarm in his head. Quickly, he made his move. Knowing he would not have time to free all of the Coda before the train stopped, he resolved to escape into the nearby woods and wait until dark.

The train was still moving when Solo jumped. His legs wavered like two thin willow branches, and he rolled several times to cushion the blow. He crawled on his belly, so as to attract less attention, and ducked behind a small tree. Much of the nearby forests had been cut down and used in buildings, so Solo found cover to be rather scarce.

The clockworkers opened the train cars and led the Coda out of Solo's sight. "I will save you," he vowed. "Even if I have to take on an entire metal army alone, I will save you."

Nearby, a rather large cat rolled its eyes and sighed.

Like a solemn marching band, the Coda prisoners lined up outside Aori's tower. The clockworkers put half of them to work as a sort of chain gang, while the other half was sent to meet Aori. One by one, they were escorted into the elevator, which lifted them to the top of the great clocktower.

"Welcome!" Aori greeted an elderly female Coda. With a smile, he said, "I hope your voyage here was not too uncomfortable. I am afraid that in our haste, we neglected to make the trains very hospitable. In the future, we will try to add sleeping and dining cars."

The Coda stared at him in wonder. "Oh!" he exclaimed. "Where is my head?" He continued, in the Codan language, "I suppose you didn't understand a word of that. Well, suffice to say, it is good to have you here, finally. Come."

Aori led her to a dark, stuffy room with a horrible odor. He lit several candles, which revealed a rotting corpse set upon an altar. The stench of death permeated the room, and Aori mumbled, "I'm afraid the smell is quite unpleasant. One day, we will have air filters to rid us of this odor." A handkerchief covered his mouth and nose, thereby muffling his words.

Aori's similarly lifeless music-machines shared Bertram's tomb. "You are to do…whatever it is you do to bring him back. Sing, play instruments; work your magic." He paused, waiting for her to begin. "I'm sorry," he said. "What is your name?"

Very softly, the Coda sang, "P... Piano."

"Pretty name. Now, Piano? Please. Time is of the essence." He walked out of the room and shut the door.

"It won't work," said a familiar voice.

"Yes, it will, Bertram."

"You're taking birds out of their natural habitats and expecting them to still sing as sweetly as before. Whether it's a caged bird or a Coda in captivity, the song is just as sad."

Aori sighed. "Please don't argue with me, Bertram. I'm doing this for you."

"Really, Aori. I'd rather you didn't say such things. For one thing, I'm not Bertram."

Aori grabbed Bertram's hand and pulled it to his face. The sweet smell of flowers filled his nostrils and erased any memory of the stench of death. He studied his friend's face, which was made up of bits of rusted metal mingled with wood and vines. "Bertram," was all he could say.

"Aori, you mustn't carry on so," Asalie's voice echoed through Bertram's flower-petal lips. "It is not healthy. Your friend has joined the cycle of Life. His life-force is now swirling around in the Great Spiral. But, he will return in a different form, Aori. Everything revolves."

"I need him now, Asalie. I need them all."

"Aori, what happens to the rain after it falls?"

"The sun causes it to evaporate."

"Yes. Then, it gathers in the clouds, gets heavier, and the rain falls again. You know of this cycle. So, too, turns the cycle of Life. The moons may die, but they return, do they not?"

Aori snickered. "If your silly allegory is meant to cheer me up, congratulations."

"Oh yes, I forgot. This one cannot think metaphorically. Must everything be concrete—and mechanical—for you?"

"Leave that Romanticism for Dolente and the others. The moons do not die. Our perspective of them changes as Aia spins."

"And they revolve around Aia, correct?"

"Yes. And they aren't seeds, as the legends tell."

Asalie smiled. "You wish to cast away all of the beliefs that have supported me all these years?"

"Ah, so you are the one who planted them? You are a tree?"

Leaves sprouted from Asalie's hair and fingertips. Her fingers grew into long branches. "Is that so hard to believe?"

"Yes. Trees do not walk or talk."

"I am not a tree now, Aori. I was reborn. I am reborn every day. Life begins at dawn. You should remember that."

"Why? It is a lie. I wake up older and older every day." He ran his finger along the wrinkled furrows of his face. "I have seen many dawns pass by, even as my eyesight withers and fades."

"Perhaps your sight left you long ago, for you are blind."

Aori's eyes narrowed. "Am I blind, because I refuse to see your truth? I am not willing to blindly accept the beliefs of others, and yet you call *me* blind? Nay, old woman. Those sheep that use the folklore and legends of others to construct their reality—they are the blind ones."

"How do you explain the recent events? How have you altered the course of Time itself, Aori?"

Aori considered his answer carefully. "Magic. Magic is an art; you perform tricks with growing things. I work my magic on the minutes and seconds."

"*Your* magic?" She massaged her brow, and the vines of her fingers began to entwine themselves with her hair. "Aori, you speak in contradictions. You wish to take no responsibility for what has happened; yet you say your magic caused the shortness of seasons. You claim that you are not a villain, but if you are not, who is?"

"Time."

"Time distorted itself? How can a concept, like Truth or Beauty, distort itself?"

"It is not a concept. It is a person... a wizard. He gave me this power."

Asalie paused to let Aori's words settle. "He is a god, Aori. You are a puppet, and he is the puppeteer. You are his scapegoat—he does whatever he pleases, and the people of Aia blame you."

"They do? But, I am just a man. I will pass on and no one will remember me!"

"No, Aori. You have made a name for yourself. Your influence will be remembered, I assure you!"

Aori grimaced at being thought of as a villain by the entire world, but a small flame flickered inside his brain. *I will live forever in their minds*, he thought. *Long after I have grown old and died, they will know the name Aori! They will remember all that I have done!* He turned his back on Asalie, and a wry grin spread across his face.

Chapter 4:02

The Living Embodiment of Death Lightens the Mood

"Wake up, boy."

"I can't," coughed Quondam. "I'm dead."

"You can't be dead, boy. It isn't your time."

Quondam tried to open his eyes, but he had the feeling of being in a dream, with no control over his physical body. At that thought, a third eye opened in his forehead, and he could see things beyond the physical. His own body, or the astral representation of it, was that of his eight-year old form. "Where am I? Is this Heaven?"

"What do Aians know of Heaven? That is an idea created on Earth."

"I must have my times crossed," said Quondam. "Munder's rubbed off on me, I suppose." He looked around, but saw nothing except swirling spirals. "Where am I?"

"Tweentime... and Tweenspace a bit too, I suppose...."

Quondam panicked and fumbled for footing to escape. "Toki? Did you pull me here again, you foul--?"

"I am not Toki, boy." An old man appeared, and though he vaguely resembled the Time god, Quondam thought he looked a bit more familiar.

"You're me? But how?"

"I'm an older you," said the older Quondam. "I thought, since none of us is currently occupying your body, that this would be a good time to come and give you some advice. But, we don't have much time," he continued. "Aori comes here often now, and if Toki spots us...."

The old man led Quondam up a spiral staircase and down a hall with many windows. Each window showed a variation of the same event; a great war, with beings of all sorts in the mix. As he looked upon the windows, Quondam was reminded of the television sets in Toki's palace. The connection made him uncomfortable.

"Be at ease, boy," the older Quondam consoled. "I know what you're thinking, and you needn't fear Time."

"But, he wanted me to be his puppet," the eight-year-old said.

"Better you than *him*," the elder replied. He pointed at an image of a much older Aori. The elder Quondam continued, "You would have saved Aia, boy. You still could, if you act quickly."

"What must I do?"

"Use your timepiece. It can turn back the age of Aia, just as it turns back your own age. Of course, you may have to give in to some god-given powers." As he spoke, his image seemed to fade into the swirling background, along with the windows and the staircase. Before it faded completely, he continued, "At least, that's what *I* would have done. Hindsight is 20/20, they say."

"So, do I still have time? Or am I destined to fail, because you did?"

Quondam's only answer was the distant flutter of wings, which drew closer and finally stopped altogether.

Acheron the Death's Head stood resolutely over Quondam's burial chamber. The cold, stale air reeked of death, but none of the denizens of this underworld seemed to mind. The breath of Life had left them, taking with it all sense of smell. There was no fire and brimstone in this underworld; in fact, the place was rather dull. Aside from the Gothic architecture and morbid décor, the place was mainly darkness and void.

Of course, there was a rather large screen and rows of chairs as one would find in a movie theatre, but none of the seats reclined and every view of the screen seemed to be blocked by either a morbidly obese woman or a fellow in a large cowboy hat. In addition, the floors were very, very sticky. Instead of popcorn and abandoned soft drink cups, however, the floor was littered with bones and decayed remains of living things.

Quondam felt rather uncomfortable in his chair, but who said the afterlife was supposed to be comfortable? Actually, many have said that. At any rate, Quondam tried to see the screen, but a couple of giant moth wings blocked his view. He reached for his sword, but found only a withered, dead twig.

"Nothing grows here," said some character in the movie that was projecting on the screen. "You're dead. You only think you're alive."

"I can move," said Quondam. His voice sounded very dull and lifeless. "I can speak...in a manner of speaking." Since he couldn't see the screen, he looked around the room. In the distance, he saw a strange light flashing.

An usher moved up and down the aisles with a flashlight in his hand. His words seemed important, but Quondam could not hear a word. He wondered briefly if he were in the wrong seat. Would he be asked to move? Could he?

He rose from his seat and stood up as tall as he could, but he still could not see past the immense form of the Death's Head moth. The pale face of Death stared back at him, and a shiver ran along his spine.

"That's what it feels like when someone walks over your grave," said the actor on the screen.

"But, I don't have a grave," said Quondam. "I'm not dead."

"That's what they all say."

Quondam tried to move his feet, but they were stuck firmly to the floor. Someone next to him shouted "FIRE!" Confusion and chaos erupted in the cramped theatre, and everyone attempted to escape the flames.

However, there were only two doors. One, Quondam could see, had a very bright light behind it. The other seemed to open up to more fire. People were running madly in both directions, but Quondam stood motionless, unable to move his feet. The usher was shouting orders and directing people to the exit, but he spoke in some language Quondam could not understand.

As the flames licked at his skin, his memory returned with a vengeance. He felt the all-consuming heat and remembered his "death" at the hands of the moth. "I was taken into the flames," he mumbled. "But, I don't remember dying. Did I burn?"

Acheron did not respond. Quondam continued, "You were the one who brought me here. Where am I? Answer me!" He held the dead twig in both hands and felt some unknown power inside him grow. The twig began to change into a large, wooden sword.

Quondam thrust the sword into the face of Death and Acheron's body scattered into many smaller moths. As the moths fluttered and burned in the flames, Quondam could see the screen. Several successive images flashed so rapidly that he could barely distinguish one from the next. He saw a lone figure with its arms spread like a bird's wings. As the projector focused, Quondam could see that the figure writhed in pain, and its wrists were pinned to a long plank of wood.

Other images followed. Quondam saw stillborn babies, diseased rats, hundreds of bodies piled atop one another, and all sorts of horrible murders in several frames per second. Images of wholesale death accompanied those of lampshades made of skin and various knick-knacks composed of bones. "Death will outlive us all," said the voiceover in the deep, commanding tone of a movie trailer. A picture of a large, black bird filled the screen, and the projector shut off.

The flames erupted and Quondam struggled to free himself from the sticky floor. The fire burned everything around him, but he felt no pain. The next thing he knew, he was underwater, and he could see that the light of the surface was very far away.

Suddenly, sharp talons grasped his shoulders and carried him out of the abyss. A great blackbird cawed, and Quondam understood it to say, "This one does not belong here." Feelings of alienation weighed him down more than the water that soaked him, as he felt alone and out of place.

Something about the blackbird struck him as strangely familiar. Quondam wiped the water from his eyes, and his fingers lingered on the wrinkles beside his eyes. "Crow's feet," he said aloud. "Crowfoot."

"Yes?" cawed the blackbird.

"Have we met before, Crowfoot?"

"Yes. You were the Demon-Sorcerer I fought as a boy."

Quondam struggled with the memory, as if he were seeing it through a deep body of water. "Leafblower" was all that came to mind.

"Alas, my tribe has been scattered, much like the leaves they blew. I shall find all their spirits someday. They were all killed in battle." He told Quondam of the fall of the Leaf-blower tribe at the hands of the Army of the Anachronist.

"I am sorry for your loss."

"The blackbird feels no loss, Child of the Morning and the Evening," whispered a diminutive figure as it stepped out of the darkness.

"I found him in the river Lethe," the blackbird cawed.

"Do you wish to leave the past behind, Quondam? The water will make you forget all your worries and concerns. It is usually reserved for the Dead, but we seem to be making all sorts of exceptions today."

"Who are you?" Quondam asked.

"I am Finis, the End, Death Incarnate, or the End of All Things, if you're not into the whole brevity thing. Most people just call me Finis."

Far from one's imagination of a grim reaper, Finis stood roughly four feet tall with a svelte and wiry frame. His dark eyes sank deep inside his skull, and an ashen grey layer of skin hung from his bones loosely. Despite his skeleton-like appearance, he glowed with a lively spirit.

"What am I doing here?"

Finis replied, "I summoned you here, where all things go after death. Come. I shall explain everything."

They passed through several dimly lit tombs. At the end of a long hallway, Quondam saw the Death's Head moth. He drew his sword and ran towards it. Acheron's tattered wings spread, and he held a large axe in both hands. Bones of long-dead warriors composed the handle of the axe, and the Death's Head emblem stared out from the wide blade. Many of Life's most stalwart champions had fallen to the Axe of the Death's Head.

Fearlessly, Quondam rushed his opponent and slashed wildly. Acheron listlessly let his axe fall, and Quondam deflected the blade with his wooden sword. They fought like bitter enemies for what might have been hours in the land of the living.

"By all means, continue to fight," said Finis. "You'll never defeat him, Quondam. Acheron is the Moth of the Death's Head. Do you really think you can kill him?" Finis laughed a deep, hollow laugh. "He is already dead. You'd have to fight to the life."

Quondam lowered his weapon. Finis continued, "He is not your enemy anyway, Quondam. None of us are. Whenever anyone thinks of Death, they automatically think we're evil. That's just not the case. I mean, sure, some spirits of Death are bad news—you wouldn't want to mess with those guys. But here, we're just doing our jobs. We work the graveyard shift, you see." The echo of his words faded to silence. "That's my little joke." Silence enveloped them like a death shroud. "What, a god of Death can't be funny?"

"So you're the god of Death?" asked Quondam.

"Don't sound so surprised, kid. But, I'm not *the* god; I'm *a* god of Death. Really I'm more of a deified man." In a loud, important-sounding voice, he proclaimed, "I am Death Incarnate; I am the Living Embodiment of Death." He cocked his head to the side proudly. "We like those contradictions. Did you know your buddy Asalie's dying? She's the Dying Embodiment of Life. I just really get a kick out of that. It's a killer."

Quondam turned his head away to deny the news. "She's not dying. Asalie *is* Life."

Finis looked at him as one does a naïve child. "We're all dying, Quondam. Everything decays."

Like a devoted believer in Asalie's rhetoric, Quondam continued, "Everything revolves in the great cycle of Life."

"The cycle is a downward spiral, kiddo. We're all headed down the drain."

"But... I have seen so much growth in the world."

"Flowers may bloom, but they all wilt in the End. Fruits rot even while they're still on the vine. This whole planet is rotting. You of all people should see the changes. When you got so old your brain began to rot, did you not see Death coming for you? Dirge saw it in you, as did Crowfoot, remember? Did you think you were growing then, boy?

"Death happens to the best of us. It took your parents and your parents' parents. Of course, the Timisters have a way of putting Death off for a while. Speaking of which, how are things between you and the old time god? Has he got you doing his dirty work?"

"I...I do not work for him."

"I've said the same thing myself, kiddo, but I'm always here to catch them when they fall. The corpses, I mean. This is hallowed ground. Every grave in the world is connected to us here. Crowfoot and Acheron handle their souls. The moth likes the way they taste."

Quondam shook his head. "What is wrong with you? How can you be so callous? I may look young at times, but I have seen more than my share of death. It is never, ever humorous!"

"Wait," said Finis. "Imagine this scenario: What if a thief painted his face to avoid recognition, and died of lead poisoning from the paint? See? An ironic death can be humorous."

Quondam was not amused.

Finis crossed his arms. His face turned a bit sterner. "Fine. Death is nothing to be taken lightly. I see, now, the error of my ways. You have enlightened me." His skin grew very pale, and a faint glow seemed to emanate from within him. "You think you have seen Death? Show us! Teach us about Death, Quondam!"

The entire tomb was bathed in the dull glow, and suddenly things that had been still for centuries began to move. Bones scraped along the stone floor to find other bones. Worms oozed out of cracks in the walls and congregated on the floor. The silent, lifeless tomb suddenly buzzed with life.

A reconstituted skeleton rose to its feet and walked toward Quondam. Soon, another skeleton accompanied it. The decomposed stitches of clothing that remained barely distinguished them as male and female. "Recognize them?" asked Finis.

"N-no," Quondam answered, obviously shaken.

"You will." Several other lifeless corpses rose from the tombs. Some seemed to grow out of the fresh soil like withered trees. Many of the corpses retained enough semblances of their lives to seem familiar to Quondam. He recognized Limbender and the chieftain-king of the Leaf-blower tribe, though their flesh had decayed considerably. Several bodies seemed to belong to soldiers of Munder's battalions.

Finis spoke in a solemn voice. "Now, do you recognize them? You have seen Death in your short life, Quondam.

You have also caused it!" As if empowered by their master's voice, the corpses marched toward Quondam. Some seemed rather disoriented and frightened by the whole situation, but the undead Army of the Anachronist drew their swords, clubs, or guns and attacked.

Quondam defended with his wooden sword, and he found that death had slowed his opponents considerably. He was wounded, but his body would not shift to other ages. "Nothing grows here," echoed in his mind. As if influenced by his new injuries, his broken hip returned with all the pain. Countless wounds split open in his body, and he remembered every time he was hurt. A lifetime of mortal wounds caught up with him, and he fell to the hard stone ground in a heap.

Finis's somber voice rose above the clatter of bones and rotten flesh. "You have spent your short life in defiance of Death, Quondam. Those injuries should have killed you, but you grew out of them." He held a skull in the palm of his hand pensively. "Let us consider a hypothetical situation: Let's say you're twenty-four, and you get shot in the chest by an arrow. You regress your age to twenty-three to escape the injury, but then you have a birthday. Is the twenty-four-year-old version of you dead? If not, how did he survive the wound?"

The skull in his hand began to speak, as though it were a ventriloquist's dummy. "What happens when you mortally wound yourself at every age?"

Several of Quondam's undead attackers spoke in monotone unison: "You cannot escape Death, Quondam. You can only put it off. Death is inevitable."

Cold, decomposed hands groped all over Quondam, aggravating his wounds and tearing at his flesh. Just as he felt consciousness fading, he saw the first two skeletons hovering over him. The process of decomposition seemed to reverse, and skin grew back over their bones. Their clothes mended themselves, and their hair grew back into place.

"Quondam," said the man. "My son."

Chapter 4:03

Sunrise, Sunset

"Father?" Quondam swallowed hard. His undead father helped him to his feet, while his mother dusted him off.

"Mother?" Due to the timepiece's power, he retained perfect memories of his childhood, and his parents were just the way he remembered them. His mother smiled warmly in spite of her cold absence of life. Her skin was pale and fair, and her eyes seemed full of sorrow, just as they had on the day she died.

His father was a noble, sturdy looking man, with narrow eyes and chiseled features. Part of his dark hair was drawn back in a ponytail, while the rest hung loosely about his shoulders. The traditional armor of an Orien samurai adorned his body, and he held a long katana in his hand. "Stay here, son. I will fight them."

Quondam watched as his father defended him against the numerous zombies and skeletons. He welcomed the protective care of parents, as he had lived most of his life having to fend for himself. He just wanted to stay in the shelter of his mother's arms, while his father battled the evil of the world.

"Quondam..." Finis's voice called him back to reality. "Your parents are dead. You know that. These are just lifeless husks; shells of their former glory."

He held tight to his mother's arms as they crumbled to dust. Tears burst forth from his eyes. "No!" he screamed. "You cannot take them away again, Demon!" He rushed toward Finis with his fists swinging.

Quondam's fists passed through Finis as if they hit nothing at all. "My apologies. In showing you the seriousness of Death, I may have caused serious damage to your psyche," Finis said calmly. He seemed to look very far away. "Sometimes, you see, it is better to detach oneself from the Death."

Quondam took a deep breath, but his exhale crumbled into several sobs. Finis placed a comforting hand on his back and said, "Come. There is more to show you."

Crowfoot's dark wings enveloped them, and Quondam felt his feet leave the ground. They passed through the dirt ceiling as if it were nothing, and soon, they were emerging from the ground of a freshly dug grave. "There are other ways of traveling here, but I thought you might not want to dig yourself out of a grave."

The air felt especially fresh and clean in contrast to the stuffy tombs of the underworld. As Quondam inhaled, he no longer felt the stifling, overpowering presence of Death. "I should be going. I need——." His thought process was interrupted by sudden pangs of hunger. Such needs do not exist in the land of Death, but returning to the world of the living brought them back with a vengeance. He reached into his pocket and found one of Ekisha's cookies. He had forgotten all about them. The cookie bore the following message:

'Tis the sunset of life gives me mystical lore,
And coming events cast their shadows before.
Campbell, "Lochiel's Warning"

Finis continued, "I know you have much to do, boy, but take your cookie's advice. You may learn more in Death than you ever did in Life. Look at all these graves, Quondam."

He walked over to a large, ornamental tombstone. A crumbling statue rested atop a marble pedestal, which was also in poor condition. "This was a rich man, who hired an assassin to kill his family. Ironically, the assassin killed him as well." He blew on the statue, and more pieces crumbled. "He had this statue built for himself years before his death; he believed it would be a permanent reminder of his life. Be sure to note its current state of decay.

"Now, look at this one." He walked over to another grave, but it had no headstone or statue of any sort. There was a small marker with a worn engraving. "This was a pure, innocent child." Finis paused, and Quondam thought he saw tears. "She has no gravestone, while...." He flung his hand despondently in the direction of the statue.

Finis walked slowly to another grave. This one had several rocks piled atop it, and it looked rather strange compared to the rest of the graves. Green grass had grown around the entire cemetery, but nothing seemed to grow above this grave. "This is the father of that child. He... killed her. Then, he killed himself."

Asalie and Aori sprouted out of a seemingly burnt-out stump in Smokywood Forest. Aori panicked. "Where have you taken me?" he demanded.

"Look." She kicked at a scorched piece of metal. "This is your train. It derailed, set the forest on fire, and killed several innocent people."

Aori surveyed the wreckage. "You mean to say that I am responsible for this?"

"Indirectly, yes. But, do not worry for the mechanical workers that were destroyed."

"I was concerned for the——."

"Ori. Do not be concerned for them, either, Aori. The damage is done. Their deaths were tragic, but they have already been reborn. Or, shall we say, *resurrected*."

"So it can be done! I can resurrect Bertram and my family!"

Asalie just smiled. "Aori, come. There is more to show you."

They walked through thick, tall grass, and Aori lost his bearings. When they exited the thick grass, they were in a completely different place. Green grass grew all around, and Aori could see several graves. "A cemetery? What have you to show me here?"

"Look around you, Aori. What do you see?"

"Death. Countless graves containing dead people. Do you propose to depress me to death, Asalie?"

"What else do you see?"

Aori grew impatient. "I need to be getting back home, Asalie. All of a sudden, I'm very hungry. I don't remember the last time I ate." He reached in his pocket and found one of the fortune cookies he had been given so long ago. Breaking it in half, he found the following message:

"Adopt the pace of nature: her secret is patience— Emerson."

Asalie's mouth branched into a smile. "Look, Aori. It is Life. It is all around you. The grass grows up from the graves of the Dead. You look around and see all these interrupted lives, but Life continues on and on. It exists in every blade of grass, every flower petal. Birds are drawn to the flowers, carry the seeds of trees, and spread the Life all around. It is a beautiful thing."

"Flowers wilt," said Finis. "Even as the flower lives, petals fall off and wither. So too, will we decay before we die. These flowers and trees produce millions of seeds in a year, and only one or two will germinate and produce Life. Futility, Quondam. That is Life. Look at the rich man: he worked his whole life to amass great fortune, but it is useless to him now. Even his expensive statue is falling apart."

"There is much to be done in a day," said Quondam, "before the sun sets."

Finis ignored his deeper meaning. "Good point. Let us go. Acheron?"

Acheron pulled a long, weapon-like shovel from the folds of his tattered wings. Finis said, "Dig," and several loyal undead servants began to dig at the grave. "Quondam, while they dig, let's you and me have a walk."

They stepped on another grave and sank into the dirt. Quondam panicked, but before he could yell out in alarm, they reappeared in a completely different cemetery. "Look, Quondam. More graves. Do you see how all-encompassing Death can be?"

Quondam shook his head. "But, it's a cycle. Some things die so others can be reborn."

Finis leaned against a great, stone mausoleum. "There is no coming back, Quondam. When Death takes you, it is final. The people in these graves are gone forever."

"What about the tale of Threnody and Volare? You brought him back to life."

Finis closed his eyes. "No." At the thought of Threnody, a bit of color returned to his skin. "I loved her; I would have done anything for her. But, Volare could not beat Death. Death is too powerful even for me."

"Then, who brought him back to life?"

"Asalie," said Aori, "I understand that nature is beautiful. But, look at all that I have created. It has its own beauty."

He took his spectacles off and handed them to Asalie. "Look through them. I created them. They did not exist in nature, Asalie."

She looked through the glasses and her eyes appeared very large. "What else have you done, Aori? Teach me, as I teach you."

"There are the clockworkers. They are made of metal, yet they move and perform simple tasks."

"We have discussed that, Aori. They have also performed horrendous acts against the people of Aia. They may respond to simple commands, but some higher power motivates them. They are not alive; they, too, are puppets."

"The train, then. Transportation has been utterly changed because of my creation."

Asalie smiled. "True. But, the birds have been getting around quickly for many years without your invention."

"But, we cannot fly as the birds do, Asalie. My Revolution will propel mankind into the future! Soon, the possibilities will be limitless! We will not be confined to Aian concepts of gravity and such."

"*Revolution*: such a powerful word." Asalie spread her arms and twirled around in a circle. "The world revolves around the sun, yet the meaning you intend is that of change. You are right, Aori; for what is Revolution, if not change?"

"And change is growth. Because of my inventions, we shall grow as a people."

"No. Growth is a form of change, Aori, but change is not always growth. You may change your clothes, but are you developing? Your eyesight has changed since before you began this work; do you feel that it has grown?"

"It has grown worse. It has regressed. Is growth always positive?"

Asalie considered the question very carefully. "Perhaps not."

Finis seemed to have aged a good deal in his time out of the underworld. Similarly, Quondam had taken on the appearance of an older version of himself. They walked through the cemetery as if they were just two old friends sharing stories of days gone by. "Decay is not always negative," said Finis.

"Of course," said Quondam. "Wisdom comes with wrinkles."

"And sunsets are very pretty, are they not?" Finis smiled. "Death can be a blessing, Quondam. I know it's hard to understand, but Crowfoot can tell you; already he has delivered trapped souls to the beyond."

"Why would anyone wish for death?"

Finis grew silent. "Some find it empowering. They feel that Life is out of their control, but Death is attainable. Of course, the universe frowns on suicide. It is too easy. It provides an escape to the decay of aging and the hardships we all endure."

Quondam followed him into another grave, and suddenly they were in a barren field of tree stumps. Decomposing bodies littered the ground, and it looked like various animals had eaten bits of their flesh. "This is where we last fought the battalion." He looked around at the carnage. "Oh no! I forgot all about them!" He looked imploringly at Finis. "I have to find my friends." He spoke their names aloud, as if calling them back into existence by remembering them. "Lithe. Munder. Connery: he fought here, too." He looked at the stumps of trees, and said, "Asalie."

"Look at this stump," said Asalie. "This is the great *asa* you cut down to make your towers. What do you see?"

Aori had to climb the stump to see its top. "It is growing! It is not dead!" Relief poured over him.

"True," said Asalie. "This is a very hardy tree." She sat on one of its large roots. "Do you know its history?"

"I have read some folk-lore, but I'm not sure if I believe..."

"Believe it. The name comes from the Orien word for 'morning,' because it grew great, yellow blossoms at dawn."

"Is it you, Asalie? Is the tree an extension of you?"

"In a way, I suppose. The *asa* is an extension of all of us. He loved the world, so he was made part of it."

"He loved you," deduced Aori. He was putting pieces of the lore together with their basis in reality.

409

Asalie looked at the stump fondly. "Yes. He begged Toki for a longer life, so that we could be together forever. We were reborn as trees. Perhaps Toki saw it as ironic punishment, but we felt that it was a blessing. Never were we as close to nature as we were then.

"But, the endless Spiral had other plans for me, I suppose. I burned down and was reborn as a spirit of Growth. Now, I wander Aia, giving a nudge here and there to aid in the development of Life."

"But, you know that the seasons come from the angle of the planet in relation to the sun, correct?" Aori reasoned.

Asalie laughed. "There you go again, trying to renounce me as a goddess. I never claimed such power. If I stayed here all year, the world would go on spinning and, yes, there would be seasons without me. Sometimes, nature needs a helping hand, however."

She gathered several seeds from her house in the hollow tree. "Look at these seeds. Each one is unique; special in its own way. Why are they not all the same? Wouldn't it be easier to just mass-produce them, as you create items in your factories?"

"No. It is an adaptation; this one grew these wing-like structures so it could travel farther." He picked up the seed and let the wind carry it away. "This fruitseed is designed to be attractive to animals, which eat it and scatter the seeds in their waste."

"Very good," said Asalie. "Life always finds a way to persevere. Adversity arises, and seeds grow wings to work around it."

"Adversity rises, and whole populations fall in its wake," said Finis. "Some members of a species must die in order for that species to grow and evolve. Death is a necessary part of growth, you see."

"Just as Life is a necessary part of decay," said Quondam, pointing to a congregation of maggots on one of the corpses.

Finis put his hands together with finality. "Well, that just about sums it up. We should be getting back now."

They sank into the hallowed ground of the battlefield and reemerged next to the grave, which looked empty. "Where is the body?" asked Quondam.

"Here," said Finis.

"You?"

"Yes. I committed such a ghastly murder that I was not allowed the satisfaction of a simple death. I lived several lives, and in each life, I was doomed to die tragically. Everyone I've ever loved has been ripped away from me numerous times. If I remain here, I will die, only to relive the tragedy with other friends, other family. I took the graveyard shift job so I wouldn't have to live as a human, with all the sorrow and grief of human death. Death is all there is for me, Quondam. So, do not assume you know something more from your experience. If you live a thousand years, you will never see the kind of Death I have seen!"

As if in response to Finis's grief, a nearby party of mourners at a funeral sobbed and wailed. Again, Quondam was reminded of Lithe, but he could not leave Finis in such a condition. He walked over to the demigod to offer condolences, but he fell into the empty grave. He fell and fell, until darkness surrounded him. When he opened his eyes, he was back in the underworld. "Finis!" he shouted, feeling betrayed. "If this is another one of your tricks…"

"It is no trick, Quondam. You have seen the truth that Death provides. It is a stark reality." Finis stepped out of the shadows.

"If I have seen all you have to show me, then why am I still here? I must go, Finis. I have to find my friends. They need me. We have to stop a madman from… from…"

"From doing what? You seek this madman, but do you know what you will do when you find him?"

"Kill him," Quondam stated plainly.

Finis closed his eyes pointedly. "Perhaps you shall," he said somberly, "but it won't prevent the End from coming."

Chapter 4:04

Time to Die, Time to Kill

For one reason or another, the gods of Time and Death often blur into the same entity. I suppose people believed that some supernatural being with an hourglass and a scythe had nothing better to do than measure the lives of each living thing. At some predetermined point in time, the scythe would fall and life would end. The Roman god Saturn is at the same time grim reaper and Father Time, as countless cultures and ideologies blended in his lore with their own.

Death is just part of the cycle, however—it's not a hooded figure with a scythe. And Time, while represented here as Toki or Tempo, doesn't count down the seconds until your demise. It's all about the delicate balance between the decay and regeneration of cells inside your body. …Either that, or it's part of some greater, unforeseen plan.

Lithe gripped her larva-spike tightly. The sharp end rested on the fleshy part of the Sphinx's neck. The moth rasped, "Kill me if you must, but it will not give you back your friend… or your time. That, I am afraid, you have squandered."

"Emmeleia, be careful," sang the Odestone through Lithe's vocal chords. "That is the spike of the Death's Head larva. If it breaks the skin, it will kill him instantly."

"Suddenly, you know all about the Death's Head, father?"

"I... have known all along. I knew your friend was dead, and I purposely sent you on an empty quest."

"Why?" Lithe squeezed the stone tightly in her hand, as if applying pressure would squeeze more information from it.

"Emmeleia, we are of the Line of Dorian. Tempo has blessed all of Dorian's descendants with supernatural posterity. We can live forever, Emmeleia!"

"But," interrupted Munder, "you're already dead. You're a rock."

Lithe said, "You may have sold your soul to Tempo, but I have not. You have no idea of his true plans. He is using you, as he has used Dorian all these years." She threw the rock across the room, and it ricocheted off several walls.

She turned back to the Sphinx, but lowered the Death's Head spike. "What must we do to retrieve our friend?"

The Sphinx was puzzled for the first time in its life. "Now, it is you who speaks in riddles. Your friend is dead! Death is final!"

"Surely you know the tale of Threnody and Volare. Shall I play it for you?"

Munder stepped in and said, "Let's not go to extremes, shall we? Calm down, Lithe, dearie. Let's go back to threatening him with the spike."

The Sphinx rasped, "I know the tale." It collapsed limply into its sarcophagus. "There may be a way." He paused, and dust seemed to settle on him. "However, you will have to die."

"This scenario was much better when the spike was at his throat and he was the one to die," said Munder.

Lithe paced about the room. Finally, she said, "So be it. I will die."

"No, you won't," argued Munder. "Look: I've known him the longest; I'll die."

"Do not argue with me, Munder. The decision is made." Lithe held the spike out and pointed it at her chest. "The pain should be quick, if the spike is as deadly as…" she trailed off as the whole room began to vibrate.

"Wait!" the Odestone sang.

"Father, you will not delay us any longer!" Lithe picked up the stone, ran up the steps to the main chamber, and exited the pyramid. With a thrust of her arm, she cast the stone high into the air.

Suddenly, a great blackbird swooped down from out of nowhere and caught the stone in its talons. The Hawk moths took to the air in a defensive pattern, but the oblivious bird continued its descent.

"I have not come to fight," Crowfoot crowed.

Lithe worked past the initial shock of the talking bird and said, "I am sorry. I was not trying to throw the stone at you."

Crowfoot cawed, "I understand. But, if you wish to dispose of a spirit, you needn't cast it away as such. Was this stone haunting you?"

The bird cocked his head from side to side, studying the rock intently.

"This one attempts to cheat one god with the tricks of another," Crowfoot continued, "And yet, this is not the spirit that brought me here. The presence of Death lingers here."

Crowfoot spread his wings and beckoned the trapped souls of the Agypsian mummies to join him. When that task was finished, he turned to Lithe. "My work is done, yet I sense something more here. You…wish to die?"

Lithe answered, "I must find my friend, Quondam. He is dead."

Crowfoot flapped his wings excitedly. "I thought you looked familiar! You are the Songmaiden who visited the Leafblower tribe." He briefly explained who he was and how he had become a carrion bird.

When he had completed the tale, he said, "Your friend is not dead, but he is in an underworld, of sorts."

"Can you take us there?" asked Munder.

Crowfoot hesitated. "I carry only the spirits of the dead." He looked at Lithe and scratched nervously at the sand with his feet. "I might be able to make an exception for the Coda, but no more. She is light and will hardly seem a burden."

Crowfoot's dark eyes gazed at Munder, and his mind placed the giant at last. "You, however, reek of Tweentime. You are the captain of his army, are you not? Your army destroyed my people! I would not carry you, even if you were dead!"

Munder glared at the bird, but Lithe held him at bay. She turned to Crowfoot and said, "This is the friend that Quondam sought. He has proven his loyalty to both Quondam and me."

Crowfoot studied the giant closely. "I simply cannot. He is a time bomb. If he dies, he will surely take us all with him. We cannot risk taking him to Death's door."

Lithe held Munder's hand gingerly. "I will bring him back, Munder. We will all meet again, soon."

Munder grimaced, as if he were fighting some inner turmoil. "Where should I go? What should I do?" His voice sounded almost childlike, and tears welled up in his eyes.

"Go to Aori. Find Dirge for me, Munder. Please. It may be up to you alone to stop Aori."

Munder swallowed hard. "I will."

Lithe walked over to the Hawk moths. "Daphni," she said, "the emperor's chrysalis is yours, if you want it. I am entrusting it and the artifact to you. Though Munder has proven loyal recently, I have my doubts when it comes to the timepiece."

Daphni bowed graciously. "It will be safe. We shall take it to Emperor Oleander at once."

At last, Lithe turned to Crowfoot, who wrapped her up in his wings. Darkness washed over her, and the bright sun of Agyp faded away.

Chapter 4:05

The Dead Sea

Several minutes had passed since Crowfoot had spirited Lithe away to the Underworld, and Munder had experienced a wide range of emotions. At first, he lashed out and kicked wildly at the sand dunes. He climbed the statue of the Sphinx and broke off its nose.

After he had burned off most of his energy, he crumpled into heap on the sand and pouted. His mind lumbered about on the subjects of death, rejection, and how even Death had rejected him. Feelings of abandonment pounded in his brain.

"Your place is here, Munder," sang the Odestone. "This is not your time to die. This is your time to live." Listlessly, he kicked at the stone. "You must accept the things you cannot change, Munder. Accept your life."

Munder picked up the stone and it continued to sing, "Good. You mustn't fight, Munder. Fighting will not change your life; only Time may do that. All we have is Time."

Daphni approached the giant cautiously. "We must go," she said. "Will you be joining us?"

Munder looked up. The sun glared behind her, creating a sleek-looking silhouette. "My place is here," he said, echoing the words of the Odestone.

"We must take our fallen emperor with us, then." Daphni nervously gripped her staff.

Munder absently placed the cocoon on the sand in front of him, and the Brahma crawled down his arm. Daphni watched anxiously as Munder's grip remained on the chrysalis. "The artifact will be safe," she assured him.

The mention of the timepiece seemed to pull Munder momentarily out of his trance. He gazed at Daphni and said, "Is that so?" He walked closer to her, and she began to feel quite uncomfortable. "What will you do with it? Will you use it?"

"No—I—." She took a step backward in order to put more distance between them.

"How will you avoid using it? A timepiece such as this one almost killed me. Look what it has done to your emperor!" He stomped the chrysalis with his heavy boot, and a thick layer of mucous covered his foot. A wicked smile spread across his face as he dragged his foot along the sand.

Daphni's wings tensed, but she tried to dismiss her anxiety with calm words. "We will keep the emperor and the artifact dormant. No one will be in any danger." In order to convince herself, she repeated, "No one is in any danger."

Munder's smile remained unchanged. "You know, I was supposed to have a timepiece of my very own. I could have had Quondam's. I could have this one. *I* am the true son and heir of Father Time."

Daphni spread her wings, and the motion made them appear invisible. Nonetheless, the iron grip of Munder's hand brought them to an abrupt stop. His eyes narrowed, and, with a quick, downward jerk, he made sure the Hawk moth would not leave the ground.

With her right wing broken and useless, Daphni winced from the pain. She struck at his arm with her staff and jabbed the other end into Munder's kneecap. With all her strength, she forced the staff diagonally into his torso, but he didn't budge.

The other *Fellfallan* knights soon recognized the danger and rushed to aid their leader. One of them dove at Munder from high in the air and cut a deep gash down the giant's back. His name was Falcatus Sicklewing, for his wings were razor sharp and shaped like scythes.

Before the others could strike, however, a timely sandstorm whirled all around them. Sand filled their eyes, and even their strong wings could not maintain control in the forceful winds.

When the winds finally subsided, Munder, the chrysalis, and the Brahma were gone. Prosperpina, one of the smaller Hawk Knights, had been cast far away from the rest of the group. When she returned, she was very fatigued. "The giant walked this way," she indicated the direction with her hands.

"Then we must follow," said Daphni.

As Munder trudged through the hot sand, he mumbled incoherently. Since no other living thing existed for as far as the eye could see, the Brahma caterpillar believed the giant had lost his mind. The chrysalis remained intact, except for the fluids oozing out of it. Each drip of the viscous substance left a noticeable trail on the barren sand. Yet, when the Brahma looked back to see if anything was following, it marveled at its findings.

They were being followed. The trail of emperor-drops followed them; each drop had grown into a small moth larva. The ones that didn't burn up immediately in the oppressive sun continued to follow the trail.

The Brahma could easily have stopped Munder at any point, but for some reason, it hadn't. Quite a while had passed since he had stolen the chrysalis, yet he had done nothing with the artifact inside. Despite the Brahma's dazzling intellect, he could not fathom Munder's intentions. *Not yet*, it thought. *I am still growing.*

Munder's skin had blistered in the sun, and his boots had worn almost to nothing, but he continued to walk.

Something drove him onward in spite of the pain and fatigue. In fact, he barely noticed any of the hardships he endured; even the sound of singing, which normally would have annoyed him, did not incur even the slightest emotion. He had no desire to improve his situation. Rather, his only motivation was to walk.

The Dead Sea stretched out before him for several miles. Its deep darkness would have inspired awe in the great giant, had he been capable of such extreme feelings. "Why do they call it the Dead Sea?" His voice was flat and monotone, so his question came out as more of a mumbled statement.

The Odestone answered, "Jump in and see."

Munder fought the urge, but suddenly felt that the water would feel very soothing against his blistered skin. He also felt incredibly thirsty. "Is the water safe to drink?"

"Only one way to find out," sang the Odestone.

"You want me to die?"

The Odestone was silent for a few seconds, but finally answered, "No. But, have you ever really felt at home in this world, Munder Timebomb?"

"Why does everyone keep calling me that?"

"Have you ever felt that everyone besides you was a tad old-fashioned? Too behind the times?"

"I... yes, but..."

"This is your time, but this is not your place. Look at the reflection in the water."

Munder could see several images reflected on the water's surface, none of which matched up with anything around him. "How deep is it?" he mumbled.

"You will see. Jump in. Take the timepiece and walk into the water."

Munder looked down at the broken chrysalis. Through its semi-translucent outer covering, he could almost make out the outline of the timepiece. He reached his hand into the gooey mess, but before he could get a grip on the amulet, he felt a sudden, sharp pain in the back of his head. He dropped the chrysalis, and his balance slowly teetered from side to side.

One of the Brahma's strange horns was embedded deep inside Munder's brain, and while it was there, the caterpillar decided to have a look around. The horn stretched out like a tree branch in all directions, and it entwined itself into the dendrites and axons of his brain cells. It experienced horribly intense feelings of hatred and the desire for violence, but there was more there than just basic evil.

Suddenly, Munder's body lost its balance and fell to the ground. The Brahma tried to see what had caused him to fall, but sand filled the air and blocked its vision. The sand settled, or was blown away by rapidly vibrating wings.

"Stop!" Daphni shouted. "You will not escape, giant. Give us the emperor's chrysalis."

Munder barely heard the Odestone sing, "You can escape, into the sea." He clutched his head and rolled around on the sand in agony. His head felt like a ripe melon, ready to burst at any moment. Something sharp stuck in his back, sending pain shooting up and down his spine. With each struggling movement, the giant got closer and closer to the water's edge.

Falcata Sicklewing walked over to the lumbering mass of giant and pulled his sickle from Munder's back. "Get up," he said.

Unable to differentiate between all of the commanding thoughts in his head, Munder obeyed. He slowly raised his head and saw Falcata's sickle-shaped wings spread ominously before him. The wings seemed poised to spring downward like a guillotine, and Munder's head was on the chopping block. Instinctively, he lunged toward Falcata and dug his massive shoulder into the *Fellfallan* knight's solar plexus.

As Falcata tumbled over backwards, Munder rose to his feet. Another knight shot towards him like an arrow, but Munder redirected him straight into the sharp wings of his fallen companion.

Munder clenched his fists, ready to charge to the attack, but something tugged at his brain. He turned around and followed the cord from his head to his caterpillar companion on the ground. "What are you doing, little worm?" He noticed that the Brahma was eating something. Suddenly, he realized, in all the confusion of the fight, he had forgotten about the timepiece! He reached for the chrysalis, but it was too late. The Brahma had consumed the entire cocoon.

With his attention focused elsewhere, Munder proved an easy target for Proserpina, who dove straight for his torso. Despite the knight's small frame, her momentum propelled both of them forward. A great splash of water filled the air as they plunged into the murky water of the Dead Sea.

Munder felt the tugging at the base of his skull again, but had no desire to look back at the world above the water's surface. With each ripple of water, Munder got a glimpse of a different world. Bubbles rose up from the darkness, and each one looked like another planet in a galaxy. *I can escape*, he thought. *The possibilities are endless.*

In the distance, he saw another world, but as the image floated closer towards him, he noticed that it was flooded with water. *Sink*, he thought. *Why won't I sink?*

"Why won't he sink?" a knight named Laothe asked.

Daphni shrugged. "I don't know. He just seems to be floating there."

"But, Proserpina sank."

Chapter 4:06

Hospitality in Hell

Proserpina sank. She struggled at first, beating her wings against the flow of water, but her panic served as an anchor. She sank deeper and deeper, and the bubbles rushed past her. In one larger bubble, she saw another world. Everything was covered in water, but Proserpina's attention focused on the sky. *Gypsy?* She tried to call out to the *Fellfallan* wanderer but got only a mouthful of water for her trouble. It tasted salty.

The bubble floated upward, farther and farther away from her, as the saltwater filled her body and she sank into the darkness. Her last conscious thought was of some great hand pulling at her wings.

Acheron, the great Death's Head moth, dragged the body of his latest catch closer to the fire. In the light of the flickering flames, he thought he had never seen such beauty. Even the recent Coda arrival, who the Master had fawned over, did not compare to the beauty of this rare creature. The body was covered in sleek, shiny armor of a greyish-green color with darker green bands. Acheron lightly touched its skin, which shared the same green-grey pattern. Long lashes stretched from its eyelids, and wet, curly hair sprawled out like dark green vines.

"No, Acheron!" Finis shouted. "No vacancies! We're not taking any more bodies today! There's no room! Only souls from now on, okay? Throw her back."

Acheron held the body close to his and shook his head. The motion raised a cloud of dust.

"Acheron, we're already up to our eyeballs in bodies." Finis knelt beside the hulking moth and inspected the newly-found corpse. He exclaimed, "She's not even dead! Throw her back."

Acheron's pale face of Death crinkled into a frown and he gestured towards Lithe and Quondam, who had just walked up behind Finis. "Yes," said Finis. "I know they're not dead. But, they are my guests."

"We really need to be going," said Quondam.

Finis looked at Lithe fondly. "Are you sure you can't stay?" He closed his eyes. "No, you have much to do. You cannot stop the End from coming, however. It is hopeless to even try."

"If I do nothing else, I must find my little brother," said Lithe.

Finis took her hand and held it to his lips. "Ah, yes. Dirge. He is my favorite. He sings to me constantly. His every breath is music to my ears." He looked off into the distance, as if seeing something very far away. "No, I will not let him die. His breath is too precious."

Finis rose and walked a few steps away from them. "It is not often that a spirit of Death grows so attached to a living thing. It is against our way. We are supposed to appreciate the cold silence of Death." He looked over at Acheron, who was holding Proserpina up by the wings as if they were a puppet's strings. "There is no place for such things here. This is no place for the living."

"You are living," Quondam said pointedly.

Finis looked up. "True. Perhaps, this is no place for me." His gaze shifted back to Lithe, and he knew that he could follow her anywhere. "Nay, child. Your brother will be safe, even if I have to give my own life for his."

Sweat beaded on Dirge's forehead. Other Coda had been called to Aori's chambers, but none had returned. He had heard hushed whispers of Aori's attempt to raise the dead, and he envisioned armies of skeletons at the bidding of a madman. "I cannot do it," he whispered under his breath. "The last time I sang like that, I started a war. Nothing good ever comes from it. The dead are meant to stay dead!" He began to cry softly.

A whisper echoed in the dark shadows of their cell. "That is not true, my child." Notturno grasped the hands of Dirge and a young Codan girl and said, "You helped us, Dirge. You brought Harmony back to the land of Concord. She would not be here, without you. We can only hope that there is still a Concord to which we can return, when all of this is over."

Dirge stared into Harmony's tender, innocent eyes, and he tried his best to smile and put her at ease. Instead, he felt only more tears.

"No," Dirge whispered through a soggy countenance. "The End is near."

Notturno tried to hide his concern for the benefit of all those around him. "No, my child. There is hope for us yet."

All of a sudden, the door to the cell cracked and light burst into the room. Notturno cringed in the corner and tried to escape the brightness. A clockworker pushed an elderly Coda into the room and shut the door.

"Piano? Is that you?" asked one of the others.

She tried to answer, but her voice had left her days ago. Her fingers were bloody stumps from trying to play various instruments, and she seemed very, very tired.

Notturno reached out, touched her wrinkled hand, and vibrated a message into it. "Don't try to speak, but can you tell us what happened?"

Before Piano could even try to answer, the door opened again. A clockworker reached in and grabbed Dirge by the shirt. Notturno rose in protest, but the light that crept in through the open doorway kept him at bay. The clockworker carried Dirge out of the cell and shut the door.

The smell struck Dirge even before they entered the tomb. It was a familiar smell that reminded him of his family. He wondered what had become of them, without his music to keep them alive. Then, he thought of Lithe. Surely she still lived. She would come and save him.

Chapter 4:07

Acheron's Call

Proserpina coughed up a black, viscous liquid and felt the air return to her lungs. Her eyes focused on the intricate facial markings of Daphni, leader of the Hawk-Knights of Nerii. Swarms of thoughts fluttered in her head, each of them trying to rush to the surface, and Proserpina found it hard to concentrate on Daphni's concerned words.

"Are you okay?" Daphni held the petite *Fellfallan* knight in her arms and felt relief at the movement of Proserpina's long eyelashes. Proserpina stared blankly at her captain and friend, but her gaze soon wandered to some distant place.

"Proserpina?"

"What is wrong with her?" The six remaining knights gathered around her, and each of them whispered a different concern. "Will she be okay?"

"Maybe she's brain-dead." The crowd turned to Munder, who was just climbing out of the water with no help from them. The lack of concern or relief at Munder's appearance made him pause. "Well, she was under for a long time. No oxygen to the brain, 'n all that."

Falcata made a move to attack, but Daphni and the others held him back. Proserpina seemed to be trying to speak. She coughed a few more times and struggled to sit up on her own. Her gaze fixed upon the Dead Sea, as if she could see all the way down through its murky depths. Her words squished out like a dead jellyfish: "Gypsy."

"What was that?" questioned Daphni. "Gypsy?"

"Gypsy. Down there." Her words trailed off in different directions from there, and she showed no organization to her thoughts.

Daphni grew more concerned. "Pross, what were you trying to tell us about Gypsy? You saw her under the water?"

"Death… great wings… pale face… beautiful."

"Proserpina, what do you know about Gypsy?" barked Falcata sharply.

Munder drove the point. "Is she dead?" Falcata's sharp wings flailed out in Munder's direction, but the human blocked passively with his wooden arm. "She'd have to be dead, if she was down there. I mean, they don't call it the Dead Sea for nothing."

The Dead Sea

One reason for the naming of that particular body of water was that it was so salty that very little life existed in it. Freshwater fish could not live there, and the creatures of the ocean all lived very far away and rarely migrated out of their natural habitats. Desert animals refused to drink the salty seawater, and even birds stayed away. Most cognizant beings found the total lack of living things to be quite disturbing. Plus, there's the fact that there were the ghosts underneath the surface of the water.

"Dead dead dead," mumbled Proserpina. Occasionally, she smiled as the words rolled off her tongue, as if she were a giddy schoolgirl saying the name of a childhood sweetheart. "Dead."

"Is Gypsy dead?" asked Daphni, trying to make sense of everything.

"Dead dead dead," the moth repeated. Then, her mantra broke into what seemed like a coherent thought. "Have you seen him? He is an Angel of Death." Of course, none of the others had ever heard the word "angel," so the reference was lost on them. "I thought he was with me. Where did he go?"

"Where did who go, Pross?" asked Laothe. "And where is Gypsy?"

"Acheron," she answered in a sweet tone of voice not normally heard in the *Fellfallan* tongue (and never with that name).

"The Death's Head took Gypsy?"

The words sank inside each of the knights. After a few moments of quiet horror at the thought of their childhood nightmare, Daphni rose. "Go: all of you. Return to Oleander with this news. It will bring him pain to hear it, I am certain, but we cannot allow him to continue his vain chase. Alas! She has finally wandered beyond his grasp!"

The *Fellfallan* knights immediately took to flight, while Daphni stayed behind and tried to glean more information from her reticent companion. Proserpina, however, seemed more interested in rambling about death.

"Not dead," mumbled Munder. "Jump in. You'll find her." As Munder spoke, the Odestone vibrated inside his pocket.

Daphni tried to ignore Munder's mumbling and focus on helping her friend. She patted the back of Proserpina's head and spoke gently, "Fear not, Pross. You are alive and well, now."

Proserpina looked at her, and a calm clarity shone in her eyes. "I am not afraid. I am not alive. He calls to me. We are one."

"Pross— " Daphni tried to speak, but the words rotted on the vine. Proserpina leapt into the air and dove straight down into the water, while Daphni looked on helplessly.

"What are you doing?" Munder said in monotone. "Follow her."

"But, I will die."

"Maybe. Maybe not."

Daphni's sleek, shiny wings sprang into their open position as if they were spring-loaded. Like a bullet from a gun, she shot into the pool with almost no splash at all.

A barren expression hung about Munder's face as he stared down into the water and watched the blackness absorb the shapes of the *Fellfallan* knights. The Brahma caterpillar detached its horn from Munder's skull and wound its way down his body in a spiraling pattern. Munder's expressionless stare fell upon the caterpillar, as it crawled around in a circle. It seemed to be trying to eat its tail end.

"You hungry, mate? You shouldn't be… you already ate your emperor." He kicked at the caterpillar gently. "Let's have it, then. Out with the timepiece, Brahmey."

As if in response to Munder's words, the caterpillar began to change. A thick membrane formed around it, which eventually sloughed off to reveal the form of a much older, larger caterpillar. The strange, winding horn structures had disappeared, and the giant worm held its head up and arched its back so as to appear more intimidating. Two large, vacant eyes stared at Munder, but the human could tell that the eyespots were just for show. Eventually, the Brahma lowered its head to the sand and stretched out, revealing the mock head to actually be a hump just behind its actual head.

On instinct, Munder climbed on the caterpillar's back and held on to the hump. The Brahma crawled across the sand with the speed of a caterpillar on hot sand. After an hour had passed and they still had not left the shores of the Dead Sea, Munder said, plainly, "Think we might speed things up a bit, Brahmey? I mean, I'm on a bit of a quest here, and time is of the essence."

The Brahma slowly began to change again. Munder almost lost his grip as a membrane covered the caterpillar's armored hide. When the membrane fell away, the hump was all that remained of the Brahma's previous form. This form looked something like a bull-herbovine, except it was much larger and had the massive hump just behind the horns. In later years, a smaller version of the creature would be known as the Brahma bull (named after this particular caterpillar, of course).

In no time, the Hawk-Knights of the Nerii touched down on the roof of Emperor Oleander's palace. In their absence, beautiful pink flowers had been planted on the rooftop, and a pleasant fragrance filled the air. As the knights rested from their long flight and admired the garden, Oleander floated over to them. He looked more regal than ever, with his normal green-hued armor now studded with emeralds and other precious jewels.

"They are called Nerium Oleander," he said, holding a blossom up to his nose. "I assure you, I did not name them myself." He smiled, and the other knights felt some of their weariness fade away in Oleander's presence. "They are quite poisonous to humans and other animals, but the young caterpillars of Nerii love them." He picked one of the plants and held it softly to his lips.

The emperor's demeanor quickly shifted to the business at hand. "My Heralds reported that my sister was not with you on your return. I trust that she is not hurt...."

"No, my lord," said Laothe. "She was well when she ordered our return. However, I am afraid the news we have will prove no less painful."

"What news?"

Laothe balked at his leader's question, but Falcata's words drove right to the point. "Lymantria, the Gypsy, is dead, Emperor."

Oleander recoiled, as if Falcata's words had truly carried the sharpness of their tone. He looked to the softer face of the knight Lugubris, who could not speak due to her tears. "Marumba?" he questioned another of the moths.

The knight, whose wings looked to be made of wood paneling, lowered his head respectfully. "Proserpina saw her in the depths of the Dead Sea, my lord. Your sister remained behind to gather more information and to tend to Proserpina."

Oleander folded his wings and sat down upon a stone block. "This is most grievous news, indeed!" His head collapsed into his hands. Lugubris knelt beside him and offered a comforting hand. "I should have known not to give my heart to a Gypsy," the Hawk Knight mumbled under his breath.

In a swift, forced movement, Oleander sprang to his feet. "Alas! Now is not the time for such concerns. There is a war brewing in the east. Rest as you may, my knights, for there will be a grand battle ahead of you all! We will defeat this despot Aori, or die trying!"

As the last of the knights flew away to prepare for the coming battle, Oleander lingered in the rooftop garden. He held one of the bright pink flowers to his lips again. "Are we doomed to spend eternity apart, Lymantria Dispar? Why must you wander so far from my reach?" Tears streamed down his cheeks, and he put the blossom in his mouth and chewed.

Chapter 4:08

The Tiny Plastic Sword
in the Sandwich of Time

"Where is it, Ekisha?"

"Be patient, Osoi. We arrived early, in order to beat the rush."

"Rush? Is there something you are hiding, old woman?"

In the Orien language (and later, Japanese), the old woman's name meant "fortune-teller." Ekisha had been the one who set Quondam on his quest in the first place, when she gave him the fortune cookies.

"Quiet," retorted Ekisha. "Asia is waking."

One of the advantages of serving as a vessel for hundreds of other beings is that the various entities can sleep in shifts. As Asia became conscious, she realized her eyes were already open, and she had that feeling one gets after "zoning out" in the middle of a conversation.

"What?" she asked, trying to get up to speed.

"Do you think it's odd that one could be too early for his or her destiny?"

Asia looked up at the hulking caterpillar questioningly. "I...I'm afraid I don't know much about destiny."

"Ah, but that's where you're wrong, my lady," Osoi replied.

"Osoi," interjected Ekisha.

"You see, my lady, it's all up there," he nuzzled his huge head against hers, "in your head."

Asia, feeling uncomfortable, took a step backwards. Her eyes shifted back and forth around her in search of her bearings. She hated feeling out of the loop. Thousands of thoughts drifted around in her brain, but she still felt at ease inside. Events outside her brain seemed to be causing the most discomfort. As she surveyed her surroundings, she noticed several machines like the ones that had captured the Ori only a few days ago. Why would Osoi have led her here?

"Be at peace, my child." Ekisha addressed Asia's unspoken concern. "Osoi will protect you from any harm."

"Why are we here? Those metal monsters tried to capture and enslave me."

Asia drew her hands together and rubbed them in a circular motion on her stomach, while Ekisha spoke calm words. "Rest, Asia. Your mind is weary from working so hard. Now is not the time to fight."

Osoi rocked restlessly from side to side. "When *will* it be time, Ekisha?"

Asia looked up at the sun, and the fortune-teller said, "When the sun sets."

"How long until that happens, Ekisha? I think it's stuck." They looked up at the sky, and it did seem that the sun had been in about the same position for a rather long time.

"No," said Ekisha. "I don't understand. This can't be."

"What? How can you, of all people, be surprised?" Osoi scoffed. "You mean, you didn't see this coming?"

"I'm trapped here. He has frozen time."

Trying to understand the flow of time results in severe deterioration of the mind; case in point: Ekisha. But, for the sake of this chapter in history, let us imagine time as a multi-layered sandwich. Ekisha is the toothpick, or little plastic sword, if you will. She exists in every layer of time, from the past to the future. However, disturbances in the continuum (such as Aori's tinkering with the timestream) break the toothpick into splinters.

"If he's stopped time, why are we still able to move?" asked Osoi, who was utterly dumbfounded.

Asia's face contorted as Ekisha worried. "Do not question the almighty Toki, you foolish worm! His ways are mysterious, even to those who serve him unerringly. You do not wish to incur his wrath!"

"Is this your doing?"

Asalie's face grew into a smile. "I thought it was your work, Aori." The sun's rays had not changed for quite some time. "You could get more farm work done this way. That is, if you still did your farm work."

Aori shrugged. "I always hated the farm; my chores just kept me from having time for other pursuits. My parents were slaves to the seasons, planting and harvesting in an endless cycle that never gave them the opportunity to do what they wanted."

"How do you know what they wanted, Aori?"

"Because I, too, am a slave to time's constraints." With finality, he rose from his seat and walked over to the *Epic* board, which had been set up in his living quarters. Some of the pieces had grown to look very familiar. One in particular looked like a much younger version of Aori. "It's been so long," he said, holding the game piece in his hand. "I don't even recognize myself."

"You have changed, Aori. In many ways, you are a different person."

He put his game piece back on the board. "Just a pawn," he said. "We're all being manipulated... we're all just pieces in a grand game of *Epic*." He moved his piece to a different point on the board. "No more! I am in control of my life! I will not be manipulated!" In his rage, he knocked over the

Epic board and pieces flew all about the room. In a similarly dramatic display, he crashed to the floor in a heap of sobs.

Asalie helped him to his feet. "If you choose to renounce your god, the machines outside will become your enemies. You know this, correct?"

Aori nodded.

"Perhaps I can help keep them at bay."

As the sun continued to shine outside, branches grew from the base of the great towers as if they were trunks of a tree. The two towers became entwined in overgrowth, and verdant foliage burst forth all over the structures. When the clockworkers attempted to enter the tower, vines and sharp thorns barred their way.

Bertram's corpse rested on the altar in a progressed state of decay. Musical instruments, most of which Dirge had never seen before, were scattered about the room. Dirge felt very alone and helpless. What could he do to stop this madman? Could he prevent the End from coming? Could he stave off the cold hands of Death?

Determined to help in some way, he took up one of the instruments and began bashing it into the floor. Of course, he could not have known that, at that time, he had just given birth to the act of guitar-smashing, which many rock guitarists would mimic in the centuries to come.

After the instrument had been reduced to pieces on the floor, Dirge grabbed one of the thin, metal strings and tensed it between his hands. *I can't raise the dead if I don't have a voice*, he thought. He tied one end of the chord to the ceiling and wrapped the other tightly around his neck. As the weight of his body strained against it, the thin metal chord dug a deep furrow in his throat. With Death in his view, Dirge tensed the muscles in his neck. Soon, his lifeblood dripped down onto the broken pieces of the instrument. He coughed and wheezed with the rattle of blood and dearth of breath. An overwhelming darkness invaded his very being.

Chapter 4:09

Stolen Time

Through a thin veil of purple, swirling energy, Petti-fogger gazed up at the sun. Only moments ago, he had been sneaking around Aori's main tower, attempting to pick the locks on the doors to his fellow gnomes' cells. He had worried that someone might come by, that he wouldn't get the lock picked in time, and then, the door opened, and mysteriously....

He escaped to Tweentime.

A few days earlier, after mentioning to the mechanical Bertram how much he missed his family, a fairly large representative sample of the gnomish population appeared on the grounds. Of course, they had arrived as all the other Aian peoples had—packed in trains like prisoners. They had been mishandled, mistreated, and locked up in the towers for days.

Fortunately, Pettifogger had managed to open the door to their room. Unfortunately, he had unwittingly opened a door to Tweentime, and the room was empty. He slipped Aori's goggles down over his eyes, and he could see blurry, lavender shadows of his friends and family, all huddled together and wracked with terror. Apparently, they couldn't see him.

One ancient-looking gnome stood out amongst the crowd. His image was much clearer, and he stared right at Pettifogger. He recognized the old gnome right away.

"Mr. Thymegarden," he said, "I've done everything you asked. When will my family be safe?"

Quartz Thymegarden, as you may have guessed, was really just another disguise of Toki or Tempo, the god of Time. Like many of his "promises" and "gifts," his deal with Pettifogger had been underhanded and manipulative. Knowing that Aori had all but forsaken him and his grand schemes, the Time-Lord had sought out other minions to do his dirty work.

And Pettifogger, while naively innocent and with the best intentions at heart, had fit perfectly into Toki's plan. Without even knowing it, Pettifogger had become a master thief, stealing the most precious, valuable prize on Aia.

He had stolen time.

Aori's eyes burned as he stared at the sun. "Impossible," he coughed. "In order for the sun to remain in the same position all day, Aia would have to stop turning. If the planet stopped, all life would be thrown into chaos. What would become of the Great Cycle then, Asalie?"

"It is not impossible, Aori," said Asalie. "Just beyond our knowledge."

Aori squinted his eyes, partly due to the brightness of the sun, and partly because of the pain he felt at his lack of knowledge. Something caught his attention in the glare of the sun, but his eyes refused to focus. "What is that? A bird?" He closed his eyes, and the colors still burned in his vision. When he opened them again, he could barely make out the outlines of several flying objects headed in his direction.

Asalie's eyes glinted in the sunlight. "Those are no creatures of nature, Aori. They are machines, just like your monstrosities below."

Aori's gaze fell to the main courtyard of his compound, where he expected to see his clockworkers laboring on their latest project. Instead, he saw them amassing for war. They had built all manner of siege weapons—catapults, battering rams, and armored vehicles—and they had augmented their own design to better serve as war machines.

Asalie placed a comforting hand on his. "They, too, have changed, Aori. Are you surprised?"

"Not at all. They are automated workers, who are also programmed for defense. It is well within their parameters." A sudden tremble throughout the building interrupted Aori's words. Looking below, he noticed that one of the clockwork catapults had just fired.

Outside, on the wall of the great tower, the wood and foliage worked diligently to repair the damage caused by the catapult. The wood reformed and left behind barely a scar.

In the factories, where clockworkers toiled away at assembling other clockwork creatures, Pettifogger watched through purple-tinted goggles. He felt a certain satisfaction at bringing life to the mechanical creations, remembering fondly how his father's metal dragonflies and bees had buzzed around their garden. He had lofty hopes that his tinkering with the clockwork army would somehow change things, or maybe even save the world.

However, something inside him knew that, even though he had given them life, Quartz Thymegarden was always the one in control. The spirit of Time was the ghost in the machine.

In the nearby forest surrounding the compound, Solo clenched his fists restlessly. "How long have we been waiting?" he asked his feline companion.

"Rrrroow."

"Go and fetch the others," he said. "We cannot wait for the sun to set."

Very near to Solo's hiding place, a monstrous, wooly herbovine trampled through the underbrush. Many others followed closely behind. Not far away, a particularly unlucky were-squirrel was foraging for nutseeds. He looked up just in time to see the herd stomp through his home and crush him to death.

The man-sized squirrel rotted in the hot sun for several minutes, and if anyone had been watching the corpse, it would have seemed completely immobile. However, not long after rigor mortis had begun to set in, some other power took over and the squirrel-man rose once again. Mindlessly, he followed the rampaging herd of herbovines to Aori's compound.

At the same time, numerous other formerly-dead creatures suddenly snapped to attention as well. In their various states of decay, they marched as one into battle. Those who no longer had flesh walked on re-animated bones, and those who no longer had bones wisped through the air as specters or phantoms.

"Come on, boy. Wake up."

Bertram's corpse loomed over Dirge's limp body. The spurting blood looked black in his shadow, and Dirge's skin grew even paler and more lifeless. Flies swarmed in the darkness, biding their time until they could hatch their maggots in the corpses. Scooping the young boy into his arms, he exited the tomb. "Tombs are no place for little boys. A mausoleum is not a playground."

Dirge whimpered. Had he accidentally reanimated Bertram's corpse, without even trying?

"What's that, boy? You'll have to speak up. These ears aren't what they used to be." To prove his point, one of his ears decayed and crumbled to dust. "Oh, wait. You can't speak up. You've severed your vocal chords. Well, anyway, to answer your question, no. I am not this Bertram fellow, and I'm not Death either. But, I'm the next best thing. I'm Finis, the End of All Things. Of course, right now, I appear

442

to be a corpse. Of course, you appear to be a corpse too. What a pair!"

Dirge whimpered.

The heavy clank of metal vibrated through his ears. "What is it?" asked Finis. He turned Bertram's head around to see a clockwork guard ambling their way. "Don't move," said Finis. "Don't even breathe… play dead."

The clockworker disregarded them completely. Some higher power, or perhaps a certain gnome's pilfered power, had called on it to join its fellow machines in the ensuing battle. It passed on through the hall without even noticing them.

In the guard's absence, several of the stronger Coda forced the door to their cell open. Notturno crept out of the dark cell into the dim light of the hallway. "Who is there? Dirge?"

Dirge whimpered.

"What has that monster done to you?" Notturno was drawn to the darkness surrounding Bertram's reanimated corpse. "Who is this?"

Bertram's jaw creaked open with Finis's words. "Dirge cannot speak. We must protect him." The zombie crept slowly towards the light of a cracked window. "And, Notturno, my good man: Can you do something about this infernal, unending daylight?"

At the unspoken suggestion of Piano, Notturno dashed to the music room, where Aori's mechanized, pneumatic organ waited to be played. The dark Coda sat down on a bench and his long, slender fingers automatically found the keys. Sound erupted from the pipes in a great and forceful burst of energy. As the music of the night spread throughout the primed

---

Finis

Interesting side-note for the mythologically-minded: Many of Aia's various cultures believed that Finis, the deity most commonly associated with Death, was also responsible for the decay of the sun (i.e. sunset). Please note the inherent irony in Finis's request for an end of the day.

acoustics of the *asa* wood, all the shady places seemed to grow and swell. Before long, the shadows outnumbered the light.

Candles flickered black with the ensuing darkness. Soon, the artificial night spread outside the walls of the tower and consumed the surrounding land. How fitting, thought those who understood, that a world born in darkness should find its end in darkness as well.

Chapter 4:10

War in the Wild Black Yonder

Through the black emptiness of the imposed night, ebon wings of an even darker pitch beat against the air. Crowfoot traversed the vast expanse from the plane of Death to the Living in a matter of seconds. As the mundane world crept in on his wings, he felt all the weight of his trio of passengers.

"Death has beaten us here, my lord," Crowfoot whispered to Finis. Miles below them, a great battle had commenced. Finis seemed detached, as if his mind were focused elsewhere.

"Who is fighting?" asked Quondam.

Crowfoot's avian eyes peered down through the miles of darkness. "I see the great wooly herbovines of those who murdered my tribe...."

"Wait!" Lithe interrupted, "Do you hear that?" Her Codan ears pierced through the whipping winds and honed in on the faint and unidentifiable sound.

Miles away, but closing in fast on Crowfoot's position, a wide array of flying objects from across time circled Aori's tower. Flickers of flames briefly illuminated the dark night as groups of metal dragons breathed fire, while futuristic bombs dropped and guns blazed. The Prochrons and Metachrons of the Anachronistic Army had brought air support.

"Now is our chance," whispered Solo. Notturno's shadows still clung to his skin and clothes, making him almost invisible in the darkness. Numerous shadowy feline forms followed him silently into battle, as if the darkness belonged to them.

Solo drew his long sword, placed it to his lips, and sang softly to the blade. Immediately, it hummed with the flow of mystical energy. Beside him, moving just as stealthily as the shadows, a large panther with black, velvety fur purred with an intense feeling of anticipation.

"The others are all in position," the panther cooed.

Solo waited, as he had done for many days now. He knew the timing was right, but rushing into a camp of futuristic soldiers was ill advised. Still, the sudden darkness had thrown the enemy into disarray, giving Solo, Caitlin, and the cats an advantage.

Careful to stay among the shadows, the Coda crept into the Metachron camp. The Metachrons had rolled barbed wire all around their encampment, and several were positioned within a deep trench. As Solo slipped over the barbed wire, he heard them speaking in languages he could not understand. Before moving on, he stuck an object, which was shaped like a tuning fork, into the ground next to the trench.

Tents served as temporary homes for the soldiers in the Metachron battalion. They had electrical generators and lights, but the mysterious darkness seemed to swallow all of the luminance. As Solo snuck into the center of the camp, soldiers did not even sense his presence. After placing several of the tuning forks in strategic locations, he slipped away silently.

As he approached a group of trees, Solo heard a low growl in response to his arrival. In the low light, the glint of two canine eyes stared at him. "We smelled y', Coda. Y're lucky the soldiers haven't such keen noses!"

Solo pulled back his black mask, and the shadows seemed to thin around his face. "Very true, Connery. Very true indeed."

"Is everything in order?"

"Yes," Solo said. "I placed several charges throughout the camp. They're designed to explode when the decibels reach a certain level. Naturally, one explosion sets off all of the others. Then, we just go in and take out what is left."

"So now we wait f'r one o' them t' shout or use one o' their weapons?" Connery's impatience was shared by all around him. He and his wolves had been preparing for this battle ever since his last meeting with the Metachrons.

"I think we will not be waiting long. These humans are a clumsy bunch—I feared that the charges would go off before I could even leave the—." His words were interrupted by a grey-furred hand across his mouth.

"Listen," whispered Connery. His lupine eyes glowed faintly in the gloom. Far over the stripped-down forest to the east, the sound of thousands of locusts droned louder and louder.

Solo turned his head to pinpoint the location of the sound. "Be on your toes, Connery. This could be just the noise we need."

"The sound is getting closer," Lithe murmured. "It sounds like ten-thousand locusts, maybe more."

"No," countered Crowfoot. Even in the overwhelming gloom, he had the best vision in the group. "It is one giant locust, made of metal."

Quondam's face flashed to that of another time. Wrinkles grew about his innocent face. "I know that sound. It's a whirligig," he said. "A helicopter." The wrinkles flashed away again, and Quondam gripped Lithe's waist tighter. "I'm… a little afraid," he whispered.

Lithe placed a comforting hand on his. Taking the words out of her mouth, Finis woke from his trance to say, "It will all be over soon."

The helicopter buzzed right over their heads, and Crowfoot had to dive erratically to avoid the whipping winds. Quondam lost his grip and began to topple, but Lithe's long, slender arm reached out and caught him by the shirt. "Are you okay?" she asked.

Quondam caught his breath. "I… yes. Thanks." Everyone watched the helicopter as it zipped out of sight to the west. Quondam thought he saw it descending in a clearing near the forest, but visibility was poor in the thick blackness.

In a blinding flash, a chain of massive explosions rocked the ground underneath the helicopter. The helicopter burst into flames and eventually crashed near its destination. "What was that?" Lithe shouted when the sound of the blast reached her ears.

"Some sort of explosion," Quondam explained. "—or a series of explosions. More signs of battle, I suppose…." The helicopter and following blast had distracted them from the commotion to the east, but a rather large reminder was headed their way. "Crowfoot…do you see that?"

Crowfoot peered into the darkness ahead of them just in time to see a brilliant blue flame cut through the black sky. In seconds, the enormous mouth of a dragon stretched open before them. In the light from its fiery breath, they could see the pulleys, gears, and cogs just beneath its steel scales. It shot towards them like a rocket, and Crowfoot froze.

The dragon's jaws clamped down on Crowfoot's body, and Lithe strained to evade and pull Finis out of harm's way. The blackbird's body dissipated into thousands of feathers, which fell peacefully on the wind in stark contrast to the destruction above.

Time seemed to slow down for Quondam as he watched his friends scatter upon the winds. Briefly, he wondered if Toki had bestowed upon him some greater power over time itself. As Lithe and Finis fell into the darkness below, Quondam noticed that the waistband of his pants was caught in the teeth of the dragon. Furiously, he beat upon the dragon's upper lip, but the monster barely noticed the assault.

Quondam took a second or two to question the hardness of the dragon's skin. It seemed that the scales were made of metal rather than—well, Quondam didn't have time to figure out the normal properties of dragon scales. Rather, he reached for his wooden sword and, gripping it with both hands, stabbed it deep inside the dragon's upper lip.

Steam whistled out of the creature's nostrils, and hundreds of compound machines activated. The jaw hinged open with a resounding, metallic creak, and a cloud of black feathers burst forth upon the wind. Quondam was lifted higher into the air, and suddenly he became aware of his dangerous altitude. Vertigo struck him briefly, but he shifted to a hardier age. Muscles ripped through his arms, and he clenched the hilt of his sword tighter.

Blue flames burst out of the dragon's mouth once more, like a blowtorch. Quondam scrambled to get his feet out of the way of the blast, and as he did, his wooden sword cut a deep gash across the dragon's face. He struggled to find footing but held his grip upon the sword. With a loud crash, his knee plunged into a glass window that served as the dragon's eye.

Two startled clockworkers stood motionless as their clocks skipped a beat. In the seconds it took for the machines to get their bearings, Quondam had shifted, risen to his feet, and hacked one of them into gears and springs. The wooden sword sliced through their metal bodies as if it had been created for that very purpose. Before long, the head of the mechanical dragon was littered with heaps of scrap metal and clock parts.

Feeling the flying machine surge downward, Quondam rushed to the instrument panel. He found a large lever and several cranks. Never, in all his many years, will Quondam ever learn to pilot a giant, metal dragon. Therefore, shifting did nothing to help.

Instead, the left side of the dragon just stopped working altogether. The monstrous machine spiraled out of control, and Quondam was thrown all about the beast's skull. The iron floor, or perhaps a wall, crashed into his head and snatched away his consciousness.

Lithe tried to concentrate on a light, airy song, but the speed of her descent preoccupied her thoughts. Finis, still in deep concentration, flopped around like so much dead weight. For all intents and purposes, he was dead. All of his life force was currently busy freeing the Coda from Aori's tower and looking after Dirge.

As Lithe struggled with the melody to her mother's Lyric of Levitation, her mandolin strained against its strap. It took on the form of a lyre and, as the wind whipped past its strings, the music triggered Lithe's memory. Slowly, her downward velocity decreased. As further proof of her weightlessness, a feather looped around and spiraled downward as it passed by her. She reached out a hand and caught it before it plummeted out of reach. Tucking the feather behind Finis's ear, she reached out to catch another.

> Strangely enough, the forgotten words to Aria's Lyric of Levitation are, quite simply, "La La La."

Soon, she had built a rather intricate headdress about Finis's inanimate head. She continued to sing her mother's song, but she knew, eventually, she would have to begin a lamentation for the dearly departed Crowfoot. Of course, she was not privy to the particularly important fact that Crowfoot was, in the strictest sense, already dead. It's extremely difficult to kill something that is already dead. Unfortunately, it is sometimes also difficult to reconstitute something that is already dead but subsequently dismembered.

A huge clump of feathers dropped into Lithe's lap as she sat cross-legged in mid-air. "Hello," said a voice from within the cluster. "Good thing I ran into you guys." As the cluster of feathers began to swell, other feathers gravitated toward it. Even the pitch of the night sky seemed to insinuate itself into Crowfoot's pieces. The darkness solidified into the forms of two beady eyes and a beak, which asked, "Where is Quondam? I thought surely he'd be with you two." The eyes darted upward, but found nothing amidst the dark sky.

"Haven't seen him. You okay?" Lithe had to be terse in her speech in order to resume her song.

Crowfoot gradually began to look less like a clump of feathers and more like a giant blackbird. "One state is as good as the other when you're dead. But, I was concerned for you guys. Of course, I didn't know you could fly."

"Me neither."

"Would you still like a ride, or are you going to just float around from now on?"

"Ride," mumbled Lithe, in between lyrics of her song.

Crowfoot spread his wings so wide that one could not tell where his feathers ended and the sky began. "Just to be safe, you should ride inside me this time."

Lithe's eyelids drooped as she succumbed to the incredibly safe and comfortable feeling of the blackbird's wings. Everything was dark inside Crowfoot, and Lithe felt the cold (but comfortable) hands of Death for the second time. With all her trust in Crowfoot, she slipped off into much-needed sleep.

Quondam felt a throbbing pain in his head and quickly shifted past it. The pain followed him for many years' worth of growth, but he eventually overcame it. Even before he opened his eyes, Quondam identified the unmistakable ticking sound of the enemy all around him. With his sword nowhere within reach, Quondam scrambled to find his center of gravity.

Apparently, the dragon had crash-landed while he was unconscious, and the rest of the ship's crew had come to inspect the damage in the eye socket. Quondam wondered, in the seconds it took him to stand, why the clockworkers had not attacked him in his unconscious (and, therefore, defenseless) state. Surely the mechanical men were not concerned with sportsmanship or a fair fight.

Quondam surmised, perhaps through his gift of hindsight, that the clockworkers had been programmed not to kill, but to detain and, eventually, retrieve him. These particular clockworkers never got a chance to explain, or even carry out, their plans, for the machines were reduced to rubble as soon as Quondam found his sword.

From the vantage point of the broken dragon-eye, Quondam could see that war had erupted all around him. Agypsian slave/pupils had escaped the prison/school and revolted against the clockworkers and time-tossed soldiers. Dinosaurs and dragons battled alongside stone-age warriors and soldiers from every war throughout history. Swords clashed, bullets and arrows flew, and fires burned.

In the center of all the chaos, Quondam's eyes focused on one fighter, and no amount of activity could distract him. The warrior fought with several different martial arts styles, yet she appeared to be around eight years old—how could she have had time to master so many different techniques?

Though her skill in fighting amazed Quondam, what held his gaze most of all was her appearance. She wore an intricate gown that, surprisingly, did not hinder her movement whatsoever. Her black hair was pinned up behind her head, but several pieces of it danced around her face as she fought. Everything about her seemed so poetic and, at the same time, very familiar. Quondam knew at once that she was an Ori, like his father.

Every Anachronistic soldier that attacked Asia fell at her feet, and nothing could get close enough to even touch her. Somehow, she seemed aware of all that happened, or would happen, around her. However, Asia's heightened awareness and foresight were obscured by her trust in her allies. An image flashed in her head, and she saw herself crumpled and bleeding on the ground. The vision disoriented her, and the next thing she knew was the feeling of a sharp spike through her back.

She fell to the ground and her blood splashed onto the battlefield. The giant, grotesque form of a caterpillar towered over her, and more of her blood dripped from his horns. Despite her injuries, Asia's mind was sharp and focused. "Osoi. You betrayed me," she spat. She felt the energies of her people escaping with the blood.

A purple mist rose from the blood that had pooled under her, and soon the crooked and worn figure of Ekisha hunched over Asia. "Hello, my dear. Welcome to your destiny."

"Ekisha...help me," Asia implored.

Ekisha gingerly brushed the hair from Asia's eyes. "I cannot, my child. For you see, this is as it must be—as it was foretold—or foreseen, by me. Everything is going along right on schedule."

"Not everything," grumbled Osoi. "Where's my timepiece?"

Ekisha ignored him and began to walk in the direction of Aori's tower. Osoi called after her, but she continued to ignore him. With a spring-like action, he bounded up in the air to attack. As he came down, however, Ekisha stepped aside and an intense blast of fire burst forth and struck Osoi down.

Quondam crawled out of the eye of the dragon and fell a few feet to the ground. With a quick shift to a spryer age, he was back on his feet and heading towards Asia. "I'm sorry I wasn't quicker—it took me awhile to find the controls for the dragon-fire."

Without turning around, Ekisha shouted, "Just in time, man-child. Just in time."

Quondam puzzled over Ekisha for a moment, trying to remember where he had seen her before (and trying to make sense of her arrival). The bleeding girl at his feet took precedence, however, so he cast the thoughts aside.

Blood continued to pour out of Asia's wound, and more of the purple mist rose from the pools. Soon, a large group of Ori had gathered around them, whispering their concerns for Asia's life.

Quondam's eyes frantically searched the crowd. "This girl needs a doctor. Does anyone here practice medicine?" Oddly, Quondam found that his words came out in the Orien language.

Asia rose to her feet. "I am a doctor," she said. "I think I still have the energy to help... us...but I will need more."

One of the Ori from the crowd spoke up: "You can have my *chi*, doctor."

"Thank you, but I will need the help of *all* Ori, I fear." Asia took Quondam by the hands. "Even you, Child of the Morning and the Evening."

Quondam felt uncomfortable. "My mother was not Ori, and I was never taught...."

"I know, Quondam. The power of the Ori flows inside you, nonetheless. We are united by blood." Asia's body began to glow, which caused the bodies of Quondam and the other Ori to radiate energy as well. In no time, the bleeding had stopped and her wound healed.

One of the older Ori said, "As long as one Ori lives, Asia will never die. She is the living embodiment of our culture— our life force—our *chi*."

The moment in which Quondam had been caught seemed to pass, and he suddenly became aware of the battle raging around them. "It is not safe here. More soldiers will be along any...." He stopped talking when he realized that the Ori had been fighting off the enemy's forces the entire time.

Asia's voice rose above the sounds of battle. "Our brothers and sisters will fight this battle, Quondam. You and I must find Ekisha. I fear for what she has planned."

"Nothing worse than Aori's plans," Quondam pointed out, "But, maybe they'll be together."

Asia and Quondam took off in the direction of Aori's towers, while the Ori and Agypsians fought against the clockwork soldiers and the Anachronist Army.

Osoi and the Timepiece

Orien folklore tells of a fearsome dragon named Osore that terrorized the villagers each year at precisely the same time. The word *osore* came to mean "fear" or "terror."

The dragon eventually met its fate at the hands of none other than Konban, Quondam's father.

The stories of Konban's victory spread far and wide, but nobody ever mentioned the fact that the dragon didn't die. It simply changed form. It changed into a tiny caterpillar and quietly crept away to live another day. Eventually, his name changed from Osore to Osoi, which means "late."

At that time, Osoi had the timepiece that eventually fell into the hands of the Emperor Saturn of the *Fellfalla*, got eaten by the Brahma, and was carried all the way to this battlefield. Osoi had used it to shape-shift for centuries, and for years after his defeat, he had sought to get the timepiece back.

However, he was always just a little too late.

Chapter 4:11

The Future's Not Ours To See

No one can be sure how many days passed between the Seer's Day Festival in Auldenton and the end of the world, but it is believed that Auldenton fell on a Tuesday. Of course, no Auldentonians lived to tell about it, so no historical records of its destruction remain.

Nevertheless, this Historian's visions of the past have revealed that Auldenton fell off into a huge chasm—the same chasm, in fact, that Munder fell in when he was eight years old. Over the course of a week or so, the chasm aged a few million years and, eventually, swallowed up Auldenton.

The chasm, as well as its devastating effects on the city of Auldenton, could easily be seen from the top of Aori's tower. Aori watched the catastrophe occur, and he realized that the chasm's growth rate would soon put his compound in jeopardy. Far from Aori's line of sight and unbeknownst to him, similar catastrophes were happening all over the world. Volcanoes, quakes, tornadoes, and hurricanes ripped through Aia and left the planet a lifeless husk.

"This is all my fault," said Aori. There was a great commotion directly outside his tower walls, but his words echoed in the stillness of his room.

In the milliseconds between Aori's confession and Asalie's forthcoming response, Pettifogger crept into the room and overheard the admission of guilt. It did nothing to assuage the bitter feelings that had been welling up inside him lately. At first, he had seen Aori as his mentor, even going so far as to think of him as a messiah or savior who pulled the gnome from certain death-by-boredom in his family home.

After spending what felt like months (but was, in fact, only a few days of real-time) listening to Quartz "Toki" Thymegarden spout nothing but filth about Aori, he had no doubt whatsoever about the culprit behind Aia's eminent destruction.

He had even seen it with his own two—albeit magically bespectacled—eyes. With the goggles he had stolen from Aori, the chasm below was like a time-lapse panoramic view of the present and near future. Pettifogger just watched in horror as the widening gash tore the planet in half.

"You must do something about it!" he shouted at the blurry, purple-hued images of Aori and Asalie. "You have the power of gods! Do something!"

"Even if they could hear you beyond the veil of Tweentime," whispered Toki, once again in the guise of the elderly gnome named Quartz Thymegarden, "It's inevitable. I've seen it happen time and time again."

"You've seen this happen before? Why didn't you try to prevent it this time?!" Pettifogger demanded to know.

The ancient gnome gazed up at Aori's blurry image. "That was the plan, long ago. It never fails; you think you can entrust the power of time to the next generation, and they end up screwing things up all over again. That's why I need you to stop him."

Pettifogger stood on his tip-toes, sizing himself up against Aori and Asalie. She was almost a head taller, though still far shorter than Aori. Of course, with a thought, she could grow to gigantic heights. But that's neither here nor there.

The goddess of Growth could see neither the gnomes in the room nor the dark future facing Aia, choosing instead to present a positive outlook. She, too, had seen cycles of birth, destruction, and rebirth, which gave her a healthy perspective on current events.

"Aori," she mollified him in a calming, congenial tone, "You haven't the power to destroy an entire planet. This is but part of the cycle." A large explosion shook the tower, and Asalie had to root her feet to the floor to avoid falling. Still, in spite of the quake, her voice remained mellow, even sweet. "Aia, like everything else, eventually grows old and dies. But, do not fear. Life will begin anew. Perhaps here, perhaps elsewhere."

Just as Asalie mentioned the planet's rebirth, a quick flash of a distant future merged with Pettifogger's goggled view of the chasm. It was too far away to see clearly, but he thought he saw a tiny seed growing deep beneath the surface of the planet.

"What is that?" he asked Toki.

"That's the reason I've promised to save your race. Only those who work with rock and herbs with equal prowess can tend this particular garden. Your people can grow a new Aia, Pettifogger!"

The aged gnome led Pettifogger to the locked room in which his family had been imprisoned. The door looked different from within Tweentime, but it remained just as sturdy and impenetrable. Pettifogger saw no keyholes or doorknobs whatsoever.

"I promised to save your family from Aia's fate, and so I shall," Toki said with a smile. He pressed an elevator button and a whirring sound came from beyond the doors. "They're now on their way down to the center of the planet, where they can start work immediately."

Pettifogger was beginning to see the catch. Dealing with Toki was like making a deal with the devil—or any other trickster god from numerous mythologies. Promises always came with a price. "You're not letting me go with them, are you?"

Toki took feigned offense to the question. "I don't know why you'd want to, my good man! Why stay here when there are so many other worlds to explore? Who knows what the future holds for Pyrite Pettifogger? Well, I do, but I'm not telling!"

Pettifogger suddenly felt sick to his stomach.

Aori could find no comfort in Asalie's words. "I wanted to change things—create new things—not destroy."

The constant attacks continued unabated, as did Asalie's calm demeanor. "Aori, let me tell you a story. Long ago, when I was still a tree, I spent most of my days stretching my roots, watching my fellow trees grow, and enjoying my long life with my true love, Asa."

"I just want to make sure I understand," Aori stopped to clarify, "You were once a tree, and you were in love with another tree?"

"Well, we weren't always trees. It is a long story with many branches."

"But, he was an *asa* tree?"

"He was the first and oldest *asa* tree on all of Aia, and their namesake." Asalie's voice turned somber, "And you cut him down to build this infernal tower."

"I'm sorry. I... didn't know."

"I believe he'll grow back eventually. Anyway, you mustn't let me get sidetracked. My stories can be very long-winded and circuitous when I get going. Stop me if you've heard it."

"Please continue," Aori urged her onward, sincerely interested in her story.

"One day, a young man climbed down Asa's mighty branches. I tried to find out from whence he came, but 'somewhere between now and then,' was Asa's only reply.

"The young man grew cold, for winter was almost nigh. Luckily, he had many stacks of paper with him, and he set them afire. A sudden gust of wind caught the paper and spread the fire throughout the forest. Asa and some other trees were spared, but I burned.

"At dawn the next morning, life began for me. I sat and talked with the young man for many hours, and he told me all about himself. He had been destined to spend all eternity writing the future on a typewriter. Two other writers wrote the past and the present, and all three typewriters were linked, so that each writer ended up recopying whatever the last one had typed. All events in time kept repeating infinitely in a loop. Do you understand so far?"

Aori nodded. "But, if the man you met stopped typing, wouldn't that destroy the loop?"

"Yes, and that was the man's intent. He wished to change things irrevocably—the papers he burned were the future he had copied. He set out to create a new future for the world. And, as you can see, that is what he has done."

"But, the world is ending. What will become of us?"

"The future is not yet written, Aori. That is for you to decide."

Aori took in a deep breath and braced himself against a wall. "I am the instrument of change here. I am the man from in between time, who creates the future as it happens. The man you met—I am that man. Yet, I have no memory of the event."

"When you left that nether-world Toki calls home, you became part of the cycle. The man I met died and you were born. Now, you understand your great importance to the Spiral."

"I do." Aori straightened his posture. Energy sprang forth inside him, and he began to move, as he had not done for many days. "I can change things. I can make things better for all of us." He paced the floor once or twice and said, "Please excuse me, Asalie. I have much to do, and very little time."

Aori took a quick glance out the window to survey the status of the war. Several flying machines—jets, biplanes, and dragons—swarmed both towers. The agents of Time had, most assuredly, turned against him. He sighed, but kept walking. "I have greater concerns at the moment," he stated defiantly, as if ignoring the enemy would serve as some defense.

Despite his worn joints and knees, he traversed four flights of the tower's stairs with little pain. "No time for pain," he grumbled as he clambered down the steps.

As he approached the music room, he heard the sound of the pipe organ. "Please," he said as he quickly entered the room, "keep playing. Don't mind me. I've just come to check on the status of my friend, Bertram."

Oblivious to Aori's arrival, Notturno continued playing. Aori peered across the room to the altar on which his dead friend had rested. He looked about the room frantically and said, "Excuse me. I hate to interrupt you, but have you seen a dead body walking around here lately?"

Without speaking or even looking Aori's way, Notturno raised one hand and pointed to the hallway. As soon as he took that one hand off of the organ, the room seemed to brighten a bit.

Aori sprinted out of the room and down the hall, towards the Coda holding-rooms. Coming out of a doorway, he saw the decayed figure of Bertram. "Bertram!" he called. "It's me, Aori!"

Finis took a deep breath and spoke, through Bertram's mouth. "Aori! Sorry I'm late. You will never believe what it took to get here!"

Aori guffawed. "Come, Bertram. I have much to do! We have very little time!"

Bertram stood rigidly in the open doorway, as only a dead man can. "I cannot go, Aori. My unlife or undeath is tethered to this room."

Aori tried tugging at his friend's arm, but soon gave up and asked, "This room? Why?"

"This boy." With a stiff gesture, Bertram motioned toward Dirge's bloody body slumped in the corner of the room. Several other Coda were busy singing soothing, healing melodies. "This is Dirge."

"He brought you back to life?"

Bertram's mouth stuttered with Finis's words. "In a manner of speaking, yes. But, if he dies, I will too. In fact, I might go so far as to say the entire world is in jeopardy."

Aori frowned. "The entire world *is* in jeopardy, Bertram. But, I think I have enough time to fix things." He stepped past Bertram's corpse into the room. "I will start with this boy."

"He has lost so much blood already," sang one of the Coda. "I'm afraid his time is short."

Aori placed his hands upon Dirge's throat. "Trust me. Time has pooled up in my idle hands." He reached deep inside himself, drew out what little temporal energy he had left, and gave Dirge the time he needed to recuperate.

Dirge's big, dark eyes opened and stared at Aori. He tried to speak, but his vocal chords were still severely damaged. Aori stood up and motioned for Dirge to do the same. "Come, Coda. We have much to do. Keep singing those soothing songs!"

He marched out of the room and down the hall a few steps. "Bertram, are you coming?"

"I suppose so." Bertram picked Dirge up and followed Aori down the hall.

Aori slowed his pace so his zombie friend could catch up. "Bertram, what has gotten into you? You just don't seem yourself today."

"Well, I'm dead. That can change a man, Aori."

As they entered Aori's living chambers, Ekisha was waiting for them on a pile of broken fortune cookies. "Right on time," she said. Then, she read the message from one of the cookies: "Whatever will be, will be. The future's not ours to see." She seemed particularly troubled by the words, but brushed them aside, along with the pile of cookies. "Sit down beside me. We have much to discuss."

"No time to talk! I have to save the world!" Busily, Aori rummaged around his room.

With an exasperated sigh, Bertram's corpse placed Dirge on the bed beside him. Asalie stepped out of the woodwork (literally) and sat next to him. "Good evening, Asalie," said the zombie.

Asalie studied the cadaver carefully. "Still dead, I see."

Bertram nodded.

"Aori believes you've been resurrected?"

Bertram nodded.

"Glad you could make it for the end of the world, Finis."

Bertram smiled. "Good to see you too, Asalie. How's the cancer?"

"Growing."

"Sorry to hear that. No offense, but I think you'd be a bit of a drag as a dead woman."

Asalie smiled. "None taken. Anyway, it's all part of the cycle."

Finis watched Aori with Bertram's eyes. "So, Aori. Do you have a plan?"

Aori barely stopped long enough to answer. "Yes." Hastily, he tossed several objects aside. "I don't have time to explain."

"Is he always so irrationally optimistic?" Finis whispered.

With a smile, Asalie rose and walked to a window. "I can't keep them out for much longer."

Finis looked out the window, but Bertram's weak eyes could not pierce the darkness. "Help is on the way. I'm bringing friends."

With some effort, Ekisha stood up and grabbed Aori by the shoulders. "You must listen to me," she shouted. "I know the outcome of this war!"

Aori struggled to free himself from her grasp. "The future is not yet written. How could you possibly know?"

"I exist throughout time," Ekisha announced. "Everywhen."

Aori shook himself loose and threw his shoulders back dramatically. "Then take another look around, because everything is about to change."

Bending over, he picked something off the floor and held it out for all to see. It was the game piece he carved on the train so many days prior. "Here it is!"

With a particularly Bertram-like air, Finis said, "I hardly think this is a time for games, Aori." Of course, he recognized the figure as that of Quondam.

"No, watch." As he held the carving in his hand, it changed slightly. Then, the figure seemed to age very quickly. "I must find this man... this boy."

Proudly, Ekisha announced, "All you have to do is wait. The Once-and-Future Man will be arriving shortly."

Still looking out the window, Asalie verified the prophecy. "It is so. For good or ill, Quondam is approaching the front door as we speak."

Ekisha held her arms out triumphantly. "See? Now that I have proven that I have seen the future, hear me out!"

Hesitantly, Aori put down the figurine and focused his attention on Ekisha's words. She ambled over to a window and gazed up at the circling planes. "Very soon, one of those aircrafts will hit the other tower. The explosion will cause it to crumble and fall." She turned and looked at Aori dramatically. "Then, a few minutes later, a jet will hit this tower, and it, too, will fall." Fanning herself with an ornate, paper fan, she continued, "After that, the world will end."

Chapter 4:12

Oroboros

The aircrafts continued circling and attacking the towers as if they had missed their cue to crash into the buildings. Mechanical dragons breathed fire, and Asalie's organic defenses ignited. As more thorns and vines grew back, the inferno would consume them, so the towers were in a constant state of flux.

Notturno's shadows absorbed most of the light from the fires, so Crowfoot's dark pinions hid the blackbird and his cargo from view. Unfortunately, his size made him a rather large target on the advanced radar systems employed by the Anachronistic air forces. Though he knew nothing of missiles, Crowfoot did his best to evade them.

As he dove to outmaneuver a missile, he crashed into the side of a large, mechanical dragon. Its rusty scales clanged at the impact of Crowfoot's body. He tried to right himself and resume his flight, but an iron claw had already clamped down on his tail feathers. The dragon's mouth opened and flames roared. Crowfoot knew he would never evade the blast in time.

The dragon choked and coughed mechanically until a large fireball sputtered out of its mouth. The flames spiraled and whirled in the wind, and Crowfoot just stared, as the flames seemed to take on a life of their own. Suddenly, a distinct hum could be heard over the grinding of the metal dragon. The regal form of a man clad in shining, greenish armor flickered inside the ball of flames. His wings beat so furiously that they could not be seen. Oleander, Emperor of the *Fellfalla*, had arrived—magically transported through the fire.

In a blur of wings and shining armor, Oleander sped toward Crowfoot and carried the large blackbird out of the dragon's line of fire. As they approached the closest of Aori's clocktowers, the structure looked like a lit match. The fire around the pinnacle of the building increased in size. Two burning wings flickered against the stark black background. Crowfoot realized that the conflagration heralded the arrival of another of the moth-people, but he had never seen one quite so gigantic.

Attacus the Atlas Moth leapt from his perch on the top of the tower and flapped his wings. As he did, flames leapt forth, flickered, and metamorphosed into scores of *Fellfallan* warriors. The *Fellfalla* scattered and joined in battle against the various enemy biplanes, jets, and helicopters.

Meanwhile, Attacus smashed into the mechanical dragon, sending them both hurtling toward the ground. The serpents on the Atlas's wings hissed and struck at the dragon, but their teeth could not break the thick metal scales.

As Attacus wrestled the dragon to the ground, Oleander and Crowfoot faced off against an Apache helicopter. It sped towards them with machine guns blazing, but Oleander effortlessly deflected the bullets with his halberd and armored wings. As the *Fellfallan* emperor's arms blurred, the weapon took on an ethereal, green glow. With several swift swipes of his staff, he had completely dismantled the propellers. As the helicopter plummeted downward, Oleander sliced open the cockpit. Before he could free the pilots, they conveniently vanished just in time.

The *Fellfalla* dominated the sky, for they could easily see through the darkest of nights. Moths of various families and sizes fluttered about, raising thick clouds of dust in the process. The pilots of the futuristic aircrafts could not maneuver in the reduced visibility, and many crashed. However, no planes had yet crashed into the clocktowers.

From the opposite direction of the main squadrons of *Fellfalla*, another moth approached. The Brahma's wings looked like tapestries woven with velvet and inlayed with gold. They shone brilliantly, even in the low light of Notturno's night.

Seated behind a golden hump on the Brahma's dorsal area, Munder rubbed his temples and tried to stop the vibrating hum that had been droning for many days. He removed his helmet, which had been a gift from the Brahma. With golden, spiraling horns similar to the larva's, the helm and corresponding armor matched the moth's color scheme perfectly. Munder shook his head back and forth, but the congestion of thoughts and voices still remained.

Suddenly, his eyes were drawn downward, to the ground. "Now," he mumbled. The Brahma did not respond. "NOW!" he shouted. "We need to go down now. We're late." The Brahma continued to flap its wings. Munder mumbled several incoherent words, grabbed his axe, and leapt from his ride.

Like a rock chained to a house occupied by a family of elephants, Munder and the Brahma plunged downward. Despite the harrowing circumstances, the giant seemed totally unaffected. Likewise, his companion adopted a similar lack of emotion as it gradually metamorphosed into a thick cocoon around Munder's body.

As Munder and the Brahma rocketed toward the ground, the situation had become quite intense on the battlefield below. The Anachronists had brought in tanks in addition to their wooly herbovines. The Ori fought valiantly, but many of them lost their lives to the technologically advanced warfare. The tanks indiscriminately plowed over everything in their way, despite the opposing will of the Ori who stood against them.

Munder's cocoon hurtled downward with such speed that, when it landed, it created a rather large crater around the crash site. In addition, the giant completely destroyed one of the Metachrons' tanks in the process. After the dust settled, Munder walked away unscathed.

The Ori began to cheer for their savior from the skies, but Munder paid them no attention. The Brahma sustained serious damage in the crash, but it reverted to caterpillar form and followed Munder out of the fray. All those who opposed the giant fell lifelessly in his wake. He would not be detained.

After hacking through several battalions of soldiers, tanks, and wooly herbovines, Munder came upon the crumpled mechanical dragon and the scorched form of Osoi. "I'm late," he said, matter-of-factly.

"You're late, I'm late. It's all over now." Osoi crawled over to the giant. "We have all missed our destinies. You have failed us!" The great caterpillar lunged at Munder and impaled the unconcerned giant with its great horn.

The Brahma sprang upon Osoi like an arrow. It chomped down on Osoi's tail end and began eating.

> **Oroboros**
>
> In Asalie's palindromic language, *oroboro* means "it consumes itself." Throughout the ages, the symbol of a snake eating its own tail has appeared in numerous cultures, including Earth's Egyptian artwork and Greek philosophy. In all aspects, it symbolizes eternity, the cyclical nature of creation and destruction, and the beginning and end of time.
>
> Interestingly, later in life, the oroboro would become Munder's insignia.

With a choked scream, Osoi snapped to attention and retaliated. Each caterpillar attempted to consume the other, thereby forming a circle around Munder. The circle gyrated faster and faster, until Munder could no longer make out which creature was which. Munder raised his axe, intending to cut down friend or foe in order to continue his quest. With one great swing, he broke the cycle and four equal pieces of caterpillar fell to the ground.

Munder lowered his eyes to his feet, but not out of pity for the fallen Brahma. Rather, he was preoccupied with the timepiece, which had been hewn from the caterpillar's body. Without blinking, Munder stooped low, picked it up by the chain, and set out for the clocktowers once again.

As Munder passed slowly out of view, the halves of the Brahma grew together. Gradually, it grew into a dark-olive-skinned old man. He sat, cross-legged, about three feet off the ground, while mystic energy swirled around him. Then, the Brahma went to sleep.

Chapter 4:13

Up the Downward Spiral

By the time Quondam and Asia arrived at the feet of the clocktowers, the foundations had grown together. Where once there had been two separate entrances, there was now no sign of any door at all. Thorns and vines choked off any hope of passage. Fires burned near the top of each tower, but the growth continued unabated below.

The more Quondam hacked at the overgrowth, the stronger it became. Between exhausted gasps of breath, he groaned, "This growth—I wonder if Asalie is involved in some way. Could she have lost her mind and allied herself with my sworn enemy?"

Asia investigated the towers' conjoined base closely. She, too, knew of Asalie, as the goddess's wanderings to her home had brought the change in seasons. "Perhaps her power is being used against her will." She attempted to clear some plants away, but she just became entangled in the vines. Thorns cut into her skin, and she shrieked. "Cut me loose!"

With every swing, Quondam's wooden sword became more entwined in the overgrowth. Soon, he could no longer distinguish his own weapon from the rest of the organic material. To make matters worse, the fire was quickly making its way down to the roots of the structure. In a matter of seconds, they would both be burned along with the thorns and vines.

Vines wrapped tightly around Quondam's wrist, and he lost his grip on the sword. Quickly, his mind shifted to a clearer state, his wrist shifted to a smaller size, and he slipped free. The blaze grew nearer, and Quondam could feel the heat on his skin. He reached for his sword, and the muscles in his arm shifted to a stronger age. Suddenly, it was as if all the vegetation in the vicinity responded. Thoughtseeds burst in his brain, and Quondam saw the vines and thorns grow and change around him. The wood of the clocktower warped and swirled. What appeared to be a knot in the wood grew larger and eventually formed a door.

Quondam touched the door lightly with his hand, but nothing happened. The skin of his palm grew wrinkles, and the wood of the door creaked in response. It opened, and Quondam and Asia rushed inside just before the fire spread to the base of the building. The vines and thorns sparked and crackled, but the *asa* wood did not burn.

Inside the clocktower, two staircases spiraled upward and wound together like strands of DNA. As he watched the staircases move, Quondam felt his stomach spin with vertigo. "They're revolving."

"Which one do we take?" asked Asia.

"I don't know. They both go up."

"Maybe we should each take one."

Though they had just met, Quondam's attachment to his new companion would not let him leave her behind. "I'm afraid I won't see you again."

"As long as there are Ori, I will be with them. You are Ori, Quondam." She looked deep inside her psyche to find a source of bravery. "Our father wants you to be brave, Quondam." As her words faded, her hand slipped out of his and a stairway spiraled up to meet her feet.

Quondam's feet met the other staircase, and he rushed up them with renewed vigor. His pride pained him, as this little girl seemed to have so much more bravery than he had, and what did she mean by "*Our* father?" For a few seconds, he wondered if he should have pushed her down and made fun of her instead.

Strangely, his archenemy and the fate of the world seemed insignificant compared to his bond with Asia. He hoped against hope that the staircases would meet at the top, and his feet moved for that purpose only.

As he climbed, the ticking of the clocktower seemed to divide into two separate sounds. One tick sounded something like the beating of heart, only more mechanical and artificial. The other ticked so slowly that Quondam wondered if it had stopped altogether. Looking up, he could see that the towers and their respective staircases diverged into two separate structures. In one side, a giant pendulum swung back and forth in time with the ticking sound. The pendulum in the other tower barely moved at all.

Asia followed her stairway up into the latter tower, while Quondam's path led straight past the swinging pendulum. He noticed that, every so often, the moving stairway would get in the way of the pendulum, which sent splinters of wood and saw dust raining down to the stairs below. Of course, the wood of the staircase always seemed to grow back after a few minutes.

Quondam waited at the break in the stairs and watched the pendulum swing. He predicted that, if the stairs continued to grow as they were, there would be no avoiding the swinging saw blade. His thoughts slowly shifted from Asia back to his role in the fate of the world as he waited for the proverbial—and almost literal—axe to fall. "I should just go home. I'm a kid. I know I wanted to be big and have adventures, but this is… preposterous." His voice matured and continued, "I've been through too much already to give up now. It's past time to grow up and get things done."

"That's right, boy," said a voice in his head. "If you give up now, Aia is doomed for sure." He recognized the voice as the eighty-year-old Quondam he spoke with in Tweentime.

"You know how it turns out, right? Could you give me a heads up?"

"Sure, kid. Get hit with that pendulum blade, and it'll hurt a whole lot."

"That's not what I meant," Quondam said.

"Listen," said the older version of Quondam, "If you keep talking to yourself like this, people are going to think we're crazy. I don't want people thinking we're crazy, so just get back to the task at hand."

The pendulum crashed into the stairway and wood split beneath Quondam's feet. As his balance left him, he lunged forward and caught a step with the tips of his fingers. The pendulum roared as it began its arc back toward him. He braced himself as the saw barely missed him and sliced through another part of the stairway.

Suspended in air by a single step, Quondam prepared for the long fall to the bottom of the tower. Miraculously, however, the step held fast to the wood of the walls. Quondam pulled himself up to get a better grip on the step and noticed that the next step up was far out of reach. He took a breath and waited. Just at the end of his patience, an opportune distraction presented itself. Far below him, a loud, booming sound accompanied the ticking. *Tick boom tick boom tick boom.*

Outside the tower, Munder rammed at the main gate with his wooden arm-ram. The fire, having consumed all of the vegetation, had been reduced to embers. Munder's knack for perfect timing held, as he had arrived at the foot of the tower during the three-minute interval between devastation and re-growth.

The Anachronistic Army approached behind him, but Munder could not be bothered. All that stood between the giant and his appointed task was a five-foot thick gate made of the strongest wood on Aia. His first few attempts at hacking the door down with his axe proved quite futile, as the wood repaired itself faster than he could chop. Surprisingly, the wooden battering ram worked like a charm—or, to put it more precisely, a key.

After three loud booms, the gate gave way and Munder fell into the opening. The hardwood floor rushed up to meet his face, and he got a mouthful of sawdust and woodchips.

Looking up, he noticed the spiraling staircases, but Quondam was well out of view. Sternly, Munder stepped upon the winding stairway, but each step he took brought him no closer to the top. Rather, his massive weight caused the steps to sink to the floor.

He tried the other stairway. No luck.

He tried taking a running leap. His face struck the floor once again.

As his face brushed the sawdust away, he noticed that something had been carved into the floor. The carving read, "You're early. Take five."

A tank rolled up to the foot of the clocktower, and several soldiers, knights, cave-people, and wooly herbovines followed. By the time they arrived, the vines and thorns had grown back even thicker than before. No matter how hard they tried, the soldiers could not get in the tower. The knights tried cutting through the vegetation, but the thorns had more luck cutting through their armor. On several occasions, soldiers became so entangled in the foliage that they were altogether lost and eventually forgotten.

As the ravenous wolves, panthers, and lions encircled them, several cave-people made up their minds to try their hands at being ripped to shreds by thorns instead of ferocious animals. As for the rest of the soldiers, knights, and whatnot, their fate was similarly brutal.

Caitlin slicked back her bristled fur and tempered her raging bloodlust. "My kin are up there. I can feel them."

Connery poignantly set aside the soldier he had been fighting and said, "Get t' climbing, then, lass. Y' won't get through those briars, o' that I am sure."

The Queen of Cats inspected the vegetation more closely and, after casting an enemy soldier into the growth as a test, decided not to chance it. "Solo?"

The dark-clad Coda strolled up, with his broadsword humming a glorious song of battle. The singing sword had sliced through armor, tanks, and herbovines in its journey to the foot of the towers, but the dense shrubbery quieted its song. Solo chopped at the vines, but they continuously grew back. Eventually, the sword became so entwined in the growth that it took the three of them to pull it free.

Connery sniffed the air. "Reinforcements," he snarled. The cavalry had arrived. Appropriately, the reinforcements were led by gun-slinging horsemen far removed from their Hollywood Western time period. Jeeps, tanks, and armored personnel carriers followed.

A bullet ricocheted off of Solo's sword with a musical chime. The bullets continued to fire in rapid succession, and the Coda managed to deflect the bulk of them. However, he could not stop the spray of sub-machine gunfire that tore through the hides of his allies. Wolves yelped, lions roared, and panthers screamed as the hot metal bit their flesh.

A grenade landed amidst the allied animals, and one of the wolves cautiously sniffed at it. The concussion of the subsequent blast knocked Connery into the thorns and burned off most of his fur. Caitlin rushed to free him from the now-burning briars, and, though he still breathed, the werewolf's breaths came in raspy growls.

In order to divert the enemy fire, Solo blitzed the cavalry and managed to knock many of them from their horses. His *alla breve* blades zipped from his hands and took out two drivers and the sub-machine gunner in the time it took for the bullets to leave his gun and strike Solo's sword.

The blade of the great broadsword screamed a harsh, visceral battle song as it met with the steel of the armored vehicles. Soldiers fell to the ground with their hands cradling their ears in anguish.

Connery howled at the sonic assault on his sensitive ears, and Caitlin tried to assuage the pain. "Solo! We have to fall back—find refuge!"

Solo glanced back at his allies, drove the great sword deep into the ground, and ran back to the foot of the tower. The vines were now smoldering and the main gate could be seen among the blackened foliage. "Go. Take Connery and the others. I will remain to hold off the attack."

"Alone?"

"It is my way."

As Caitlin darted through the main gate, barely evading bullets and burning briars, she heard a deep, powerful song echo across the battlefield. As Solo sang, his sword responded with a sonic boom that shook the ground.

But, even as Solo made his final stand against the onslaught, he was not wholly alone. The fallen corpses of the war's casualties rose again to join him in battle, and the skeletons of long-dead warriors dug their way out of Aori's cemetery to fight again.

While Caitlin curiously inspected the winding stairway, the double-doors to a nearby room slid shut. Munder stared at the blank walls of the tightly closed-in space, but he felt no panic or discomfort. Rather, he determinedly turned a crank, eased a lever into place, and felt the elevator ease upward.

Meanwhile, the elevator containing a small representative sample of the gnomish population hurtled downward at a speed that might seem impossible if one had not already extended his or her suspension of disbelief past the breaking point. At this point, anything goes, right?

In that case, suppose a certain familiar gnome with a penchant for escaping and sneaking around undetected had somehow slipped away without the god of Time noticing. Then, that little scoundrel also managed to maneuver through space and time quickly enough to catch up to an elevator at its terminal velocity. While we're at this logic-defying threshold of plausibility, let's just say he managed to forcibly gain access to the elevator and reunite with his long-lost family and fellow gnomes.

Far above the elevators, Quondam heard the commotion of gears turning and chains grinding, but he chose to focus on the sudden growth of his stair-step. In the short time he had been waiting, it had grown and carried him up two more flights of stairs. At times, it seemed more like a tree or ladder than a stairway, but Quondam managed to keep his grip as he ascended.

At the top, branches of stairways spread out in many directions, but Quondam could tell that only one led to another floor. He noticed the black of the night sky through several windows along the wall. Seeing the windows immediately reminded him of the televisions in Tweentime. The darkened sky lit up with explosions and dragon-fire, but Quondam was trying to look deeper. He needed some reassurance that his friends and allies were okay.

As if in answer to his thoughts, one of the windows showed Lithe, but the war-torn sky in the background seemed to vanish. Everything around her was grey and lifeless, and she crouched among a pile of corpses. Quondam shook his head to clear the eerie images away.

In another window, he saw Munder, but the giant no longer looked like his lifelong friend. Rather, he had two large horns that spiraled out of his head like the horns of a ram. His features looked more animal than human.

"These are windows into the future, boy," said the old man's voice in his head. "Keep looking, if you truly want to see what transpires. Or, you could keep walking and find out for yourself."

After shifting his legs to relieve his weariness, Quondam sprinted up three more flights. As he climbed, the building began to look more like a clock and less like a tree, as it had before. Gears and other simple machines wound around and turned other cranks and pulleys. Quondam marveled at the liveliness of such lifeless objects. The paradox distracted him just enough that the first of the clockwork traps caught him completely by surprise.

A wooden plank under Quondam's foot applied just enough pressure to raise the opposite end of a balance, which turned a wheel, which caused numerous other chain reactions leading up to the release of two giant, gyrating saw-blades aimed directly at Quondam.

Metal teeth gashed his shoulder and tore his tunic, but the wound quickly shifted to another age. The second cog rolled toward him, but quick reflexes allowed him to jump aside just in time.

Quondam stopped to rest, which gave his brain a chance to reflect on his environment. "I've been here before," he whispered in a deep, adult voice. "I know my way around." And, to prove it to the younger parts of his body, he leapt upon a moving gear, which lead him to a conveyor belt, which lead to a catwalk, which lead to a ladder.

Climbing the ladder took him to a six-sided room containing six bells of varying sizes. His boyish curiosity compelled him to gently knock on one with the back of his knuckles. Suddenly, the room hummed with motion and the bells began to clang and ring. He shifted his ears to an age with hearing loss in order to avoid the overwhelming pain.

The walls of the room turned clockwise around him. As they clicked into each new position, Quondam noticed an opening on one wall. Through the opening, he could see that another set of walls surrounded the room. The other walls moved clockwise as well, but they moved at a slower rate.

"There must be an opening in the next set of walls as well. They probably only match up at a specific time." Though his words were lost on his own deaf ears, several other concerned parties paid careful attention.

Chapter 4:14

Nothing Frees Up Your Schedule Like the End of the World

"He's coming," said Aori.

"Any minute now," Ekisha mumbled, "And right on schedule."

Aori paced the room. "There is still time to save Aia. I think your prediction was wrong, time-witch."

Ekisha muttered, "I have seen it. The two towers will fall."

"The aircrafts have been circling for hours now, and the building still stands."

The fortune-teller's forehead wrinkled with the worry of multiple ages. Since she arrived in this time-forsaken tower, she had felt trapped in this era. Tunnel vision limited her view of the future.

Finis whispered in her ear, "And you reek of death, my dear."

Ekisha tried to ignore him and continued to stare out the window at the flying objects in the sky. A click on the other side of the room caught her attention for a second, and in that time, a large, black figure blocked her view. The watched pot had finally boiled.

With a loud crash, Crowfoot shot through the opening. Glass shattered and filled the air, as time seemed to ebb to a crawl. Ekisha's face contorted as the bird's beak pierced her heart and darkness enveloped her. Black feathers danced with shards of glass in the air, and almost a lifetime passed before they finally struck the floor.

In that time, Quondam managed to enter the room through an opening in the wall, drew his sword, and put it to Aori's throat. However, before he had time to make the kill, Asalie shouted, "STOP!"

Every living thing in the room obeyed her command. The glass crackled and tinkled as it hit the floor.

"Quondam, stand down," said Asalie.

Quondam's eyebrows crashed together with incredulity. "What?" He looked at the faces around the room to find some sort of sense in Asalie's command. Crowfoot's eyes darted around with confusion, and Lithe struggled with newfound consciousness. Finis, once again occupying his own body, looked down solemnly at his feet, while Bertram stared as blankly as a corpse.

"He's the enemy, Asalie. He must be stopped. He has already done enough damage." Quondam looked to each of the others in the room, searching for corroboration. His gaze fell on Dirge, who now sat up in bed and looked back at him.

Lithe rushed to Dirge's bed. The scar on his neck smiled at her innocuously. He touched his sister's hand to communicate with her, and Lithe reported, "He...he's okay."

Quondam eased the sword off of Aori's neck and slowly backed away. Still pointing the tip of the wooden blade towards his sworn enemy, Quondam moved to be with the others. To Finis, he asked, "Has Asalie truly lost her mind?"

Finis smiled. "We all have, Quondam. The world's cracking up, and so are we. It's all going to end."

"No, it's not," insisted Aori. "Your interruption has cost me valuable time, but there is still a chance."

With more speed than a man his age should have, Aori dashed across the room. Instinctively, Quondam sprang to attention. "No, villain! Not another move. I will kill you, no matter who tries to stop me! Your madness will end here!"

Silence piled up around them. After the weighty pause, Aori closed his eyes and sighed. "Quondam, give me the timepiece. Now."

Time seemed to stop in the room again, as all its inhabitants held their collective breath.

The real world washed away like a watercolor painting, and a watered-down hue of purple took its place. The sworn enemies slipped between the last few minutes before apocalypse. In Tweentime, they could continue their battle for eternity, if necessary.

The two men stared at one another, and both of them seemed to age countless years in the struggle of wills. Father Time's prodigal sons gauged their respective opponents unrelentingly. Quondam had the physical advantage, but would he have time to attack before Aori dodged or unleashed some sort of magic? One of them would have to back down eventually.

The unbroken windows in the room revealed the current events in the war below similarly to the television coverage of wars of the future—only without the incessant ticker at the bottom of the screen providing extra news. "Look around you," said Aori. "The windows show what's happening to your friends in the real world. Funny; they never seemed to work before. I suppose it's because all my friends were dead."

Chaos continued to spread outside the tower. In the air, the *Fellfalla* kept Time's forces in check, while the Undead, the Agypsians, the Ori, and Solo fought valiantly on the ground. Unfortunately, Solo's last-ditch sonic boom had exacerbated the huge crack that had been spreading from Auldenton.

Attacus and the great clockwork dragon had stomped all over the battlefield in an all-out brawl, but the giant Atlas moth had managed to force the machine into submission.

The ground opened up between Attacus's feet and swallowed up his opponent, but the Atlas stood firm. He increased in size and clutched the ground with multiple hands and feet. With all his might, he strove to hold the world together.

Though the room remained still, Crowfoot cawed. "There is death all around. I am needed." Finis nodded, and the bird took flight. The souls of Aians everywhere leapt up at his call, as if they had been waiting on him for days. His wings spread wider and wider to make room for the load of spirits.

Osoi's soul struggled with its metamorphosis, as he had in life, and finally left the corporeal world in his usual state of flux. Nearby, the Brahma continued to expand its essence to make room for its enlightenment. It transcended one form after another and, finally, grew four heads and took flight on the back of a swan.

Time for a Transcendental Meditation Break.
Smoke 'Em If You've Got 'Em.

This form of the Brahma, with four heads, represents the Hindu creator deity of the same name. It is believed that the Brahma creates and destroys worlds in an endless cycle. That, and he rides a swan.

The question is, did Brahma cause the creation and destruction of Aia, or was that all because of Toki, Aori, and the Chronoclysm? Only Time will tell, I suppose. In other words, keep reading!

Oleander surveyed the destruction of Aia from miles above. "My darling Gypsy, I shall see you soon." Like a bullet from a gun, the hawk moth dove toward the clocktowers. Missiles came at him from all sides, and the explosions tore large chunks from his armor.

Aori's other tower shook as Oleander and the missiles struck it, but it did not fall. As the last noble of the *Fellfalla* crashed through a window in the center of the tower, glass filled the air. The shards of glass fell to the floor at a normal speed, but shards of Oleander continued to flutter around the room. The moths scattered all over the place, taking refuge in closets, gathering around light sources, and some even strayed outside the tower.

One of the Oleander moths fluttered to Auldenton to witness its destruction. One monitored the battle between the Agypsians and the Prochrons. One watched as Caitlin and Connery met up with Asia in the second tower and the three of them fought the remaining clockwork soldiers.

Another fluttered over to Aori's chambers, where the air still hung stagnantly. Aori and his nephew flickered in and out between normal time and Tweentime. Aori shouted, "The timepiece, Quondam! It is my birthright, and only I know how to use it!"

"What will you do with it? Save yourself from old age? Death? At a time like this, you only think of yourself?"

Aori considered the question. After a pause, he said, "You are right; I am old. I have aged more in the last few days than I should have in a lifetime. This morning, I might have been tempted to erase all the effects of age, yes. But now, there are more important concerns. Hand it over!"

Quondam clutched the timepiece obstinately, as if he were a child unwilling to share his favorite toy. "You will have to kill me first!" With that, he lunged at Aori. The blade hit Aori with all the threat of a wooden, toy sword. His wrinkled, thin skin broke at the assault, but only as much as elderly skin is apt to do when hit with a blunt object.

"Your sword has lost its magic, boy."

Shocked, Quondam stared at his sword, and implored Asalie with tear-soaked eyes. "How could you? I worshipped you, Asalie, and you betray me?"

Asalie's face seemed bright and warm in spite of the tragic destruction all around them. Like tendrils on a vine, a smile spread through her wrinkled lips. "It is all a part of the cycle, Quondam."

Quondam reached for the timepiece. "I—can't. He is evil, Asalie. If he gets his hands on this…"

"…The world will end? Kiddo, it's already over."

487

Everyone in the room turned to the open doorway, where Munder filled up the entire space. His head bumped into the high ceiling, but he seemed rather complacent. He plodded over to Aori and pushed Quondam aside. "Sorry I'm late. You wouldn't believe the traffic out there."

Aori seemed just as confused by the giant's words as everyone else had been. Proceeding to shock and appall the members of his audience, Munder held out his timepiece by the chain. It dangled peacefully in front of Aori's face, and all of history and the future teetered on a similar, momentous, thin chain.

"Munder, no!" Quondam screamed. "What are you doing? Am I the only sane person left on this planet?"

At this point, even Asalie seemed concerned. Up until that point, everything had seemed to fall together into the Spiral's great plan. Suddenly, however, the unknowns of the universe struck her with all their immense weight. "The Spiral... ineffable..." she muttered.

"Effing ineffable," added Munder. "Take it, boss."

Aori looked at him questionably for a split second, but he should have taken a second or two more to weigh the consequences. For, as he took the timepiece in his hand, he began to age a year for every millionth of a second. After his body had withered almost completely, it cycled back to that of a fetus.

Munder snatched up the timepiece by the chain and ripped it from Aori's newborn fingers. The rapid aging cycle stopped, and Aori remained only a few days old.

Chapter 4:15

The Final Countdown

As the world rapidly decayed, the vines surrounding the clocktowers withered. Asalie seemed to wither as well, for what is Mother Nature without the natural order of the world?

Gravity abandoned Aia as its orbit became more and more distorted and its composition decomposed. Everything that was not firmly planted to the ground was flung from Aia's surface.

The roots of the clocktower receded, and Aori's tower slowly began to rise. It floated up, through the sky and clouds, into the stratosphere. The other tower shot off like a rocket and soared through the sky in a hundredth of the time it took the first tower.

The crack in the world continued in spite of Attacus's efforts to hold it. Eventually, his body crumbled under the immense strain, and smaller Atlas moths were scattered about the universe. The cracks spread throughout the world like wrinkles on a dying person's face.

"But—wait," you say, "What about Pettifogger?" You'll remember that he was last seen climbing onboard an elevator hurtling downward through the tower. As it sped toward its destination at the center of the planet, this historical account asked more and more of its reader's suspension of disbelief.

At this point in your already-suspended disbelief, would it be crazy to suppose that the girl of his dreams, a gnome by the name of Daylily, just happened to be on that elevator? What if your humble narrator had never mentioned her before, and she seemed to be just an opportune coincidence-bordering-on-contrivance? How about this? Pettifogger had never even met her before, but, through the use of the stolen spectacles, he could literally see himself marrying her one day. Now, throw in the little tidbit that Daylily's last name was Thymegarden, and that might get a couple more wheels turning.

Whether or not you're a gifted seer, surely you see where this is going.

Exactly. They all make their way to the center of the planet, where they craft a number of random-yet-precise explosions that start the metal core spinning again. Though completely out of left field, this hairball scheme corrects everything that was wrong with the world, and everyone is saved from utter annihilation.

You're right— nothing that absurd would ever really work. Instead, the gnomes, including Pyrite Pettifogger, his mother Cinquefoil, his sister Daisychain, his future wife Daylily, and several other gnomes just rode the elevator down to the center of Aia. There, they did what they did best— tend to the gardens and work with the stone.

All that remained of the planet Aia was one plain, otherwise boring seed. To be exact, it was a nutberry.

Epilogue

Here, at the end of all things, questions still linger in the minds of those who see across time. Perhaps the questions are what drive so many *Everseers* to lunacy. Could Quondam have saved the world from its fate, if he had used his timepiece as his older version had suggested? Or, if not for Munder's intervention, could Aori have been the hero and savior? On that note, did Munder act of his own will or as part of some greater scheme?

Unfortunately, the sides in the story of Aia's last days are not as black and white as Quondam=good and Aori=evil. The "villain" of the story was stopped in the end, but that didn't result in a happy ending.

However, cheer up, faithful reader and history student! Our heroes yet live! Well...

"I'm dying," said Finis, with an unusually cheerful look upon his face. "I haven't committed any heinous act, and I haven't taken my own life. I'm dying, and not in a tragic way! The curse is finally lifted, and I can rest in peace!"

As you'll recall, Finis gained his deified state as part of a curse involving an endless stream of tragic deaths and suicides. He had killed family members, committed atrocities, and avoided a life of guilt by killing himself numerous times. Of course, when one lives life over and over, one can never escape the guilt.

Asalie crawled over to the spirit of Death as he stared out the window at the destruction of Aia. "We are the last survivors of an entire planet. Our lives and energies are linked to that planet. Old friend, I am afraid there is plenty of tragedy to go around."

Lithe cradled the infant Aori in one arm and held Dirge close with the other. Dirge looked up at her with frightened eyes, and she tried to vibrate soothing songs to set him at ease.

"How can you mother our enemy, Lithe?" Quondam felt as if everyone he knew had betrayed him.

"Aori's not the enemy, kid." Munder pushed the boy into a wall, as bullies often do. "You need to grow up."

"You...you need to *shut* up!" Quondam retorted.

"Alas! It all comes full circle. Now Quondam's the one without a witty comeback," sang Lithe. She set Aori down upon a bed and led Dirge to the music room, where Notturno continued to play unabated. The trio's Requiem for Aia would last for years to come and score their entire voyage to a distant and growing planet with many similarities to their former home, but just one moon.

While it's unfortunate that Aia had to meet its end, it is all, as Asalie continued to mumble absently for the next seven years, "part of the cycle."

ABOUT THE AUTHOR

 Jared Kitchens, M.Ed., is a Gifted and Talented teacher from Smyer, Texas. After visiting a science fiction/fantasy section of a local library, he thought "I could do that!," and thus began The *Anachronist Chronicles*. He lives in Lubbock, Texas with his wife and their two little kitchenettes. He's an avid collector of all things Pez, Star Wars, superheroes, and any other thing his wife deems "nerdy." When not writing or teaching, he enjoys playing video games and researching etymologies for an hour and a half.

Be sure to check him out on Facebook, under KitchensInk, as well!